THE SKILTHORN CONGRESS

BOOK FOUR OF THE SHATTERED MOON

JON SPARKS

CONTENTS

For Jonathan, Julia, Jago, and Thea.

PART ONE
CHANGES

CHAPTER 1

RAILU

"It's not broken," said Railu. "But that's a nasty gash, and there'll be a lot of bruising."

"Yow 'xpect horses to kick," said Arclant. "Not cows."

"I don't know, I think I've seen more injuries due to cows. Anyway, let's get this cleaned up and then I'll put a few stitches in."

As she worked she sensed movement in her peripheral vision. Focused on her patient, she didn't give it much thought until she heard herself addressed. "Miss Railu..."

"I'm kind of busy right now, Lutrin."

"Yes, ma'am, but I thinked yow should know. There'm a message come on the wing."

"For me?"

"Yes ma'am, Rhenya knows how yowr name looks in writin'."

Rhenya was better at reading than she usually let on. It could be a dangerous thing for a slave to admit, but Lutrin wouldn't blab. "I'll look at it in a minute."

"Yes ma'am. An'..."

"There's more?"

"Some ladies come. Askin' for yow."

That was more of a puzzle, but *first things first...* "They'll have to wait a few minutes too. Or did you leave them back at the house?"

"Rhenya's lookin' after most on 'em, but one come wi' me."

Railu, readying the first suture, did not look up, but she did raise her voice. "I'll be a few minutes." *Whoever you are.*

"I can wait," came the reply. "Take as long as you need."

The voice itself was unfamiliar, but the accent took her back fifteen years. *Dawnsingers...*

She finished suturing, bandaged the leg and issued strict instructions not to put weight on it for at least a week. Finally she looked at the newcomer. She was a tall woman, a head taller than Lutrin in front of her. Face and neck had a spare leanness just the healthy side of gaunt. Twin braids of dark copper hair framed the face; if she was a Dawnsinger, it must be a wig. Behind her, a rangy roan mare cropped avidly at the grass, ignoring Railu's own mount a few yards away.

"Railu," the woman said, making the sun-circle gesture of the Dawnsingers. "Pleased to meet you at last. I've heard a lot about you. But let me introduce myself. My name is Evisyn."

"Oh my... you're the Master Prime!" In that moment Railu felt like a Novice again. She had to remind herself that she was no longer a Dawnsinger, had not been for nearly half her lifespan. Keeping her gaze level, she said, with perfect honesty, "I'm honoured to meet you. Jerya speaks very highly of you."

"The regard is mutual," said Evisyn.

They mounted. Railu aided Lutrin to get up behind her. The girl gripped tightly around her waist as the horses swung into motion.

"Speaking of Jerya..." said Railu, "Did you bring the message with you, Lutrin?"

"I did, ma'am, but... it's in my pocket."

She saw the problem. "And you don't want to let go till we stop."

"No, ma'am. Not less'n I have to, ma'am."

That was brave: she knew how Lutrin felt about horses. "It can wait," she said. "And, Lutrin, you really don't have to call me ma'am all the time."

Back home in the kitchen, Railu settled her glasses on her face, then opened the message. A skinny strip of paper, stubbornly trying to return to its tight curl around the pigeon's leg. On the outer face, her name in capitals, 'Duncal by Drumlenn' the whole of the address. She turned it over and smoothed it out, wondering if she would require the second pair of glasses, the magnifying ones, a notion she'd got from a friend of Lady Pichenta's, an accomplished painter of miniatures. But the message was brief, meaning it could be written large enough. *R. Would be most grateful if you were able to come as soon as convenient. Love, J.*

That was enigmatic, and perhaps concerning, but it didn't sound like an emergency.

✳

"I don't suppose Jerya's here at the moment?"

"No. We don't see so much of her these days, now she's... Have you come straight from the Crossing?" Evisyn confirmed that they had. "Then you won't be up to date with the news. I'll fill you in in just a moment. But you'll be needing some refreshment."

She showed them through to the parlour, encouraged them to make themselves comfortable, then extricated Lutrin from the brewhouse. *"Dem gotten guests,"* she Pattered. *"Chai, kahvi, cake, presto. She prend?"*

"Me prend ben," said Lutrin, evidently delighted to be relieved from cleaning duties.

Railu returned to the parlour. "Analind isn't with you this time?"

"No," said Evisyn, wigless, massaging her scalp. "Having had tantrums until the Conclave agreed I could make the Crossing myself, I thought I should leave my most trusted Masters in situ. But I have brought someone you'll remember." She looked to her right. A small brown woman, still wearing a dark wig, was smiling at Railu.

Recognition dawned. "Oh, my word. Tutor Yanil?"

"The very same."

"I'm so happy to see you... and Jerya will be thrilled."

"Happily, the Healers judged me sufficiently spry to make the trip. And the refuges do mitigate the hardships now... it's nothing to what you and Jerya must have endured."

"It had its moments," agreed Railu. "One word of advice, if you don't mind. You might pass more easily if there was a little grey in your wig."

"Well, no need to worry about that right now." Yanil pulled off the wig, just as Lutrin came in, bearing a tray. She stopped abruptly, mouth falling open. Railu understood; they must look like a bunch of slaves disporting themselves in the master's parlour. In most households, any slave caught doing anything of the kind would be lucky to escape with a mere whipping. "*No fret,*" she said quickly. "*She-she be'st...*" There was no Patter alternative. "Dawnsingers," she finished in Plain. "*Prend?*"

"*Me prend ben,*" said Lutrin, springing into action again.

"Well," said Evisyn as the door closed again. "Am I right in thinking that it's another day's journey to Jerya's home—Kirwaugh, isn't it?"

"Yes, but she isn't there. She's mostly at Skilthorn these days. Hedric's uncle died in spring, so he inherited, which means she's Countess now."

"You'll have to explain what that means."

Railu smiled. "I think Jerya's still trying to fathom that herself."

"Is it further from here?"

"I haven't been yet. Jerya's only been there for a few weeks herself and she's thrown herself into work, making changes—well, you know Jerya."

Evisyn smiled. "I only knew her for a few weeks, but she left a vivid impression."

"Renovating the slave quarters and—but your question was how far it is. Yes, it's further. It's possible in a day's ride, given a good horse, but you'd need to start at first light, even at this time of year. Right after Dawnsong," she added, recalling who her guests were.

Evisyn pursed her lips pensively. "And is it on the way to anywhere else?"

"Not Denvirran; you could say it's on the way to Troquharran. It's not too far from a river, so you could take a boat. That's usually quicker than riding, at least downstream."

"All in all," said Evisyn, "I'd like to see Jerya first. Get her view on things, what's changed since last year. And give myself a few days to see more of the Five Principalities. It's all very well listening to briefings and reading reports, but I still believe there's no substitute for seeing for yourself. Well, that's why I'm here."

"Well, you want to see Jerya, and she's just asked me if I can go to see her too. Maybe we can travel together?"

Evisyn smiled. "I'd like that; but we had planned to go to Denvirran first. Maybe we'll see you at Skilthorn?"

Chapter 2
Jerya

As usual, Elleret said only the minimum she thought needful. "There's a girl askin' to see yow."

Jerya had just picked up the latest *Proceedings of the Denvirran Society for Natural Philosophy*. Now, with an inner sigh, she laid it down again. "A girl?"

"Young lady, should say. Speaks proper ladylike, anywise."

"Did she give a name?"

"No, m'lady. Jus' said 'twere very impor'ant."

That was highly unusual. Any lady calling on another would give her name, usually send in a calling-card. Unusual... and intriguing.

"Oh well, it's not like I have anything else to do." She smiled, and Elleret grinned back, recognising the irony. "Send—no, *bring* her in. And then stay close, in case I need to send her packing again."

The girl was not tall, but she might not even be full-grown. Sandy-gold skin went with light red hair; you could almost call it pink. Both hair and skin, thought Jerya, had received plenty of exposure to the sun, which could bleach the one as it darkened the other. She was dressed in a decently-cut riding-habit, garnet-coloured in the lamplight. Jerya noted the divided skirt, and approved, as the girl executed a well-schooled curtsey.

"Thank you so much for seeing me, Countess." As Elleret had said, *proper ladylike.*

"I'll admit I was curious." *And more so now: what are you? Sixteen, seventeen?* Few ladies of such tender years would ride out alone, still less call on a Countess unannounced. "We haven't met before, have we?"

"No, Countess, though I have long wished to make your acquaintance."

"I'm flattered... but something tells me you haven't ridden here today just in hopes of a brief chat."

"No, Countess. The fact is I need your help."

"*My* help?"

"I couldn't think of anyone else I could turn to."

Again Jerya sighed inwardly, or mostly inwardly. *Sounds like a complication; and so much to do already...* She could not, however, deny that she was intrigued. "Sit, please. And begin at the beginning: your name."

"It's Irmavel, Countess... My friends call me Mav, my Mamma hates it. And my Mamma is... well, she's the main reason I'm here."

"I surmise she doesn't know?"

"You're quite right, my lady. I... the only way to say it is, I've run away from home." She said it with a flourish, full of her own youthful daring.

"How old are you, Irmavel?"

"Seventeen, Countess. Eighteen in four months." Jerya could have believed her even younger. But there was something about the way she said 'eighteen'...

"And eighteen is important because...?"

"Because on that day they'll no longer be able to marry me off."

"They?"

"My mother and my uncle. They're determined to wed me to some man twice my age."

"Irmavel, you've captured my attention. Now... have you come far?"

"I've been riding since first light."

"Hungry?"

The girl's face answered before she could form the words. Had they been at Kirwaugh, or back at Duncal, she'd simply have taken Irmavel down to the kitchen and fed her there. There were three kitchens at Skilthorn, but none had the right homely warmth. She ordered sandwiches for one—'whatever's easy for the cooks' and Elleret departed.

"Why here?" she said to the girl. "Why me?"

"I thought if anyone would understand you would, Countess. You believe in greater freedom for women, for girls."

"That's true, but I'm hardly alone in that."

"I hope that's true, but I don't know anyone else who... whom I thought would understand. I believed you would. That you would sympathise with my plight."

Elleret came in then with coffee, which she would have brewed in a nearby pantry, under the stairs. The sandwiches would take longer.

"I've read all I can find about you, Countess," said Irmavel as Jerya poured. "But the accounts don't always agree on everything."

"Are you surprised? Half of the authors never even spoke to me. One day, if I can ever find the time, I'll write my own story."

"I would love to read that. But may I ask you now, is it true that you were once a slave?"

If nothing else, thought Jerya, it was one more chance to set the record straight. "Yes... but also no."

"I beg your pardon?"

"I'll try to explain. Well, you know why we say 'enslaved', to remind ourselves that it's something imposed on people, not in their nature. You understand that?"

"I think so."

"As to my own story... I am officially freeborn; the law has recognised that I was taken as a slave in error. In that sense, I never was one. But I was shackled, I was put on a platform, I was *sold*. And, believe me, the experience of being seen as property stings far longer than any physical indignity I experienced.

"I was fortunate; I was bought by a liberal-minded owner, our living conditions were... well, no worse than I'd known before. We weren't overworked or abused. But still, we were not free. Until you've experienced that, you can't know what enslavement is."

"My mother intends to marry me to a man I do not know and do not care for," said Irmavel, her voice a dull overlay masking deep bitterness. "And then I will belong to him, will never be free of him. I think I may have some notion of how it feels to be unfree."

Jerya let this settle in her mind. "I understand, but I still believe the two things are different... And why are we talking about this at this time? They will be looking for you. What do you think I can do?"

"I know it's a great deal to ask, Countess, but... I'll beg if I have to. I need to stay out of sight till my birthday."

At eighteen she would be of age, could not be forced into marriage. Though, reflected Jerya, there were many forms of coercion short of outright imposition. "I do sympathise. But do you really think that we can hide you, that the unexpected addition of a young lady to our household, even in a house this size, can go unnoticed for... how long did you say?"

"Just shy of four months." Before she could respond, Irmavel had another question. "Countess... how long were you... how long did you live as an enslaved?"

"About the same, four months. A bit longer."

"And... of course, the arrival of a young lady in your household would attract attention. But the arrival of a new enslaved?"

How did I not foresee that? thought Jerya, simultaneously wondering if Mav were truly serious. "You want to be an enslaved?"

"If I can pass myself off until I am of age... it's like hiding in plain sight."

"When did you think of this?"

"Just a few moments ago, when you spoke of your own experienceprecision."

"I need to think about this. And so do you. But there's one other thing we should attend to. You came on horseback?" The girl nodded. "Horses are as recognisable as people, to those who know them."

"Yes, of course... I didn't take my usual riding horse, but this one will be just as recognisable."

"Then we had better do something about that." She rose. "No, you stay. Your food will be here shortly."

❋

"Nothing happens tonight," said Jerya, returning to find that Irmavel had disposed of a plate of sandwiches and an apple. "It's a drastic step, you only just thought of it, you should sleep on it. But... if you do go ahead, there'll be no half measures: you'll live like the other enslaved in this household. And that means... I don't mean that I don't talk to the staff. I do. It's important; I talk, and I listen. But one new enslaved doesn't get more time with me than any of the others. There won't be any more cosy chats after this. Is that clear? It's not just a case of making you look like a slave in case anyone is looking for Irmavel, daughter of—."

"—I understand. You lived as a slave and that's one of the reasons I admire you."

"There will always be a difference. When I was thrown into that life, I had no way of knowing I would ever get out of it. That's the reality for all who are truly enslaved. A few are granted manumission, usually at an advanced age, but most live and die as slaves. You can walk away on your eighteenth birthday."

Mavrys nodded soberly. She had taken the point.

"Anyway, no more cosy chats after today. So this is your chance."

"Thank you, Countess. I... most of all I would like to ask you about the Dawnsingers. Do they really rule over the Sung Lands?"

"Well, it's more complicated than that. But there is no higher authority."

"It must frustrate you that we—women—are *powerless* here."

"Well, I hope that this ridiculous title, Countess, will bring more chances to make things happen. But even in this privileged position, even as a Countess, I cannot own a house, an acre of land, the horse I ride... it's not mere frustration I feel, it's anger."

"Of course. I understand. But the reality of the Five Principalities is all too familiar to me. I want to know about the Sung Lands, about the Dawnsingers... if you don't mind talking about them, I mean."

"I don't mind. Oh, maybe there are moments I don't care to relive, but mostly... I was only there, in the College, for a few months, but it changed my life entirely. I suppose it changed *me,* probably has a bearing on everything I do to this day."

"How old were you?"

"A little older than you. Nineteen. Normally, girls are Chosen much younger, at ten or eleven. But I arrived knowing little more of the world than most of that age—and I mean the Sung Lands, because that was all the world we knew."

CHAPTER 3

MAVRYS

"Perhaps you should have a new name, too," said the Countess, testing the edge of the blade against her thumb.

"Yes, of course."

"Think about it while I do this. Above all, hold still. It's a while since I've done this... Sorry. That probably doesn't inspire confidence."

"I have complete confidence in you, Countess."

"No more talking. Just thinking."

She could think of any number of names, but one thought kept coming back to her. It kept her mind from the utter strangeness of the sensations; the blade whispering across her skin, the cool touch of air spreading across her scalp.

One thought: she'd actually said half of it yesterday. *It's Irmavel... My friends call me Mav, my Mamma hates it.*

I'm Mavrys. I'm Mavrys. I am Mavrys.

She thought again of what Countess Jerya had said; *no half measures.* And, later, *We can do this, I'll support you, but only if you're fully committed. You aren't disguising yourself as an enslaved, you aren't playing at being an enslaved, for the duration of this you* are *an enslaved.*

My name is Mavrys. I have no other name, answer to no other name.

My name is Mavrys. I am an enslaved. I do as I'm told. I go where I'm sent.

My name is Mavrys.

Once more her hand found its way to her scalp, once more she felt a kind of shock even though she was expecting the smoothness. The Countess had warned her about this too. *You'll probably do it a hundred times. I'm sure I did. Just try not to do it when anyone's watching.*

"This is Mavrys. Mavrys, this is Shevra. Put her to work, will you, please? Wherever you need help the most."

Broad-bodied and broad-faced, Shevra had ruddy skin and a Crest of silver hair, its braids more precise than the Countess's own.

"Thank yow, Ladyship. We c'n allus use an extra pair o' hands."

She curtseyed and Irm—*I'm Mavrys, I'm Mavrys*—hastily followed suit. Shevra waited until Jerya had left before turning back to face her newest slave.

"*Mavrys, em?*" she said. "*She ben trav kitch, laund, scrubben?*"

"I'm sorry, I don't understand."

"*She ken parl Patter?*"

"I'm really sorry, I still..."

Shevra gave a theatrical sigh, heavy shoulders rising. "Them dun't talk Patter wher'ver yow was afore?"

This was still hard—Shevra's accent seemed thicker now than when she'd been speaking to the Countess—but she could decipher it. And it wasn't hard to work out what 'Patter' meant.

"No, I'm sorry, I never learned."

"Yow'll pick't up. Yow'll have to... I was askin' where yow worked. Kitchen, laundry, cleanin'?"

Draff, what do I say now? And why didn't I anticipate this? "A little bit of everything." It was true, if polishing tack counted as cleaning. She'd pulled her weight around the stables for most of her life.

"Countess'd pro'ly ask what yow *likes* doin'." Shevra sniffed, as if she disapproved. "Me, I'm askin' what yow're best at."

I'm best *at caring for horses*, thought Mavrys. *But I don't suppose I can say that...* She thought about the 'accomplishments' of a young lady. A succession of governesses hadn't entirely failed to drum some skills into her. But she didn't think there was much demand for slaves who could bash out a few simple tunes on cimbalom or dulcimer. "Needlework, I suppose."

"Thatso?" Shevra arched a black brow. "Might try yow in th'linen room, then. But not right yet. What we need now is cleanin'." She snapped her fingers, turning. "Follow."

Vireddi was surely younger than herself, slight and pale. She'd seemed shy when Shevra first brought Mavrys to her. It didn't take her long to grow bolder. *"Nen, nen! She mun't go for duss likeso."*

"I'm sorry, I... I dun't parl Patter."

Bright green eyes widened. *"She dun't parl Patter? Wo she ben trav prev?"*

Mavrys shrugged helplessly. "I'm sorry," was all she could think to say.

Vireddi's expression softened. "Ben't yowr fault, reckon. Appen I c'n help yow learn?"

"Thank you... thank *yow*."

A sudden laugh pealed out, stifled hastily with a hand over the mouth. "Dun't ken what manner o'place yow trav'd afore, Mavrys, but yow sounds more like one o'th'fine folks than th'likes o'me."

"I guess I spent a lot of time around the fine folks. Picked up their way of speaking." A truth that felt like deceit.

"Well, mebbe it cud help, sometime. If they puts yow on waitin' tables, servin' drinks." She straightened, angled her head back, adopted a nasal intonation. "*May I po-ar yew some mo-ar wine, yewer ladyship?*"

In spite of everything, Mavrys laughed. "I don't sound like that, do I?" Vireddi only looked at her, head on one side. "Oh, draff... do I?" *No one's going to believe I really am a slave...* "What can I do?"

"Lissen, mostly, reckon. Lot o'th'time yow dun't have to say anythin but 'Yes, my lord,' 'Yes, my lady.'"

"But what about... Patter?"

"Patter ben't hard." Vireddi grinned. "*She go for ken parl notime.*"

"'You're going to learn to speak it in no time'?"

"*So, so! She semb apt for ken.*"

"Why's it always 'she' and not 'you'?"

Vireddi shrugged. "*So's ever ben't. Me, she.*"

"What about plurals? I mean, more than one person."

"*Parl* and *trav*," said Vireddi firmly. "*Viz: liff, duss, reput. She ken?*"

"*Me ken.*" She lifted a vase, passed the duster across the surface, replaced the vase.

"*Brav. Go for keepon... Me-me, she-she. Or he-he, or he-she.*"

"*He-she not she-he?*"

"*As she like.*"

They worked on, and Vireddi chattered cheerfully, and almost continuously; in Patter as much as possible, sometimes aiding comprehension with gestures or little mimes. She switched to Plain when she saw that Mavrys wasn't following. And so the morning passed, and by the time they went down to the slaves' dining room for lunch, Mav was able to follow, or at least catch a sense of, maybe half of the talk around her.

Much of it was about the new Earl and the new Countess and the changes they were instigating. Though the Earl, if she'd understood correctly, was absent, had been for over a week; somewhere far-off, she thought, though she hadn't fully understood beyond that. *I could have asked the Countess last night*, she thought. *No chance now.*

The free staff were no longer permitted to discipline the slaves physically; a couple of overseers had already been dismissed. Everyone seemed glad of that, and everyone seemed happy with improvements in the food they were served, though it was still plain fare. *Or have I just never thought what slaves might be served before this day?* she wondered sheepishly.

There was more doubt about the new sleeping quarters that were being planned, though as far as Mav could tell nothing had been decided. It seemed that everyone would have their own room, but not everyone wanted to sleep alone. *I wonder if I should tell the Countess?* thought Mav, and then remembered that she too was now a slave and presumably no more supposed to voice an opinion than any other.

I'll just have to wait and see if she asks, she thought, running a hand over the strange new smoothness of her scalp.

❈

After a few days she began to forget she had been Irmavel. She woke, usually to Vireddi banging on her door, dressed hastily, and followed her friend downstairs. Depending which queue was longer, they would go first to be shaved or to the breakfast counter.

To her, the food still seemed plain, though wholesome enough, but she continued to hear frequent expressions of pleasure. Just how bad, she wondered, had it really been before?

Conversations might be conducted in Plain, or in Patter, or in a mix. Sometimes one person would parl and the other reply in Plain; sometimes the same person would mingle the two in the same speech, even in the same sentence, to the extent that Mav began to wonder if they even saw a clear distinction between the two dialects at all.

At first it was confusing, but by and by she began to find it freeing. She tried to keep learning, to parl as much as possible; but this in itself became easier when you knew you could always drop in a Plain word or two when you were stuck.

While most words in Patter were recognisably derived from Plain, though truncated or warped or shifted in meaning, there were some she found more mysterious, like the numerals she recited to herself as she worked, until she knew them backwards: yann, tann, tetha, metha, pym, setha, letha, hotha, dotha, dyz, and so on. You had to be careful because 'tann', particularly in a broad Wolden accent, sounded a lot like 'ten', but you could nearly always tell from context which the speaker meant.

Vireddi took great delight in being her tutor. *My governess*, thought Mav, scarcely able to credit that she had occasionally fretted about the social stigma of being a gentleman's daughter who had no governess. As a young girl she had been schooled two days a week with the daughter of a neighbouring estate, by their governess; later, her mother had taken on the role herself—when she could prise Mav away from the stables. Vireddi, to Mav's eyes now, was a better teacher than either, patient and kind, and above all delighted by the responsibility. Perhaps responsibility was a new feeling for her; for sure she took it seriously.

And perhaps, she thought now, *she just likes* me.

Chapter 4

Railu

"**G**hastly, isn't it?" said Jerya, with a kind of breezy resignation.

Railu pondered a moment. Politeness might suggest that she disagree; but this was Jerya. "The basic proportions are fine, I think. It's just all the extra ornamentation."

"I suppose. But it's also the sheer scale of the whole place... You know, Kirwaugh was generous, I always thought. But Kirwaugh had five main bedrooms; that's still more than enough for two people."

"It won't always be just two."

"No... I still can't quite feel it's real. I don't think I will until I've told Hedric."

Railu squeezed her hand briefly. "And you often had other people there. Astronomers, campaigners, Dawnsingers. Even me."

"Especially you," said Jerya, returning the squeeze. "Yes, we tried to make something of it. And, you know, I'd grown very fond of Kirwaugh. I don't believe I'll ever feel like that about this place. If Kirwaugh had five bedrooms, Skilthorn must have six times as many. Draff, I haven't even *seen* them all... but four dining rooms, three sitting rooms, a picture gallery *and* a sculpture gallery... we even have two libraries."

"I wouldn't have thought you would ever think there could be such a thing as too many libraries."

Jerya *humphed*. "Most of my childhood I slept in a cave. In a cell so small I could touch both sides at once—when I was grown, I mean. I slept on a shelf of rock with just a thin pad stuffed with goat's wool. Then at the

College, I got an actual bed. I even had one to myself for a few weeks." She grinned impishly. "But we never really had many possessions to call our own, did we? At Duncal, well, there was the slave-quarters at first, but then I got my own room. And it wasn't fancy but it was twice the size of the one you and I shared in the College."

"Twice the floor area, maybe. But you couldn't stand up in half of it."

"Well, anyway... and then Kirwaugh, and suddenly I'm mistress of a whole estate. Five bedrooms, a morning-room, a drawing-room, a dining-room and a library. Oh, and forty-odd slaves; five in the household, serving *me*. *That* felt like a big adjustment. Took me a while to get comfortable with it... and I've never quite settled whether I *should*. You know, how can I be comfortable as a slave-owner? Whether it's one slave or a hundred or two draffing thousand?"

"Technically it's Hedric who's the slave-owner."

"*Technically*, yes. But I can't use one injustice to get me off the hook for another."

"Jerya... I can't know exactly how that feels. Half the people I meet still see me as a slave. I doubt I'll ever be in the position of an owner. Or an owner's wife, which is the closest I could get. But I do know something about *being* a slave. I lived that life, if you don't mind me saying, a lot longer than you did."

"I *mind* that you lived it, not that you remind me of it."

"Well, I'm not living it any longer. I can do some good in the world now. And so can you. You *are* doing. Didn't I hear you're planning on remodelling the slave-quarters?"

"I don't know whether to renovate what we have or build a whole new block. That'll have to wait till Hedric's back. But there are things that need fixing now. Leaky roofs..."

"How long have you been Countess now? Five weeks? You can't do it all overnight."

"Six weeks tomorrow... But if that's one step, what's the next one? All those other rooms, and just the two of us—when Hedric's here—but that's the question. What can we do to make this place *mean* something?"

"Well," said Railu, "Evisyn and I had a talk at Duncal. And it gave me an idea. I was going to put it to you and Hedric together, but since he's not here..."

※

Jerya looked tired, and by the time Railu had finished, a little overwhelmed. She sighed. "It's a good idea, but can we really do this now? Get enough people from all over the Five Principalities to travel here on a week or two's notice? Especially... our housekeeper's just given notice. She doesn't approve of what she calls 'laxness'."

"From what you've told me, I suppose anyone who could stomach working under the old Earl might not think much of your new broom."

"I'm not for sweeping anyone away just for working here before. I dare say some shut their eyes and carried on because they needed a job. As long as they adapt to new ways... it's bad enough losing the housekeeper; if we lose too many it'll be chaos."

She turned suddenly, faced her with a glint in her eye that Railu knew all too well. "Any ideas where I might find an experienced housekeeper? Someone I can trust? Someone who believes in a better life for the enslaved?"

Railu hadn't anticipated the suggestion, but somehow she wasn't surprised. There was a logic to it. However... "I'm sorry, Jerya, I'm really not inclined to leave Duncal just now, just when I've managed to build up some sort of practice."

"There'd be plenty of people needing your care here too."

"But I can't see how housekeeper here could ever be a part-time position. Even at Duncal it really only works because Rhenya's so capable; and Lutrin's shaping up pretty well too.

"There's another thing, too. I can't help thinking coming here to work for you—to be employed by you—would be, well, strange. I'd have to call you 'my lady', wouldn't I?"

"Rai, I'd never want that."

"But how would it look, calling you 'Jerya' in front of your staff?"

Jerya snorted. "*Laxness...*"

"I wouldn't do it—and then I'd worry about calling you 'Jerya' in private, in case it slipped out in public."

Jerya sighed. "You're right, of course. But then, draffit, what am I going to do? And how can I even consider inviting... I don't know, maybe *dozens* of panjandrums, from all across the land, when I don't have a housekeeper?"

"Is there not some other capable person? Someone who knows the house, the routines... a deputy, perhaps?"

"Gillas was second housekeeper when I first came here. She only advanced to first about a year ago. I'm now reliant on *her* deputy, and she's clearly inexperienced. She seems permanently flustered, and she leans heavily on her lead slave, Shevra."

Railu sighed. "We both know how much responsibility some slaves carry, and how rarely it's recognised... Jerya, I won't come and work for you permanently, but I can see you need help. I'll do whatever I can while I'm here, and if you do decide to go ahead with the congress, I'll do my best to come back for that too. It was kind of my idea, after all."

"Thank you. It means a lot to me. Well, let's think a bit more. See if we can thrash out some sense of how big this thing could be, who we could invite... and whether they'd come, of course." Her clear laugh rang out and a second later a faint echo came back, presumably from the great slab-facade of the house. "Just imagine if we got all hot and bothered about it and then nobody turned up anyway!"

Chapter 5

Railu

"I cared for him, five year'n'more. Cared for him fai'f'ly, I did. I spoke for him when no'un else could und'stan him." Her eyes almost met Jerya's. "Well, yow saw, yowr ladyship."

"I did, many times." Jerya looked at Railu. "Three or four times a year, over four years... I saw a good deal. You were faithful, Dortis. More than he deserved, I always thought."

"I dun't know about 'deserved', m'lady."

"I thought—and Hedric saw this before I did—*that girl has the soul of a healer.* Well, I wrote to you, didn't I?"

"You did," agreed Railu.

"But ever since he died... I feel bad about it, Dortis. I saw how things were but there always seemed to be something else I had to do. Trying to change things around here... but it's not a good enough excuse. The way you cared for the Earl was extraordinary. And I don't suppose he ever thanked you for it. I'm not sure that man ever thanked anybody for anything in—what is it?"

The girl was weeping now. Railu slipped an arm round her shoulders, felt the bones all too present under her hand.

"What is it, Dortis?" asked Jerya again.

"I can't tell yow, m'lady. Yow'll think I'm wicked."

"Tell me," said Railu. "You don't know me, I'm not part of this house-hold. And I'm a healer, I know something about difficult patients. Though I don't think I ever had one like the old Earl, from what I've heard."

She glanced over Dortis's bowed head. Jerya got the message, stayed where she was as Railu gently steered Dortis to the far end of the room. There she turned her around till they faced each other, hands resting lightly on the girl's shoulders.

"Are yow truly a slave?" asked Dortis. "Yow're not one o'them Dawnsingers?"

Railu smiled. "I'm not one of those Dawnsingers, no." *Not for fourteen years...*

Dortis frowned. Railu was well aware that she was a puzzle to many people, both slaves and frees. Dortis would see someone who looked like a slave but spoke to the Countess as an equal, a friend.

Perhaps Dortis needed just a little more encouragement. "I'm not going to think you're wicked, no matter what you tell me."

Dortis hesitated, then evidently made up her mind. "Yow know how I spoke for him? How I could und'stan' him when no'un else could?"

"I heard about that, yes."

"Right at th'end it were just a mumble. Last month or so. Couldn't make out more'n one word in..." Dortis shrugged. "Ten, twenty, dun't know."

"From what I've heard, it was like that for everyone else a long time before. Jerya told me about the first time she met—"

Dortis was looking at her with renewed suspicion. "Yow mean th'Countess?"

"Her name is Jerya. And I've known her a long time. Fourteen years, near enough."

"But yow said yow're a slave..."

Railu sighed. "I just said I wasn't a Dawnsinger. And I'm not a slave, but I've lived that life. I know what it feels like. And I'm also a healer. That's why J—why the Countess and the Earl, the *new* Earl—that's why they wanted me to meet you. They told me about you a long time ago. But you were taken up with the old Earl, caring for him day and night." She gave a little shake of the head. "But that's not the point right now. The point is... I'm a healer. And there's a thing called confidentiality. It means if someone tells me something when I'm caring for them I don't tell anyone else."

"But I was carin' for *him*. That means... what yow're sayin' is, I can't tell yow, can't tell nobody, what he said to me."

Draff, thought Railu, *have I just scuppered my own strategy?* She tried to think fast. "I said I'm a healer. I was *trained* as a healer. I took a Physician's vow—a healer's vow. That's when I swore to protect the confidentiality of every patient. I don't believe you ever... did you ever have any training?"

"Doctor told me a few things... Doctor Aiskin."

"But that's all. And you never swore any vow?"

"No, never."

"Then you're not bound the way I am. It's between you and your con- science. But if something he said is weighing on you now, if that's why you're not eating properly... then I think you need to tell me. Listen, Dortis, you can trust me. I promise I won't tell another living soul. Not without your permission."

Dortis gazed at her. Railu could see the longing to tell someone, how it warred with her sense of duty. It was long seconds before she decided, but from the moment she began, the words spilled out of her in a torrent.

"It were one o'th' last things he said. That I could und'stan', I mean. It were gettin' hard by then. Often he had to say things two or three times. It made him mad. Not with me, mostwise, just mad. Mad wi' th'whole world, belike."

"I get the feeling he was already like that a lot of the time."

"I dunno, rightly; mostly I only saw him after he were sick. Then, for- sure, most o'th' time he was mad wi' some'un or somethin' or just, like I say, wi'th'whole world. But this time, time I'm talkin' of, he didn't seem mad. More sad, yow know? Like he knew he din't have long. And this thing he said to me..." Dortis wrapped her arms around herself. She looked past Railu as if examining the bookshelves. "Took a long time to get it all out. Like I said, had to repeat ever'thin' two, three, e'en four times. But it came down to this: *Yow've been my voice for years now, girl. Don't know what I'd ha' done wi'out yow. But my voice will be silent soon, and I want yow to honour my silence. When I'm gone, go to the slavemaster an' tell 'im... Tell him yowr tongue's to be clipped."*

Railu took a pace backward, feeling as if she would fall down if she didn't. Dortis's last words struck her like a physical blow. She stared at the girl and for what felt like a full minute she could not speak.

And Dortis—*oh, you poor thing*—looked at her as if Railu were blaming *her* for failing to comply with that barbaric order. "I know I done wrong," she said rapidly. "But I thought, if'n I jus' kept silent anyway, mebbe I din't have to..."

"I had no idea... by the moons, he wasn't a man, he was a monster. How you could care for him, *speak* for him, for five years and more... I don't believe I could have done it for five minutes." She pondered briefly. "You need to tell J—the Countess."

"Yow promised yow wun't tell nobody."

"I did, and I won't. I said *you* need to tell her."

"She'll have me called out for disobeyin'—"

"—She won't, I promise you." Dortis gave her a doubting look. "Listen, she's my oldest friend. I knew her long before she was a Countess, before she was Mistress of Kirwaugh, before... well, it's quite a story and this isn't the time. She'll be as horrified as I am. With him, not you."

Jerya was struck dumb. *And that doesn't happen very often*, thought Railu. It had to be a full thirty seconds before she could speak. At last she shook herself like a wet dog. "Come over here, Dortis. Sit down with me."

"We en't to sit in th' presence of our betters, yowr Ladyship."

"And who told you that?" Jerya was smiling now. "Is there someone whose orders have more weight than mine?"

"We always was..."

"*Was*. In the past. Things are different now." She guided Dortis to one of the armchairs that stood around the hearth. In the grate a fire was laid but not lit. Jerya hitched up her skirts and knelt before it, drew a box of matches from the firestand, and struck a flame.

Railu watched Dortis, almost quivering in her chair, the thought as plain as if it was printed on her brow: *I should be doing that.* She smiled at the girl, shook her head gently.

It was a warm afternoon, no real need for a fire, but she knew Jerya was making a point.

The Countess of Skilthorn sat back on her heels, gazing into the flames as they began to lick at the larger logs, sparking highlights like glowing embers in her hair.

Finally she returned the matchbox to its drawer and got easily to her feet. She took the chair facing Dortis and gestured Railu to the third. "Things are different now," she repeated. "Lots to work out still, can't change everything overnight, but we always knew where we were going to start.

"The day he died, the very first thing we did, as soon as we got here... we issued instructions to all the overseers, all the staff, on all Skilthorn properties. From that moment on, there would be no more clipping of tongues. No more flogging. No more mutilation of any kind."

Dortis looked at her as if she didn't dare believe her ears. *Looking for the trap*, thought Railu. "But it were his dying wish, yowr Ladyship."

Jerya waved a hand, dismissing the notion. "If it had been written into his will, then we would have a problem. And at this moment I don't know how I'd have dealt with that... but it wasn't, so we don't have to worry. And to change his will, the witnesses would have had to be assured he was of sound mind. Tell me, would a man in his right mind really give such an order to the person who above all others had cared for him for five years and more?"

CHAPTER 6

MAVRYS

And then the Dawnsingers arrived. The Countess had let it be known a couple of days before, and there was much anticipation among the slaves. Like the rest of them, Mav had never seen a Dawnsinger, but she had read about them almost as avidly as she had about Countess Jerya, and she soon found herself correcting some of the wilder rumours. Yes, they were all women; and, yes, they were all bald, just like slaves; but no, they couldn't tell how long you'd live or who you'd marry just by looking at you. Without saying *how* she knew, it was hard to convince everyone that she did know what she was talking about; in the end she resorted to, "Where I was afore, I heard th'Mistress talkin' 'bout them." It was true, as far as it went; her mother had been Mistress of Carinnan, and she had expressed opinions on the subject of Dawnsingers. She didn't say that the gist of those opinions had been, 'It sounds unnatural, if you ask me.'

On the expected day of their arrival, there was an unusual spectacle: slaves petitioning Shevra for cleaning duties in the front rooms. Everyone wanted that first glimpse of these exotic females; but Shevra was not to be moved. "I has my rota in my head," she declared, "And I's stickin' to it. Only way to be fair to ev'ryone. And I dun't want to catch anyone sneakin' off to the front what ain't rightly workin' there."

To their delight, Mav and Vireddi were rota'd for upstairs front that day, but delight soured when they were tasked with bathroom duty. It was never a favourite anyway, but today it was frustrating because the windows were of patterned glass. Good for guests' privacy, bad for slaves who wanted to see any comings and goings.

When Mav grumbled, Vireddi got a knowing look, and disappeared for a minute or two. "*Brav*," she said on return, "*Cherrin she go for yap soonas she see she-she.*"

"*Brav*," said Mavrys from her kneeling position, and returned to wiping the tangle of pipes and valves behind the water-closet. After a moment she added, "*Who go for clean ahind thim afore? She nen go for do prop'ly.*"

They were on the third bathroom when the call came, and rushed to the nearest bedroom to find that the group of riders were still a good way off, only just this side of the lake. When they came nearer, Mav and Vireddi looked at each other, puzzled. There were eight, which fitted, as the slaves had been told to prepare eight rooms. But...

"*She-she ben't bal'*," said Vireddi.

"*En ben bal'*," said Mav, pointing to a rider near the front of the group. "*Appen she slave.*"

Mav wasn't so sure. "*Me-she see quan she-she in-come.*"

They did see. A couple of slaves had been in attendance as the Dawnsingers were welcomed into the house, and a dozen more were peering over the balustrades from the higher floors. All agreed that by the time the party entered, all were revealed as bald.

"Wigs," said Mavrys that night at the dinner table. It was beyond anything she could do in Patter, either to explain what a wig was or to conjecture why the Dawnsingers might wear them. "S'pose they make 'em less..." Was 'conspicuous' a word a slave would use? "So people take less notice of 'em. But I never saw eight women riding together, no men with 'em."

"Ben't got no men in den Sung Lands," said someone, casually mixing Patter and Plain.

"*Nen!*" she said now. "*Ben't vrai. Sung Lands got men, jussame den Princ'pal'ies.*" She switched. "And most women ain't Dawnsingers neither. Girls get Chosen—that's what they call it—when they're *dyz* or *yann-a-dyz*. And they dun't choose more'n a few each year."

"*How-be she go for ken allmuch?*"

"*Me gotten shellies,*" said Mav, tapping an earlobe.

She wasn't the only one with ears, or eyes, and more reports were being shared in the shaving-queue next morning. They had names for some of the Singers now; the tall one was Evisyn, and someone said she was called 'Master' as well.

"Woman can't be Master," said an older woman, whose name Mav thought was Tehir. "Yow mus' mean Mistress."

"I hear 'em," said the other, lifting his chin. "Close as I am to yow or Mavrys now. One o'th'other Dawnsingers, 'twere, the one with eyeglasses. 'Master', she say. I knows th' differen' from 'Master' and 'Mistress'. And 'twere a bit more. Master-somethin'... Master-prize, sound like."

"Master Prime?" said Mavrys.

"Appen, yem."

Could that be true? she wondered as she settled in the chair for her turn. *The Master Prime of the Guild here in the Five Principalities? Here at Skilthorn? That ought to be in the papers...* Of course she didn't get to see the papers now. Not that she'd been a keen newspaper-reader before; but she had read *The First Crossing. The First Crossing of the Dividing Range by the Southerly Route*, to give its full title, except that only the first three words appeared on the spine, and even on the title page the rest was in far smaller type. When she'd realised the implications of this, Mav's indignation had been thoroughly roused on behalf of Jerya—not then a Countess—and she felt stirrings of the same ire now.

"Hold still," said Felleth.

Mav calmed herself. That was old news, anyway. She had taken much more from the book, had found the references to Jerya; a few lines only acknowledging her as the pioneer of the true First Crossing, but rather more covering the part she'd played around the first meetings between Dawnsingers—including Master Prime Evisyn, she seemed to recall—and men from the Five Principalities.

As the Countess had warned, there was much to be done. Every bedroom—every one of the 'fine folks' rooms—had to be made ready. The beds were always made up, but they had to be aired, which meant lighting a fire in every room, opening the windows, and folding back the eiderdown and top sheet.

Supervising all this was one of the Dawnsingers' party. The one, thought Mav, who had not worn a wig riding up the drive. She seemed unlike her companions. After arrival, the others had soon changed into white clothing, but this one appeared in a rust-red skirt and a blouse of pale primrose yellow.

Miss Railu, as they'd been told to call her, was wearing the same the next day. She came along the passage, looking into each room, perhaps making a note if the room was empty, but always seeming to have a pleasant word or two for any slave she found at work. A couple of times she heard laughter.

As she appeared at the door, Mav dropped into a curtsey. "Really," said Railu, "There's no need for that. I was a slave myself for ten years, you know."

Mav, rising, looked at her curiously, but remembered she was a slave and held back the questions that flocked to her mind. Railu smiled. "And now you're wondering why I'm still bald."

"Appen so, Miss."

"Well, let's get this bedding sorted and I'll tell you while we work."

Railu wasn't far into her tale before Mav realised. In her excitement she quite forgot about sounding like a slave. "You're the... I mean, you were Jerya's companion on the First Crossing. The *true* First Crossing."

"You know about that, do you?"

"I read every—" She broke off, feeling a blush heating her cheeks.

"Something tells me you're a little different from the other enslaved I've been talking with."

"I try not to be, Miss. Not to be different, I mean."

"All the same, I think you have a story to tell, too."

So then it was her turn. As they worked, Railu listened attentively. When Mav was finished, she said, "Thank you for sharing that with me, Mavrys. I wish I had more time but there's so much to do. I hope we can talk again soon."

"I hope so too, Miss."

CHAPTER 7

JERYA

Jerya settled into a chair in the Lesser Library, which had quickly assumed the standing of her favourite room in the house.

My dearest, she read.

Bastil has just announced his intention to send a man down to scurry up some more supplies, which means he can take mail also. Of course he wanted to send the fellow off at once, and took some persuading to allow me twenty minutes to scribble this hasty note to you.

So much I would like to say, and so little time. But I must get on and say something rather than waste the time chewing my pen and staring at the screes. It is a bleak enough prospect, a gritty little flat space where we are pitched, a jumble of scree and boulders above, rearing high enough to block most of the peaks that bound the valley. Behind us the stream curls across the flat, its water opaque and blue-white. We have ascertained that this is due to an abundance of sediment, as fine as flour. Fascinating as a clue to the processes going on beneath the ice. of course, but a darned nuisance from the point of view of drinking and cooking. We have nothing fine enough to serve as a practical filter, and we have established that the sediment takes an interminable time to settle, so much of our servants' energy has been consumed traipsing back and forth more than a mile down the valley to a clear spring.

It is almost as far upstream to the beginning—or rather the end—of the glacier. And when you reach it, a rough journey, first impressions are hardly inspiring. Indeed, you might wonder whether you have reached the ice at all, so overstrewn with rocky debris is it. You must recall, as I do, those distant glimpses of ice from our peak on our Crossing, all white and shining. Here it was only by climbing some way above the glacier that we were able to see its full extent and observe, higher up, that clean white glimmer.

It will no doubt amuse you to hear that in this company I have been nominated as the climbing expert. Really, of course, Lallon is the best man for the job, but Bastil is not inclined to take advice from, still less submit to leadership from, a slave.

Blast the stiff-necked old antique! I know he's not really so old, and he is spry enough on rough ground, but he's so set in his ways he gives the air of a much older man. It's this same side of his character that made it impossible for both you and I to accompany him on this expedition. And, as matters have unfolded, you may well think I should not have been so stiff-necked either, insisting that my promise to him trumped my obligations to you, and to all the people of Skilthorn. I'm tempted to throw the blame on my uncle—really, could he have chosen a more inconvenient moment to make his final, and otherwise unlamented, departure?—but I know that's mere deflection.

And I am daily haunted by the thought that you would love it here. It is, as I say, a cheerless spot in many ways, and as lacking in comfort as any of our camps on the Crossing, but there is so much to see and, most importantly, to learn.

Bastil is looking significantly at his watch, and I really think I must humour him and close this letter soon. Let me say this: among our observations and our collection of samples, we have embedded a number of wands in the ice, some way up 'stream', and taken careful bearings on each from our high-point, as well as sketching reference points on the rock buttresses above. The intention is to return, possibly at the end of the season, possibly next spring, to see if we can confirm, first of all, that the glacier does move. I cannot see any credible account in which it does not; the ice melts, and we have seen chunks break off at the very end, around the blue cave-like aperture from which the stream emerges. If the ice does not advance, how does this eroding terminus remain in place from year to year? And how did the thing reach so far below the summer snowfields in the first place? The argument is compelling, at least in my view, but argument is not proof.

Well, my dear, there is every reason to return in due course, but I have studiously avoided making any new promises to Bastil. He may be a sound philosopher, but I find his company wearing. More importantly, I have no wish to repeat so long a separation. I can justify my presence this time, at least to myself, on the grounds that I was cozened into making a rash promise. I cannot defend making the same mistake a second time, and I would not want to.

Let us come here together as soon as we are able, my dearest. I know you will be struck, and fascinated, and I am sure you will have many original suggestions as to the most rewarding observations we might make. Most of all, I believe you will love it. But beyond all that, I think it would be unconscionable of me to abandon you as I have done these last weeks. I hope it goes without saying that I have every confidence in you, and unhesitatingly granted the widest possible proxy responsibilities, but with every day that passes I feel more strongly that I should be at your side, most particularly at such an early stage of our custodianship of the Skilthorn estates.

I have yet to engage in a serious discussion with Bastil about the date of our departure, but I shall do so very soon, and to argue for the earliest possible. I do not know if I shall be able to give you fair warning of my return. It is not very likely that Bastil will agree to another despatch of mail from here, and even when we reach civilisation again, notification always depends on the weather allowing either a heliograph or avian service to function. And there is really only one place from which either could be sent, before I am within half a day's ride of home, so it is very much unknown. So you may or may not have any advance warning of my return. Let me only assure you that I long for that day and I feel sure that you do too.

Bastil's shadow has now fallen across my page and I fear he might detonate if I turn to a new one, so I really must end here.

I fondly hope that all is well with you and yearn to see you soon.

From the bottom of my heart

Hedric

CHAPTER 8

RAILU

Two days after their first meeting, Railu encountered Mavrys on the back stairs. The girl stepped aside and curtseyed; it looked like a reflex, as if she'd been a slave all her life.

"How are you, Mavrys?"

"I'm quite well, Miss." For a moment that seemed to be all, but then Mavrys blurted, "May I ask you a question, Miss Railu?"

Railu cocked her head, considering. "Is this a question I can answer in one minute?"

"Probably not... I'm sorry, Miss, it's an impertinence, I shouldn't have asked."

"It must be important, or you wouldn't have... What time do you finish your dinner? Half after six?"

"I can be finished by then, Miss."

"Jerya mentioned a place... a grove opposite the West front. Meet me there."

"Thank you so much."

✳

What Jerya had called a 'grove' was actually a narrow wood, at right angles to the house. Before they had gone more than a dozen paces, they found their path descending, decanting them into a shady dell where a tiny stream trickled over a rocky bed.

Railu stooped to lay her hand on a smooth shield of dark rock, dry now but clearly smoothed by water. "I can see why Jerya likes it here," she said. "The living rock... I suppose it reminds her of the place she grew up."

"Delven."

"I see you've paid attention to your reading."

"It fascinated me, Miss. To think of all that the Countess has done—and you too, of course."

"Call me Railu, at least while we're here. Now... I came late, and I dare say both of us need to be back soon. So, please, tell me why you needed to speak with me."

"I won't waste a moment more of your time than I must. It's just one question. It it possible... do you think *I* could be a Dawnsinger?"

Railu hadn't anticipated that question. For a moment she was silent, concentrating on the path as it descended over rocks, not looking at Mavrys. She trailed her fingers over dark green foliage springing from a crevice in the rocks. "Maidenhair spleenwort," she said. "It's a fern, but you wouldn't necessarily think so, would you? Lots of ferns here. Shady and damp, it's just the place."

She glanced back as the path broadened, motioned Mavrys to come up alongside her. "And now I'm wasting *your* time babbling about ferns. But I needed a moment to think... Tell me, what makes you ask that?"

"Because... When I came here, threw myself on the Countess's mercy, all I could think of was getting away, finding some way to hide out until my birthday. I never really thought past that. But what happens when I do turn eighteen? I can refuse to marry that man, yes, but what then? Do I go back to my family? Maybe they couldn't *force* me to marry him, but they could still put a lot of pressure on... I just know my mother would keep saying she's not angry, only disappointed."

Railu smiled. "I can see that would sting."

"But if I don't go back there, what can I do? Where can I go? I can hardly go on living off the Countess's charity indefinitely."

"You aren't. You're earning your keep, like every other enslaved. Earning your keep and a lot more. Enslaved built the house, put carpets on the floors and paintings on the walls. You ask Jerya. Remember, she's been a slave too. She'd say, it's not you living off her charity, *she's* living off your hard work." She stopped, looked into Mavrys's eyes. "If that's all that worries you, why not carry on being a slave?"

"Because..." She stopped.

"I was a slave for ten years, and now I've been free for four. And most of the time my life doesn't feel a lot different."

Mav opened her mouth then shut it again, bemusement plain on her face..

Railu gripped her shoulder for a moment. "I'm sorry, I'm confusing you. I suppose you were thinking *in a few months*... how long, Mavrys?"

"Three months now, near enough."

"*In three months I'll be free; but free to do what?* That's the question, isn't it? And I suppose that's why you thought about becoming a Dawnsinger?"

"Yes."

"You know they normally Choose girls at ten or eleven?"

"Yes, but the—Jerya was older, wasn't she?"

Railu smiled, glanced at her wrist. "We'll have to start heading back soon... Yes, she was older. Older than you, indeed, nineteen... But why do you think you want that life? How do you know you'll be suited for it?"

"I don't, if I'm truly honest. Don't know enough about it. I hoped you could help me with that."

Railu only looked at her, until Mavrys added, "I've seen the Dawnsingers around the house, the last few days. And of course at first glance they look like slaves—"

"—Just like me."

"Aye, but you're not, and you can soon see they're not. It's in how they carry themselves, the way they talk. And they rule over the Sung Lands. So it seemed to me that must be the one place where women are truly free."

"If you're saying that women here *aren't* free, I completely agree. Maybe a few of us manage to chip out some kind of freedom for ourselves, but it's hard. But... remember, Mavrys, we left the Sung Lands and came here. I didn't know what I was going to find, of course. Not the faintest idea...

"Now, though... I've lived on this side nearly half my life. Think I know something about both."

"I could go back, you know. Master Evisyn—the Master Prime—told me herself. And don't think there's no temptation..." She sighed. "You might wonder why I don't. I wonder myself... I suppose I have all summer to think about it. But somehow I think... I'm rooted here.

"But listen, Mavrys, what I really need to tell you... don't go imagining that Dawnsingers are free. As a Postulant, a Novice, an ordinary Singer, your life's very ordered. Dawnsinger say: *you do what you're told and you go where you're sent.* Maybe after twenty or thirty years you might rise to the position where you're one of the ones giving the orders, rather than taking them, but even then... Do you think even the Master Prime is truly free? Do you, or I, any of us, really even know what freedom is?"

"Don't take this wrong. The life of a Dawnsinger is a fine one in many ways. But... it's not all one life either: a Singer in a remote village has a very different life from one in the College in Carwerid. I knew the College life, but when they told me they were sending me off to the other, I was... well, never mind that. We probably should be turning around, and I've hardly even begun to answer your real question."

They began to retrace their steps. Overhead the trees sighed in a breeze unfelt in these depths.

"I was at the College for eight years," said Railu. "You know Jerya was there for four months, don't you? Even a little less. Though I think she might have learned more in that time than some people did in as many years."

"She's extraordinary."

Railu smiled. "That's one word... Being Jerya's friend isn't always plain sailing, but it's never dull... But you didn't want to talk about Jerya, you wanted to talk about the College and the Guild.

"The first thing I should tell you is that in eight years I never saw another girl Chosen after the usual age. Maybe that's just Jerya being *extraordinary* again, but I think... Sharess, Jerya's—Delven's Dawnsinger—she was the one who Chose her at that age. And..." She sighed. "To be honest, I've never been sure Sharess was quite well at the time. In her mind, I mean. When I met her, after those same four months, she was much better, but by then I think even she herself had some suspicions. We knew she'd been bodily ill and weak at the time, but I've never fathomed out what that illness might have been, so I can't say for sure it affected her judgement. In the end all I know is that what she did was very unusual, even unprecedented.

The path narrowed as they approached the steeper section at the end of the dell. They had to go single file, picking up their skirts to negotiate the steps made by rocks and roots. But Railu kept talking, throwing words over her shoulder. "I don't want to throw cold water on your dreams, but I strongly doubt the Guild would accept another late Postulant. After what happened with Jerya it's doubly unlikely. For there even to be a chance, they'd have to be sure you were absolutely committed to it."

"That's the thing. I don't know enough about it to know for sure that it *is* what I want."

Railu glanced back at her. "Then you're not off to a good start."

"But maybe if I knew a bit more...?"

"Tell me, why do you think it might be for you?"

"I... I just want to do something that means more than being married to a stranger. You know, you're a healer, J—the Countess has done all sorts of things. And seeing the Singers, these last few days, even from a distance. The Master Prime... she's like a Prince or something. *And...*" She rubbed a hand over her scalp. Railu remembered how shocking that had been at first—and how quickly it had ceased to be. "And they look like me now.

You too. Almost like I'm halfway to being a Dawnsinger already. But most of all I just want to... to *do something* too."

"Well, that's admirable. I wish more girls in the Five Principalities felt that way. I know Jerya does too. I know education for girls is one of the things she wants to... but you should talk to her about that."

"It's a lot harder to get time with her than with you."

Railu smiled. "I'm the next-best thing, am I?"

"I'm sorry, I didn't mean it like that... Really, I think you're amaz—"

"Don't worry. You're absolutely right, she's extraordinary. I couldn't compete with her if I wanted to, and mostly I don't want to. She carries a heavy load."

"But you save lives every day."

Reaching level ground, they stopped before the last of the trees.

"Not *every* day... But we're straying again. You wanted to know about being a Dawnsinger. Let's come at it another way. Tell me, do you... do you like reading?"

"I do," said Mav, obliging but clearly puzzled.

"What kind of books? History, natural philosophy?"

"Oh... mostly stories. But I always thought stories meant for boys were much more exciting than the ones meant for girls. I found a collection of books my father had when he was young." Suddenly she was blinking furiously. "But true stories, too. I told you, I read everything I could find about Jerya. And I read the Duke of Selton's *The First Crossing*, too. Though it should be called *The Second Crossing*, really."

"The Third, if we're being picky... no, the Fourth."

"The Fourth?"

"Ah, that's... not exactly a secret, but we don't talk about it often. Jerya and I weren't alone on the First Crossing. And our companion, Rodal, went back about a year later."

"On her own?"

"His own, actually, but yes, alone. Therefore Jerya, Hedric and Lallon made the *Third* Crossing."

Together they left the trees and hastened across the lawn, now in the shadow of the house; passed into sunlight again as they followed the South front. Conversation and music drifted from open windows. Just before they reached the steps, Railu stopped.

"The First Crossing, we didn't know what we'd find. We didn't even know that such things as Countesses *existed*... Seven years in the College of the Dawnsingers and we were barely prepared for anything we found here." Railu chuckled softly. "Maybe it's not such a complete education after all."

Part Two
The Congress

CHAPTER 9

SKELBER

There was something not quite right about the horse's gait; hardly a limp, but a distinct hitch. And either it was getting worse, or he was starting to notice it more.

Since Fulmer was only half a horse behind him, he turned in his saddle. "Your pardon, Doctor Fulmer..." One must always be sure to address him as 'Doctor'; otherwise he was all too apt to take offence. "I wonder if you could do me a kindness?"

"What is it, Skelber?" He was not so punctilious about returning the courtesy of the title, but he came up alongside.

"Would you be so good as to look at my horse for a few moments? There's something uneasy in his stride."

"That's the thing with post-horses," said Fulmer. "Never know what you're going to get."

That was true, though in no way helpful; but Fulmer did at least deign to observe the horse for a minute or so. "Might be favouring his right fore a little," he said finally.

"Thank you, I was forming the same impression. How far to the next staging post?"

'Three miles at the last milestone."

"I should think he'll manage to carry me that far, then. And I'll mention it to the ostler when we arrive."

"Likely he'll know the horse; it probably spends its life up and down this same road."

Aye, Doctor Fulmer, I know how post-horses are worked. But really, he thought, it had been a perfectly innocent remark; he might have said it himself had the roles been reversed. It was just that almost anything Fulmer said could feel like salt on an open wound.

The mystery was that Skelber had not thought of himself as bearing any open wounds.

❋

Fulmer having trotted on ahead to confer with Le'ast, he had the liberty of the remaining couple of miles to consider this. The loss of Selence was a wound, of course, but surely it was a scar, not an open sore. *Twelve years...*

Was it, then, that Fulmer was just one of those people whose nature was fundamentally at odds with his own? There had been fellows at school, at the Medical Academy, who had irked him beyond reason; and others who seemed to find Skelber himself equally provoking. Maybe it was that; but he could hardly hope to evade Fulmer's company for the next two weeks.

No, the three of them, the official delegation of the Denvirran Medical Association, would be very much together. *I should have thought about that before...* Though it would hardly have been politic to decline. To be invited onto the delegation to Skilthorn was a great honour, and hinted at prospects for advancement; to turn it down would surely vitiate those.

Besides all that, he was intrigued to see the famous—sometimes infamous—Countess Jerya; and perhaps even more so to see Dawnsingers. And on a personal note, he would hate to disappoint Le'ast. He could only hope that his respect for the older man would compensate for his less noble feelings toward the younger.

Perhaps. But he knew there was more behind his dislike than mere personal incompatibility. Fulmer had to be five years his junior, if not more. It could be as much as ten. How, then, did he come to hold a higher position in the Association?

But, then again, was it really higher? Arguably they were of equivalent ranking; it was just that Fulmer, being in the Administration office and working directly under Le'ast, tended to assume the air of the insider. *As if Ethics and Enforcement were any less essential to the good conduct of the profession.* He managed to avoid grinding his teeth. It had been his habit once, until his dentist had given him a stern talking-to.

Yes, Fulmer had a way of implying that E&E was somehow... peripheral. Not that he had ever said anything explicit; the closest he had come was in his first greeting when their party assembled: "Ah, Skelber. So they've managed to spare you for this jaunt, eh? Well, I suppose some can be spared more readily than others."

It had been all he could manage not to retort, "I see Admin's managed to spare *you*, Doctor."

❋

Skelber was glad to find that his new mount had a more regular gait. The ostler had nodded sagely: "Aye, 'appen he's been overworked this week, and th' gen'l'man what took 'im yesterday... well, he'd nigh of made two of yow, sir. We'll give 'im a day's rest."

It was a pity, he was thinking now, that the lunch they'd been given hadn't been equally satisfactory.

It seemed as if Le'ast was thinking along similar lines. "Well, Doctor Skelber, I hope tonight's inn will be more salubrious than that last one."

Skelber throttled the thought that Le'ast himself was the reason they were spending two nights on the road rather than one. Admittedly, Denvirran to Skilthorn was a good distance; and perhaps, if he were honest, he wasn't quite as riding-fit as he had been. There wasn't much call for it in the city. He thought wistfully of his days in a country practice... but city life had to be better for Sumyra, especially with his own sister just a few streets away.

He made some anodyne reply to the older man and Le'ast nodded rather absently. His mind was already running on to something new. "Dawnsingers... Have you ever seen any of these... remarkable ladies?"

"Once or twice, at a distance. At least, I believed them to be Dawnsingers; what else is one to think when one sees a group of women with bald heads, all dressed in white, being received at the main gate of the University?"

"Just so... Well, I too have not had the pleasure."

"Do you call it pleasure, then, sir?" asked Fulmer, coming up on Le'ast's further side.

"I call it a most... intriguing prospect, at the least. I must say I really do not know quite what to expect."

"What about you, Skelber?" said Fulmer.

"I try to keep an open mind," he said, quite aware that he had omitted to add 'Doctor'.

CHAPTER 10

MAVRYS

She was halfway shaved when the commotion began. Seconds later someone stuck their head in at the door. "Countess is comin'."

The strokes of the blade across her scalp speeded up unnervingly, and Imress abandoned her entirely to rinse and towel herself. By the time she arrived in the dining hall the Countess was already speaking.

"…will mean a lot of extra work for everyone. It's quite possible every bedroom will be filled. I know there haven't been large numbers of guests here for ten years at least. So Mistress Meryth and Shevra and I will be doing the rounds this morning to weigh up exactly what needs to be done. And I wanted to say a thank you in advance to all of you by making today a holiday, for everyone who can be spared."

Vireddi guided her to a bench by the lake. Mav pulled off her shoes and pressed her feet into the grass. Vireddi was looking around, and Mav realised she was checking they couldn't be overheard. The nearest people were a group perhaps forty yards away. One was patting the ground; she said something, and they all settled to the grass. Unless you counted the moorhen that was poking about in the reeds near their feet, there were no eavesdroppers.

"People been talkin'," said Vireddi.

"Talking?" Then light dawned. "About me, you mean?"

"Appen. Some dun't reck yow can be a true slave."

Mav sighed. "I suppose it's the way I speak?"

"That. An' yow dun't know the work."

"I should have known... but I've been trying so hard."

"I know it. But... yow can see why they wonder. Some are sayin' yow're a..." She halted, obviously reluctant to say the word.

In a nasty moment of clarity, Mav saw what it was. "A spy?"

"Yem. A spy for th'Countess, some reck."

"She's not like that," said Mav hotly, and then saw Vireddi blink. *I've said too much...*

"Most people dun't want believe that. So they reck yow mun be a spy 'gainst her."

"I suppose you wonder too."

Vireddi shrugged. "I'd like not to..."

And I very much want you to trust me. "But I can see why you would." She took a deep breath. "Vireddi, if I tell you something, will you promise not to tell anyone else?"

She took Vireddi's hands, small and cool, but work-hardened. She'd begun to think Vireddi was probably older than she'd first guessed, but still she could hardly be older than herself. Seventeen, probably, and already bearing the callouses of labour. It didn't seem right. She had a conviction the Countess would feel the same, but not even Countess Jerya could put the whole world to rights at a stroke.

"Promise?" she said again.

Vireddi met her gaze squarely. "I promise."

"They're right. You're right. About me not being a slave, I mean. Although I'm trying very hard to be one. To be a good one. But I'm not a spy, not for anyone. I suppose if you want one word, I'm a fugitive."

Then she wondered if Vireddi knew that word, but she got a nod, and that set the whole tale spilling out. She held back only one thing, that she'd borne another name until the day of her arrival at Skilthorn.

When she'd finished, Vireddi sat a long time silently gazing across the water. A small duck drifted past, poised on its own reflection; a teal, thought Mav. She looked down and saw their hands, left and right, only a inch apart on weathered wood that might once have been the same colour as the flash on the teal's head.

She felt a strong urge to bridge that inch. But in the instant she was debating it, Vireddi stirred.

"I thowt yow talked like a lady."

"They wanted me to *be* a lady."

"And you din't?"

"All I ever wanted was to go on as I had been, with Father and the horses."

"An' now yow're a slave..."

"Trying to be."

"But what after... what'd yow say? Twelve weeks?"

"Eleven, now." She looked into her friend's face. "Honestly, Vireddi, I have no idea."

They walked on, rounding the lake. A breeze was springing up, riffling the water that had been such a perfect mirror. A female mallard shepherded a brood of ducklings, little round fluff-balls seeming to skitter across the surface rather than swim. Vireddi gazed at them as if enchanted.

"How often did you get chance to do this before?" asked Mavrys.

"Never been down here afore."

Mav had expected it to have been a rare privilege, but 'never' shocked her. She took Vireddi's hand, squeezed. "Did you get out at all?"

Vireddi shrugged. "To th'orchard, when they need hands for pickin'. That sort o'thing."

"I'm sure it'll be different now. Today's only the start."

"Mav..." Something in Vireddi's tone made Mav come to a halt. "Place you was afore..."

"Carinnan."

"Aye... was it like this?" She freed her hand to make a wide gesture: the lake, the wide bright lawns dotted now with drably-garbed figures, the huge house.

"Shebb, no. The only bit that was at all like this was the stables and the paddocks. The house wasn't a tenth the size of this."

"But yowr father was master."

"Yes..."

"And after yowr birthday yow could go back..."

"No, V, didn't I say it clear enough? My uncle's master there now. And the way he's going he'll probably have to sell the whole place." *Maybe he has already*, she thought with a pang. But Carinnan was lost to her already, too much of what had made it special gone, too much of what had made it *home*. Could she express that in words Vireddi would understand? "Right now, it feels like this is the only home I have."

"Even as a slave?"

"Even as a slave."

The more she thought about it, the more true it felt.

✳

They spoke of other things for a time. She told Vireddi the names of the birds, teal and moorhen and mallard, the buzzards above. Trees too, as far as she knew them; alders fringing the stream that fed and drained the lake, oaks and elms and limes dotted about the lawns.

They walked back up the slope, beyond the carriage-drive; the trees were less scattered here and the grass longer, swishing rhythmically around their skirt-hems. They both saw the deer at the same time, a dozen or more, resting in the dappled shade under a wide-spreading oak.

"What are they?" whispered Vireddi.

"Deer."

"I know that. But there's diff'rent kinds, ain't there?"

Mav reminded herself not to underestimate Vireddi. She was illiterate, essentially uneducated, but she had an innate sharpness. And, as Mav had seen already today, an appetite to know more. "Fallow deer."

"Ben' safe go a bit closer?"

"I'm not sure... if it's mating season, or they have young—fawns, they're called—they're probably more nervous. But I don't know when those seasons are." Vireddi gave her a surprised look. "I told you, our estate wasn't like this. And what land there was, was for horses, not deer."

"Horses?"

For a moment Mav was lost for words, but then they seemed to tumble out of her. "And now I've been here a month and the nearest I've been to a horse is looking out from an upstairs window."

They lingered a few minutes, watching the deer, and being watched in return. They were clearly alert to the girls' presence, which Mav took as sufficient sign not to attempt a closer approach. As they began to walk again, Vireddi glanced across and said, "Yow like the horses, then." It wasn't a question.

"I do. Really, I love them."

"And yow miss 'em, I can tell."

Having seen how eagerly the slaves had embraced the freedom of the grounds, the Countess let it be known that the right of access applied whenever they had free time. 'Free time', Mav gathered, was itself a novel concept for them.

Vireddi's response was to spend every possible minute out of doors, whether it was wandering the park or investigating the orchard and the rose-garden. Mav was surprised to find that, though her friend hardly knew a goose from a swan, she recognised many of the varieties of roses, from handling the cut flowers. Mav, by comparison, could only confirm identification by looking at the names inscribed on small wooden markers.

Ironic, she thought that in this Vireddi came closer than she did to the kind of accomplishment her Mamma had tried to instil. *Perhaps you'd have been a better daughter for her*, she thought.

Next morning, looking across the breakfast table, she saw, "You're getting freckles."

"Freckles?"

"Those spots on your face." They were spreading across the scalp, too.

After that nothing would satisfy Vireddi but to march straight to the shaving room. Away from the fine folks' rooms, Mav realised, it was the only place slaves had access to a mirror. As they resumed their interrupted meal, she explained that freckles were a natural response to exposure to the sun, and nothing to worry about. "I think they're beautiful, in fact."

A little later, once they'd received their duties from Shevra, Vireddi leaned close as they filed out in the crowd. Keeping her voice confidentially low, she said, "Mav..."

"Yes?"

"Yow're in th'end room, aye?" She knew very well, of course; she'd banged on the door most mornings. "An' there's a second bed...?"

"There is."

"Would yow... *she brav go for sharem*?"

"I asked ole Ilam could I move," said Vireddi as she hung her spare dress on the rail. "She sort of shrug and sigh an' say, *'seems like this new Countess say we can do whatever we want'*. An' I look at her an' she say, *'so how's we to know what's what now, then?'* An' then she shake her head an' say, *'don't yow go gettin' used to it. Reckon all these changes ben't goan last when th'Earl come back.'*"

Mav snorted. "He's nothing like his uncle."

She could read the thought behind Vireddi's glance: *how do yow know?* "Did you ever see him, V? The new Earl, I mean."

"'Course I did. He were comin' here reg'lar afore they were wed, long's I can remember. Visitin' th'owd Earl, like. He dun't much semble him, and I dun't reckon he take after him any way around. Master Hedric—what he was afore—he were always kind. That Lallon, his 'tendant, he'd say th' same. I saw myself how he—Master Hedric—stood up for slaves what might of got a beatin'. Stood up for that Dortis, you know, when..." Vireddi moved closer, dropping her voice, as if about to impart a grave secret. "Yow dun't tell no one, right? Promise?"

"I promise."

"I heard she used to speak for him—th'owd Earl—when no one else could understand him. 'Cause she was with him all th'time, like... like a nursemaid, I s'pose. He were ill, last few years, couldn' hardly leave his room. An' he tole her after he died she was to be tongued."

Mav started violently, as if someone had dumped a bucket of cold water over her. "*Tongued?*"

"'S what I heard."

"Why?"

"Said she'd been his voice and now his voice were goin' to be silent."

"That's... *wicked*." Mav had long known, in an abstract way, that tonguing, and other mutilations, occurred, but they'd never been practised at Carinnan. And she'd seen Dortis, stood behind her in a breakfast queue; a few years older than herself, she seemed a gentle soul. Soft-spoken anyway. Wanting to silence her entirely... She shuddered in revulsion. "He wanted it, but it didn't happen?"

"Yem," said Vireddi, still hushed. "Th'Countess put a stop to it. Her an' that one they call Railu..." She shook her head. "Can't figure her out. Ain't a slave, ain't a Dawnsinger, why's she bald?"

"I can tell you something about that. But finish the story. They put a stop to it... but how do you know all this?"

"Someone heard more'n she was meant to. If I tell who, d'yow promise not to tell no one else? It'd get her in a pack o' trouble, belike."

"Of course. You can always trust me, V."

✻

"What *are* yow goin' to do when yow turns eighteen?"

There was only one honest answer: "I don't know." The idea of being a Dawnsinger hadn't survived five minutes' conversation with Railu. Mav wasn't sure she had ever been convinced by it herself. It smacked of desperation... but what else was there?

"Yow can't go back to yowr family? Yow said they can't make yow marry this man after yowr birthday."

"They can't legally compel me, no." She wondered if Vireddi understood words like 'compel', but her friend was nodding. She reminded herself again not to underestimate her native wit. *And she's a slave; she knows about compulsion.* "But there are other ways..." Guilt, and shame, and fear.

Fear, in fact, she could supply for herself. What future was there for a girl of eighteen, alone, with no skills beyond a profound knowledge of horses? That apart, she had the beginnings of competence as a housemaid, and housemaids in places like Skilthorn were, as far as she knew, invariably slaves.

"I told you once, didn't I, this feels like the only home I have? Carinnan's gone, and my uncle's house... it's the place I fled from. I don't ever want to go back there. Here... honestly, I don't feel any less free than I did there, latterly. And here... " She looked firmly into Vireddi's grass-green eyes. "Here I've found a true friend."

Vireddi blinked. "Yow're a true friend too, Mav. And I'll say it true, yow sayin' yow might wanter stay on after yowr birthday... it fills my heart. But is that *really* what yow want? To go on bein' a slave when yow dun't hafter?"

Mav reached for her hand. "If it's a choice between being a slave with you and being free without you..."

Vireddi did not speak, but her grip was so tight it hurt.

CHAPTER 11

JERYA

"Countess, I am here to tell you that the Sessapont delegation is approaching."

"How far off?"

"A couple of miles, my lady."

"How do you know, at that range?"

"I stationed a slave on the roof with a spyglass, my lady."

I wouldn't have minded that job myself, she thought. *Make a change from small talk and keeping everyone happy.* "A good idea, Evril."

"Thank you, my lady, but there is more."

"More?"

"The carriage is a gilded one, my lady, and there is an outrider carrying the Standard of Sessapont."

"Meaning...?"

"Meaning, my lady, that the Prince of Sessapont has come himself."

Jerya's stomach performed a manoeuvre she would not have thought possible. *Draff*, she thought. *Does this mean...?* "I need your advice, Meryth. Your honest opinion, please."

"Of course, my lady."

"Do I need to change my dress? Draff, do I need to put on a *corset*?"

"I venture to suggest, my lady, that it would be unreasonable for any guest to expect you to anticipate an unannounced arrival to that extent. And I have no grounds to suspect that the Prince is an unreasonable man.

Later, of course, it would doubtless be appropriate for you to change, but no doubt you always intended to do so for the welcome banquet."

Corsets. Hip-rolls. Banquets. *Hedric, Hedric, Hedric, why aren't you here? Or... why aren't I there with you among the glaciers?* She sighed. *Oh, to be cold and uncomfortable and hungry again.*

✻

Prince of Sessapont was the title generally accorded him in the other Principalities. In Sessapont itself he was the High Prince, as if claiming precedence over the other Principals. In formal address, a string of other titles followed, like a flotilla of small ships.

Jerya's experience of Sessapont was limited to three fairly brief visits, the first being her sweetmoon. As gateway to the islands, and the ocean beyond, she had been thrilled by it, but much about the city itself, and the wider Principality, had given her a more jaundiced view. She could not say she had high expectations of the Prince himself, but her first impression was at least gently encouraging.

He was, she thought, about ten years older than herself, skin bronze, once-black hair just beginning to grizzle. He wasn't over-tall—no taller than herself—but trim and erect. *I will not cringe*, she told herself, but she did sink into the deepest curtsey she felt she could safely manage.

"Countess." He took her hand as if helping her to rise, then touched his lips to her fingers. "A true pleasure."

"Welcome to Skilthorn, Your Highness. We are honoured by your presence. A most... unexpected honour."

"Ah," he said, with just a hint of a smile. "Word has not reached you?"

"I'm afraid not, Your Highness."

"The weather has not been favourable for the heliograph relay, has it? And one can never entirely rely on birds. Hawks and eagles must live too, one supposes."

"Indeed. So it's very fitting... we've had some interesting discussion already about ways we might make rapid communication more reliable. More rapid *and* more reliable." *Don't babble, Jerya,* she told herself sternly.

"I look forward to many fascinating discussions," he said, that faint smile still teasing at the corners of his mouth.

Jerya knew one awful second of not knowing what to say next, before she was rescued by an arrival at her elbow. "Your Highness, may I present Master Evisyn, Master Prime of the Guild of Dawnsingers."

If the Prince felt, as most did on first meeting a Dawnsinger, the reflex association of *bald equals slave,* he concealed it adroitly. "Master Prime. A pleasure indeed. I cannot express how avidly I have looked forward to this meeting."

"As have I," said Evisyn. She did not curtsey. Dawnsingers did not curtsey to anyone. *But I did. Is a Countess then less than a Dawnsinger?*

She banished the thought. "Your Highness, Master Prime. I have taken the liberty of ordering refreshments to be prepared. Shall we go in?"

✳

"I have been here before, you know," said the Prince.

"I did not know, Your Highness. That would have been in the time of the previous Earl, I suppose?"

"Indeed."

"I only knew him in the last few years of his life, and by that time he was having great difficulty in making himself understood. No doubt there were many things he would have wished to say to me if he could."

The enigmatic smile was there again. "You surely have the right of it there, Countess. The man I knew—however briefly—I cannot but think he and you would hardly have... seen eye to eye? If you have that expression in this part of the world."

"We do, Your Highness, and you are quite right."

"Yes, it is interesting to consider... my impression of him was a man of, how shall I put this...? A man of more energy than refinement. Whereas you, if I may venture an opinion on such brief acquaintance, are a woman of considerable refinement."

"Thank you, Your Highness. Though I hope I am not lacking in energy."

"I have scarcely had time to form a judgement by my own observation, but your... reputation certainly suggests no dearth of energy. But we were speaking of refinement. What intrigues me... the previous Earl was a man of noble birth, with all the advantages that breeding, upbringing, and education can confer. On the other hand, if I understand correctly, your origins were much more humble. Indeed, you were once a slave, were you not?"

Jerya blinked, took a sip of wine. She dare not drink too much, especially so early in the afternoon, but the taste calmed her, as if by association. "Legally, Your Highness, that is not correct. My friend and I were taken in error and our listings in the Slave Rolls have been voided. But I do know something of the... of the taste of enslavement."

"I see..." he said, musing, eternally half-smiling. He sipped his own drink. "Well, Countess, I hope to have the pleasure of talking with you again, and at greater length. I am avid to hear more of your remarkable exploits. But a Prince is never entirely free to indulge himself, and duty requires that I circulate; take the measure of all the protagonists, you know."

"Of course, Your Highness."

"There is one small matter I would mention first, however."

"Please..."

"Speaking of my previous visit, and your noble husband's predecessor. I must say I found him most obliging in matters of my personal comfort. Specifically..." He sighed. "I dare say this would be easier to say if your husband were here."

"I hope he will be here within a few days." Now more than ever, Jerya longed for Hedric's return.

"A hope I share, but in the meantime... a Prince, you know is in many regards a man like any other, with a man's needs. And as I say, the previous Earl was most obliging in ensuring that my needs were met."

"I am not sure I understand you, Your Highness."

The smile finally slipped from his lips. "You are, as I have said, a woman of great refinement, and that is wholly admirable. However, as we have also established, you are a woman of unusually wide experience. I find it a little hard to believe that you could be so innocent as to fail to understand me."

"*Draff!* What the hell am I to do now? I've spent the last weeks telling the enslaved that things are different now. I can't just turn around and say 'but now I need to pimp one of you off on this... smiling, charming, festering boil of a man.'

"Of course you can't," said Railu.

"Of course I can't. It would make a mockery of everything I've said, everything we've tried to do, not just in the last few weeks but ever since we were married. It would undermine everything we want to do in the future. How could I ever look anyone in the eye and talk about making life better for the enslaved? How could I ever look *you* in the eye again?"

"You have bigger problems than what I think about it."

"Yes, you're right... because what happens if I refuse him?" She could not keep still, began to pace up and down. "I was starting to be charmed, you know. Drawn in by the smile and the honeyed words about how refined I am... well, *piss* on refinement if this is what it means. But everyone says he's a man who likes to get his own way. Moons only know how many women he has at his disposal back in Sessapont. Draff, why couldn't he have brought one along with him? Then we could turn a blind eye..."

Jerya stopped, leaned on the heavy oaken table. "If I say no to him and he takes it badly—which he probably will, being used to getting his own way—it could throw this whole gathering into jeopardy. Sessapont's the

richest of the Principalities and he's the one absolute ruler. And the Master
Prime's here for the first time. Think about that. The Master Prime is here,
at Skilthorn. The Master Prime of the Guild of Dawnsingers has never left
the Sung Lands in all of recorded history. There'll have been opposition
from the Conclave, don't you think? They're not all Evisyn-loyalists, I've
seen that. If she comes back empty-handed, her authority could be chal-
lenged. Perriad's still lurking in the background somewhere, and she's not
the only one who wants the Guild to 'stabilise', not go forward."

"Jerya, I know you always want to fix everything. But the Guild is
Evisyn's problem, not yours."

"Maybe. But I can queer the pitch for her, can't I? This *meeting* is my
problem. Your idea, you and Evisyn, but I took it on. I couldn't even ask
Hedric. I just merrily said, hey, suddenly I'm Countess of Skilthorn, let's
do something useful with this ugly great monster of a house.

"Countess of Skilthorn. For two months. One minute I'm saying I can't
even make sense of being called Countess... the next I'm inviting moons
know who to discuss moons know what. And now it could all come crash-
ing down because I can't turn flesh-peddler on one of my own people."

"Pardon me, Countess, may I speak?"said a new voice.

Jerya spun around. "Mavrys! I didn't know you were there!"

"I'm sorry. I did knock, but you were talking, I guess you didn't hear me.
But you did order coffee..."

"Yes, put it on the table, please. Thank you."

Mavrys complied, but instead of withdrawing immediately, she lingered.
"May I speak, Countess?" she said again.

"This is hardly the time."

"With the greatest of respect, my lady, I think it might be. I didn't mean
to overhear, but I did. And I believe I see a way past your dilemma."

"What? How?"

"Send me to him."

Jerya knew she was staring, open-mouthed; Railu too. It seemed an age before she could speak rationally. "Send *you*... No, Mavrys, you can't know what you're offering."

"With respect, Countess, I believe I do. Maybe many girls of my age and class are ignorant of... carnal matters, but I grew up in the country. My father bred horses, when he... and since I have been here, well, slaves talk in a very different way. I may not understand everything they say, I am still learning the Patter, but I have heard them talk about how the old Earl used them, when he was able, and how he offered them to guests.

"And you know what I thought when I listened to those conversations? What's the difference between him doing that, and what my mother wanted to do to me? He treated women's bodies as chattels—the law says they are his property—but so did she."

"And you ran away," said Jerya. "The idea revolted you so much you ran away here. It repelled you so much you'd rather shave your head and live as a slave."

"Yes, but it wasn't the thought of... the carnal side... that appalled me. It was the thought of being shackled for life to a man who doesn't respect me. A man who laughs when I say something he deems ignorant or ill-informed. Calls it *charming*. Compared to that..." She squared her shoulders. "You saved me from that, Countess. I've never known how I might repay you. Now I do."

"But still..."

"Countess... Jerya. I offer myself of my own free will. For one night, or a few nights. Not as a slave, or a chattel, but a free woman."

Railu stirred. "Mavrys, I gave myself to a man once. I mean literally once. And I got myself with child. Have you thought about that?"

"Is that likely?"

"Not likely, perhaps, but it's certainly possible, as I proved."

"No," said Jerya. "That's my final word. We'll find another way. I can't let you do this."

CHAPTER 12

MAVRYS

Early sunlight slanted in where the curtains didn't quite meet. Outside, birds were limbering up for the day. Mavrys lay back, listening, luxuriating in the feel of fine linen against her skin, thinking of nothing else. But something nagged... curtains? Her room had no window, only a skylight streaked with birdlime.

But thoughts and memories began slowly to intrude. They were not comfortable, but they would not go away. She remembered how the opportunity had suddenly presented itself. She had chanced to overhear another of the household slaves being ordered to carry a tray of dainties up to the Prince's rooms. She had followed the girl, caught up with her in an empty passage, said, "*Me go for tekem for she?*"

"*Why she go for doso?*"

"*She semb apt for go crib. Me... me yen go for looksee em Prince.*"

The girl had shrugged, as if she could look at a Prince any day of the week, and handed over the tray with mumbled thanks. Her name was Kopani, or something like it.

Well, you're in for it now, girl...

The hardest part, she thought, was remembering to speak like a slave when she presented herself at his door. Not in Patter, but equally not in the refined version of Plain that came most naturally. "Th' Countess thowt Yowr Highness might 'preciate some 'freshment. An'... an' I'm to remain, too, if t please Yowr Highness."

The first time, he had said hardly a word, only terse instructions as he placed her against the footboard of the bed, obliged her to bend over until her face almost touched the bedspread, then lifted her skirts. A moment later she felt sudden pressure, then a momentary stabbing pain, gone as quickly as it arose. Then just the weight of him and the absolute *strangeness* of something inside her. A few quick thrusts, then he was done.

"By the stars," he'd said a moment later. "A virgin? Seems I misjudged your mistress. I thought she seemed loath to send me anyone at all. Instead she was saving me a peach."

There'd been a knock on the outer door then, and he'd left her without another word. She'd stood up, rearranged her skirt, looked around. Two chairs flanked an ornate cabinet of—she thought—walnut. Plush mulberry-hued upholstery, gilded woodwork slightly worn. She sank onto one before remembering that slaves did not sit on the furniture in the fine folks' rooms. But there were voices in the other room now, and she thought she would get a few seconds' warning before anyone entered. She could risk sitting, as long as she remained alert. She needed to think about what had just happened.

In one way, it was strangely familiar... no, not familiar, that wasn't quite right: it had been as expected. Growing up around bloodstock, she'd been familiar with mating for years. Her mother would surely have been horrified, but Mavrys (Irmavel) and her father had kept some things to themselves. What had just happened to her was really remarkably like what horses did; the stallion mounting the mare. It was nearly always over as quickly, too. With a frisson of something close to horror, she wondered if his member extended in the dramatic way a stallion's did. (Her mother *had* caught sight of a stallion in such a state a few times, had always reacted by turning hastily away, tight-lipped.) No, surely not: the thing inside her had felt big, yes, but not half a yard long.

Well, she thought finally, *if that's what it's like, there'll be no joy in this for me, but I can bear it.* If it helped the Countess's cause and the progression of the Congress, it would be worth it.

But how did he know I'm a virgin?

A moment later she amended the thought: *was a virgin.*

An hour or so later, he'd returned, laughing to find her where he'd left her. She'd leapt up and reassumed her place at the foot of the bed as soon as she heard his guests leaving.

"Not this time, girl," he'd said. "Don't you know variety is the spice of life?"

He'd talked this time, though she'd barely taken in a word, her senses being fully taken up by the feel of his hands as he undressed her. Long-fingered, elegant hands, beautifully manicured and multiply beringed. Beautiful... but also terrifying. Somehow this slow buildup frightened her more than the coolly businesslike swiftness of the first coupling.

A moment later she'd learned that humans did not always couple as animals did, that they could also do so face-to-face. And that it could take longer, could take many minutes rather than a handful of seconds. She had learned that the stabbing sensation did not occur every time. She had learned that the act could provoke a whole range of feelings. That utter strangeness remained; to feel part of another body inside her own, invading her, as if displacing her own flesh. There was terror, too, not so much of the act as of the man. Whether inside her or not, he had her in his power; and no one knew where she was. Perhaps Kopani would recall that she had taken the tray, but she would have no reason to think that Mavrys would have done more than deliver it and leave.

But there had been something else, too; another sensation. She had thought that it would all be about enduring, but some part of her was feeling something that felt very much like... pleasure. The experience as a whole felt like something to be endured, but some fickle part of her took a different view.

Then he had pulled out of her, rolled off her. With the sudden release of his weight, she felt she could breathe again. For a few moments he'd just lain alongside, panting lightly, then turned toward her, propped himself on one elbow, and smiled. "You're quite a find, girl. If I had you in Sessapont, I'd put you on a leash, take you everywhere. I wonder if your mistress would entertain an offer?"

Terror gripped her, sudden and absolute. *Grief, what have I done?*

Reliving that moment, she thought of another thing. If the Prince *did* say something to the Countess... she could well imagine Jerya's reaction to the sudden revelation. *I have to get to her first...*

With that, she stirred. She was naked in the bed, and had no idea where her clothes were. Could he have hidden them to make sure she could not leave?

Then she heard voices in the outer room. That gave a partial answer to the question she had been formulating. She could not leave now, not without the Prince's permission, nor without her clothes.

Then some stray words reached her and curiosity took over. Silently she slipped from the bed and crept to the door, which stood just an inch or so or ajar. She had little fear that she would be seen lurking there, but if anyone moved toward her she would know, be ready to dart away in an instant.

And what she heard filled her with a new dread.

Chapter 13

Jerya

She knew how to address nobility and gentry; the only difference now was she had to stand up and speak the words aloud instead of writing them in a quiet room. She had argued a case in front of the Conclave of Masters of the Guild of Dawnsingers; pleaded for her liberty, too. She had faced a fierce antagonist then; she had ground to hope there was no one so inclined here. *I can do this*, she told herself. Railu's look, and a swift press of her hand, carried the same message.

Jerya took a final sip of water, gathered her papers, glanced at the top sheet once more, then laid them down on the table as she stood.

"Your Serene Highness, Master Prime, Dawnsingers, gentlemen, it is my great pleasure to welcome you all to Skilthorn. Perhaps I should say 'welcome you to my home'... but I have not lived here very long and I can hardly say it feels like home to me, not yet. It is certainly very different from any home I've previously known. Be that as it may, I hope Skilthorn will serve us well as a place to talk, for generating better understanding between the Five Principalities and the Sung Lands.

"I am aware that this has all been arranged at remarkably short notice. I must pay tribute to the tremendous work of all our staff, free and enslaved, without which this gathering would not have been possible at all, and I must humbly beg you, our guests, to make allowance for any rough edges which may remain. If you do have any concerns, please bring them to me. I am sorry my husband is not also here to welcome you, but I'm sure most of you know he is honouring a prior commitment. Word has been sent, but he is beyond the reach of normal postal services, and there has hardly been time for the message to reach him and for him to return."

She could not dwell on it now, but it remained a sore point. It had been a real coup being invited by Bastil, but he'd stated that he wanted someone with experience in mountains—of which Jerya had far more than Hedric. But Bastil was a pillar of rectitude and would never have gone on expedition with a female even if he could be convinced of her merits.

Jerya's price had been the Deed of Proxy. 'If I sell Skilthorn for half its true worth and move us back to Kirwaugh, you'll never complain,' she'd said in barbed jest. 'We could fund a few decent expeditions for that,' he'd joked in return. They both knew, of course, that any move as drastic as that would almost certainly precipitate a legal challenge to her proxy status. Ferrowby, brooding rancorously on his own estate, would see to that if no one else did.

She'd made play of her disappointment, of course, but privately she'd consoled herself that it would have clashed with the likely arrival of visitors from the Sung Lands. She hadn't wanted to miss that, and her pleasure had been heightened by Yanil's inclusion, as well as the presence of Master Evisyn. That other things had flowed from it... well, neither she nor Hedric could have anticipated that, so it would be unfair to blame him.

The Deed of Proxy gave her authority, but authority, for a woman existed solely by male dispensation. It grated to say it, but some of the guests might need reassurance. "Be assured that I have full authority to administer the estate in his absence."

Sighing inwardly, she forged on. "I'm equally conscious that all of our Five Principalities guests have revised prior arrangements to be here, and that many of you have travelled at least several days. I'm very glad to know that we do have representatives from all five of the Principalities.

With a nod toward Evisyn, she went on, "Of course, none have undertaken a journey quite equal to the Crossing from the Sung Lands. I've made that journey myself, so I know from experience.

"It remains to be seen how much we can accomplish in the coming week. For myself, I shall be well content if we can lay solid foundations for future exchanges. Perhaps we can look to a time, not too far distant, when Dawnsingers may be more than just summer visitors to the Five Principalities. Like swallows, whose arrival heralds the summer and whose departure always fills me with melancholy...

"Above all, I trust that we all come to this gathering with open minds. I know both sides better than most, and it's my firm belief that each has much to learn from the other. I trust that, starting from this recognition, we can make things better for the people—all the people—of both the Five Principalities and the Sung Lands. Thank you."

❊

"Countess, please, I really need to speak with you."

"Mavrys, I've given you a lot of leeway, but I really don't have time, and this is not what you agreed to."

"I know, my lady, but this is not about me—and I truly believe you need to hear this."

Jerya sighed. Even to herself it sounded theatrical. "All right, I'll try and find ten minutes later. Maybe after lunch."

"That might be too late."

She's persistent, if nothing else. "Tell me in one sentence, then."

"The Prince is talking about war, my lady. About invasion."

"What are you talking about? And how would you know anyway?"

Mavrys hesitated, swallowing visibly. Jerya had a sharp intuition that she wasn't going to like what came next.

"I heard him talking to someone, my lady. Early this morning. Couldn't see the other man but he was a Troqu'er by his accent. And I couldn't get away to tell you before, because I couldn't find my clothes."

"Find your..." Jerya seized the girl's upper arms in a fierce grip. Mavrys winced but Jerya wasn't in a mood to care. "Don't tell me—wait, not here."

Releasing one arm, she almost dragged the girl into the Lesser Library, inclining her head to Railu in a request to follow. She knew the old Earl had not been much of a reader, and a slightly musty air lingered in the room, as if it had been the private sanctum of some previous lord, neglected for decades.

Railu closed the door and Jerya confronted Mavrys. "Please tell me you didn't go to him, after everything we said. After I *commanded* you not to."

"I'm not sure you said that exactly, Jerya—

"Don't! I think you just forfeited the right to call me by my name."

"I'm sorry for that, my lady, truly. But..." Mavrys drew herself up straighter. "I am deeply grateful for all you've done for me, but in the end I am not your slave."

She has backbone, I'll give her that. But... "I could argue that 'my slave' is exactly what you agreed to be. You can't have it both ways, Mavrys . But tell me what you heard."

"I didn't hear it all, m'lady. But I heard him say something about the Defile, and I know that's a feature of the Crossing. And the other one said, *You can get as many men through as you want, but not quickly. Too many places where they have to go one at a time. Perhaps if you had a few ladders, and ropes, it would be quicker, but it's still a narrow way.* And he said, *but beyond the Defile, there is ground to reassemble the force.* And I thought: *force? Why does he say 'force'?*

"But the next thing he said was even clearer. *And there is truly no army? No militia?* And the other said, *Nothing of that kind at all, your Highness.* Then the Prince said, *They let themselves be ruled by women, I suppose it's to be expected.* He was quiet a moment, and then he said, *We wouldn't even need a large force. Quality, not numbers. A hundred trained and well-armed men can defeat any number of rabble, or eunuchs.*

"Then... I think they sat down. I heard papers rustle, like unfolding a map. They spoke more softly after that and I didn't really hear anything more. But I thought I had heard enough. I had to find my clothes... it turned out he had kicked them under the bed. By then they had gone, so I came to find you."

Jerya just looked at her for a moment, head buzzing with things that needed to be said, to be done. "I need to find Evisyn," she said finally. "She needs to know this before her address later. Can you stay with her, Railu?"

CHAPTER 14

MAVRYS

Mavrys stood at the back of the room, against the wall, as inconspicuous as she could make herself. She could only hope no one would call for food or drink. It was likely everyone would be focused on the front during Evisyn's address.

Jerya stepped up. "I first met Master Prime Evisyn—Master of Peripatetics then—four years ago, in Carwerid, and I was immediately impressed. She was the first of the Guild's leaders to truly recognise the challenges and opportunities inherent in relations with the Five Principalities." She paused, looking around. Just for a moment, Mav thought, Jerya's eyes rested on herself. "Today, and in the next few days, we will truly begin to understand those challenges and opportunities, and how we can best deal with them. There is one thing though, of which I'm certain: the Sung Lands could have no better representative. Please welcome Master Evisyn, Master Prime of the Guild of Dawnsingers."

Polite applause ushered Evisyn to the podium. "Many thanks, Countess. I wonder how many of you really know how much Jerya, as I first knew her, risked to bring the news to the College back then. The Guild and the Sung Lands owe her a great deal. I think the Five Principalities have good reason to be thankful too.

"And now, now she is Countess Jerya, we owe her renewed thanks for inviting us here, and for ensuring that everything has gone so smoothly, even at such short notice. I must echo her earlier thanks to all the staff here at Skilthorn, free and enslaved, without whose hard work I suppose none of us would have beds to sleep in or food to eat. And I must not forget our friend Railu, who originated the notion in the first place.

"I'm sure all of you have had to rearrange your schedules. I know that at least a few of you have had to abscond from planned holidays and precious time with your families. I may not have a family of my own, at least not in the sense in which you use the word, but I understand your sacrifice. I can only reiterate my appreciation, and hope that everyone will leave feeling that it's been worthwhile. But that's up to all of us, isn't it? To ensure that this gathering leads to real progress, to the benefit of the people of both the Five Principalities and the Sung Lands.

"I must particularly mention one honoured guest. We don't have Princes in the Sung Lands—nor for that matter, do we have Countesses—but it has been made clear to me that the presence of His Serene Highness the Prince of Sessapont is a remarkable honour. It surely demonstrates how highly His Highness values the enterprise we are engaged in, the quest for greater understanding, the sharing of knowledge to mutual benefit.

"Your Serene Highness, Countess, Sisters in Song, nobility and gentry. As Master Prime, one thought occupies my mind above all others: peace. Under the Guild's guidance, the Sung Lands have had several centuries of peace. My knowledge of the history of the Five Principalities is, I'm afraid, more limited, but I'm assured that only the oldest of your people will have any memory of the wars and skirmishes which once raged here. In the succeeding three-quarters of a century, your lands have flourished. Peace is the soil in which progress and prosperity grow. In the discussions to come, I have an open mind on almost every question, but I will do nothing which jeopardises the peace of the Sung Lands, or of yours."

She sipped water, scanning the room, eyes never lingering on any individual.

"Peace has been the watchword for the Guild of Dawnsingers throughout its centuries of existence. The Guild grew from the misty memories of terrible conflict which ended the Age Before; our mission was forged in the absolute resolve that such things should never happen again. The ancients surely had powers we still do not understand, some of which we might dearly wish to emulate. In the end, though, their powers were turned to destruction.

"This is the perspective from which we view our quest for knowledge. The Guild is the *custodian* of knowledge, and we constantly remind ourselves of the potential that learning holds, for good *and* ill." She looked around again with a quirky half-smile. "I think it's fair to say that among my Sisters, and among my fellow Masters, there are two schools of thought. For some, the instinct is to hoard knowledge; for these, the question is always, is this understanding safe to share? On the other hand, there are those whose first inclination is to disseminate learning, who ask not why we should share but why we should keep it to ourselves.

"By temperament, I incline toward the second group, but as Master Prime I am not free to follow my instincts. In all major decisions I require the consent of my Conclave. They put me in this position and they can as readily remove me. Something similar may apply for many of you. We all proceed with caution.

"And we all have much to learn. It occurs to me that there are two people in the world who discovered fourteen years ago that there was civilisation on both sides of the mountains, and both of them are in this room." A few heads turned, surely knowing the Countess's story but wondering who the second might be; but the Master Prime was still speaking, reclaiming their attention. "For the rest of us, it's only four years since the truth was revealed. As you know, this is my first time in the Five Principalities, and I have yet to venture beyond the Principality of Denvirran—but I certainly intend to do so and I have already discussed prospects for further travel with several of you.

"We all have much to learn from each other. That is both the central reason for this congress, and the reason why we proceed with caution. But nothing will be achieved unless we all enter into this in the right spirit. We can look upon the exchange of knowledge as trade, as barter... or we can look upon it as the free exchange of gifts. How much difference this makes in practical terms, I am not sure, but I, for one, would very much prefer to take the second view. And in that spirit I am making a commitment, here and now, that we will be passing on significant chunks of our learning in several areas, including medical science and also horology."

The Master Prime paused, sipping water. "It's only four years since we learned the truth of what lies beyond the mountains. There were those in the Guild who refused to believe Jerya when she brought the news, but we soon had verification, with the arrival of the Duke of Selton and his companions. Thanks to Jerya, we had at least a little forewarning, but we still had no real notion of what to expect. We hoped for the best, but—please do not take this amiss—we had to prepare for the worst."

She smiled. "The Duke and his companions made a favourable first impression, but we still felt we had to be prepared for all contingencies. One of my first steps after our visitors had departed was to despatch several of my best Peripatetics to take a good look at the Crossing route. They were charged with assessing both its difficulty for future exchanges, and the possibilities open to us should we need to close off the route. I repeat, we had no reason to *expect* any hostile incursion, but nor could we rule out such an eventuality with any certainty. Not at that early stage."

A new, sweeter smile. "I am happy to state now that such concerns have receded far into the background. But for the record, should anyone be interested, we found that the nature of the route, especially the Defile, makes it readily defensible. Having passed through there myself just a couple of weeks ago I am entirely assured of this.

"But let us not dwell on concerns which are now entirely hypothetical. I have no wish to dampen the spirit of this gathering."

She was clearly winding up, returning to her hopes for an exchange of 'gifts'. Mavrys's attention shifted. By sidling a pace to her right she could see the Prince. At first he was angled three-quarters away from her, but then he turned to say something to his neighbour. There was no smile on his face now, not even the customary half-smile. The Prince was not happy with what he'd heard, and Mavrys knew exactly why. His notion that an incursion into the Sung Lands would be easy seemed to have been strangled at birth.

A twist of fear curdled her stomach. He might take at face value Master Evisyn's statement that she, and the Guild, had contemplated the possibility four years ago; but then again he might not. If not, and he began to wonder how the Master Prime had come to consider it now... where might his suspicions lead?

She tried to reason that, to him, she was just a slave-girl, a bed-warmer who'd shown no particular signs of intelligence, who'd never spoken unless spoken to. Mavrys knew that, to many among the owner-class, slaves were effectively invisible most of the time. She could hardly exonerate herself; she'd known the names of the household slaves at Carinnan but, with rare exceptions, had known little about their lives beyond their duties. Would the Prince make the mental leap from seeing her as a passive creature to imagining her eavesdropping on his conversation, grasping its import, and then having sufficient initiative to pass it on?

She couldn't be sure; but the more she wrestled with the question, the more one thing became clear. He would be a lot more likely to suspect if she failed to appear that night.

She sighed. *I don't want to go back, but I have to. At least once more. For my own sake, and for the Countess.*

When she woke, his hand was on her throat, thumb resting right on her windpipe. She went rigid, unable to speak, pleading with her eyes. Had he guessed, after all, her role in revealing his plan?

"You think I'll hurt you, girl? Why would I do that? As a Prince, sometimes I must hurt people, or order them to be hurt. But I don't take pleasure in it, and I never do it needlessly."

His half-smile flickered in in the soft candle-light. "No, my girl, I was only thinking how well you would look in a gilded collar... Shall I tell you a secret? Most people in Sessapont think that my slaves wear golden collars. Quite apart from the fact that there probably isn't that much gold in all the Five Principalities, have you any idea how *heavy* the stuff is? I myself wear a golden torc for certain ceremonies, and I am always heartily glad to shed the cursed thing afterward. I am kinder to my slaves than I am to myself: their collars are merely gilded.

"Yes, you would look exquisite in such a collar. You would be a delightful addition to my collection... which is why I am sitting here debating with myself whether to take you with me, with or without your mistress's agreement."

Or mine... A strange clarity had settled on at least part of her mind. *If I were truly a slave, my permission would mean nothing—but taking me without Jerya's permission would be common theft.* She almost smiled: when princes did it, it surely wasn't 'common'. Perhaps he wouldn't even see it as theft. But... *As I am not in fact a slave, it would be... what would the law call it? Unlawful seizure? Abduction?*

Another thought; her mind was racing even as she held her body quite still. *I am not a slave, but I let him believe I am. And I let him use me like one. Three times last night.*

Three times, always from behind, like a stallion, with the same almost brutal swiftness. There had never been the same pain as the first time, but she would hardly call it comfortable, even if something akin to pleasure had flickered for a few moments each time. It felt like treachery from her own body; it almost added to the humiliation.

And you still don't know my name. Either of my names.

His smile grew wider; she glimpsed teeth, almost *too* white. "To be a Prince, one must decide."

His hand returned, over her face now. There was something in it; something that pressed down over mouth and nose. Her world filled with a scent that she could not name.

Then there was nothing.

Chapter 15

Skelber

My darling, he wrote.

Please forgive me if this is ill-written; once again the hour is late. It's true that I spend all day sitting behind Le'ast and Fulmer and saying nothing unless referred to for an opinion; but still, the time is not my own. And Le'ast always requires further discussion after dinner, to review the day and consider prospects for the morrow. The only time left for writing is late at night, or before breakfast, and as you well know I have never been by inclination an early riser.

I have not forgotten that you particularly wanted to hear all that I could relate about the Countess. It must have been a disappointment to you that I could tell you so little in my first letter. As I said, I could barely see her during her opening remarks on the first night, and most of what she said was quite conventional. As the first week ends, I hope I can now do better for you. I know she is a figure of some fascination for many women and girls; would it be fair to say that the fascination, especially among the older generation, is sometimes of the appalled variety? (Ask your aunt!)

So: Countess Jerya. Of course you have seen many descriptions of her, and saved more than one engraving from the illustrated journals; but, as we have discussed, these engravings are by no means always drawn from life; I should say more often not. Therefore I trust you will be interested in my own impressions, now I have had greater chance to observe her.

She is a tall woman, though not so extraordinarily tall as one of the more lurid journals portrayed her. I should put her at close to my own height. She carries herself well, attempting neither to emphasise nor minimise her height. When she wears her hair piled high in the fashionable manner, she gives an impression of greater stature, but so far I have seen her so adorned only twice; for the welcoming banquet, and after the unexpected arrival of the Prince of Sessapont. (I shall of course have more to relate on the subject of His Highness, but I think I may have to leave that for another letter. It was the Countess you wished to know about, and your wish is my command.)

Her skin is of a middling shade, and with a warm tint: deep gold, one might call it, or honey. Her hair appears black but in direct sun or under a bright chandelier it reveals an auburn gleam. It is beyond my capacity to describe her features in a way that will serve to give you a true image, but I think now that the engraving from the Denvirran Illuminated News is the most accurate of the ones in your scrapbook. Even so, it shows her in a moment of stillness, and I should say such moments are rare. Only the greatest of artists could hope to capture a subject in animated moments; perhaps we may hope that now she has attained high rank, such an artist may be drawn to Skilthorn.

(Forgive me, my dear. 'An artist may be drawn'. Truly, I intended no pun. As I say, it is late.)

I say that repose is rare for her; that is undoubtedly true at this Congress. It appears she is everywhere, or trying to be, endeavouring to follow every discussion and ensure that every aspect keeps flowing smoothly. I do not know if she always walks so briskly, but that is what I have observed this week; she goes with a full stride that traditionally-minded observers, like your aunt, would doubtless call masculine. Other than for the banquet I alluded to, she does not hamper her freedom of movement with restrictive clothing. Her skirts are not excessively full; I am hardly an expert, but for your sake I do my best to observe. Save on the most formal occasions, she relies solely on pleating to give fullness around the hips, and her skirts skim an inch or so above the floor rather than trailing upon it. Again this might strike some as approaching too closely the dress of working women or slaves, but it seems to me merely sensible, and she remains perfectly respectable. Given the prominence she has recently *attained, I wonder if her tastes may have an influence on the ladies' fashions of the next few years. I should be interested to know your thoughts on this, as on any other matter.*

Again, I cannot speak with authority but I suspect that she has a naturally slender figure and does not rely heavily on corsetry to maintain her outline. Perhaps not at all. (Now I know your aunt would not approve!)

Her speaking voice is contralto rather than soprano, and when she addresses the gathered delegates, as at the opening banquet, it carries readily throughout Skilthorn's expansive ballroom. At first hearing, you would take her for an educated Denvirraner, though not necessarily an aristocrat. However, on careful listening, I discern underlying traces of a different accent, presumably harking back to her origins in the Sung Lands.

There is much more I could say, but it is past midnight, and we must be done with breakfast and ready to begin again by nine. And I am aware you were equally agog for my impressions of the Dawnsingers. Rest assured I shall return to the subject of the Countess in future letters.

As you know, Dawnsingers are easy to identify; they are bald and wear white. It is of course a curiosity, for those used to the ways of the Five Principalities, to see bald women who are not slaves; what is interesting, even surprising, is how quickly one becomes acclimatised. I have heard men express concern that any slave could now put on white clothing and pass themselves off as a Dawnsinger, but I am certain it would not be so easy. Ten seconds' converse would be more than sufficient to dispel the illusion. It is not just how they sound; I mentioned traces of an accent in the Countess's speech, but the Dawnsingers do not all sound alike. On reflection, this is hardly unexpected. The Sung Lands are, I think, at least as extensive as the Five Principalities, and you know how a Denvirran accent is distinguishable from that of Troquharran or Sessapont, even between those of similar class and education.

While the white garments and bald heads confer a certain sense of unity, which is probably exactly what they are intended to do, in other respects the

Dawnsingers are as diverse as any group of eight or ten might be. Tall and short, stout and slender, dark and pale.

I should say that when they arrived they did not look as I describe. They wore a range of colours and they hid their baldness with wigs or scarves. It was said that they did this to make themselves less conspicuous while passing from the vicinity of Drumlenn, where they emerged from the mountains, to Skilthorn. On the other hand, there was not a side-saddle among them; all of them rode astride, which would attract attention. They wore what I believe are called divided skirts. The Countess had, I gathered, ridden out an hour or so to greet them and welcome them in, and she also rode astride and wore a riding-habit along the same lines (with an elegant jacket, all in a shade I think one would call aquamarine). There, you can no longer upbraid me for never noticing what a lady is wearing.

Perhaps, my dear, you would be able to enlighten me on the difference between a divided skirt and, not to put too fine a point on it, a pair of trousers. Is it simply that a divided skirt has sufficient fullness that when the wearer is walking it (mostly) appears to be a regular skirt? Still, in logic, I do not see that represents a fundamental difference.

Such idle thoughts occupy my mind as a clock somewhere strikes a quarter to one... I really think I must end soon, and save further observations about the Dawnsingers for my next. If I persist much longer I shall not be fit for duty in the morning; and you will probably find my ramblings increasingly illegible—and sufficiently incoherent as to not be worth the effort of deciphering them.

One final thing. I can imagine that this talk of divided skirts and riding astride fires your imagination, and I have no intention of quelling your interest. I recall a conversation once with a veterinary friend, whose decided opinion was that, whatever the pros and cons from the rider's point of view, side-saddles were decidedly bad for horses. I must look into the argument further, but I know it will carry weight with you, and if the evidence holds up, with me also. And, as I have already noted, the current public interest in our new Countess may well mean that where she leads others are likely to follow.

Still, having said all that, I must urge you with all force to do and say nothing until we are reunited. I doubt very much there is an astride-saddle (if that is the correct term) suitable for your pony, and I will not commission one until I am fully satisfied that it is the correct course of action and that we know precisely how to instruct the saddler. I would suspect also that both you and the horse may require additional schooling before it is safe to let you ride astride. It will not be so very many weeks more, my dear, so please restrain your understandable impatience.

You will also understand that your aunt will likely be scandalised. I do not intend to be ruled by her prejudices, but I also wish to retain her good opinion. I do not say this solely because she is useful, in giving you a home when I am away. As long as I am employed by the Association, some absences from home will continue to be inescapable, but in general should only be for two or three nights; it is hardly necessary to bundle you off to your aunt every time for so short an interval. I wish to retain her good opinion for worthier reasons. She does feel genuine affection for you, however cross-grained her way of showing it; her strictures are her way of demonstrating her care for you. You are her only niece, after all, and I have no doubt you remind her of the sister whom she sorely misses (as do we all). I would not put her through the pain of an estrangement if it can possibly be avoided.

So hold your peace and keep your own counsel, my dearest, until I am reunited with you. I shall raise the subject with her, but you must rely on me to, as the saying is, break it gently. I am sure that in time she will see that, if it is good enough for a Countess, it is good enough for her niece. And if it genuinely is better for the welfare of the horse, you know she has a kind heart under all her bluster and bombasine.

And now I really must be away to my bed; I have burned through most of my candle writing this. Remember that every day brings us closer to our reunion.

Sighing, even a little moist-eyed, he signed off, blotted the final lines, and folded the paper.

Chapter 16

Jerya

"I believe, Countess," said Maedler of Troquharran, "That on your return to the Sung Lands five years ago you carried with you a copy of the *Proceedings of the Denvirran Association for Natural Philosophy* ?"

"I did."

"And I imagine that even a single volume would represent a significant addition to your burden when everything had to be carried on your own back across the mountains?"

Jerya smiled. "I was not sorry to leave it as a donation to the Guild Library before my return."

"Thank you, Countess, you make my point admirably. I have not, I'm sad to say, made the Crossing myself, though I hope to rectify the omission soon—"

Jerya heard the door open behind her. Railu appeared at her side. A few whispered words were enough to bring her to her feet. "Dawnsinger, gentlemen, you'll have to excuse me. Something has come up. In any case, Dawnsinger Kelsaq is more familiar than I with the Guild Library, and her experience of the Crossing is five years more recent."

Outside in the passage, she faced Railu. "Tell me again."

"The Prince is clearing out. That's the first thing. And... Mavrys seems to have gone missing."

Jerya stared at her a moment, then puffed out a big breath. "That girl... But I suppose I'll have to deal with His Pestilential Highness first. What do you know?"

"He ordered his carriage brought round... it's ready now, and his servants are bringing his boxes down."

"There was no suggestion of this last night."

Railu shrugged; Jerya had an intuition that she cared much less about the Prince than about Mavrys. "All right. Take any staff you can stir up, start a search. You could try the dell; you took her there, didn't you?. I'll see to His Royal Reprehensibleness." *I don't need this, not on top of everything...*

By the time she reached the front entrance, the Prince's carriage was waiting. His baggage-wain was already rolling away, and the Prince was standing beside his four-in-hand, a well-matched set of dapple-greys, watching idly as his coachman adjusted a back-band.

They made their farewells with punctilious politeness but scant warmth. He stepped up into the carriage and two liveried slaves took their places on the rumble-seat. The coachman swished his whip, not touching any of the horses, called something, and they took the strain. The carriage began to move with the usual lurch before the four settled to a steady trot.

As soon as they were at a decent distance, Jerya hurried back inside. Railu, who had continued the search in her absence, met her with a dour shake of her head. "We're mobilising everyone we can. With these numbers it won't take long to search inside, but if she's wandered off somewhere out of doors..."

She stopped. "Jerya? What are you thinking?"

"Only I can't see her wandering off. She's been conscientious enough about her duties."

"She defied you with him. The Prince."

"Because she thought it would help. Foolish, but—" She broke off. Railu watched her face. "What if she went *back*? Who was she sharing quarters with?"

"Vireddi, m'lady," said Elleret.

"See if you can find her, please."

Elleret hurried off, while Jerya and Railu hastened up the main stairs and along to the rooms that had been the Prince's. They had already been searched, of course, but Jerya was now looking with different eyes. She went first into the bedroom, but could see nothing that might be classed as a clue. When they emerged into the sitting-room, she found a slave-maid clearing the fire-grate.

"Wait!" she said sharply, then recollected herself. "Sorry." The girl looked startled—an apology from a Countess?—but laid down her tools, scrambled to her feet, curtseyed. "What have you got there?"

"Looks like some rags or summink, m'lady."

"Look again. Doesn't it look a lot like what you're wearing?"

"I dessay yow're right, m'lady."

"Remains of an enslaved's apparel," she said to Railu. She knelt, began spreading the charred shreds on the hearthrug. The maid looked shocked, whether at the mess it might make of the rug, or the notion of a Countess getting her hands covered in black char and ash. "A female enslaved. We can say that much."

Before she could examine the evidence further, Elleret appeared, a slight, pale-skinned young slave in tow. "Your name is Vireddi, I believe," said Jerya.

"Aye, m'lady, if'n it please you."

"*All name brav for me.*" Vireddi's eyebrows shot up to hear the Countess parl Patter. "*She, Mavrys, go for kip same room?*"

"Aye, m'lady, if'n it please you." The girl was clearly not quite ready to parl back.

Shrugging, Jerya reverted to Plain. "Was she there last night?"

"No, m'lady, not fer last three nights."

"Do you know where she was?"

"First night, I know she came here, m'lady."

"You know for sure, or you know that she *said* she was coming here?"

"Beg pardon, m'lady. She said."

"And the second and third nights?"

"Very sorry, m'lady, I dun't rightly know."

"No need for apologies. I think that's all—unless Railu has any questions? Thank you, Vireddi. Please remain a little longer, just in case we think of anything else."

She and Railu moved away a few paces to confer privately. "So Mavrys wasn't in her proper bed last night," she began. She felt like grinding her teeth at the girl's persistent heedlessness. "And now we have the incinerated remains of..." A thought came. "Vireddi, would you look at those fragments? In case there's anything to tell us they were definitely Mavrys's clothes."

The girl crouched, Jerya briefly envying her suppleness, and examined the scraps of fabric with commendable thoroughness. After a few minutes she straightened. "This darn here, m'lady." She brandished one of the fragments. "It looks a lot like one I watched her do. If'n it please yowr ladyship."

"It doesn't, exactly... But you do," she added hastily as Vireddi's face fell. "Thank you again."

She turned back to Railu. "That seems conclusive. We have no sign of Mavrys, she wasn't in her right bed last night, and here are her clothes burned in the fireplace. I smell a rat. A large royal Sessapontine rat."

"There's another question, isn't there?"

"Aye." Jerya looked down at the fragments littering the hearthrug. "If her clothes are here, what's she wearing now?"

She thought for a few moments, then snapped into action. "Elleret, please run to the stables and ask them to get Oronsa saddled and ready. I'll be there as soon as—no, in fact, get them to bring her to the front. Make clear it's urgent." Elleret nodded and darted from the room. "Vireddi, thank you for your help. Please gather up those remains... but we'd better keep them for now. "She looked around. "Take a pillow-case from the bed. Put them in there. When Elleret gets back, give them to her for safe keeping. Then if you could take that rug and see what can be done about cleaning it..."

"Very good, m'lady."

"Thank you."

Jerya turned away and began heading for her own room to change. Railu fell into step with her. "What's your plan?"

"We may as well keep the search going for a little longer. Just in case we're wrong about this evidence." Not that she had any real doubt, and the dread about what might have befallen Mavrys almost had her breaking into a run.

"That's not why you're changing into riding gear, though."

"No. I think I need to have another word with His Exalted Highness."

Chapter 17

Jerya

In a straight chase, she would have doubted her chances of overhauling a coach-and-four. Fortunately, on an early visit to Skilthorn, Hedric had showed her the hill-track, a much more direct route than the carriage-road's devious course around the hills and the mazy meanders of the Horris Brook. The track, in places, was too steep for wains or carriages to negotiate safely; even pack-mule trains tended to avoid it.

Even a feisty mount like Oronsa slowed to a stately walk at times. Trusting her horse's instincts, Jerya made no attempt to push her to greater effort. The short-cut would gain at least an hour, even if the Prince's four-in-hand were being driven apace. Perhaps it would moderate its speed to allow the baggage wain to keep up, but she could not rely on that.

Even so, she was nervous, biting her lip as another steep descent eased and Oronsa picked up pace once more. What she could do if she failed to waylay the Prince at first attempt, she really was not sure. *Come to that, I'm not exactly certain what I'm going to do if I do catch him...*

Her first worry was soon assuaged as they breasted a slight rise. They passed a stand of trees on the crest and a clear view opened up to the left. At once she saw rising dust, apparently from two vehicles travelling close together. She patted Oronsa's neck. "Easy, lass." They finished the descent at an ambling trot, reached the junction, and turned onto the highway. Less than a hundred yards along, trees clumped close on both sides. Here Jerya reined in. She found a wizened carrot in her pocket; evidently it had been there a few days, but Oronsa didn't mind.

It felt like an age before the carriage hove into view, but in reality it had surely been less than ten minutes. Sensing her rider's nervousness, Oronsa shifted her stance and snorted. "Easy, lass," said Jerya again.

She could not believe the coachman would drive right over a lone woman in the middle of the road. Even if he, or his master, cared nothing for her or her mount, even with superior momentum, there'd be a high risk of injury to his own horses. *Worse for us, of course. But he won't try it.*

He didn't, first slowing to a crawl while gesticulating to her to get out of the way. When it was clear woman and horse were not about to budge, he applied the brakes. The carriage halted, the leading pair perhaps four metres away.

A head—not the Prince—leaned out of a window to speak to the driver. There was a brief exchange. Voices were low and she could make nothing of it; perhaps they were speaking a Sessapontine dialect. The head withdrew; she heard still fainter voices from within the coach.

A different head appeared; the Prince. He peered at her with affronted curiosity. Something about his gaze made Jerya wonder suddenly if he were short-sighted. She knew how Hedric looked without his glasses; but he was never too vain to wear them. "Greetings, Your Highness," she called.

"It is you, Countess. I must say this is a quite unexpected pleasure."

"Unexpected, certainly. I am not so sure about the 'pleasure'."

"Whatever can you mean?"

"I believe you have something that belongs to me." She had resolved during the ride that she would not mention Mavrys's true status. It would only muddy the waters; and if the Prince did not respond to the challenge of an affronted owner, she doubted he would be any more swayed by consideration of Mavrys's ambiguous freedom.

"Have I?" he said, a perfect pantomime of bemused innocence.

"It is unedifying to conduct this conversation by shouting, Your Highness. Might I approach? If you will give me your royal pledge not to drive on when I am no longer blocking your path."

He shrugged. "My word on it."

A few moments later they were standing by the carriage, and Oronsa was cropping the strip of grass between road and plantation.

"So, Countess, what is it that you believe I have inadvertently purloined?"

Jerya had no belief whatever in the 'inadvertent' part. Either she was completely in error and would have to apologise in the most humiliating fashion... or Mavrys had been taken quite deliberately, and with forethought. "The slave who... came to your bed the last three nights?"

"Yes, a lovely specimen. But what about her?"

"She's missing."

"Unfortunate. Are you saying she's run off?"

"It's possible, I suppose." Inwardly, she marvelled at how calm she sounded. She felt anything but. "There is an alternative explanation, however."

"And what would that be?"

She could hardly have expected him to make this easy for her, yet the longer he parried her approaches, always with that same sardonic half-smile, the more certain she felt that he did, at least, know something about Mavrys's fate. Mentally, she squared her shoulders, stiffened her resolve, commanded herself to overlook the fact that she was quite alone, on an empty road, facing a haughty autocrat and at least five of his minions. There was the coachman, the two slaves on the rumble-seat, and two brawny handlers with the baggage-wain; and his chancellor, watching from the shadowy interior of the coach. He would be of little use in a physical struggle, but the Prince had more than enough already. If it came down to that, she wouldn't stand a chance.

She had to make sure it didn't end that way. "The facts are these, Your Highness. The girl was in your rooms last night. She is nowhere to be found this morning. If that information, by itself, were to reach the newspapers... you can imagine the conclusion that many people will draw." *Common theft is how most will see it.*

He shrugged, but the nonchalance was starting to look just a little forced. *I hope I'm not imagining it.* "Why should I care what fancies the bourgeoisie of Denvirran might get into their heads?"

"The bourgeoisie are not the only ones who read newspapers, Your Highness. And Denvirran is not the only Principality that has them."

Another shrug. "A few days of speculation, then everyone loses interest, moves onto the next fleeting sensation." His eyes narrowed. "Besides which, Countess, you are not unique. Anyone can spread speculation and gossip."

"Quite true. Though I have several impeccable witnesses to every statement I would make."

"Nevertheless... I might suggest that you consider the risks, all the same. Your reputation already has a somewhat... sensational tinge in some quarters."

It was Jerya's turn to shrug. "Perhaps. But I believe, in the world of newspapers, to be first with the story counts for much. It's an hour's ride back to the house, and there are gentlemen there who could have messages on the wing very shortly after. I doubt you can match that."

The Prince still wore his increasingly infuriating smile, but the nearer of the two slaves on the rumble-seat was looking at her in a manner surely intended to be menacing. Generally, for a slave to look at a free person that way, still less a member of the nobility, would bring swift retribution.

"I'm sure no one is thinking of doing me harm," she said. More than ever it was an effort to keep her voice level. *I should be grateful to Perriad*, she thought. *Gave me some practice in facing up to bullies.* "If they were, I'm sure they'd reflect that many people at Skilthorn know where I have gone. And if I fail to return in a reasonable time that would be a much more sensational story."

She let him consider that for a moment. 'There's one more thing. One more piece of evidence which points in one particular direction. We found charred remnants of the girl's clothing in the fireplace."

Finally his smile vanished and Jerya had a glimpse of just how dangerous this man might be. It was an unsettling moment, but his anger was directed elsewhere, toward the unseen occupant of the carriage. "You pestilent fool, Couzel! I'll deal with you later," he snarled, before turning back with smile restored.

He even offered her a small bow. Jerya could not imagine he was one who bowed often. "You are a formidable woman, Countess. I shall remember never to underestimate you... Now, I don't suppose you would care to save us both any further time and trouble, since the girl is already in my possession, by agreeing to sell her to me."

"She's not for sale."

He spread his hands resignedly. "There will be other noble visitors requiring entertainment, no doubt."

"That's not what..." She bit back her fury. "Let's save time and trouble, as you said, and just move directly to the part where you return her to me."

"As you can see, she has not been harmed," he said when the baggage-slaves had hoisted the trunk down to the ground and lifted the lid. Jerya noted how it had been propped open to allow ventilation. Mavrys was curled up inside, nestled among colourful silks. The burly slaves lifted her out, their handling neither rough nor overly gentle, and laid her on the grass. The girl was naked; Jerya was dismayed, but not surprised.

She crouched beside Mavrys, anxious to reassure herself that the girl was truly unharmed. She was so intent on trying to rouse her that she hardly noticed anything else until the rumble of wheels and creak of harnesses penetrated her awareness. The carriage and baggage-wain were lurching into motion.

You could at least have left me something to clothe her with. She thought of shouting a protest, but decided it was futile. If the mighty Prince of Sessapont took satisfaction in such a petty act of revenge, so be it. He had lost the greater prize.

Even a firm slap on the cheek could not rouse Mavrys. Still, there were no signs of injury, and her breathing was steady, exactly as if she were in a comfortable slumber. Oronsa stepped closer, bent to nuzzle at the girl's bald head, huffed out a warm breath. Mavrys—Irmavel—had spoken about her upbringing, and Jerya remembered that she had grown up with horses. Maybe she imagined it; maybe the unconscious face relaxed a little.

She scratched Oronsa below one ear. "You're doing your best, lass, but you'll not be offended if I still want Railu to have a look at her. I see no obvious cause for alarm, but all the same... The question is how do I get her on your back?"

She looked up and down the road. Eastward, dust still hazed the air where the Prince and his retinue had passed, but there was no sign of other traffic. West, the road was empty. If someone did come, she thought, it would be embarrassing; hard to explain how the Countess of Skilthorn came to be standing at the roadside with a naked and comatose teenage slave. That would be grist to the gossip-mills, for sure.

She considered her own jacket, but even on Mavrys, who was shorter than herself, it would only reach just below the waist. Decency would hardly be satisfied. Perhaps once they were mounted she could contrive something with the spare fabric of her divided skirt. The first and most important problem was *getting* mounted.

This, however, proved impossible. Jerya could, with a mighty effort, get the girl in her arms and get to her feet, but she could find no way to manoeuvre the limp body onto Oronsa's back. As she rested, breathing hard, Mavrys again curled at her feet, she recalled her own introduction to the Five Principalities, how she and Railu had been slung behind the saddles of the freebooters. But those mounts, she know now, had been stocky hill-ponies, shorter than Oronsa, and it had taken two men to do the slinging.

If there was a mounting-block, it would be easier, she thought. Unsurprisingly, there was nothing of that kind in sight, and it was not the kind of country where one might find a handy boulder. She looked around for fallen trees but the plantation was young, the trees slender. She wondered briefly if she could contrive some sort of sled, so that Oronsa could haul Mavrys rather than carrying her on her back; but how would she lash the spars together? How would she harness it?

She was still pondering, with increasing desperation, when she heard the sound of hooves on the road behind her. *Oh well*, she thought, *have to face it now.*

She turned to look, and as she recognised the approaching rider her shoulders sagged in relief.

✻

Railu was off her horse almost before it had stopped, crouching over Mavrys.

"I've tried to rouse her," said Jerya. "She doesn't look injured, but..."

"Not all injuries are visible. But I'm inclined to think she's been drugged."

"They had her in a box... a trunk."

Railu glanced up, visibly shocked. No doubt she was thinking, as Jerya had, of the time they themselves had been taken. They had been caged, and then chained, but they had never been crammed into a box smaller than a coffin.

"I know..." said Jerya. "You think you've seen the worst, but there's always something else."

Sighing, Railu returned her attention to Mavrys. "I can try smelling-salts, but when I don't know what she's taken—or been given—it's probably best to let her sleep it off. But that could take hours..."

"D'you think between us we can get her into the saddle? And have you anything we can cover her with?"

"I've got a saddle-blanket."

"Draff, and I've got a numnah, but I never even thought of it."

They had to leave Mavrys on the grass while they removed the saddles and retrieved the blanket and the sheepskin pad.

Even with two it was a struggle getting the girl onto Oronsa's back. After one futile attempt, they decided that the best way was for Jerya to mount first, not least because it encouraged Oronsa to stand still. With one pushing and one pulling, the thing was done. Jerya wrapped one arm around the girl to stop her slumping forward.

They arranged the blanket to cover Mavrys's dignity as best they could, with the numnah partly beneath her for comfort and partly doubled around the top of her legs.

Jerya took the reins in her free hand. "We'd better go back the long way," she said, turning Oronsa's head to the West.

"I came that way," said Railu. "I thought I'd get along as well on a good road as on a rough track, especially on a horse I don't know."

"No need to apologise. I'm just glad you're here."

CHAPTER 18

JERYA

As they approached Skilthorn, Jerya had been wondering how to protect whatever remained of Mavrys's dignity. The lodge at the main gates offered an answer. She reined in and asked Railu to go on ahead.

Mavrys had been stirring for a while, but Jerya had limited herself to general assurances and admonitions to keep still. Mavrys herself had hardly spoken, but she had asked the horse's name. Now Jerya asked, "How are you feeling? Does it hurt anywhere?"

She clearly felt the girl's shudder. "I don't like to say, my lady."

"I doubt anything you can tell me is going to shock me now. But I think I can guess... if he used you often, or roughly...?" Another shudder told her all she needed to know. "Can you bear it a few more minutes? It's just the length of the drive now, but it's still nearly a mile."

"Aye, my lady. It's uncomfortable, but not *too* sore." Jerya suspected Mavrys was putting a brave face on it, but said nothing. She tightened her hold on the girl, and for some reason found herself thinking of the child growing inside herself. Even odds it, too, would be a girl, and what a difference that made to the chances and opportunities it—she—would have in life. Whether in the Sung Lands or the Five Principalities, the lives of males and females were profoundly different. Her own life had embodied that; Mavrys surely knew it too. Had it always been the same, or had there been a time, in the Age Before (the Long-Ago, as it was often called here), when men and women had been truly equal?

If there's anything I can do... Her mind returned again to the idea of a school for girls. She was about to ask Mavrys how she would have liked that, when they saw Railu returning.

Railu had brought a long coat, obviously a man's. It was much too big for Mavrys, but none the worse for that, and its tails covered her legs down to below the knees. With the blanket repositioned as a kind of apron, she was as decent as they could make her for the final stretch.

People were milling about on and by the main steps. A discreet arrival would have been too much to hope for, she thought resignedly. And then resignation turned to incredulous joy as she recognised one of the figures, turning away from a conversation with Master Prime Evisyn as the horses approached. For now, she could give Hedric no more than a flashing smile. Their real reunion would have to wait a little longer.

It was at least fifteen minutes before things were squared away. Railu and Mavrys were closeted in the room that was set to become Hedric's workroom, a slave standing by the door with strict orders to allow no one to enter. The sole exemption was Vireddi, who had been hovering in agitation until Jerya dispatched her to find clean clothes for Mavrys.

Finally she and Hedric were able to ensconce themselves in the Lesser Library, and give each other a proper greeting. For a while nothing was said.

Then, lifting her head from his shoulder, she said, "Your timing leaves a little to be desired, my lord. I could have done with you an hour ago. Draff, I could have done with you a week ago."

"Had I but known..." he said in his usual mild tone. "But it seems there's a lot I didn't know. I get back to find the house full of strangers, including half a dozen Dawnsingers. Well, Evisyn's no stranger, but... Couldn't get much sense out of anybody, except Railu... but even she gave me some tale I couldn't quite follow about you haring off after some Prince... But whoever that girl is you were hauling, I swear she's no Prince."

"Her name is Mavrys," she said. "As to the rest... It's a long story. Gossan, where to begin? Well, I suppose it started when I sent Railu a message on the wing. I had a suspicion I wanted her to confirm..."

❋

An hour later, Hedric was still looking mildly stunned. She ascribed it primarily to the news of his impending fatherhood, but there had been much else for him to ingest.

Mavrys, who had joined them a few minutes before, looked almost the calmer of the two. "Railu tells me you'll recover fully in a day or two," said Jerya. "But how do you feel, yourself?"

"More than anything, my lady, I feel... relief. Immense relief. And gratitude..."

Jerya shook her head. "There'd be no need for either if... I can't decide whether to admire your initiative or to remind you that you're still supposed to be a slave."

"I'm sorry, my lady. I didn't exactly plan any of it."

"I suppose not... But then acting on impulse seems to be very much your standard way of doing things."

"I'm very sorry, my lady. I will give it my very best efforts."

Jerya nodded, but she hadn't finished. "I've heard one or two of our esteemed guests grumbling about all this fuss over a mere slave. It could really have affected the mood of the whole thing. Especially if I'd succumbed to temptation and told them what I thought of their heartlessness."

Mavrys blinked hard, and Hedric frowned at Jerya. She took a deep breath. "I'm sorry. It's hardly your fault they're heartless. Hardly your fault the Prince is... well, something worse. I can only hope kidnapping one slave was the extent of his revenge."

"Revenge?" repeated Mavrys, echoed by Hedric.

"Nothing to do with you," said Jerya. "Not as far as he knew, anyway. Though you *were* the reason we knew about his plans. Well, that he was at least *considering* an invasion, or some sort of incursion. But I'm sure he didn't suspect your part in it. Evisyn was clever in her speech... and if he *had* suspected, I fear you might have suffered even more dire consequences."

Tears welled in Mavrys's eyes. "I've caused you so much trouble. And all because I didn't listen to you."

"I've always found my wife very much worth listening to," said Earl Hedric. "But at least some good appears to have come of it this time. We *do* know of his scheming."

There was a tap on the door, and a moment later a slave entered. "The 'freshments yow ordered, m'lord, m'lady."

"Put them on the low table, please," said Jerya.

She did as instructed, though she could not entirely conceal her bemusement at seeing Mavrys—just another slave, for all she knew—sitting with the master and mistress; and, even more unheard-of, being allowed to eat with them too.

"Thank you, Aynwick," said Jerya, and the girl bowed herself out.

"I don't know if I'm hungry..." said Mavrys, looking down at scones, butter, jam, and soft white cheese.

"Try a little," said Hedric. "You often don't realise until you start."

CHAPTER 19

MAVRYS

Mavrys didn't know how long she'd been sitting on the bed before Vireddi came in. It was the first time they'd been alone together since...

Vireddi sat down beside her and stretched an arm around her shoulders, but Mav felt herself flinch, and Vireddi hastily pulled away.

"Sorry." They both said it in near perfect unison, which should have made them smile, but failed to do so.

"*She nen brav?*" asked Vireddi, but Mav didn't have the energy to cast her thoughts into Patter.

"I'm fine, really. Tired, but not hurt. It's just... I... I don't know."

"Dun't know how yow feel?"

"Yes, that's it. Almost don't feel anything, really."

Vireddi said nothing. After a few moments, Mav felt the light touch of a single finger against hers, where it curled over the edge of the thin mattress. That was all right.

More time passed, and Vireddi's hand advanced by tiny increments until it was covering her own. Not a word was spoken. Mav felt a little as if she never wanted to speak again.

How would that be? It was going against orders that had got her into a mess. If she had only listened... Why not, from now on, be one who did nothing but listen? Listen and obey. Be a good slave. But slaves had to speak sometimes. *Speak when you're spoken to.* She thought of Elleret, the Countess's personal attendant; someone had said that she'd once been tongued. There was no separate word for it in Patter, so she couldn't be mistaken about that. Elleret's speech was sometimes indistinct, but she could make herself understood. Still, from what Mav had seen, Elleret was not one to open her mouth unless she needed to.

Vireddi broke into her thoughts. "Yow had aught to eat?"

Speak when you're spoken to... "Some scones, a while ago."

"And ... like a this mornin'?"

But Mav couldn't remember the morning, or didn't want to. She shook her head mutely, miserably.

"Seems to me yow might need some feedin'."

"It's too late for dinner, isn't it?"

"I c'n find yow somethin', if yow likes."

Mav shrugged, but then felt ungracious. "If you don't mind."

"S'all cold," said Vireddi, settling onto her own bed. "But's better'n nothin'."

"Much better," said Mav, lifting a delicate-looking little tart. "Asparagus? Must be the last of the season."

"I wun't know 'bout that."

'Yes, sorry..."

"No fret. Just eat."

The tarts were delicious, and she'd eaten three before she stopped to think. "You didn't get these from the sla—from our kitchen."

"Nen, from th'frees kitchen. S'always a better place for leftovers."

"They don't mind?"

"Not if'n yow asks nice-like."

"That means you've walked further... I'm truly grateful."

"No fret. For yow, Mav..." Vireddi stopped. Mav looked up, hand arrested over a fourth tart. Vireddi blushed, but sat up straighter. ""For yow, I'd do anythin'."

Mav could only stare at her.

"I dun't know what he did to yow," said Vireddi, "And less'n yow wants to tell, I dun't care to know. But yow can tell if'n yow wants."

"He put me in a box," blurted Mav, surprising herself. A vow of silence was never going to work. "A trunk. Portmanteau. Whatever you call it. It was a box. Jer... the Countess told me that. But I remember: he said he was going to put a collar round my neck. Soldered, so it would never come off. A gilded collar, but a collar all the same. Put me on a leash and lead me around like a... like a dog."

Then she broke, and wept, and Vireddi had to leap forward to catch the plate as it slid from her knees. "I'm sorry," she sobbed.

"What for should yow be sorry? That cull'n of a Prince oughter be sorrying yow."

For some reason that only made Mav weep the harder. Vireddi set the plate down on the chest between the beds, then dropped to the floor, only the worn rag-rug for padding under her knees.

"Mavrys," she said. "Belike yow don't want touchin'. I don't... I don't rightly know what yow wants, but whatever 'tis..."

"Oh, Vireddi, I don't want to push you away. I just... I don't want to feel like he made me feel."

"If'n I just sit aside yow?"

"You can hold me, if you want. Yes, just... just hold me."

Vireddi wasn't tall, and she seemed slight, but there was strength in those arms. Mav, though really the larger, was glad in that moment to feel small, to feel herself wrapped in warmth and strength and care.

After a while she squeezed Vireddi's hand and said, "You're worth a thousand of him."

Chapter 20

Skelber

*M*y dearest one, he wrote.

There are many things I had intended to tell you about, but all must give way to the latest to-do. I do believe old Sivrenn would have called it 'a right kerfuffle'. He smiled as he wrote this, sure that Sumyra would smile just the same when she read it. *It all revolves around the Prince, and as I had pledged in my previous letter to say something of His Highness, I may at least partly fulfil that promise here.*

It is clear that no one had anticipated that Sessapont's Prince would attend in person, and no advance notice had been sent by bird or by heliograph, which would have been normal. (Or, of course, something was sent, but not received.) The first that was known of it, therefore, was when a watcher on the roof of the house spotted the carriage, with an outrider bearing the Royal Standard. Everyone, I think, was aware within minutes of the stir this created, but no one had much time to prepare and neither the Countess nor anyone else had time to change their dress. I wonder if his intent was to catch us all off guard, but that is mere speculation... and from what I was able to observe, albeit at some distance, the Countess handled the moment with customary aplomb.

He went on to sketch the Prince's appearance and then, before relating the sensational events of the previous two days, he felt it necessary to issue a caveat.

Let me caution you now to be very careful about relaying any of this. In fact I strongly urge you not to speak of it with anyone until I return. By then we shall know what, if anything, has reached the public prints, and I shall have a better notion of what it is advisable to say openly. I place my trust in you, Sumyra, and the delicacy of the whole matter will be clear to you.

Before the events I am about to relate (just a little more patience, my dear!), I should say that the first days of His Highness's sojourn passed without incident. He appeared amiable to all and, as far as I could tell, well-satisfied with proceedings. Something changed on the night before his departure. I cannot say what, but his accustomed smile was conspicuously not in evidence following the Master Prime's address to the assembly, and he had previously given no indication of an intention to leave the next morning. I do not think even the Countess had much warning.

As to the rest of what happened, much of it remains obscure; if I learn more I shall communicate it to you. For now I shall relate what I know as plainly as I may. As I say, you will appreciate the delicacy of it all. Your aunt would doubtless say that it is far too shocking and I should preserve your innocence, but it is my belief that you need to know what kind of world we live in and what kind of men live in it—even, sometimes, occupying the highest positions in the land.

And I would be surprised (although part of me might be relieved), if you did not already have some inkling of the ways some men use their slaves; specifically, their female slaves, and even more specifically, in most cases, their younger female slaves. I would be surprised if you had not heard, perhaps in whispers, that such practices are particularly prevalent in Sessapont. Previously I might have cautioned that such whispers may be no more than slander. Now, after what I have seen, I have no doubt that the Prince himself not only condones but actively practises such incontinence. If the highest in that land does so, who may doubt that others follow?

He paused a moment, looking back over the previous paragraphs. They represented a full page of preamble without ever getting to the point. He could readily imagine Sumyra's impatience, but he hoped she would see he was trying to prepare the ground, to soften the shock that the truth must carry. Still, he could not put it off for ever; time, ink, and paper were all finite.

This is what I know, between direct observation and corroborated report. I will attempt to relate the tale in the order events occurred, though some only became clear to me later.

He then ran through an outline of the tale, as best he could put it together.

What is somewhat puzzling, he added in conclusion, *given her evident condition, is that neither Le'ast, Fulmer, nor I were called to attend her. Knowing all we do of the Countess, and the lengths she had gone to to rescue the girl, it is not credible that she would subsequently neglect her medical needs. But we also know that there are not, among the company of Dawnsingers, any of what they call Healers (our discussions, of which I must say more soon, have been with Master Prime Evisyn and Master Yanil, whose subject is Mathematics). If there had been, this omission would have been explicable. As it is, it remains a puzzle, albeit a small one among the greater.*

Well, my darling, this has become a long letter indeed, and I fear once again I must postpone for another occasion all the other tales I have wished to relate for you. At least I shall hardly want for subjects when next I pick up my pen, and even then I suspect there will be much more that will have to wait until the longed-for day when we are once more together.

He sat back. Was the whole tale too lurid, too rich, for Sumyra's innocent eyes? He had better not seal the envelope just yet. He'd find time to reread and reconsider in the morning.

CHAPTER 21

MAVRYS

Morning felt brutal.

Miss Railu had given her 'something to help you sleep', a packet of powder. Vireddi had scurried off for hot water to dissolve it. Last thing Mav could clearly recall before sleep took her was her friend's watchful face. Her last, vague, woolly thought had been *it's good to have a friend.*

There had been a few dreams, she thought. Dreams of smiling men; it was probably a mercy she remembered little more than that. That was easy to explain. More of a mystery was an episode when it seemed she heard heavy grinding sounds. Could it be some memory of being carried, like some piece of cargo, on the Prince's baggage-wain?

In a box... Mav shuddered in her bed, and knew that there would be no more sleep. Rubbing her eyes, she sat up, and as soon as she could see, one mystery was explained.

At some point in the night, Vireddi had shifted the weighty chest out from between the beds, and then moved her own bed right up to Mav's. Mav thought about the mass of an iron bedstead and mattress, and Vireddi's slight frame, and marvelled.

She thought again, *it's good to have a friend.*

❋

Vireddi, however, was nowhere to be seen, and her bed was cool. Looking out into the passage, Mav realised from the slant of the light that it was well past the usual time for slaves to rise—even though, as she'd learned, this was an hour later under the new régime than under the old. She'd have missed breakfast for sure, and it was far too late to join the line for shaving. She ran a hand over her scalp, felt the friction. There was no real expectation to be shaved every single day, but she'd missed two days in a row. *And I want to be a* good *slave...*

Still, just now, she didn't mind missing the meal, or the closeness of the shaving room. There was other company to be sought.

Her legs felt wobbly at first, but by the time she had descended the back-stairs she was moving more freely. She knew that if she was fit enough to do what she was doing she was probably fit enough to return to her duties, but the body's recovery was not the whole story.

It felt almost like another betrayal. The Countess had done so much for her. It seemed she had ridden out alone—alone except for Oronsa—to confront the Prince. Mavrys had not clearly understood how she had managed to persuade the Prince to relinquish his prize, but she could not imagine it had been easy.

Yes, it felt like another act of defiance, but she needed to do this.

She passed other enslaved on the stairs, nodded to those she knew, but kept moving. She kept moving too in the passage that led to the back-yard. A slave who looked idle, purposeless, would surely attract attention; one who moved like she had a place to be, work to get to, would pass unnoticed. She thought guiltily of how often in her old life she had barely even seen the slaves who kept the household running—her *old* old life, when the house held a dozen slaves, when her father still lived, when the stables were busy and the horses throve.

The horses...

She stopped short of the stable-yard, leaned on a paddock-rail. Surely that was Oronsa at the far side, tail swishing idly as she grazed? Rose-grey was an unusual colour; it might be strong in Skilthorn bloodlines, of course, but she had not noticed any others when she first rode up to the place... how long ago? Three weeks? She almost laughed; it seemed ridiculous. So much had happened, it had to be longer.

One of the other horses, a leggy roan filly, trotted over, obviously hoping for a treat. Mavrys wondered if she could have filched a carrot or two on her way past the kitchens. "I'm sorry, lass, I've come empty-handed." The horse snorted reprovingly, then trotted a few paces, staying by the fence; stopped, looking back at her. Mav quickly realised she was being led. Twenty yards away, by the paddock gate, a bin stood on a short post. Lifting the lid, she found it stocked with chunks of carrot.

"You're a smart one, aren't you?" she said as she gave the filly her reward. "What's your name, I wonder? I called my first pony Feathermane, when I was little. He had another name, of course, but he learned to answer to it. It'd serve for you too, wouldn't it?" She scratched that place many horses liked, by the root of the jaw, and the filly tilted her head a little as if to say *harder, please.*

A harsh voice broke the moment. "What yow think yow're doin', wench?"

Mav spun round, an indignant retort dying on her lips as she recalled just in time that she was a slave. "Just talkin' to th'horse."

"An' feedin' her. Who told yow to do that?" He had the compact build of a jockey, though one who'd retired and grown a little heavier. His skin was weatherbeaten; hard to tell what his original colour might be. Black brows were drawn down in what looked like a practised scowl.

"No one told me. She was hung—"

"—Oh, an' I s'pose yow knows all about it?"

Remember you're a slave was getting harder by the moment, but she tried. "Beggin' yowr pardon, sir, but I *do* know summing 'bout horses."

"Is that so?" His tone said he didn't believe it for a moment.

"'T's true, sir. Ask me anythin'."

"I dun't have time to waste on slaves with ideas above their station. Be off back to where yow belong an' maybe—*maybe*—I'll forget about this afore I run into anyone in author'ty over yow."

She longed to defy him, to show just how much she did know, but she knew it would not end well. She looked like a slave; for the remaining time till her birthday she had to *be* a slave. And slaves did not argue with frees. She'd gotten into enough trouble by failing to heed Countess Jerya, but Jerya was a lot more sympathetic than most people would be.

Mavrys turned away, sick at heart. The place she'd come for comfort had turned sour on her. The filly paced alongside her as far as the corner of the paddock. *She knows I'm good with horses,* she thought. One bit of carrot hadn't purchased her affection. Horses could sense how you felt about them.

She was halfway back to the house, trudging along half-blind with tears, when another voice broke into her doleful reverie. "Hello, is that you, Mavrys?"

Mav brushed her eyes, saw who had addressed her, dropped into a hurried curtsey. "My lord."

"There's no need for ceremony, not out here, just the two of us. Besides, Jerya told me your story. I know you're not enslaved."

"No, my lord, but then again... for the next eleven weeks I *am.*"

He only nodded. "And you were... just taking the air, like me?"

"Not exactly, my lord. Truth is, I came to see the horses."

"I see."

His voice was gentle, seeming to invite frankness. "Aye, my lord. Ever since I was little, I've turned to the horses when I'm in need of solace. Horses never judge."

He smiled. "I'd say they judge pretty well who cares for them and who doesn't." This so precisely echoed her own recent thought that Mav found herself smiling back at him. Slaves weren't supposed to look their masters in the eye, let alone grin right in their faces... but he had said *no need to stand on ceremony.*

"You're right, my lord. But I thought at least they wouldn't judge me for what I did."

"With the Prince," he said quietly.

"Yes, my lord, with the Prince." She paused, half-expecting, wholly dreading, that he would say more about that, but he only said, "But you didn't find the solace you were seeking?"

Her answer was lost to fresh tears.

The Earl considered a moment, then said, "Come this way." He led her to a small door near one corner of the garden wall, and ushered her through. She saw immediately that the nearest sector of the larger garden was given over to herbs.

They sat side by side on a wooden bench. Belatedly, Mav recalled that slaves were not supposed to sit in the presence of their betters, but she supposed the Earl had implicitly granted permission.

"I used to come here when I was a boy," he said. "My mother... I believe she was the only person, beyond himself, that my uncle ever cared about, but even so, he could be vile to her at times, and it upset me very much. She used to bring me here and... close your eyes, Mavrys."

That took her by surprise, but it was an order. Like a good slave, she obeyed.

"Now," he said, "Take a few moments, and then tell me... What can you smell?"

"Lavender, my lord."

"Always the first you notice, isn't it ? But not the only..."

She sat, inhaling through her nose, and began to unravel the weave of scent. "Rosemary too... well, there's a bush right next to me, I saw it before I even sat down."

"I could call that cheating." His voice sounded as if he were smiling, though, so it was all right. "But go on. What's in the bed behind you?"

The scent was there, but what was it? "Oregano?"

"Well, I'd have said marjoram, but you may be right. I'm no botanist, nor much of a gardener."

With a little more gentle encouragement, she picked out thyme and bay; then he asked her what she could hear. "Bees," she said at once.

"Besure, as my wife would say." He chuckled. Had he made a pun? Bee... sure. Was she meant to laugh? Would a good slave laugh? But he had barely paused. "She knows a good deal about bees. Did you know that she was a beekeeper in the village where she grew up? Helped with the hives, anyway... But we're not here to discuss her. What else can you hear?"

"A waggon in the yard."

"Aye, a delivery of flour, I think. What else can you hear in the garden?"

"Birds, my lord."

"Aye, and I'm a better ornithologist than botanist. Are you? Do you know them by their song?"

"Not well, my lord. But there's a blackbird..."

"There is. Fine musicians they are. Anything else—ah, did you hear that?"

"A buzzard."

"Passing right overhead. And there's a robin looking right at us, but you can hardly be expected to know that. Well, you can open your eyes, if you want."

She was almost reluctant to do so, and then it was all a dazzle for a few moments. But she had not forgotten her manners. "Thank you, my lord."

"Feel better?"

"Very much so, my lord."

"Well, I'd still like to check on my horse, if you feel like wandering back there. Or you can stay here, if you'd rather? I gather my wife has made it clear the grounds are open to all."

"I didn't know if that included the walled garden, my lord."

"I shall take it upon myself to say that it does, and I shall speak to the gardeners. It seems to me that all members of the household should have access, not only to these gardens, but to other facilities. Why should slaves only be permitted to look at the sculptures when they're dusting them?" Mav, who'd experienced that very duty, merely nodded. "And then there are the libraries..."

"But slaves don't—" She cut herself off, feeling heat in her cheeks.

"Slaves don't read? But you're a slave, aren't you?"

"Yes, my lord." She said it firmly, striving to believe it.

"Yet you can read, I'm sure."

"Yes, my lord."

"And you're not the only one. The law says a free person may not teach a slave to read, but when was any law universally obeyed? Besides, not every slave is born to that station. You know that some are subject to punitive enslavement, and there is voluntary enslavement too."

"Voluntary enslavement?" she echoed, her mind seizing on the words.

He gave her a curious glance, but at that moment a chime rang out from the bell above the yard door, and then another.

"Two already," said the Earl with a sigh. "And I must be back before four and sprucing myself up, ready to make conversation with people and pretend I have the faintest idea what they've been talking about this past week." He rose. "I'm going to the stables, Mavrys. Will you come with me, or stay here?"

She had no need to think about her answer. "I'll come with you, my lord, if I may."

Master and slave walking side by side was another breach of decorum, but if the Earl encouraged it, no one else could object.

"May I take you back a little?" he said. "Jerya said something about your father breeding horses?"

"Yes, my lord. Birtler of Carinnan, he was. You may know of him...?"

"I've heard the name, I'm sure... but I confess I don't much follow the finer points of breeding. And racing too, I think?"

"Very much so, my lord. Especially the 'chase."

"And yourself?"

"I spent every moment I could down at the yard with him. My mother didn't think it was 'ladylike' but she couldn't do anything as long as he was alive. I loved him and I loved the horses. When he died... they were my only comfort. But then my uncle came in, and... within a year the yard was empty, grass growing between the setts. Half the horses had been sold right off, to whoever came along. Two of his best steeplechasers are pulling carriages now. I could have told him how to find a better buyer. Not just better for the horses, he could have made a much better return. I could told him which of the mares needed serving when, and when they needed to go to another stud, not one of our own stallions. I had all the bloodlines in my head. I could have... but it would never occur to him that he might take advice from a female, let alone a mere slip of a girl." She snorted. "If he could only have listened, he might have kept my mother in the style she was used to and she wouldn't have been so desperate to marry me off."

This speech—which, she realised, she had failed to punctuate with a single honorific—had brought them back to the paddock, and the hungry filly was waiting at the corner. Once more she paced alongside as they continued to the the feed-bin.

"Renfrith objected to you feeding her?" the Earl asked.

"Renfrith, my lord?"

"The stable-master. *Our* stable-master, now. It's still new to me, you know. I've been coming here all my life; I knew these stables before Renfrith arrived; but they weren't mine." Mav had no idea what to say to that. He smiled, regarding her through his spectacles. "Curious... He's never once said anything when I, or Jerya, gave them a treat or two. Why do you suppose that is?"

"Is that what they call a rhetorical question, my lord?"

He chuckled. "I dare say it is, though Rhetoric was never my subject... Well, from your knowledge of horses, would you say this one's hungry? Or merely gluttonous?"

"Horses aren't like dogs, my lord. Dogs—many of them—don't know when to stop eating. Horses mostly do."

"Interesting. It's true, you see plenty of fat dogs, but I don't know that I've ever seen a fat horse. I wonder if that's a difference between carnivores and herbivores."

"I don't know about that, my lord."

"Well, if she's not one of the rare gluttons, she's hungry, wouldn't you say?"

"I'm sure of it, my lord."

"Then have at it." He nodded toward the feed-bin.

"Do you know this one's name, my lord?" asked Mav as she was feeding the filly.

"I'm afraid not. Lot of guest-horses here at the moment. We can ask Renfrith, though."

Mavrys glanced over her shoulder, saw the stable-man once again approaching. Denying him the satisfaction of acknowledging his presence, she returned her attention to the filly.

She heard the Earl say, "Ah, Renfrith. We were just admiring this fine filly. Whose is she?"

"Came in from Drumlenn, m'lord. One o' them Dawnsingers on her."

"Do you know her name? The horse, I mean, not the Dawnsinger."

Mavrys was glad she had her back to Renfrith. She met the filly's gaze and imagined the horse was grinning too.

"Sorry, m'lord," said Renfrith, "Can't say as what I do."

At that she couldn't stop herself swinging around. Not knowing the name of a horse in your care, even temporarily... her father would have deemed that unacceptable.

The Earl looked at her with a hint of a frown: a warning? No, it would not be wise to antagonise the stable-master. With the earl's countenance, as she had just realised, she might, at least, be permitted to come down here when she could. Just to spend time with the horses would do her more good than any medicine.

His frown cleared, giving way to a smile. "Hello, here's an old friend."

Oronsa had quietly made her way over while Mavrys had been focused on the filly. Now she stretched her neck over the rail, nuzzled up to her.

"Seems she remembers you," said the Earl.

"Of course she does." After a second she remembered, "My lord." There was a small sound from behind, presumably Renfrith. "And I remember you, don't I, beauty?"

"That's her ladyship's favourite," said the stablemaster. "Brung her wi' her from Kirwaugh."

"Who rides her when the Countess hasn't the time?" Mavrys was fairly sure yesterday's unplanned outing had been Jerya's first ride since her own arrival. When had the Countess ever had a free hour? She felt a pang of guilt at the way she herself had added to the demands on her time.

"Mostly no-one," said Renfrith. "We walks her up and down twice a day. Rest o'th' time she's free o'the paddock."

"That's nowhere near enough exercise, not for a horse like this."

He looked startled, and Mavrys remembered that she was meant to be a slave. "I beg yowr pardon, Master." Earl Hedric must have heard every word, but he said nothing.

The stablemaster was aware of the Earl's observation; he might also reflect that his master had brought Mavrys back to the paddock for a reason, though nothing had been said. "I'll not say yow're wrong," he said after a moment. "But she dun't like a heavier rider."

Mavrys hesitated, but the Earl caught her eye: was that a faint nod? "I'm not a heavy rider. I dare say I weigh less than her ladyship."

"Yow can ride?"

"I've been riding since... I can't remember a time when I couldn't." *And I've quite forgotten about sounding like a slave...*

"Well," he said dubiously. "I'd want to see yow on some less precious horse first. And I reckon, rightly, I'd need her ladyship's say-so."

"You leave that to me," said the Earl. He gave Mavrys a smile. "Now, Master Renfrith, how's my Revelin? He had a long run yesterday."

✳

"Might I ask you a question, my lord?" she asked as they began walking back.

"By all means."

"You mentioned... voluntary enslavement?"

He stopped in mid-stride. "Don't tell me you're thinking of *that*...?"

"I hardly know what I'm thinking, my lord. But... it does happen?"

He gave a quirky smile. "My wife was right; you're a very determined young lady. Well, then... when is your birthday?"

"Eleven weeks away, m'lord."

"As I may have said, Jerya has told me something of your story. And whatever else I may think about voluntary enslavement, you cannot submit yourself until you are of age. Only your parent or legal guardian can do that. And from what I've heard, I assume you wouldn't want your mother or your uncle involved?"

"No, my lord."

"So nothing can be done for those remaining weeks. If you still feel the same by then..."

CHAPTER 22

MAVRYS

The Countess was frowning. "I wonder just how many times I'm going to have to speak to you about acting on impulse."

"I'm truly sorry, my lady. It won't happen again."

The Countess looked doubtful. "We'll see... But I suppose I can't fault you overmuch for wanting to spend time with Oronsa."

"It isn't only Oronsa, my lady."

"Just as well, or I might have to forbid you on grounds of making me both jealous and envious." She smiled to show she wasn't serious, but Mav still felt some further strictures were impending.

She was relieved, therefore, to hear a knock at the door, but her relief crashed into dismay as she recognised the voice that came to her ears. "Please forgive the intrusion, but my master requests to speak with you, my lady. As soon as conv—" Brellas stopped. His jaw moved but no sound emerged.

Mavrys had seen him a couple of times before, but kept her head down and relied on the usual invisibility of the enslaved had. This time, unprepared, she'd failed to do so. And there could be no doubt that he had recognised her.

"Irmavel?" he managed at last. "Is it really you? But how...?"

"My name is Mavrys," she tried, but it was futile. No doubt he recalled the timbre of her voice as well as her face.

"My lord," said Brellas. "My lady. I do not begin to understand what is going on, but I must make you aware that this girl is no slave. And she has been missing for several—"

"I am aware of her origin," said the Countess.

"I fear, my lady, you cannot be aware of all the circumstances. Irmavel—"

The Countess held up a hand. "A moment, please." She turned back to Mavrys, her eyes steely. "One question. Is there anything of significance that you have omitted to tell me?"

"No, my lady. Nothing. I left home of my own free will; I came here and threw myself upon your mercy. I agreed, of my own free will, to live as a slave until I attained my majority."

Then she made herself meet Brellas's gaze. He was staring at her. "You would rather be a slave than be my wife?"

"I would rather live as a slave until I am of age than be dragooned into marriage—for life—with a man I hardly know and do not care for."

"Brellas," said the Countess gently. "You did say your master was anxious to speak with me?"

"I beg your pardon, my lady. This... seeing my fiancée here like this... has made me forget my duty."

"I understand. Where will I find him?"

"I can take you to him, my lady."

"Thank you, but I think I can find my way around my own house. I'm sure you need a little time to get over the shock. And perhaps, if Mavrys is willing, if she feels up to it, you can hear her explanation." She looked at the earl, a look for him alone, full of unvoiced messages and shared understandings. *That is how a marriage should be*, thought Mavrys as the door closed behind the Countess.

Brellas nodded slowly. "Irma—or am I to say Mavrys? Would you allow it? Please?"

Well, he did say 'please'. "On one condition."

"What is that?"

"Under no circumstances will you tell my mother where I am. Not before my birthday, at any rate."

"I'm sure she's deeply worried for you."

"I'm sure she's worried. I'm not so sure she's worried about *me*."

"What do you—"

"—Forgive my intrusion," said the Earl, standing. "I will be at the other end of the room, reading over the minutes of the meetings so far. I still have much catching up to do."

"Please, sit," said Mavrys, pointing to the nearest chair, then thought, *A slave shouldn't be inviting a gentleman to sit...*

But Brellas sat. "How am I to understand all this? I thought everything was fine, we had a clear understanding... and then I hear that you have disappeared. No one even knew if you'd been abducted or you'd absconded... though the fact that a horse was also missing did suggest the latter was more likely. And then... nothing. Not a word. Until today, until just now, when I find you sitting here, looking like a slave and calling yourself by another name."

She sighed. "You said we had a clear understanding. The fact is, you and *my mother* had a clear understanding, not you and I."

"But surely... your mother has your best interests at heart."

"I wish I could believe that."

He shifted uncomfortably. "What is it you are trying to tell me?"

"It's simple enough. This marriage was entirely my mother's idea, in cahoots with my uncle. She never offered me a choice in the matter. And as far as I can see her interest is all about ensuring her own comfort. Oh, no doubt she made sure I'd be comfortable too, but her own security is her first concern." She looked at him, wondering just how much to tell. "I don't know exactly how much she ever related of our circumstances...?"

"I know that things became... stretched... after your father's passing. For which I'm sure I have extended my condolences before, but please allow me to express again—"

"—Thank you. But did she ever tell you how and why our affairs became so *stretched,* as you put it? It's a good word, by the way. Stretched, threadbare. Last winter we could barely afford to heat the house so we spent most of the time visiting distant friends and relations of my mother... I'll give her credit, she sewed with her own hands, altering some of her own dresses so that I could be decently attired when you came calling. But why were we in that predicament in the first place? We'd always been comfortable when my father was alive and well. Not exactly wealthy, but we had a good few slaves, we travelled, I had a new dress every few months.

"Breeding horses wasn't a hobby for my father, as it is for some. It was what sustained our household. And I shared it as much as I could. Being with him, with the horses, it was all one, really. And I learned a lot about the business. I'm not saying I could have run the yard singlehanded, but he had good staff." *Could have run the yard...* The thought lingered

"But when he died, of course my mother couldn't inherit; it passed to her brother, and he took the horses away to his own estate, didn't take the men who knew the horses, the bloodlines. I could see clear as day he was wrecking everything my father had built up, but he'd never have taken my advice. Within a year he'd turned profit into loss, sold most of the horses for half their true worth...

"Most of the household staff were 'let go', just like the stable hands. My only education was what I could find for myself in books, and then most of our library was sold. The house soon followed, and we were moved into a smaller place. I—well, I needn't bother you with all the details. My mother hated it, but she never acknowledged that she might bear any responsibility, even though it was *her* brother who was frittering away everything we had."

He sighed. "You know, if you had told me this before..." He didn't finish the thought.

"How could I? I didn't *know* you. For all I knew, everything I said might have gone straight back to my mother."

"I will say this, you paint a very different portrait of your mother to the impression I formed for myself."

"I'm not surprised. She can be... she *is* charming."

"And so are you." No doubt he meant it, but then he looked at her again, at the shaven head and the homespun clothes, and his face showed uncertainty. That flicker of doubt was enough to dispel any lingering doubt in Mavrys's.

"You seem like a decent man," she said. "But I never knew that before. I never had the chance to know anything about you." *I never had the chance to know any other man either.*

"Is that... Do you mean that there's still a chance?"

"Would you still want me? A bride who steals a horse and runs away? Would you want a bride who looks like I do now?"

Again there was that betraying flicker of expression; maybe not outright rejection, but definite hesitation.

"When I left home, I was thinking only of one thing: to get away, to be free. But since then so much has happened." *And I'm not about to tell you all of it.* "I have, as you see, lived the life of a slave. Just as Countess Jerya herself once did. I am sure she would agree, a person cannot have that experience and not be altered by it. But *how* it has altered me... I don't know. I may not truly know for a very long time... I said I ran away to be free. But running is not freedom, 'away' is not a destination. I think... I think I may have experienced more of real freedom living here as a slave than I ever did before."

She saw that he was frowning. "I don't expect you to understand this. I'm still trying myself. Irmavel, Mavrys, who am I?"

❋

After Brellas had gone, baffled and slope-shouldered, Mavrys simply sat for a while. Perhaps lingering traces of the drug explained her lethargy, but also she was striving to understand what she herself had said, especially the question she had raised at the end.

Eventually a discreet cough pulled her from her reverie. The Earl was looking down at her, eyes full of concern behind the lenses. "Are you all right?"

"I am well enough, thank you, my lord. Just rather confused."

He gave a soft chuckle. "As am I. I am not confident I will ever fully catch up with all that's been done and said in my absence. Still less when I shall find time to write up my notes from the expedition." He gestured. "May I sit?"

"It's your library, my lord. And I am—"

"—You are confused. And sometimes things become clearer when you tell someone else about them." He shifted the chair, setting it roughly at right angles to hers. "Also, since I despair of catching up with the wider story, perhaps I can do better with yours." He settled more comfortably. "You know that this has been the first time, since well before we were married, that I have undertaken a significant journey of exploration or discovery without Jerya?"

"I didn't, but I am not surprised."

He smiled. "And what happens? I spend a month scratching around on glaciers. All very interesting, of course; there aren't many who've had that experience. Still... you might expect a glacier to be all white and dazzling, like freshly fallen snow, but I can tell you now, they're remarkably dirty places. Like the last drifts at the side of the road when the thaw comes, but on a giant scale; boulders instead of pebbles. So my trip was a lot less glamorous than I had envisaged, and meanwhile all manner of momentous events are happening right here in my own house. I only hope Jerya appreciates the irony."

"You know her infinitely better than I do, of course, but I think she will. And I think she might have been happier grubbing around in dirty snowdrifts with you."

He smiled, but there was a shadow behind it. "I don't think her own happiness has been her first priority for a while. Least of all since we inherited this place... But that's my problem. And I am meant to be hearing your story, not burdening you with my own complaints. If, that is, you wish to tell it."

"If you truly wish to hear it."

He lifted one hand in a kind of shrug. "I seem to be superfluous to proceedings elsewhere. And I think your tale will interest me. Why did you come here, to Skilthorn?"

"Because... I had read everything I could lay my hands on about Countess Jerya. Since the very first time I heard of her, I had hoped to meet her one day. And I thought, if anyone would understand my predicament, it would—"

"—Start from the beginning, if you please. I may have some pieces of the picture, but I don't know what I'm missing. Your predicament...?"

"My mother was determined to marry me off to Brellas."

"That young man who was here just now?"

"He's twice my age."

"True, I suppose. What are you, seventeen? And he must be somewhere about my own age, when I think of it. But I do still like to think of myself as young..."

"I meant no offence, my lord."

"I'm sure you didn't. So, your mother was determined you would marry him... and I surmise you were equally determined not to?"

The story unfolded by degrees. The Earl was a sympathetic listener, only interrupting when clarification was needed, until they reached the point where Mavrys presented herself at the Prince's door. Then he sat back in a way that made her stop. He remained silent for some moments, shaking his head slowly.

"I know it was foolish," she said. "I thought I knew what I was letting myself in for. I understand much better now."

He sighed. "Jerya wants to do something about the education of girls. As do I, of course... but we haven't gone far in considering exactly what should be taught. Now I'm thinking..."

As he fell silent, she said, "I grew up in the country. My father was a breeder of horses. I knew from an early age what happens between stallion and mare. And yet I never fully considered..."

"That humans are animals too? Mammals, to be more precise. Yes, and of course you were never encouraged to think about it... If you had known, would you still have done it?"

"No," she said as a reflex, only then pausing to think about it. "No, in truth, my lord, I am not sure. It was not a happy experience, but it still seems... the Countess was in an impossible position, and I thought I could help her out of it. But, doing so, I defied her express wishes, and now she is angry with me."

He smiled. "When Jerya has a moment to reflect, she will see... and if not, I will ask her: *does Mavrys remind you of anyone?*"

"I'm not sure what you mean, my lord."

"You know Jerya's story, you said. So you know she did something that most people would never dream of, against all common sense, against explicit instructions—and against a solemn Vow she had taken... because she was convinced it was the right thing to do. And then she walked right out of the only world she knew. When we went back—when she went back, I mean; obviously it was my first Crossing—I saw with my own eyes just what an undertaking that first journey was... I wonder if she needs to be reminded that you're not the first young woman to take a crazy risk. And even then she was older than you are."

"I don't know if I could say that to her."

"I think you could take that risk too... But, you know, if Jerya seems angry, it really isn't you she's angry with. You just catch a little of the backwash. She has—we have—bigger things to be angry about. Men like the Prince, and the way they treat people, for starters."

"And women who would sell their daughters in marriage to ensure their own comfort?"

"I don't know your mother, so I'd rather not pass judgement on her. But it does seem to me... that fellow Brellas seems decent enough."

"No doubt he is. But I don't want to be shackled for life to a man of whom I know nothing more than he's *decent enough*."

"No, of course not, and I don't for one moment suggest that you should. How many of us, at seventeen, eighteen, nineteen, really know what we want, who we are?"

"Jerya did," she said, and then thought she might have overstepped. "Railu said much the same."

"Aye. Railu has her head screwed on. Although..." He chuckled. "She *did* follow Jerya across the mountains. I should say, she's had her head screwed on since I've known her." His face grew pensive. "They've been very close for a long time. I'm sure it pains them both that since our marriage they see each other more rarely."

"And now Railu's here but Jerya's got so little t—I mean the Countess. I'm sorry."

"Don't apologise. Call her Jerya; call me Hedric, if you like... it's all very new, this 'Earl and Countess' business. We aren't too comfortable with it; maybe we shouldn't be. Just remember there's a time and a place..."

"Yes, my lord."

"Now you're pushing your luck." But he grinned. "I imagine you've learned a lot from even just a few weeks living as a slave. Or enslaved, as Jerya wants us to say. You understand why she says that?"

"Because it's something that's done to you, not what you *are*."

"Just so. I couldn't wish for a more succinct summation. It seems Jerya's found an apt pupil..."

She'd expected a test, and she couldn't fault Renfrith for that, but this was taking it to extremes. Dalster was huge, even by the standards of cart- and plough-horses. Mavrys could easily have believed him close to twenty hands high. He was also beautiful, a light chestnut with flaxen mane and shaggy fringes around his feet. Feet, she noticed, surely as large as her own head.

Like most heavy horses she'd seen, his temperament appeared placid; he stood patiently as blanket and saddle were thrown over him—and 'thrown' was the word. *Perhaps someone will throw me up there too*, she thought.

When the other hands—a pair of lads both brawny enough to remind her of Renfrith's comment about heavier riders—had finished, Mavrys stepped forward, going first to the horse's head. She could hear her father's voice: *always introduce yourself first*. She gave him a carrot she'd pocketed earlier, stroked his nose, gave him her name. Only then did she move rearward, checking the tack, lengthening the stirrup on the left side as far as it would go.

"Yow ben't meaning to ride him like that, surely," said one of the lads.

"I can't ride him at all if I can't get on his back," retorted Mavrys. She could of course have led Dalster across the yard to a mounting block, but if Renfrith had meant for her to use it, she thought they'd have begun over there anyway. Besides, she had a plan.

Even with the stirrup low, it was a high stretch to get her foot in, and when she straightened her leg the pommel was still a stretch. She double-checked that the girth was secure; she'd seen stable-lads prank newcomers that way more than once. Including a time when the sudden shift of the saddle had spooked the horse and earned the unfortunate victim a kick in the thigh to add to mere embarrassment.

Satisfied, she grasped the knee-roll and launched herself upward.

Lengthening the stirrup had been a good solution to the first problem, but left her too low to comfortably swing a leg over the animal's broad back. Even with a firm grip on the pommel, her only recourse was to momentarily rest her belly on the seat before swinging herself around and then upright.

With her right foot securely in that stirrup, she could finally lean down and adjust the length of the other. She checked that everything felt right, that both stirrups were now the same length. Even a slight imbalance in the rider could unsettle a horse, though she doubted her light weight would trouble such a heavy horse however she shifted.

Then she made herself comfortable. She was aware that her skirt was ill-suited to straddling a horse, especially one so broad, but her riding-clothes were tucked away with the rest of her belongings, somewhere in Jerya's custody. She arranged the skirt as best she could, but still she was showing an unseemly amount of leg. Perhaps it mattered less for a supposed enslaved than it had for a gentleman's daughter; her father had insisted on proper riding-clothes, made a new habit his regular gift every Wintermas since she was about six. This last had been the first time she'd received no such gift.

Her eyelids prickled, but she spoke sternly to herself. *Don't think about him. Don't think about this being the tallest horse you've been on.* It felt like twenty-five hands now, though she knew that was impossible. *Just don't... Just get on with it.*

Finally, she gave the reins a twitch, heeled the horse's flanks, and said, "Walk on."

Nothing happened. The beast felt like a slow-breathing statue. She looked down—a long way down. The two lads were grinning broadly, nudging each other, but Renfrith's face was serious.

"Do you say something different here?" she asked.

Renfrith said nothing, but one of the lads obliged. "He's more used to hearing 'pull'. But 'appen that'll confuse him when he's not in th'traces. He did learn 'walk on' when he were schooled. He should remember; it's not that long ago."

So the vast animal was still young. Had he even finished growing? *That was a notion...*

She thought a moment. *He's a big horse. Massive. Maybe he just needs more...* She repeated the process, exaggerating each element far more than usual; she dug her heels in with a force she'd be scared to employ on any ordinary mount, said 'walk on' with all the command she could summon, almost barking the words.

This time it worked, and as Dalster eased into motion she felt the sheer power of him.

She'd been on thoroughbreds more times than she could possibly count, or even estimate. She knew the power that dwelt beneath those sleek, rippling hides. She'd felt it translate into speed, into the fleeting airborne exhilaration of a jump. This felt different. Slower, almost ponderous, but immense. She could scarcely imagine Dalster clearing a hurdle, or breaking into a gallop, but she also felt that if he did he would be well-nigh unstoppable. And who needed jumps when her feet were almost level with the others' heads anyway?

"Take him out that gate and into th'paddock," said Renfrith. "Trot 'im round a couple o'times,"

At a trot, Dalster proved to have a surprisingly fluid gait, and just by the sheer size of him he covered the ground quite quickly. She found herself reluctant to rein him in and walk back to the yard. This time, she didn't ask, simply guided him over to the mounting block. It could still have done with an extra step, but she could make a reasonably dignified dismount.

"Well," said Renfrith when she stood by the horse's head. "If her ladyship really wants yow to exercise Oronsa a time or two, I won't be telling her again it."

He didn't sound happy about it, but Mav was quite happy enough for both.

CHAPTER 23

RAILU

She'd only thought to wander down to the stables, see how Mavrys had fared her first time exercising Oronsa. The girl appeared to be fully recovered, in body at least, from the Sessapontine drug and whatever other indignities she had suffered. Horses seemed to be her refuge from the mental trauma, and Railu could see how riding, and caring for the beasts, might well be therapeutic.

A pleasant sunny stroll to the stables, a cheerful chat with Mavrys, an encouraging report back to Earl and Countess; it all sounded delightful. Instead she found herself witness to disaster.

She'd caught a distant glimpse of Mavrys heading in, but the girl was already off the horse and leading her into the stable as Railu arrived. Her attention was distracted by voices behind her, in the paddock. She turned just in time to see one of the stable-lads on a dark bay horse, kicking it into stride towards a jump. The other lad was nearer the rail, shouting something that sounded more like derision than encouragement.

Then Railu realised that the rider was mounted bareback. She was enough of a horsewoman to get around, but had no experience over jumps. Still, surely that was no way to go about it?

Time seemed to slow as the horse took its last few strides; the rider bunched his fists in its mane. Abruptly the horse dug its feet in and half-skidded to a halt. The horse stopped; the rider didn't.

Railu glanced back toward the yard, saw no one. "Help!" she yelled. "Rider fallen!" Then she took off running, as fast as her dress skirt would allow. Afterward she could never remember whether she had opened the gate or scrambled over it.

Her practised eye appraised the situation. The horse was standing a few yards away, snorting and pawing the ground uneasily. The rider lay still, his friend kneeling by him. She saw blood, bright on his breeches, already darkening on the ground.

"You," she snapped. "Secure that horse."

"I don't take orders from slaves."

"Are you a healer?"

"No."

"I am, so get out of my way. The last thing your friend needs is a frightened horse running loose."

He stared at her for long seconds, doubtless still wrestling with the idea of 'taking orders from slaves'. But then, presumably, he saw the sense, though he couldn't resist a snort of disgust as he levered himself upright.

Two things were immediately apparent. The lad's right arm lay at an unnatural angle: dislocated shoulder. And there was a sharp splinter of wood protruding from mid-thigh of his right leg.

One of Sister Berrivan's first lessons came back. There had been perhaps six or seven of them in the room, second-year Novices who'd chosen to specialise as Physicians. This was their first introduction to trauma.

Mostly, said Berrivan, *we talk about triage in relation to numbers of patients. But you can apply the same principle to an individual patient too. Often there can be more than one injury. First, identify the most serious. Is it life-threatening? Then that's your priority.*

Beware, however, it's very easy to be drawn to big obvious injuries and miss something that may be less spectacular but more dangerous. However urgent the obvious one may be, take a few moments to check you aren't missing something else that you should be tackling first.

A dislocated shoulder was not a life-threatening injury. The splinter in the thigh didn't appear to pose an immediate threat either. Blood was dripping from the wound, not pumping out.

With the swift but careful touch Berrivan had taught, she ran her hands over his other limbs; no obvious sign of fractures. She pulled up his shirt to check his abdomen. No evidence of internal bleeding. She knew that deep internal injuries could take time to manifest at the surface; she would need to keep checking every few minutes.

A voice: "What the hell are you doing? You said you're a healer, why aren't you *doing* something?"

She had probably heard it a thousand times; the panic in the voice of the bystander, the friend or lover or family member. "I am a healer," she said, trying to keep her tone firm but not antagonistic. "And there is a right order in which to do things."

"But he's bleeding to death."

"No, he's not. There are at least eight pints of blood in most human bodies. A biggish lad like this, could be eleven or twelve. He hasn't lost even half a pint. He *isn't* bleeding to death. But if I don't take that splinter out exactly right, it could get worse."

There were footfalls behind her, more voices. But just at that moment the fallen lad gave a long moan and began to stir. A few seconds later he was whimpering and thrashing about, clutching at his shoulder.

"Lie still," said Railu urgently. "I can't help while you're writhing about like that." There was no reaction, as if he couldn't even hear her.

She glanced up momentarily. Mavrys was there, an older man behind her.

"All right," she said. "It's a dislocated shoulder. They hurt like hell, and that means he won't keep still... So I have to reduce the shoulder before anything else. We need to keep him still as we can. Mavrys, you hold his other arm. You—what's your name. Get down here and put your weight over his chest."

"I don't take orders from slaves," he said again.

"She's not a slave," snapped Mavrys. "And, by the way, neither am I. So either shut up and do as you're told, or make way for someone who *can* help."

Railu could have laughed out loud at the look on the lad's face, but she deferred that pleasure. "Don't put weight on his belly, keep it over his ribs. Now it will probably hurt him worse, for a moment, when it pops back in, so be ready."

She moved into position, grasping the hand and wrist, thinking about the configuration of the head of the humerus and the socket. Again she recalled Berrivan's teaching. *Once they're aligned correctly, the same muscles that were pulling it askew should now pull it back in.*

Steady traction; simultaneous rotation... The click was audible, but she'd heard louder. The patient's scream, however, was right up with the loudest she'd heard.

"You're killing him!" said the other lad.

"No," said Mavrys. "Look."

The scream had been appalling, but there wasn't a second one, just a few whimpers. Then the lad lay still, white-faced and panting, but no longer thrashing about.

"Now," said Railu, "Has anyone got a knife?"

"What the hell do you want a knife for?"

To slit your throat if you don't stop fighting me at every turn... Through gritted teeth, she said, "I'm going to cut strips from my skirt so I can immobilise that shoulder before I look at his leg."

The older man, who still hadn't said a word, produced a short stubby knife. It wasn't surgically sharp, but it was good enough to make the initial cut to allow her to tear her skirt. She tried not to think how much it had cost.

As she set to work binding the arm across the chest, she glanced up. "I'm going to need clean water, clean cloths, and alcohol. The purer the better."

"We have rubbing alcohol," said the man. "I'll go."

"And someone needs to go to the house," added Railu. "Mavrys, d'you know where my room is? No? Then find J—the Countess—or Elleret, to direct you. Bring my bag." She described her physician's satchel. "Fast as you can."

With a nod the girl was off. It wasn't how Railu had anticipated checking on her, but she seemed to be fine. Railu watched a moment, noting how freely Mavrys moved in her divided skirt; a pointed contrast with her own heavy—and now ruined—dress.

Within a few minutes the older man was back, arms full of cloths. "Bottle in my pocket," he said. "Tek it, Tharshin. Pass it to th'lady."

The lad, Tharshin, complied, but with a grudging air. "And tek that sour look off o'yowr face, lad. Reckon yow're in enough trouble a'ready."

"What for? Wun't me on that horse."

"No, but I dun't need to ha' bin here to know yow was eggin' him on. In fact... I want yow out o'my sight. Tek th'horse back to his stable. Give him a real good rub down, a pail o'watter, then a couple o'handfuls o'feed. Stay wi' him and keep him calm. I'll talk to th'both o'yow later when Mardom's on th'mend.

"Pair o' spraggin' idjits," he muttered as Tharshin and the horse moved away. "Beggin' yowr pardon, m'lady."

"I'm hardly a lady," said Railu with a smile.

"Oh... that lass, Mavrys, said yow wasn't a slave. And seems like yow knows what yow're doing around an accident... I thowt yow must be one o'them Dawnsingers."

"I was, once," she said.

"Oh, I..."

"Don't worry. My name's Railu, by the way. And you are...?"

"Renfrith, ma'am. Master o'Horse."

"And the lad's Mardom?"

"Aye, ma'am." Railu shrugged inwardly: 'ma'am' would have to do. She bent over the patient; green eyes turned to her. "Mardom, my name's Railu and I'm a healer. I think your shoulder's feeling better?"

"Aye, ma'am."

"Good. Now, I'm going to take a look at your leg but I probably won't do much with it till Mavrys gets back with my things. I hope she won't be much longer. But listen to me, I'm going to need you to stay as still as you can. It might be very important, understand?"

"Yes, ma'am."

"Good. Now, this may sting..." She dripped some alcohol onto the wound. Instinctively the lad flinched. "Try not to do that again. Renfrith, could you hold his leg? Around the shin. Keep it as still as possible."

Originally, the wound had probably been a clean penetration, but Mardom's earlier writhing, the associated flexing of the thigh muscles, had opened it somewhat. It would have been painful, but doubtless he hadn't even noticed it beside the agony of the shoulder. She splashed more alcohol into a cupped hand, rubbed it over both hands, felt the chill of evaporation. Then, gently, tentatively, she probed at the edges of the wound. Mardom moaned, but Renfrith's firm grip on the lower leg quelled any movement.

She sighed. "I can't see how deep it goes. But I daren't just pull the thing out, it might do more damage. I'm going to have to open the wound a bit to get a better view, but I won't do that till Mavrys is back."

"'Appen she wun't be too long," said Renfrith. "Reckon I can see her now, in fact."

"That was quick... but I'm not surprised."

"Yow knows her?"

"We've talked a few times. I think she—" She turned at the sound of running feet.

Mavrys thrust the bag at her before slumping to the ground, too out of breath to speak.

"Thank you," said Railu, giving her a smile as she delved into her bag. "Now, let's have a proper look."

A few minutes later there were more footsteps, and then a voice. The kind of voice she'd heard far too many times in her life, the kind that thought it was acceptable to own people. "What the devil do you think you're doing?"

She sighed, wondering how many more times she'd have to explain herself. "I reduced a dislocated shoulder and now I'm looking at getting this splinter out."

"Move aside and let me do it. I'm a doctor."

She glanced up just long enough to gain an impression of elegant, and doubtless expensive, clothes, rather at odds with an unruly shock of dark red hair. About forty, she guessed. "I am a trained healer. And right now I have my fingers in this lad's thigh and this splinter is a fraction of an inch from one of the main lateral branches of the femoral artery. Do you really think it's less risky to attempt to change places than to let me continue?"

He only grunted, then after a moment crouched down next to Mavrys. There was something familiar about him, but there were more than thirty delegates at the Congress.

"Mardom," said Railu. "I'm going to take this thing out now. It shouldn't hurt like your shoulder did, but it may still be painful. But it's more important than ever that you keep really still."

"I'll hold his shoulders," said the newcomer.

"What can I do?" asked Mavrys.

"Hold his hand and keep telling him to lie still."

"Would you kindly accept my apology for my earlier rudeness?"

Railu glanced up from the pan that was just approaching a boil, the farrier's forge providing a convenient source of more than sufficient heat. As it reached a simmer she dropped the scalpel and forceps into the water. "Do you have a watch?"

"A watch? Why... yes."

"Then could you please tell me when ten minutes have elapsed?" She grasped the pan's handle with a well-wrapped hand, moved it a little further from the centre of the fire. Finally she turned to meet his gaze. "Your apology is accepted."

"Thank you. In that case, might I take the liberty of introducing myself? My name is Skelber of Brinscal."

"I'm Railu. Railu Kermey."

"Miss or Mistress?" he asked. "If you do not consider the question impertinent."

"Miss," she said, thinking, *I don't know about 'impertinent', but it does seem irrelevant.*

"It is a pleasure to make your acquaintance, Miss Kermey. And if I dare presume on your good nature for just a little longer, my curiosity is still unassuaged... you described yourself as a trained healer?"

"I trained for seven years in Carwerid."

"Oh, you're a Dawnsinger? I thought you always wore white."

"I trained as a Dawnsinger. I'm not one now."

"Ah..." There was that air of light suddenly dawning. "I believe I begin to understand... and to recall. Have you not been advising the Dawnsingers in the medical discussions?"

"I have... and you..." That was where she had seen him before, seated behind Le'ast and Fulmer, taking notes and engaging in whispered consultation, much as she had been doing for Evisyn and Yanil.

Having finally agreed that they recognised each other, he returned to her history. "It is well-known that the Countess was once a Dawnsinger. And most people, I think, also know that she did not make the First Crossing alone. Would I be right in supposing...?"

"We were Novices together in the College of Dawnsingers. Of course, as you probably know, Jerya was only there for a few months."

"And when you say you are a Dawnsinger no longer... Might I surmise you left the Sung Lands at the same time as she did?" Railu nodded.

"In any case," he said, with a beaming smile that made her reassess her earlier estimate of his age. "It is not only a pleasure but an honour to properly make your acquaintance, Miss Kermey."

She dropped her gaze from his cool grey eyes. "How's the time?"

"Almost seven minutes gone... might I ask why you are doing this?" He indicated the simmering pan.

"Virtually the first thing I learned as a Novice Physician was the importance of cleanliness, sterility. I've seen doctors here start on a procedure without washing their hands. I've seen them pull instruments from their bag and start straight in on cutting. They wouldn't last five minutes in the Guild of Dawnsingers. We were taught to sterilise everything for ten minutes before every use. Clean your hands, clean every wound, apply an antiseptic. Of course if you have to do an emergency procedure in the field you may have to compromise somewhat."

"As you did today..."

"Yes, but then it's even more important to get the patient to proper care as soon as possible. And fortunately, perhaps because the previous Earl was in poor health for some years, the facilities here are the equal—in quality, if not quantity—of most hospitals this side of the Dividing Range."

"Well," he said, when the ten minutes were up and Railu had lifted the pan away from the fire, "I should very much like to prolong this conversation, but I fear my superiors will be wondering where I have got to. And since my presence at the scene was entirely surplus to requirements, I shall have difficulty sustaining a plea of clinical exigency..." He smiled.

"I shall have to go soon too. Perhaps we could walk back to the house together?"

"That would be delightful, but the walk is all too short... I wonder if you would consider joining me at dinner tonight? As you must know, there are smaller tables in the second dining room. If we get there early, we should be able to dine tetatet."

Railu's smile felt slightly forced even to herself. "If my patient is progressing satisfactorily, and J—the Countess doesn't need me..."

"And always presupposing there are no more unfortunate accidents. I understand perfectly. A doctor's life is never entirely his own." He smiled. "Or *her* own."

And that, she thought, *is the closest any doctor in the Five Principalities has ever come to acknowledging me.* She gave him a warmer smile. "Let's hope there are no other idiots trying to jump fences bareback, or any such foolishness."

※

Railu was finding it unusually hard to concentrate. She wondered if Skelber was feeling something similar.

The strangest thing was how they had barely noticed each other before. Perhaps he had simply always kept his head down, taking notes, as he was doing now every time she looked his way. But surely, in a situation of such novelty, even the most assiduous note-taker would look up occasionally, look at the women who sat across from him.

He can hardly think we all look alike. Evisyn was tall, bronze of skin, brisk. Yanil was a head shorter, walnut-brown, her face deeply lined. She herself sat between, in both stature and colour, and of course she did not wear white. True, she sat behind the others, had never addressed the room, communicating with Evisyn and Yanil by passing notes or in brief whispered consultation. But she was not invisible.

Perhaps he had taken her for a slave, as so many in the Five Principalities inevitably did—as indeed he had seemed initially to do when he found her attending to the injured stable-lad. Slaves could be almost invisible, until they were needed. A moment's thought must have shown him that she was no slave. The notes that passed to and fro were sufficient proof of that.

Literacy was rare among the enslaved, but not as rare as most free-folk surely imagined. Railu knew a good deal about it; she had helped teach more than one slave to read and write. Skelber might have no idea of the truth; but what was certain that no slave would let themselves be *seen* reading or writing, except among those she trusted implicitly. He must have seen her doing so; ergo, he could not dismiss her as a mere enslaved.

If he thought about it... That, perhaps, was the crux. The habit was deeply ingrained in the minds of the free-folk of Denvirran and the other Principalities. Some, she knew, had struggled to overcome it even though they were fully aware, in their rational minds, that the women they were dealing with were Dawnsingers.

And Dawnsingers wear white.... The old habit might reassert itself when the bald woman you were looking at—or not even really looking at—wore a dark red skirt and butter-yellow blouse. Her second-best; the damaged dress was now in the hands of Skilthorn's seamstresses. The woman in charge had looked at it and frowned, but had not altogether ruled out the possibility of repair.

It won't be ready for tonight, though... In just a few hours they were due to be dining together. The thought was so strange that for a moment she did not realise Yanil had turned, leaning closer, to ask her something.

Chapter 24

Skelber

"Miss Kermey..."

"You know, no one calls me that. I only said it because I had to say *something*. It's the name of the village I came from, but I left before I was eleven years old, when I was Chosen to become a Dawnsinger. I never went back, after a few years I never thought of it. The College was our whole world. I hardly remember anything about Kermey. I just remembered that Jerya, when she needed a second name, chose the village of her childhood... but she didn't leave till she was nineteen. It meant a lot more to her... and that's far more detail than you expected, isn't it? I'm sorry, I seem to be babbling."

"Not at all." He smiled. "But how, then, should I address you? Miss Railu?"

She seemed to hesitate, even gave the slightest hint of a shrug. "That's what most people do."

"I suppose you have had other titles."

"Yes; once I was Postulant Railu, after that Novice Railu, even for a short time Singer Railu. And then, for some years... I suppose I had no title at all." It was unmistakably a reference back to her time as a slave, which he could acknowledge only by bowing his head.

She took a sip of wine. Perhaps she, too, found it steadying in the well-intentioned awkwardness of the moment. Then she said, "I think this is the moment where I ask you if you are married."

"I was," he said, holding up a hand. She took note of the ring, as if for the first time.

"You say 'was'?"

'Yes," he said, turning his glass between his hands, looking into it, the ruby gleam of refracted candlelight. "I'm a widower."

"I'm sorry..."

"It was a long time ago. Twelve years." His eyes caught hers, just for an instant. He would have liked to say more, but the words eluded him. He resumed his fiddling with the wine-glass.

"You've never thought of marrying again?"

At once she looked concerned, as if fearing she had asked an overly personal question, but he was not sorry. "I may have *thought* of it a couple of times, but nothing came of it. In the end neither woman seemed to measure up to my wife, to be—" Again he fleetingly met her eyes; again he wished he knew what more to say.

It was almost a relief that their soup arrived at that moment. They tasted it, made comments about it, though Skelber suspected that five minutes after finishing he would be unable to recall what flavour it was.

There was a short silence. He was trying to think of a question that would assuage his curiosity, his earnest desire to know more about her, but without probing too deeply. Perhaps she was grappling with the same problem. And then, inevitably, they both began to speak at the same moment. At least they could laugh about this, and that made everything a little easier.

"Please," he said, "After you."

Railu shrugged. "I was only going to ask if you've always lived in Denvirran."

"I was born and raised in a small town in the South-West, close to the border with Velyadero. We took holidays there, around the Velya Lakes. I doubt I'd seen Denvirran, the city, more than a handful of times till I went to school." He'd been sent away to school somewhere within the orbit of the city. Sent away, just as Embrel had been—just as she herself had, in a sense.

The thought seemed to strike both of them at the same time. "And you were—" "I was—"

"Please," he said, deferring politely.

"I can't say we thought of it as being 'sent away'. I know I... I was Chosen, and that was it. Never went back, like I said."

He nodded, reminiscent. "Chosen... I think I would have liked that, to feel special, rather than thinking my parents had ceased to love me. Ah, but my mother's face when I came home after the first semster... that dispelled that notion."

The soup plates were cleared and main courses delivered, lamb roasted with juniper and rosemary.

"When I arrived at school," he continued after a first taste, "I... experienced a lot of ribbing on account of the way I spoke. They said I sounded like a Velyan." Railu understood: the upland Principality had a reputation for backwardness. He shrugged. "I changed the way I spoke soon enough. I don't suppose there was anything like that at the Dawnsingers' College."

She drew breath, started, stopped; shook her head and then began again. "I was going to say there wasn't, and... it's true I don't remember anything more than mild teasing from my own Postulant year, but then I remembered the time just after Jerya's arrival. She did suffer rather more, for a while."

He made suitably concerned noises. She waved a hand. "It didn't last too long; Jerya saw to that. But I won't... I think that's her tale to tell. Though I will say I think that was where our friendship really began." After that, and another sip of wine, she steered the conversation into calmer waters. "I've heard a good deal about the life of a schoolboy in Denvirran from Embrel... my employers' son. I wonder how much you know about life in the Dawnsingers' College?"

"Shamefully little, I confess."

She began by explaining the terms she had already mentioned: Postulants and Novices. Girls were Chosen as young as eleven, consigned to a life dedicated to learning. He could not but ask how they took to it at such a tender age. "I don't think we would have been so ready to devote all our time to books and lessons."

Railu smiled. "I think some in the Guild would call that evidence that females are better suited to the life of the mind."

He considered that as they caught up on their food. "A view, I think, not widely shared in the Five Principalities. Very few men, certainly... and I honestly beg leave to doubt, from my experience, that many ladies would agree either."

To his relief, she only nodded at that. "On both sides certain things are seen as self-evident... but not the same things."

The discussion took them pleasantly through the main course. There was a momentary bump in the road just after desserts had been served. Skelber stopped with his spoon already sliding into his syllabub, asking, "And you have never married?" When Railu shook her head, he asked, "Never thought of it?"

"Dawnsingers don't. And I suppose in some ways I'm still a Dawnsinger."

It was an answer, and probably a true one, but he suspected not a complete one. Perhaps the question had been too abrupt. When, the meal done, he enquired if she would like more wine, she declined. "I've had a most pleasant evening, but—" He never discovered what she would have said next, as she broke off at the approach of Doctor Le'ast.

"I do beg your pardon, madam," he said with a bow that could hardly have been more courtly had he been addressing the Countess herself. "But I need a few minutes' converse with my colleague."

"Not at all," she said. Le'ast skipped to draw her chair back as she rose. "I feel the need for a short walk before I retire." *Alone?* he wondered.

She seemed to have divined his thought. "It will be light for a while yet," she said reassuringly, "And I have walked in places far wilder than the grounds of Skilthorn."

That, he thought, was irrefutable. *And I should very much like to hear more about it.*

⁂

My darling, he wrote.

Once again I must apologise for substandard penmanship. My excuse is the same as always; it is late, I am tired, and I must take myself to my bed soon. And as always there is much I wish to tell you. I must not try to cram in every last detail; I don't suppose the finer details of our discussions, however momentous they seem (and may very well prove) to be, are of first interest to you. Besides, if I say everything in my letters, there will be nothing left to tell you when I do get home. Which is now just two weeks away.

I have already written at length concerning Countess Jerya, knowing she holds particular interest for you, as she does for so many (young ladies above all, I suspect). Having read much of what has been published about her, you are undoubtedly aware that she was not alone on the famous Crossing of the Dividing Range. You may have wondered, therefore, why more has not been said about her companion.

I can think of several possible reasons for this. One, I am sure, is that only one of them is married to a man who has recently inherited an Earldom. The newspapers have always paid more attention to the nobility than to other strata of society. And newspapers, I suppose, print what people want to read.

I also have reason to believe that said companion is not the sort of person who courts publicity. In fact I would go so far as to say she shuns it. You may ask how I can know this, and the answer is simple: not to prolong the suspense any longer, I have become acquainted with her. As I say, she has not received one tenth of the publicity that has followed the Countess, but I do believe that you will find her equally fascinating. I certainly hope so, because I am going to devote the bulk of the following pages to her.

Her name is Railu. I think she was mentioned in one or two of the newspaper accounts, but only ever in passing. Knowing that she was with the Countess on the first Crossing, you will hardly be surprised when I say that she, too, was at the College of the Dawnsingers. Unlike the Countess—just plain Jerya then, fifteen years ago—Railu was there for the full eight years which is the normal span of a Dawnsinger's training. At the end of this time, she was Ordained, as they call it, thereby becoming a fully-fledged Dawnsinger.

That being so, you may naturally now be asking why she then chose, very soon after, to join Jerya on a trek into the unknown. A good question, but not one I can yet answer. I very much hope to have more conversations with Miss Railu soon so perhaps I'll know more when next I write.

But I am getting ahead of myself. Let me tell you how I came to make the acquaintance of this most interesting woman.

Quickly, he wrote an account of that encounter, his hand almost degenerating into a scrawl as the words flowed. He winced a little to recall his initial brusqueness, but smiled at the memory of Railu's gracious acceptance of his apology.

The upshot was that we arranged to dine together that night. Tables are set for various numbers and by arriving early we managed to secure one for two persons. Miss Railu was a little wary at first. Perhaps she had spoken to one of the Dawnsingers. Their advances in medical and related science are one of their most valuable bargaining counters and it is quite understandable that they would not wish this information to be carelessly given away in casual conversation. I assured her that I had no wish to compromise her standing with her colleagues and would be perfectly happy to discuss other matters, about which indeed I felt much curiosity. As, I am sure, do you. In the spirit of candour, however, I reminded her that she had already made reference to the great importance the Dawnsingers' Healers attach to cleanliness and what they call sterilisation, and then said, 'If I may save more of my patients simply by washing my hands more thoroughly, then I would surely be derelict in my duty not to do so.'

She looked briefly troubled. 'There's a lot more to it than just washing well, though that's an excellent start. But the real reason I'm hesitating... there's a dilemma I've already considered, and I am sure Master Evisyn and the others have too. If we withhold information, people may die who might have lived. Others might lose limbs that could have been saved. But to give it away and get nothing in return...' She paused, drank some wine.

He paused also, remembering that moment, remembering how the light of the chandeliers burnished her smooth brown scalp. His breath had caught in his throat. Never before had he seen quite how beautiful a bald head could be.

But there were some things he would not say in a letter to Sumyra. Indeed, he could think of no one with whom he could share this realisation. Perhaps the one person to whom he would like to say it was Railu herself, but even with her it was far too soon.

What possibilities might be enfolded within those two simple words: *too soon*? But he could not consider that tonight. It was late, and getting later, and the letter needed to be finished.

She said that the first purpose of the Guild of Dawnsingers was the increase of knowledge, of which the Guild considers itself a custodian. As she said, everything we know about the time of the ancients suggests the great peril that may follow if too much learning falls into the wrong hands. Incidentally, in saying this, she revealed that the Dawnsingers' understanding of what they call the Age Before bears out our legend that there was once but a single Moon, which was shattered by weapons of which they still have little understanding. Their aim is the conservation of knowledge, but this historical perspective makes them highly conservative in sharing it, if you will forgive a small play on words.

I said that I grasped the dilemma, and I understood that her role is as an adviser to the Master Prime and the other Guild delegates; she is not an official representative, and she is certainly not empowered to make policy decisions on their behalf. She then said, 'but when I've said all that, I find it hard to think of you going back to practice and perhaps seeing patients die of sepsis when I could show you in a few hours most of what you need to do to avoid it. It seems like there could be no harm in that if I had your word that it would go no further.' Then she stopped and considered. 'But then I only transfer the dilemma to you. What's the ethical thing to do? Where's the greater good?'

I said that I was not currently active in practice, and in any case we were here for another week at least, so there was no particular urgency, that she had time to think about it and if she wished consult with the Guild delegation. She seemed grateful for this, but asked if we could speak of other things. I was happy to agree, and of course I thought of you and how much you would like to hear about what it is like to live in the Sung Lands, and in particular what it is like to be trained as a Dawnsinger.

He related how she'd enlarged on that topic. It occurred to him then, thinking Sumyra would be interested, to ask why girls were Chosen so young. '

I know I was sent away to school at the same age,' I said, 'But I think becoming a Dawnsinger is not the same?'

'No,' she said, thinking about it as she spoke. 'Embrel—my employer's son—is away at school now, but he comes home twice a year and he'll leave when he's eighteen. Dawnsingers—Postulants and Novices—don't have vacations. In fact they never really leave the College until they're Ordained, except for visits to the Observatory.' This Observatory seems to be on a mountain, perhaps a few hours distant from the College in Carwerid; I did not gather exactly how far.

She hastened to assure me that the College is not unduly cramped. The grounds are extensive, with orchards and gardens, some parkland and some wilder areas. There is even a resident family of foxes, who have been observed during Dawnsong, as if they come out to listen.

'Still,' she said, 'It is a drastic change in a girl's life. And the Guild's way is to make it a clean break. No trips back home, no visits from family, no personal letters. The rules can be waived but only by special permission.'

'That seems harsh,' I said, wondering how you would have felt about it.

She thought about it. 'I suppose it does seem... rigorous... to me now. But back then, as far as I recall, I took it in my stride. The College was where I wanted to be and I was excited to learn whatever there was to be learned. I suppose that's what the Peripatetics look for above all, at Choosing; not so much what a girl knows already, her accomplishments, but that overriding curiosity, the hunger to learn.' She smiled. 'Jerya came late to us, of course, but she had that hunger, no doubt about that.'

I wondered what happens, in the Sung Lands, to boys who also feel that kind of drive to acquire knowledge, but that was a question for another time.

I asked instead, 'What happens to girls who... fall short? There must be some, surely. Everyone changes between eleven and eighteen.'

Again she gave it some thought before answering. 'Some, yes. Not too many, if the Peripatetics have done their job properly. Well, I think that's one reason why the first year is distinguished from the rest, why those girls are called Postulants. If a Postulant does not measure up, or if she seems irredeemably unhappy, then usually she will be encouraged to become a Lay Sister instead.' She explained that Lay Sisters remain sworn to the service of the Guild, which they can perform in many ways, but they take no further part in the training. While young, they live in a house attached to the College, but when older they may choose to live elsewhere in the community and some even—she said 'even'—marry and have children.

If a girl progresses to Novitiate, however, and takes those vows, then, she said, 'It's more of a problem. By the third year, they start to know things which are not to be shared outwith the Guild. And also, of course, by then they're marked for life.'

I asked what she meant by that and she said, 'By then they're permanently bald.' She ran her hand over her own head as she said it.

I realise that in my account of my first meeting I somehow omitted to mention that Miss Railu is also bald. And now I am puzzled by my own omission; it is not something one can fail to notice. For us, until these last few years, a fully bald head has only ever meant one thing: its bearer is a slave. Here at Skilthorn, with seven Dawnsingers in attendance, I have rapidly had to learn that it can have a quite different import.

I thought of another small puzzle. Miss Railu left the Guild fifteen years ago, quite irregularly, but she (like the Countess) clearly seems to have been—shall I say 'forgiven'? Well, there are depths here that will no doubt take time to plumb, and I did not want to mar my pleasant evening by being over-inquisitive. I did, however, dare enough to ask if being bald, in a land where it is the mark of a slave, troubles her. She looked surprised at my question—and that surprised me—*because it surely must be something she has thought about. Perhaps it was my boldness in asking that set her aback.*

Be that as it may, she answered readily enough. 'I feel like I've always been bald. I know I must have had hair before I was Chosen, but I don't remember. I am a bald person; that's who I am.' She smiled. 'I remember when Jerya was bald, and it was hard to see the hair as an improvement.'

He looked up, realised the crick in his neck. He laid down his pen, stretched his fingers also. Then he glanced at his pocket-watch, lying on the desk nearby. Could that really be the time? Well, the watch might not be quite to the standards the Dawnsingers claimed, and it was decidedly bigger and heavier than the ones they wore on their wrists; but it had never gained more than a minute a day. It would surely not have gone haywire all of a sudden.

In the silence left with his pen no longer scratching on the paper, he had a sudden sense of stillness, the great house hushed in slumber. Somewhere, no doubt, there would be slaves still working; in the laundry, perhaps, more likely in the bakehouse, already kneading or proving the bread for the morning. In a few hours—too few!—there would be mouths to be fed. Forty delegates, near enough, at the Congress itself. A few handfuls of frees among the household staff. And how many slaves? Slaves, too, must eat. Probably three or four, if not more, for every free. Well in excess of a hundred, all told—and did laundry or bakehouse serve the field-hands too, or the stable-lads?

It occurred to him then that a great house like this, a great estate, was like a clock or a watch, innumerable parts whirring, oscillating, meshing together. To an uninitiated person, the workings of a watch were unfathomable. The workings of a great house seemed no less complex, no less finely balanced.

It was a nice thought, unless his sleep-deprived brain was making too much of it, and he thought that Sumyra would like to share it... but then he looked again at the time and thought that was better saved for his next letter.

He stretched again, massaged his hand, thinking wearily of the hours of note-taking that doubtless awaited him tomorrow (though it was already today, really). He picked up his pen and knew that he had no real choice.

There is so much more I could say, my darling, but the hour is atrociously late. I am sure you were sound asleep hours ago and at this moment I can but envy you. At least I know I will have no shortage of things to relate in my next letter, and I will compose another one as soon as I can find a spare moment. I long to hear from you (that is not a rebuke, but maybe it is a hint!) but I shall not wait till then.

I trust and with all my heart I hope that you are well and enjoying the air of Ramsridding. If all goes to plan, we shall be finished here in another week, though there still seems to be so much to discuss that there has been talk of extending proceedings for a few days. A prospect I view with very mixed feelings. I know that the congress itself is of the highest importance, and it would also give me more chance to observe the Countess and the fascinating Miss Railu—all to report to you, of course... but on the other hand any prolongation of my separation from you will be hard to bear. Ah well, one way or the other any decision is out of my hands; it will be made by Countess and Master Prime and the highest among the Five Principalities delegations. All I can do is try to make the best of it either way.

Sleep well, my dear

As he stretched again, it occurred to him that he had said nothing about Miss Railu's skill in performing the appendectomy. And in a sickening moment it came to him why that might be.

It had been in the best interests of the patient, he had no doubt of that. But still... *Pesk! What in the world am I to do now?*

He began to think sleep might be long in coming.

CHAPTER 25

RAILU

Her first thought had been to revisit the dell, but as soon as she stepped outside she could see that it would already be half-dark under the trees. In boots and trousers, like she'd worn on the First Crossing, she might still have dared it, but it was no place for polite shoes and second-best skirt. She knew there was a good path all the way around the lake and that seemed both more practical and more enticing. She wanted to think, and not solely about where she was putting her feet.

The question was Skelber, of course; it had merely been thrown into sharper relief by his abrupt enquiry over the syllabub. *You never thought of marrying?* Well, no, she hadn't, or only ever in the most abstract way; the idle fancy of a spare moment, picturing herself in another life. Or, more usually, failing to picture herself. The life she'd have led if she'd never been Chosen; she couldn't really visualise it, but she could rationalise it: still in Kermey, or one of the neighbouring villages, married to a fisherman, a vague swirl about her skirts that was as close as she could get to imagining the inevitable shoal of children. A particularly pungent irony: she *was* a mother, yet she could not imagine herself as one.

It was hardly more possible to imagine a life in which she and Rodal were still together. If she and Jerya hadn't been taken—Taken, not Chosen—if they had managed to learn the state of affairs before their bald heads condemned them to... well, to all that had followed. If, if, if... If Rodal had stayed with them, he could not have missed what happened to her over the next nine months. And neither of them could have pretended that he wasn't the father, not for one moment. How then would Rodal have reconciled his promise to Annyt with the duty he would have felt to her and to the child? To Embrel... though if all that had come to pass, then the boy wouldn't even bear the same name. Nor would he have grown up as heir to a substantial estate. Would he have been better off? It was hard to think he wasn't better off than he would have been as the child of a slave, as she had been for nine years.

She crossed the bridge and turned onto the path that skirted the lake. The water, green in the daylight, was now a mirror for the evening sky, a blushing veil of thin cloud. The sun had just dipped behind the Wold that rose charcoal-dark beyond the house and its flanking trees.

If not Taken; she followed that thread. In that case, she supposed, she and Rodal would be married. Though it was pure fiction, pure speculation, she still felt a pang of guilt about Annyt; but what else could they have done? Cross back to the Sung Lands? Everyone said the Southern Crossing was impassable in winter, and their Northern route would surely be worse. Jerya, still the only person who had traversed both routes, would know best how they compared. But even if it was passable in winter, it would be a different story for a pregnant woman.

But this was speculation piled on top of speculation. And all for a simple question: *You never thought of marrying?* No, because by the time she knew she was with child, Rodal was far away, seeing places she had never seen, Troquharran and Sessapont, the Inner Reach and the Outer Isles. She would have liked to have heard some of his tales of those travels. To have sat a few nights at the kitchen table with a jug of ale and shared those stories... but how could they have introduced him to the household, how could he have spent any time there, without encountering Embrel? One look at the lad and surely he would have known his own son. By Jerya's reckoning, that would have been only right, but Railu had always set her face against it. To this day, she would struggle to articulate *why* the secret needed to be kept, but from the first she had been sure that it did.

Marrying Rodal was just about conceivable, if she stretched her imagination, though she had little sense of what that life would actually have been like. Marrying anyone else... somehow it had never even been a question.

Apart from that one time, all her experience of love had been with women—with girls, in the beginning. Freilyn the first of any consequence; aye, she had thought she loved Freilyn until Jerya came along. Perhaps she had, childishly, but what she'd felt for Jerya was something else. Jerya, in those early days, with her wide-eyed air of wonderment, her frequent protestations of knowing nothing... and her seemingly unshakable sense of who she was. Jerya had changed greatly since then—they both had—but there was something at her core that was solid as rock.

Freilyn and Jerya were not the only ones, of course. There had been couplings before Freilyn; and then there was Rhenya. For over eight years she, Jerya, and Rhenya had been the points of a triangle. Perhaps never an equilateral, a triangle that had stretched and shifted and reformed innumerable times—until Hedric came along.

Railu smiled to herself in the gloaming. *Geometry as metaphor; Jerya would be proud.*

The Western sky was dimming to a greenish glow. Two swans drifted past, silent as ghosts—not that Railu believed in ghosts; Postulants had superstition drummed out of them before they took Novitial vows. Their passage broke the mirror-stillness of the water, stirring the gold of the lighted windows into the sapphire of the sky. The path ahead of her was still clear enough, the compacted gravel paler than the grass, but Railu knew she should keep moving, and briskly.

It was almost surprising she hadn't been resentful toward Hedric. *Well, maybe I was, a little, for a while.* But he was a hard man to dislike, and she had seen how he had reawakened things in Jerya that had been dormant too long. If she had shed a tear or two at their wedding, she'd had no difficulty persuading herself that they were tears of joy.

And I was still the first person Jerya turned to when she suspected she was with child.

There had been no more triangle, not where physical intimacy was concerned; just Railu and Rhenya, and that had all been sweet and simple. But now Rhenya was being assiduously courted by a slave from the estate, a woodcutter who worked mostly on an outlying parcel of land, several miles from Duncal and several hundred feet higher on the broad-backed ridge. In consequence, they had few chances to meet, but because Duncal was a liberal estate its enslaved had gatherings twice monthly, in a redundant barn that they had cleaned out and prettied up themselves. Railu was not a regular at these, and if she did attend she usually left relatively early, before the dancing really got under way, but she heard all about them anyway; Rhenya made sure of that.

Railu, following the pale path as it curved around the head of the lake, gave a mental shrug. Padon could give Rhenya the one thing she couldn't: children. And Rhenya's thoughts had increasingly turned that way since the investigations into her age. She thought thirty a good age: *'best not leave it much longer'.* Railu wondered momentarily how she'd react on learning that Jerya—three years older—was pregnant?

The enquiry as to Rhenya's age had been prompted by the prospect of her manumission, which the law only allowed for slaves over thirty. But that would create its own problems: there was no legal way a slave could marry a freed person. For Padon to be freed also would seem obvious, but fell foul of the limits on how many slaves an estate could free in one year. Duncal was a comparatively small estate, so the limits were correspondingly tight.

If it came to that choice, Railu knew, Rhenya would far rather remain enslaved. Like the old Cook before her, it was what she knew, and maybe, apart from licence to grow her hair, freedom would make very little difference. What had Cook said? *'Saying I's free... Dun't hardly know what it means. What do I want that I ain't already got?'*

Railu had overcome any resentment she'd felt against Hedric, and she'd do the same for Padon as long as he treated Rhenya decently. She had no true right to be jealous over Rhenya, or over Jerya; neither had ever belonged to her.

But it all meant that for the first time since she was fifteen she hadn't shared her bed with anyone for months. *Maybe it's time I moved on too.* Easy to say... but did that mean Skelber?

She was more than half way into her walk, and she had only just returned to the question that she had particularly wanted to grapple with. Which wasn't *You never thought of marrying?*, not really. It was Skelber himself. It was *what does he want?* And, maybe even more crucial, *what do I want?*

What did he want? That, of course, she could only surmise. He seemed very interested in her, and he had, politely and gently, asked some searching questions. She was in no position to say for sure, but she didn't think a gentleman would ask such questions unless he had some serious intent.

Railu knocked gently at the outer door. She didn't think Jerya would already have gone to bed, but if she had, she would rather not disturb her. She was pregnant, and she had been working non-stop to get the congress going and keep it running smoothly.

It was Elleret who answered, and the hairbrush in her hand told its own story.

Jerya turned in her chair. The smile when she saw Railu was probably more relief than anything, but she perceived quickly enough that Railu had serious matters in mind. "No reason to keep you from your bed any longer," she said to Elleret. "Railu's done my hair many a time. Hundreds, I should reckon."

"Most nights since it grew long enough," Railu agreed. "Right up till you got married. More like thousands than hundreds."

"I hope you don't mind one more," said Jerya as the door closed on Elleret.

"Not at all. I've missed it, if anything."

She ran her hands lightly through Jerya's tresses to be sure no pins remained, then began brushing.

"Still," said Jerya, "I don't reckon you're here just 'cause you miss brushing my hair."

"No, you're right... can I ask you a personal question?"

She had to react quickly or the brush would have pulled painfully on Jerya's hair as she turned sharply in her seat. "How long have we known each other?"

"Fourteen years."

"Aye, and I don't suppose there's much we don't know about each other. So I can only assume this is a *very* personal question."

She faced the front again and Railu resumed brushing, using the slow, even strokes to collect her thoughts. However she began, she knew it would be awkward. She took a deeper breath. "Before Hedric, you'd never been... intimate with a man at all." It wasn't even half a question.

"Well," said Jerya, "It depends what you mean by 'intimate'. There were moments on my first journey, with Rodal, that I might call 'intimate'. But if what you really mean is making love, no, not even close. Not before Hedric."

"So that was ten years—more?"

"More."

"Over ten years that you'd only ever made love with women."

"You and Rhenya, no one else. Is that the same as 'women'?"

That was too philosophical just now. "Anyway, you'd never made love with a man before Hedric." She laid down the brush and began gathering Jerya's hair preparatory to braiding.

"True," said Jerya. "But that's not your real question."

"I don't know exactly how to ask... was it strange?"

"Strange?" Jerya shrugged slightly. "I... maybe a little, in a way. Had to get used to... a few things." She smothered a laugh. "Don't know if that's the same as strange." She reached forward, tilted her mirror so she could meet Railu's reflected gaze. "Thing is, Hedric was a friend, a colleague, well before there was anything physical between us. We knew each other, trusted each other, we were comfortable with each other...." In the mirror her brow furrowed. "This is about Skelber, isn't it?"

"Is it that obvious?"

Jerya shrugged again. "Hard to miss that you were dining tetatet tonight. And looking very interested in each other."

Railu wrapped a ribbon round the end of Jerya's braid, tied it off, thinking. "Interested in each other, yes. But what kind of interest? I have no idea what he might want, where he might want to go next."

"What about what you want?"

Railu moved around, dropped onto a low stool alongside the dressing-table. It left her looking up at Jerya, but that didn't matter. "I don't know. Hardly know my own mind better than I know his. What experience have I? That one time, with Rodal, but that was out of the blue."

"An anomaly."

"Yes, exactly. There was that; but I've never walked out with a man, promenaded in Drumlenn on a Hindsday evening. Never dined tetatet before tonight. Never... well, you know. I hardly need to list all the ways I don't know about men."

"And before I met Hedric I'd have said the same," said Jerya, quiet but firm. "And when I did meet Hedric, I didn't immediately know what he was going to mean to me. I liked him, I knew that soon enough, but it was a while before I began to think we might become more than friends and collaborators." She smiled reminiscently. "There were quite a few nights out on the terrace, just the two of us and the telescope—we gave it a lot more use than the Squire ever did—but he was always very correct. If he touched my hand accidentally, adjusting the focus or anything, he'd always apologise."

"When did you know?"

"When did we really know? I don't think it was until we were on our way to Delven... when he slipped on the ice and I thought I might lose him.

And... this is something I never told you before. The first time we made love was in Carwerid."

"Before you were married?"

"Well, of course it was... you're not shocked, are you?"

"Shocked? No. I *am* surprised. You knew what happened to me after just one time."

"We didn't do it that way. Didn't do that till we were married. No, I showed him how women do it... the way you showed me, that first time."

Railu was suddenly aware that, for all her medical learning, there were things she didn't know, particularly about male anatomy.

"Look," said Jerya. "You barely know the man. Don't expect to be sure of anything right away. People talk about love at first sight but I don't know if it's real. If it is, I'm sure it's rare. Take your time, get to know him better. That's all I can say." She grinned impishly, and Railu was suddenly reminded of the girl she'd known, getting on for half their lives ago. "There you are, love, that's the sage counsel of the Countess of Skilthorn. You'd never have thought of that for yourself, would you?"

CHAPTER 26

JERYA

Evisyn arrived at Jerya's side. "Do you have a few minutes? We would appreciate your opinion." She gestured to a table where Yanil and Railu were already seated.

She picked up the thread almost before Jerya had joined them. "You remember I spoke about an exchange of gifts. I'm just becoming concerned that in the matter of the healing arts we are giving significantly more than we are receiving."

Jerya took a swig of coffee as Railu added, "I really wonder if that's because they don't have much to give. I admit my experience is limited to what I've seen of the local practitioners around Drumlenn, but I've always thought they know less than I did straight out of my Novitiate. But I don't know if they're representative of the wider profession. The hospital isn't particularly well-regarded even locally."

"Don't you see the medical journals?" asked Jerya.

"Occasionally. I suppose as a free woman I could subscribe in my own name, but it's expensive..."

"It strikes me that the knowledge and practice of medicine here isn't only restricted by sex," said Yanil.

Jerya looked at her and, not for the first time, wondered about the state of medical knowledge in the Sung Lands, outwith the Guild of Dawnsingers. Yanil must have read her thought, because she shook her head with what might have been a hint of embarrassment.

"Of course it's been slow going anyway," said Evisyn. "Half the time we don't even call diseases by the same name. But for Railu, I wonder if we'd have made any progress at all."

"We have that in every area," said Jerya. "Dawnsingers use metres, they use feet. We're building up concordances and conversion tables, but it slows everything down." She smiled at Evisyn, sure she too would remember the time in Carwerid four years before, when building a concordance of maps had been one of the key tasks. "Maybe we have to accept that doing so is important in itself. Maybe that will stand as one of the key achievements of this Congress, even if it doesn't sound very glamorous." Evisyn nodded slowly, Yanil with more enthusiasm.

"Another thing that occurs to me… We never expected that the two sides would be equal in all aspects. What I've heard from Railu, I always thought the Sung Lands were ahead in the healing arts. But the Five Principalities are ahead in other things, aren't they? Like… I don't know? Shipbuilding? I'm sure they've voyaged more widely.

"You know, Master Prime, when you talk about exchange of gifts—which I thought was inspiring, by the way—it surely has to be considered across the board. Give more in one area, receive more in another." She thought a moment. "If I may suggest… perhaps if you took a step back from the medical discussion and caught up with some of the others?"

"I think you're right," said Evisyn. "When we reconvene this afternoon I'll mention it."

"I thought of something else," said Railu quietly. "I dare say it applies in other areas too, but it's most obvious in healing and medicine. If we have knowledge they don't—knowledge which could alleviate suffering, save lives—have we any right to withhold it?"

"But to give it away and get nothing in return…" said Evisyn.

"You said, Master Prime, that we would be passing on significant knowledge. Are you regretting your words?"

Evisyn stared at her water-glass as if wishing it were wine. "Regretting? I don't know. I am thinking... what will the Conclave think if I have to tell them we gave this, this, and this, and got..."

"That's why you need to see what's happening in other discussions," said Jerya.

"For me," said Railu, "There's another side to this. I know I broke my Dawnsinger's Vow. But there's another pledge which I've always held to: my Healer's Vow. You know, one of the things that most appalled me about being sent to Delven was that I would have so little opportunity to practise my Art."

"Sending you to Delven was a travesty," said Evisyn. "It made a mockery of your Vow. And yet Perriad prates about the sanctity of that same Vow..." She almost growled. "I tell you Railu, my pledge as Master Prime; if you were to return to the Guild now, and reaffirm your Vows, there would be no further sanction against you."

There was silence at the table. The sounds of other diners seemed distant, as if there were walls of glass around the four of them.

Railu stared at Evisyn for long moments. Finally she let out a slow breath. "Thank you, Master Prime. From the bottom of my heart... But I think, unless something changes, I'll stay here. It's my home now. My family is here." Her gaze flickered, but did not quite meet Jerya's. "I have a practice now, of sorts. More than I'd ever have had in Delven, anyway."

Evisyn sighed. "Well, I can't say I blame you. I can promise you no formal sanction, but I can't say there'd be no ill-feeling. Especially with Perriad still—" She broke off with a violent gesture. "By the Seven, that woman did the Guild no service when she lost us the two of you."

Jerya had no love for Perriad, but in fairness she could not lay all the blame for her defection on one woman's shoulders. But perhaps in Railu's case it was fair.

There was another moment of silence. Railu sipped at coffee which must be half-cold by now, and said. "May we return to my Healer's Vow? Which says, in essence, that I will always, to the utmost of my ability, avoid any action which will harm a patient; and then, equally important, that I will *not* refrain from taking action in the best interests of my patients. I got the reputation of a turbulent Novice by asking if that, in conjunction with the Guild Vows, meant we should be giving proper care to everyone in the Sung Lands. And now I have to ask, if by sharing what we know we can help people in the Five Principalities too, are we not bound to do so?"

Evisyn fixed her with that raptor gaze. It might intimidate some, but Railu met it steadily. "I'm more convinced than ever that you were a great loss to the Guild. I don't know if I completely go along with your argument... the Guild Vow very specifically says 'the land and community we are consecrated to serve', and you surely aren't going to tell me that means anything but the Sung Lands? But, as Jerya and I saw five years ago, sometimes there are wider moral arguments which conflict with a strict reading of the Vow. Some would say *I* broke my Vow back then, or at least bent it out of all recognition... and yet the Conclave made me Master Prime.

"Railu, I see the force of what you're saying, but I'd like a little time to mull it over. Perhaps Yanil and I will have a private chat." She turned toward Jerya. "Which make me think, more than ever, that your suggestion that I take a break from our discussion is a good one."

"Maybe all of us could benefit from a pause to reflect and take stock."

"Very possibly."

"I'll say a few words before dinner tonight."

"I'm speaking now, not as Countess, not as your hostess, but purely as a scientist. Furthermore, almost uniquely in the Five Principalities, a scientist who received some of her training in the College of the Dawnsingers." What a relief it was, not only to shed the load of the title for an hour, but to call herself a scientist and to be listened to.

"The first work my husband and I did together—before he became my husband—concerned the distance to the moons. Fixing this is, in essence, a matter of triangulation, and all triangulation rests on accurate measurement of the primary baseline. It was beyond our resources to go out and measure it for ourselves, so we relied on existing maps.

"For precision, we wanted to work from the largest scale maps we could get. It turned out that the largest scale used across both Principalities, Sessapont and Denvirran, was two inches to one mile.

"At that scale, our baseline of two hundred and eighty-nine miles is equivalent to over forty-eight feet. Just to lay all the necessary maps out together required a room larger than any we then had available." She saw a few smiles, even heard a chuckle or two. "I don't need to detail all our problems; let me just say that more than half of the paper we wrote was devoted to such considerations.

"We did the best we could, and we arrived at our measurements; and at least I can say that if we were to repeat the observations in five or ten years' time, the length of the baseline is hardly likely to have changed. If we made a mistake, or the maps were less than perfectly accurate, we can at least say that the those errors do not invalidate comparison between past and future measurements. If there are indications that Cintilla—what Dawnsingers call simply The One—has moved away or drawn closer, we can place some trust in them."

She drew breath, sipped water.

"Five years ago, when I returned to the Dawnsingers' College after a long absence, the paper we wrote about this work was part of the evidence I brought to prove that there was indeed civilisation East of the mountains. Naturally I thought about the possibility of creating a much longer baseline spanning both the Sung Lands and the Five Principalities, but it wasn't for this reason that we—I mean myself, and the Guild's cartographers, under Master Skarat... that we applied ourselves to creating a concordance between Guild maps of the Sung Lands and the maps I'd brought showing parts of the Principality of Denvirran bordering the mountains.

"Our first purpose was to suggest the most likely places where the Selton expedition might appear. As anyone who's read His Grace's book will realise, we succeeded. Unless it was by sheer chance that a party including myself and Master Evisyn was in place to greet them when they emerged from the now famous Defile.

"Now why am I rehashing this history for you? Because it illuminated something for me. Establishing a concordance of maps required more than just looking at them side by side. There was—there still is—a large swathe of the Dividing Range which hasn't been surveyed properly from either side. A few of the highest peaks have been sighted from East and West, which gives us some kind of fixed point—but the same mountain may look very different from these two aspects, so the identification requires corroboration.

"The other immediate problem we faced was that of scale. Not simply that the maps were drawn to different scales, although they are, but that the scales were recorded in different units. Feet and miles in the Five Principalities, metres and kilometres in the Sung Lands. Fortunately this wasn't insuperable as the common folk of the Sung Lands mostly use feet and yards and many other of the same units that we know here.

"But there's a potential trap here, isn't there? How could we know, just because they were called by the same names, that a foot in Carwerid is precisely the same length as a foot in Denvirran? Or, for that matter, that a Denvirran foot is precisely the same as a Sessapontine foot? How, indeed, do we know the length of anything? What do we mean when we say I am five feet nine inches tall? What do we mean by a foot in the first place?

"There are deeper philosophical questions here, but however fascinating they may be, I don't think this is the moment to go too deep into them. My point now is that, in science, we need to be sure that when we use a word, whether it's a unit of length, or temperature, or barometric pressure—or any other term—that we always mean the same thing by it. And this applies with renewed force in the kind of dialogue we're engaged in here. Merely because we use the same word for something, can we be sure we do in fact have the same quantity or phenomenon in mind?

"And then, of course, there are all the instances where we *don't* use the same words. It wasn't long after my arrival in this land that I learned that people used different names for the moons and the planets. By contrast, it was only yesterday that I realised how many common diseases are also called by different names on different sides of the mountains.

"It was that revelation, really, which set me thinking along the lines I've just sketched for you. And it occurred to me that, if we're looking for real and lasting achievements from this congress, one approach we should at least consider is to at least make a decent beginning on the kind of concordance I've referred to. On glossaries or dictionaries to help readers from one side understand books and papers from the other. Perhaps it's not the most glamorous outcome to wish for, not the most likely to make headlines in the newspapers, but I believe it's something that many, many scientists in years to come will be grateful for."

CHAPTER 27

SKELBER

"What's his name?" asked Railu.

"Ranguest," said Skelber.

"Symptoms?"

"Severe abdominal pain, rapid onset. Localised to the the right lower quadrant, very sensitive to palpation."

"He seemed fine until lunchtime," said one of the bystanders.

When was that? An hour ago? "Roll him onto his left side—gently." Again she palpated. "Does that hurt more?"

"By thunder, yes," groaned Ranguest.

"Can you straighten your right leg? Does that make the pain worse?"

This time he didn't manage to utter a word, but his face and the tension in his neck told the story.

"All right, try and relax, whatever position feels most comfortable." She rocked back onto her heels, looked up at Skelber. "Raised temperature?"

"A degree and a half outside normal range."

"Loss of appetite, nausea, vomiting?"

"He didn't eat anything at luncheon," said another delegate. "Took one sip of his wine, made a face, rushed off."

To throw up, no doubt, she thought. Railu got to her feet. "Your diagnosis, Doctor Skelber?"

"Acute appendicitis."

"I concur." She looked around at the delegates jostling for a better view. "You can relax; appendicitis is not contagious."

"Could it be the food?" asked one.

"We've heard he had nothing at luncheon," said Skelber. "If he'd been been affected by something he had at breakfast we'd expect to have seen symptoms earlier—and probably in several of us. No, appendicitis is one of those conditions which can arise without any apparent cause."

"That was debatable, she thought, but only said, "You think this requires an appendectomy?"

"I do. And the sooner the better."

"Indeed. If it ruptures, the outlook is much less hopeful."

"You'll do it, Skelber?" asked Ranguest.

"I think it would be better if Miss Railu took the lead."

"A woman?" demanded the ailing man querulously. He took a ragged breath, then forced out more words. "You'd let... a *woman*... cut me open?"

Skelber dropped back to a crouch beside him, then glanced up. Railu, grasping the implicit invitation, joined him. "Miss Railu, how many appendectomies have you performed?"

"I couldn't say exactly without reviewing my logs, but over two dozen."

"And how many patients have you lost?"

"One," she said. "I arrived too late and the appendix had ruptured. There was peritonitis, and rapidly developing sepsis." *And if I'd had all the resources of the Guild Infirmary, he might still have been saved..." One? he thought. Only one, out of twenty-five or more?* That was a remarkable record, if she spoke the truth... and he could not doubt that she did.

Skelber looked back to Ranguest. "I've done barely half that number, and I've lost more patients. And I haven't had a scalpel in my hand for six years. I strongly suggest that Miss Railu here is your best chance."

"Is there not... a surgeon... in the town?"

"There is, but sending someone to fetch him will take a couple of hours. Assuming he is at home and available. That delay markedly increases the risk to you."

"Damn you... Skelber... you'd better be... right about this."

CHAPTER 28

MAVRYS

I t had always been Mav's way: when she wanted, or needed, to think, she went for a long ride. Other times, just riding, with no particular mental agenda, thoughts and ideas would come to her anyway.

Last night she had said to Renfrith, "D'yow reckon Oronsa could do wi' a longer ride now an' then?" She'd learned that phrasing it as a question made it more likely he'd agree. Sounding less like gentry and more like an enslaved seemed to oil the wheels too. He must have heard her, tending to the injured Mardom, say she wasn't a slave, but seemed to have forgotten it, or dismissed it as fantasy.

He'd stroked his chin as he thought. It being near the end of the week, the stubble rasped audibly. "Y'know, th'Countess allus likes to give her a longer run once a week, like."

"But she's so busy jus' now..."

He nodded. "If yow c'n get all yowr other duties done too, yow c'n tek her for t'mornin' tomorrer."

"I'll come back f'r an hour after supper tonight. Get ahead wi'th cleanin th' tack."

"Reet, then. 'Appen if yow taks her up to th'road an' along to th'East, yow c'n pick up th' back track through th'pinewoods. Tha's a fair mornin's work." By now it was sounding almost as if the thing had been his idea all along. It grated, but if she got a good ride, it was worth it.

Now, as she rode, Renfrith himself seemed a good starting point for her thoughts.

He was a fair horseman, she thought. Words like *reliable* and *competent* came to mind. But he wasn't inspired and she very much doubted he loved the horses the way she did. He certainly didn't know half as much about their bloodlines.

Take Oronsa, for example, beneath her now with her glossy rose-grey hide and lovely flowing gait. Renfrith knew nothing of her breeding. In fairness, he'd mentioned that the Countess 'brung her from Kirwaugh', so the horse had not been in the Skilthorn yard more than three months.

But if a horse like that came into my *yard*, she thought, *I'd want to know her breeding. I wouldn't wait six weeks. I wouldn't wait six* days.

Then Mavrys thought about those two little words: *my yard*.

She thought about them as she rode down, past the lake, across the ornamental bridge, and up again to the public road. She continued thinking about them as she turned Oronsa to the right. The road tracked roughly North at first, threading between the grounds of the great house on her right and fields and woods on her left—all, she thought, still part of the wider Skilthorn estate.

My yard. Of course, under the laws of the Five Principalities, no stable-yard could ever be literally hers. Women could not own real property. It was usually up to their fathers or husbands to decide whether even such things as dresses and jewellery were considered as the woman's own, or merely enjoyed by the grace of the true owner.

If I'd been a boy... But that was profitless. She'd 'become' a slave by shaving her head, shedding her fancy clothes, and changing the way she spoke, but she couldn't become male so easily.

And even if she had been male, she'd only been fifteen when her father died. There was still no chance her mother and her uncle would have let her take control of the yard. Or him, that theoretical boy-Mav. Mavrem, perhaps, or Mavviam?

But, she thought, guiding Oronsa onto the broad grass verge to pass a couple of slow-moving lumber-wagons, *if I had been a boy, they'd have had to hold the property in trust for me till my majority. The house, the stables, everything. I could have held them to account for squandering it. And they'd never have tried to marry me off like they did.*

No two ways about it, being born female in the Five Principalities was a misfortune. She wondered if high-born females, valued solely for decoration and procreation, weren't worse off than their humbler counterparts. Right now, riding down the long road alone, the slave Mavrys felt freer than the gentlewoman Irmavel.

She did have two examples of women whose lives had meaning and purpose. But was it significant that neither Jerya nor Railu had been born in the Five Principalities? Things were clearly different in the Sung Lands, but were they different for all women, or only Dawnsingers? Or did the Dawnsingers have any use for a woman who knew horses better than... *better than anyone I know,* she thought.

There ought to be a way. I know what I can do. I know what I'm good at.

Mavrys thought suddenly of Shevra: '*Countess'd ask what yow likes doin'. Me, I'm askin' what yow're best at.*' She almost laughed out loud. *They're the same thing.*

There has to be a way...

But she knew that wishing doesn't always make things true.

She knew she hadn't found an answer, but maybe she had eliminated some of the possibilities. She was never going to be a Dawnsinger, for one. *Though I'd love to see the Sung Lands...*

She was thinking about the Sung Lands, the descriptions she had read and the pictures they had painted in her mind, as she came to the next junction. Oronsa seemed inclined to take the wider road to the left, and Mav reflected that it was the way to Kirwaugh. Oronsa, and Jerya, must have ridden that road many times. The horse might still think of it as the road home. Having made her feelings known, however, Oronsa seemed amenable enough to being steered onto the narrower right-hand road, flanked by pine plantations on both sides.

Mavrys was trying to recapture her previous train of thought, those images of the Sung Lands; perhaps she was being a little inattentive. Perhaps that was why the men seemed almost to appear out of nowhere, though presumably they had really just slipped out from the shade of the trees. Half a dozen of them, and somewhat rough-looking. It was a relief to see that they wore the blue badges of Rangers pinned to leather waistcoats or felted jerkins.

"Well, well," said one, perhaps the leader. His face was red-brown but the skin that showed in the V of his shirt was pale. Straggly beard, deep-set dark eyes, shoulder-length hair trained behind his ears with a leather band. "What have we here? What's a slavey doin' on such a fine horse?"

A quiver of unease clutched at Mav's bowels, but she kept her voice steady. "I'm exercising her for my mistress." The man raised an eyebrow and she realised she'd forgotten all about sounding like a slave.

"An' who might she be, yowr mistress?"

"Th' Countess o' Skilthorn."

"Tha' so? Aye, looks a fit mount f'r a Countess." He barely sounded the 't', so it almost came out as Coun'ess. "Well, missy, if'n yowr on yowr mistress's business, yow'll have a docket, wun't yow?"

"A docket?" she repeated blankly.

"A. Piece. Of. Paper," he said, as if addressing someone very stupid. "Wi' writin' on. I know yow can't read, but yow knows what writin' is, dun't yow? A piece of paper wi' writin' on tha' says yow has permission to leave yowr master's proper'y."

"No one gave me one..." she said, trailing off as she thought, *why didn't Renfrith think of that? He sent me on this route.* But then another thought crowded that one from her head. "It's all Skilthorn property. Both sides o' th' road."

"But not th' road itself," said the man with a triumphant air. "Public road, in't it? Th' Principal's Highway, tha's th' proper name."

"Why're yow wastin' time arguin' law wi' a slavey trollop?" asked another man. "We all know how this goes."

"Listen," she said urgently, all thoughts of 'sounding like a slave' fleeing her head again. "If the Countess doesn't get her horse back, she'll be—"

"Oh, she'll get her *horse* back," said the ringleader with a nasty grin. "Aye, we'll be quite the heroes, wun't we, lads? It wun't easy, were it? Found 'im runnin' loose, all in a lather, din't we?"

Are you blind? she thought furiously, *She's a mare not a stallion.* She had just enough self-command left not to say it. Instead she stammered out, "The Countess'll miss me too."

"Oh, yow're her favourite, are yow? Little pet, is it?"

"Better mak sure we looks high and low, then," said another, to general amusement.

"So sorry, yowr ladyship," added another.

Cold sweat ran oil-slow down the hollow of Mav's back. She might only have seconds; a minute at the outside, before the men tired of mere verbal taunting and moved on to. She knew, too, that if she got down from the saddle she was lost.

There was only one chance... and that depended entirely on Oronsa.

A moment's distraction... She forced a curdled smile. *Speak like a slave.* "In't there some way we c'n mak this easy... for *yow* an'—"

And in the space of one syllable she dug in her heels, remembering the kind of kick Dalster had needed. Either Oronsa took that message, or she responded to Mav's fear. *She can probably smell it on me.* The horse surged forward, from standstill to full gallop in half a dozen strides. Mav had a glimpse of the man holding the rein; time slowed so she could track the thoughts across his face, the realisation that if he held on he would either be dragged along or, quite possibly, have his arm ripped from its socket.

"Ride," she crooned, laying her head low to Oronsa's neck. "Ride like the wind!"

Afterward she realised that the Rangers—if they were indeed genuine Rangers—had made one tactical error, leaving their horses under the trees.

If even one or two of them had remained mounted, her chances would have been slender indeed. Yes, Oronsa was probably the fastest horse; she certainly felt now as if she had never gone faster. Risking a glance back, she saw the men running to free their mounts, saw the first swinging up into the saddle. Her lead was still less than a hundred yards, and if any of the men had bows, she might still be in dire trouble.

Either none had a bow, or none had the ability to shoot from the back of a galloping horse. *Or maybe*, she thought wildly, *they're trying and the shots just aren't coming near.*

She told herself not to look back again, to concentrate on keeping her seat, urging Oronsa to maintain her furious pace. She had no real idea how long the horse could keep it up. Oronsa was built for speed, for sure, and probably lighter than any of the pursuing mounts. On general principles, a horse like this could maintain a good gallop for a couple of miles, maybe a little further. But right now Oronsa was probably pushing beyond a regular gallop, into something more like the final sprint of a 'chase.

A chase is exactly what it is, she thought with grim amusement. *A chase for my life.* She could not kid herself that only her virtue was at stake. *And when did I become someone who can say 'only my virtue'?* An image of the Prince, perpetually half-smiling, flickered in her mind.

Then the lodge loomed up, so suddenly that they were almost past before Mav could check Oronsa's breakneck course, turn her onto the new heading. The gates stood ajar and she saw no one, but as they slipped through she yelled, "Close the gates! Quick!" Perhaps, hearing a voice that sounded like gentry, the keeper would comply. Perhaps. If he was there. If he heard. If he wasn't chopping wood in the back yard or...

Risking a quick glance as they turned, she'd seen two of the pursuers had pulled ahead of the others. Lighter riders or faster horses, perhaps both. She might have gained fifty yards on them; it might be only twenty: and now she could sense Oronsa's reluctance to pick up full speed again. "Please," she said. "Please. One more effort, you wonderful girl."

And with all the heart she possessed, Oronsa broke into a gallop again. Mav couldn't bring herself to demand any more, not unless she saw her pursuers closing in. But the track wound gently between low wooded hills and rarely could she see more than fifty yards back. The surface was sandy, so there would be no sound of hoofs to inform her. She could only hope their mounts were as near to exhaustion as her own. *And how near to the house will they dare to follow?* Surely they wouldn't chase her all the way to the stable yard. They could hardly be that stupid.

Oronsa powered on. She was still fast, but Mav no longer had that feeling that she had never gone faster on a horse. *And if you've never gone faster on a horse, you've never gone faster on anything.* She had a fleeting urge to laugh, but quelled it. Another glance back; was that movement, beyond the trees that pressed up to the last bend?

Then, suddenly, she was in the open, grass under the hooves, as the parkland that surrounded the house on three sides opened before her. Deer, grazing close to the track, scattered hastily. She looked back once more. Two riders at the edge of the trees, then a third, but they had reined in. A moment more and they turned, melted back into the shadows.

At last she dared pull back on the reins, allow Oronsa to ease down from gallop to canter to trot. Only now did she really sense the deep heaving of the horse's flanks between her legs. "I'm so sorry, girl," she said. She laughed, heard the edge of hysteria. "He said *exercise* you, not run you into the ground. But you were wonderful."

As they trotted on, she let her head rest against the swaying neck. It was a precarious position, and stretched her back awkwardly, but she had to let Oronsa know the depths of her gratitude. "Five more minutes," she murmured. "Five more minutes and you're going to get the best rub down you ever had. I promise."

❇

Pesk, I'm going to break my promise.

One look at Renfrith's face was all it took. The way his jaw dropped when he saw her. It wasn't the fact that the horse was lathered in sweat, that she was still panting; it was the fact that Mavrys was still on her back. *And he... he told me exactly the route to follow.*

Two seconds later she was kicking Oronsa into motion again—no more than a trot, now—and heading towards the main house.

She looped the reins around the stem of a tulip-shaped planter and ran up the steps.

"Stop!" barked an outraged major-domo. "You can't just come in the front door like you own the place."

Mav ignored the rebuke. "Where's the Countess?"

"The Countess is meeting with... why should I even tell you?"

"All right, where's the Earl?"

"Who the blazes do you think you are, girl?"

"What's going on?" said a familiar voice: Railu, approaching at a brisk walk.

Mav thought she had never been happier to see anyone in her life. "I need to speak... to Jerya or Hedric," she said, realising for the first time that she was almost as breathless as the horse had been.

Railu ignored a shocked gasp from the major-domo. "I really don't think we should disturb Jerya, but I think I know where Hedric is. Come on."

Mav followed Railu down a passage to the right, eventually turning to the left. They were somewhere in the East Wing, but Mav's slave duties had never brought her this way. Her knowledge of the geography of the great house had run out well before Railu knocked on a plain door in a relatively plain corridor.

A voice called them into a largish room, light slanting in dusty rays through windows that looked into the central courtyard. There were stacks of boxes, ranks of larger crates, piles of papers and books on a long bench beneath the windows.

The Earl turned toward them, shirtsleeved, hair awry, cradling something in his hands. Some sort of scientific instrument, by the look of it. "I promised Jerya I'd have all this squared away by tonight," he said with rueful good cheer. "Doesn't look likely, does it? Not unless you've come to help..." He stopped, taking a better look at Mav, then laid the instrument down on top of some papers, took two steps toward her. "What's the matter?"

Haltingly, pausing often to catch her breath, she spun the tale. Hedric's face grew serious, then alarmed. Once he put a hand out toward her, then shook his head and drew it back. She was vaguely aware of Railu moving closer, a hand grasping her arm.

When the tale finally reached Renfrith, Hedric's demeanour changed again. He spun, took half a dozen strides away from them, came back. "How sure are you?" he asked. Mav could not tell whether he believed her or not.

She took a deep breath. "As sure as I can be, my lord. He really wasn't expecting to see me, or not so soon."

"It couldn't just be that you were back sooner than...? I mean, if you'd done half the ride at a mad gallop, you would be."

"It's more than that, my lord. I'm sure of it."

"Very well," he said, squaring his shoulders. "I shall speak to him."

"May I come with you, my lord?"

"I'm not sure if that's the best idea right now..."

"There's Oronsa. She really needs to be back in her stable. After what she's done for me, I have to see her right."

He gave her a quick smile. "I admire your priorities, Mavrys. Very well, where is she now?"

"Outside the main entrance."

"We'll go that way, then. I dare say the walk will help you both cool off."

❋

"Th'girl's got some wild notion in her head," protested Renfrith. "That's all it is, my lord, some crazy idea she knows more about horses than what I do." He snorted. "It's not enough that I give her a chance, 'gainst my better judgement. Not enough that I backed her when th'lads were grousin'. Is she grateful?"

He looked at the Earl's face, seemed less than encouraged by what he saw. "Surely, my lord, yow ain't goin' to take the word of a slave agin mine?"

I would, thought Mav, *and I fancy Earl Hedric might do also.* She said, however, "I'm not a slave, I'm a gentleman's daughter. In fact my father was Birtler of Carinnan. You might even know that name." She couldn't resist twisting the knife. "So maybe, possibly, I *do* know more about horses than you do."

He had a chance, still; apologise for the latest remarks, perhaps throw in a bewildered enquiry about why a gentleman's daughter should be masquerading as a slave, then renew his protestations of innocence. The route he had suggested was a perfectly plausible one, and his reaction when she arrived back could indeed have been nothing more than surprise at her early return, compounded by concern at the state of the horse. In fact, she thought, a true horseman would have focused on that right from the start. But if he stuck to his guns, she knew she had no proof.

Before he could say any of it, the doorway darkened. Everyone looked round to see Mardom's broad frame almost filling the entrance. "May I say a word, my lord?"

"If you have something to add, please do."

"It's true what th'lass says, my lord. Mavrys. Master Renfrith were proper shocked when he saw her. I mean... yow know how folk says, it were like he'd seen a ghost. Beggin' your pardon, my lord. An'... th'other evenin' I saw him talkin' to a fellow wi' a Ranger's badge, out round th'back. Like they dun't want anyone else to see 'em."

"You didn't hear any of what they said?"

"Sorry, my lord, I din't."

"What did he look like, this fellow?"

Mardom wrinkled his nose in thought. "Ord'nary, like. Not big, not small. Long hair, but tied back. And... bit of a beard, but not a proper one."

That was close enough to the description she'd given of the ringleader, and she could see the Earl knew it; no need to remind him.

Even in the secondhand light of the tack-room, it was easy to see how the colour drained from Renfrith's face, brown fading to a green-tinged grey. *The colour of guilt,* she thought.

It seemed the Earl did too. "Renfrith," he said, voice very far from his usual cheery tones. "There's a coach passing the main lodge at four of the afternoon. I'll have a wagon ready to take you and your belongings up there at a quarter after three."

"My Lord..." The protest was feeble. Renfrith had no hope left.

"Tell me one thing. Those men. Were they genuine Rangers?"

"Far as I know, my lord."

"Then I shall have to speak to the local commander. Shebb! We pay a levy to support the Rangers. I wonder how he'll take it if we tell him we're withholding payment in future?"

He stood straighter. "Renfrith, get out of my sight. You—Mardom, isn't it? Thank you for that."

"You have my thanks too," said Mav quickly. Was that a blush stealing over Mardom's already ruddy countenance? She had to suppress a smile.

"Mardom," added the Earl. "One more thing, please. Keep an eye on Renfrith. Just in case he takes it into his head to walk off with anything that isn't his..."

"Aye, my lord."

When both had left, the Earl settled back, resting his rear against the saddler's bench. He gave a heavy sigh. "I can't say I knew the man. He'd tended to our horses, of course, even when we were just visiting. Always seemed decent enough at his job... Pesk! I wonder if we've any more undesirables lurking on the staff?" He sighed again. "And I have another problem. With all the visitors on top of the residents, we must have fifty horses here... and I've just dismissed our stable-master."

"My lord," said Mavrys at once.

"Yes, what is it?"

Say it quick, before your nerve goes. Like the first time over a big jump. "My lord, when I said I know more about horses than he did... it wasn't an idle boast."

For long suspenseful moments he just looked at her. The light from the door made mirrors of his lenses, making his face inscrutable. But then, slowly but unmistakably, a smile began to spread. "Not a stable-master but a stable-mistress? 'Twould be a bold choice, to be sure... you really think... it's one thing to look after one horse, another to run a stable of fifty."

"We had fifty in the yards at Carinnan, a couple of years back..." She blinked a few times. *I can't cry now.* "I know how it goes."

He turned away, paced the length of the combined tack-room and saddlery. When he came back, his face was earnest. "Mavrys, I do not for one moment doubt your skill and knowledge around horses. When you said, *I know how it goes*, I believe you. However... you are very young, and..." He stopped, looking embarrassed.

"And I am female," she said, an acrid taste in her mouth.

"Do not mistake me. I do not discount your abilities on account of your sex. Look at the woman I married. But look around you too. Look at the other hands here. Do you think they will take orders from you?"

She did not want to admit it, but she knew he had a point; they hardly even knew her. Mavrys sighed. "I fear you are right, my lord."

"Then I suppose we shall have to see what Haldrow makes of the position."

CHAPTER 29

MAVRYS

"Commander," said Hedric. "Thank you for coming so promptly." He pitched his voice to be easily audible from the reading-nook where Mav sat concealed.

"Happy to help, m'lord."

"Well, I certainly hope you can."

"Yowr message din't say much o' what this is about."

"I'm sure you know how written messages can fall into the wrong hands. I wanted you to be the first to know. Apart from the guilty men, of course."

"Guilty, m'lord? Guilty o' what?"

"The road that passes North of our grounds runs through a longish stretch of forest. You'll know where I mean. Yesterday, in the middle of the afternoon, a member of my household was accosted there by six men wearing the badges of your brigade. There were clear threats of... molestation. And, as I understand it, an unmistakable implication that she would be... disposed of when they had... finished with her. Do you need me to spell it out more clearly?" Mav suspected he was trying to spare her feelings, but fudging the description didn't change what had happened, or what might have followed.

"Tha's shockin', m'lord, but... I find it hard to b'lieve any o' my men would do such a thing."

"As I said, they wore badges."

"Wi' respect, m'lord, 'twouldn't be th'first time some'un's faked a badge."

"I don't doubt it, but the question's easily resolved. The men didn't wear masks—which supports the idea that they didn't intend the young woman to be alive to bear witness. She is confident she can identify at least two of them. Bring your men here—or we'll come to you—and we'll see if she recognises anyone."

There was a heavy silence. The Commander had to be working out how to respond. Mav wished she could see his face.

"I dun't like pullin' all my men in at once, m'lord. Leaves th'roads unprotected."

Hedric's reply was cool. "If there's even a small possibility that some of your men were responsible for this outrage, it raises serious doubt about what kind of *protection* they're really providing. I would have thought you'd be anxious to set the record straight as soon as possible."

"Yes, m'lord. But... wi' respect, are yow sure this young woman din't get hold o' th'wrong end o' th' stick? Yow did say 'threat' and 'imp... implication'. Dun't sound like any actual harm were done."

"She could hardly have been clearer about what happened. And there was no question in her mind about their intentions... was there, Mavrys?"

"None whatever, my lord," she said, stepping out of the nook.

The Commander was a man of about fifty, still fit-looking, age showing in the lines of his face and the grey of his stubbly beard. Sweat showed on his brow. *Well,* she thought, *it's a warmish day, and he may have ridden hard to get here.*

"Mavrys," said Hedric gently. "I know it may be hard for you, recalling the incident, but would you please tell us what made you so certain that those men meant to do you harm?"

"Some of it was the way they spoke, the way they looked at me. But there were particular moments. I said something about how the Countess would feel if she didn't get her horse back. And one of them—the one I thought of as the ringleader—said *Oh, she'll get her* horse *back.* Like that: the horse would come back and I wouldn't. He said they'd spin some tale about finding her running loose—and how they'd looked for a rider but found no one. It was absolutely clear what they meant to do."

"Wi' respect, m'lord, yow din't tell me she were a slave."

Hedric's voice had sounded cool before. Now, it was cold and sharp as an icicle. "I sincerely hope, Commander, that you aren't suggesting that this kind of thing isn't to be taken seriously just because the victim might be an enslaved person?"

"No, m'lord, o'course not. But..."

"Think very carefully about what you say next."

Well, frankly, m'lord, a slave testifying agin free men, th' justices'd give less weight to it. And even if they did find guilty, 'appen they'd give a lighter sentence, too."

"I may have to have a word with the local justices," said Hedric. "Remind them who holds a veto on their appointment... But I'm speaking to *you*, Commander... You'll be aware, of course, that we have a number of distinguished visitors here at present?"

"Aye, m'lord. Tha's why we've had extra patrols on th'roads hereabouts."

"And you'll be aware that several of our important guests are Dawnsingers, from the Sung Lands?"

"Aye, m'lord...?"

"Are you also aware that Dawnsingers are always female... and that they are always bald?"

It looked as if the Commander had stopped breathing. He stared at Mav, colour literally draining from his face, tan fading to a sickly pallor.

"Yes," said Hedric. "I can see that puts a different light on the matter... for you. For myself, I happen to believe that any such aggression toward any guest, or any member of this household, is unconscionable. I'll not waste my time debating whether some outrages are more unconscionable than others. Now, Mavrys, are you in fact a Dawnsinger?"

"No, my lord."

Just for a moment, the Commander's face betrayed relief, but it was short-lived as Hedric continued. "Are you, then, a slave?"

"Again, no, my lord."

"Would you kindly tell our visitor who your father was?"

"Birtler of Carinnan, my lord."

"The noted breeder of horses?"

"The very same."

He turned back to the Commander, by now looking completely lost and confused. "How soon can you assemble all of your men? Would the tenth hour tomorrow be too soon?"

"I'm sorry, m'lord, but 'appen it would. Some squads are out in th'field. They might be passin' th'night at an inn, or sometimes one on'em's got kin wi' a farm or—"

"I don't think we need all the details, thank you. How soon *can* you assemble them?"

"T'd' be late afternoon, m'lord. I'll answer for four o'th clock."

"Then that will have to suffice. Thank you again for coming and good day to you."

When the door had closed behind the Commander, who had barely managed not to run from the room, Hedric sank into a chair before the fireplace, gesturing Mav to join him. He shook his head with a rueful smile. "I'm very much afraid I enjoyed that altogether too well."

"Too well, my lord?"

"Yes. It may have been the right thing to do, to bully that man, but I don't want to start enjoying it. I do not want to turn into my uncle."

"I don't see much danger of that, my lord." She thought a moment, decided to dare. "If nothing else, your wife would have something to say about it."

He gave a hearty laugh. "By thunder, she would, wouldn't she?

"You know, if you had in fact been enslaved, no doubt the Commander was correct that the Justices would view the matter less seriously. And, what you may well think is worse, they would view it primarily as an offence against *me*—an abuse of my property—than against the slave herself."

Mavrys found herself thinking of Vireddi, that gentle soul who had taught her so much. "That's monstrous."

"I'll not dispute it... but that's the world we inhabit. We may wish to change it but we know it will be a struggle, and a slow one. Till then... well, the one good reason I can give myself for continuing to own slaves, instead of giving them up altogether, is that as their master I have some power to protect them from the abuses and indignities this world offers." He sighed. "Sometimes that's enough, sometimes it isn't."

Mavrys was suddenly very glad of the veil Jerya had provided. Initially, while appreciating the anonymity, she had felt a subtle but distinct claustrophobia. Now, it felt not claustrophobic but *safe*. She could clearly see the face of the ringleader, without feeling that his shadow-set eyes were boring into her.

"It's him," she said, keeping her voice firm. "He was the leader."

"Are yow quite sure, m'lady?" The Commander had been calling her that since the moment of arrival. As she was gentry, not nobility, the correct address would have been 'Miss' or 'madam', but she hadn't felt like correcting him.

"He's shaved his beard since then," she said. There were audible intakes of breath from several of the men around him. *Yes*, she thought, *how would I have known that if I hadn't seen him?* "But I'll not forget him in a hurry." *Maybe I never will.* She'd had the smiling-man dream again last night.

She moved on. Three places further on down the line, she found the other. "And this is the one who held the horse's head." The Commander didn't even try to question the identification this time.

She knew it was probably futile, but she finished her walk along the line of men before she admitted it out loud. "I can't be sure about any of the others. But those two, I'm absolutely certain."

"Thank yow, m'lady." The Commander sighed, then squared his shoulders. "What am I to do wi'em, m'lord?"

"It's hardly for me to say; I am not the injured party here. But I suggest, Commander, that you put those men in your cells for now, while the lady and I discuss what should happen next."

"Very good, m'lord. An' I'll be takin' their badges."

He turned away, began barking orders, as Hedric gently grasped Mav's arm and guided her along the street. "The tavern there's rather on the rough side, but there's a better one just round the corner. I thought maybe you could use a drink."

The fire was not lit, but the inglenook still felt like a cosy spot, insulated from the bustle of the main taproom. There was just room on the bench for the two of them to sit without feeling overly intimate. She pushed the veil back from her face but left the head-dress in place. A close observer might still notice that she was bald underneath, but it would have to do.

A girl—a buxom brown enslaved—bobbed a curtsey before them. "What may I bring yow, m'lord an' lady?" *Not a close observer...*

Hedric looked at Mav. "I'm not much of a drinker," she said. "Just small-beer, really."

He nodded to the girl. "A half of the brown for the lady, if you please, and a fuller for me."

"At once, m'lord." She curtseyed again, scurried off.

Mav heaved a deep breath. "So what will happen to them?"

"Well, we have a choice. Really, I should say, *you* have a choice. Do you wish to press charges or not? There are no other witnesses, unless one of the men chooses to turn Principal's Evidence, which I deem unlikely, so it really rests on you."

"I wish it didn't."

"I cannot blame you. But a choice must be made."

"So if I don't...?"

"If you don't press charges, then I think the Commander will dismiss them from the service and banish them from Skilton Riding."

"That seems... mild."

"Perhaps. In light of what they intended, you might well think so, but just consider what that means. Men with no job, in a place they probably do not know, where no one knows them; and having been dismissed, they have no character. You understand what that means?"

"Yes. I saw my father interview for new stable-hands. I saw how he always asked for their character... I suppose anyone would do the same."

"Surely. A man without a character will find it hard to gain honest work. And then the main choices before him are *dis*honest work, or voluntary enslavement."

Mav thought about that as the girl delivered their drinks. She sipped at the stoup, finding the beer stronger than she was used to, but with pleasantly fruity overtones. "If I do elect to press charges, what then?"

"Then all I can say for certain is that it will go before the Justices. I cannot say exactly what they will decide, but their favoured recourse is punitive enslavement."

"They would make them into slaves?"

"Yes, but punitive enslavement is different from the usual kind. Absent a life sentence, such men—and women—are put to work for a fixed period. For that time they are, in theory, treated just the same as any other slaves, but at the end, subject to good behaviour, they are restored to freedom."

She sipped again, thinking hard. "But at that point, are they not in the same position as they would be if they'd been banished? With no work and no character?"

"There is one difference: absent permanent banishment, they can return to their homes, to their families. If there is a family farm, some other family business, there may be work for them." He shrugged. "Sometimes an employer may believe that if a man has served his term, he deserves another chance."

"So... what I thought was the milder punishment might easily turn out worse for them than being tried before the Justices."

"Very possibly, but there's no certainty either way."

"Then how am I supposed to decide?"

He set down his larger stoup, brushed his hand across his top lip. "There is one more thing. Leave it to the Commander, and they will be gone tomorrow and you should never have to see them again. I can well imagine you would wish to put this episode behind you as soon as possible. However, if you elect to press charges, it may take a few weeks before they are tried, but then they will have to stand up and answer for their deeds. Everyone in town, in the wider parish of Skilthorn, perhaps further afield, will know exactly what they did and how they abused their position as Rangers.

"I suppose... I suppose they should be held accountable."

"Of course, for the same reason, our worthy Commander would prefer you to make the other choice. He would no doubt argue that airing this matter in public serves only to weaken trust in the Rangers."

"If this is how some of them behave, then they hardly deserve the public's trust."

"Quite so. And a trial, making the issue public, would likely also give the Commander, and probably his superiors across all the Ridings, a strong incentive to get their house in order."

He drank again, set his mug down on the broad arm of the bench, turned to her. "It's not an easy choice, Mavrys. I don't envy you... Perhaps, in the end, it is best if you think purely of your own interest. Will you feel better if you can tell your own story and see them held to account, or would you prefer to have them gone tomorrow and never have to think about it again?"

She lifted her own stoup, realised that she had almost drained it, finished it in a single swallow. "I don't think it will leave my mind so easily as that. I think... it might seem easier, right now, to have them gone immediately, but I think in the end it will be better to see them tried."

"And I think, Mavrys, that you are wise beyond your tender years." He raised his mug toward her. "Oh, but you're empty. Would you like another?"

"I think I might *need* another." He smiled and raised a hand. The girl saw and came quickly over, threading her way deftly between the tables. "But just another half, please, my lord. Then I must get back to the stable."

CHAPTER 30

SKELBER

"I'm intrigued," said the Earl. "Why come to me? You can hardly expect me to be entirely neutral."

"No, sir. I know Miss Railu is a close friend of the Countess. But I already know, well enough, what my colleagues would say: I am bound by my oath as a physician."

"They are oath-breakers, you know," Observing Skelber's startlement, he added, "I'm not telling you any secrets. You can find it in print, though maybe not in the popular versions. Jerya and Railu had sworn Dawnsingers' Vows, no less solemn than your Physician's Oath. Maybe even more so. And still they left.

"It's not my place to plead my wife's cause. She's more than capable of doing so herself, and she's worth hearing. But I'll say this much. She felt that her Vow demanded something that her conscience could not accept.

"You might wonder why I married her; she's already a vow-breaker, how could I trust her wedding vows?" He shrugged. "I do not need vows to trust her. I have, quite literally, trusted her with my life. But as to vows, I know that breaking her Guild Vow was agonising for her... and it has made her more, not less, determined to honour any future vow.

"In the end, I don't know if this helps you at all, but I believe she would say this. Breaking a vow, or an oath, is a terrible thing, but it's not always the worst thing."

"Thank you, sir."

He made as if to move away, but Hedric laid a restraining hand on his arm. "A moment, doctor. Remind me of the wording of the Physician's Oath."

"The relevant line is *to uphold at all times the highest standards and necessary disciplines of the profession of physician.*"

"That does not say anything about women practising medicine."

"No, that is true. The Oath itself does not say anything about who may or may not practise. However, in mentioning 'disciplines', it is understood to require adherence to the rules and regulations of the governing body in the relevant Principality."

"And do those rules and regulations stipulate that women may not practise medicine?" The Earl turned away as he spoke, running his eyes along a particular shelf.

"Not directly, but they do stipulate that only those who have undergone approved training and been licensed by the governing body may practise."

"And that training is not available to females..."

"No. The schools of medicine, which exist in four of the Five Principalities, only admit men."

The Earl had found the book he had evidently been seeking, and was now leafing through the rearmost pages, presumably searching the index. "I think I'm right in saying that your specific purpose here is to exchange information on medical and related matters with the Dawnsingers?"

"Yes, absolutely."

"I'm also led to believe that their learning and their practice is at least the equal of the Five Principalities, and may in some respects be superior?" He chuckled softly. "Of course my source here is my wife, who might not be a wholly unbiased observer..."

"I could not possibly cast aspersions on the Countess's impartiality, sir. And I would say that we are still at a stage where all judgements must be provisional." He suddenly recalled Railu's insistence on 'sterilisation' of hands and instruments and more. If she was right, how many patients might have suffered, and in some cases died, for want of a few simple actions? How many times had he, just as she said, seen a surgeon take far greater care washing his hands *after* an operation than before? He shuddered inwardly.

Perhaps he shuddered outwardly, too. The Earl was looking at him with concern. "Are you quite all right, Doctor?"

"Quite well, thank you, sir." He hastened to move on. "I think I can say that my early impressions are that their skill and knowledge is at least equal to our own. In areas relating specifically to... ah... female concerns, they are no doubt ahead of us."

"As a man who loves his wife, and whose wife is with child—"

"—I did not know that, sir. May I offer my congratulations?"

"It has not been generally announced, and I'll ask you to keep it to yourself. But thank you. Though it must be said, the woman's part in this is a great deal more onerous than the man's." Skelber smiled. "Are you married, Doctor?"

"Widowed."

"I'm sorry to hear that. Any children?"

"One daughter."

"And by year's end there's an even chance I too will have a daughter... anyway, you will surely agree that you and I both have a clear personal interest in the best possible care for women and girls."

"Yes, indeed so."

"And therefore I venture to suggest it is a matter of urgency for the doctors of Denvirran, of all the Principalities, to learn whatever they can from this too-brief opportunity?"

"Again, I am bound to agree."

"Would you also agree that many women would feel more comfortable, and would perhaps be more likely to consult a doctor, if female doctors were available?"

"Your logic is compelling, sir, but in practical terms there is no immediate prospect of that. It takes five years to train a doctor, and the young men who are admitted to the medical schools have already benefited from years of education."

"Yes, there are wider issues here, are there not?" The Earl regarded him keenly, his eyes slightly magnified by the lenses of his spectacles. Skelber acknowledged the point with a nod. "On the other hand, when there is one woman who has undertaken seven years of training at the College of the Dawnsingers... but perhaps you knew that?"

"I knew she was trained by them, yes."

"But because she's modest to a fault, you probably don't know that she was rated by the senior Healers as one of their brightest prospects. And you probably don't know that in her years on this side of the Dividing Range she has continued to study. I've had some modest hand in this myself, helping to obtain textbooks and journals for her."

"I have no doubt that she is most impressive. I've seen her work and I could not have done better myself; perhaps not even equalled her. But you see, sir, that's at the heart of my quandary. You make cogent arguments in her favour and indeed I have thought of many of these points already. However... leaving all questions of sex aside, Miss Railu is not qualified to practise under the rules of my professional association. If I fail to report her, and it becomes known—as it very well might—I risk losing my own licence to practice. People talk. If Doctor Le'ast hears a rumour, before he's heard anything from me..."

"I see your difficulty," said the Earl. "Worse for you—and no better for her—if someone else tells. But if *you* report it, what will she think of you?"

"Especially as I encouraged her to lead the appendectomy. I will seem... duplicitous."

"Conscience is a plaguey thing, is it not? But consider this." He lifted the book he had found, opened it at a page he had kept with a finger. "Being unacquainted with the Physician's Oath, I looked it up. And I found this: *I will treat all patients under my care according to their clinical need, without fear or favour according to their rank or position, and without consideration of my own pecuniary interest or personal advancement.* I cast no aspersions on you personally, Doctor, but across the membership of your association would you say that clause is universally observed?" He watched Skelber's face a moment. "I have to say, in my experience when my uncle was ailing, his doctor—who, in broad terms, I count a good man—was forever available to him at short notice. But ask him to turn out for a slave, or any humbler member of the household, and he was not always so alacritous."

※

"Thank you for bringing this matter to my attention, Doctor."

"It's nothing more than my duty, sir." *And never has duty tasted more bitter...*

"Still, you are a conscientious man, and that is to your credit." Le'ast beamed at him and Skelber felt emboldened to make his request.

"Might I make a suggestion, sir? To convene a hearing can take up much valuable time and effort; for you, for the secretariat, for the witnesses. Matters can drag on for weeks, sometimes months, to the good of no one. And natural justice surely demands a speedy resolution."

"I cannot argue with any of that," said Le'ast, pulling ruminatively at one of the long side-whiskers, white against his dark skin, which gave him the air of an engraving from an antique book. "But you said you had a suggestion?"

"You have men here of more than sufficient eminence to mount a tribunal—yourself, of course, pre-eminent. The putative defendant is here, and an abundance of witnesses. Surely it would be more convenient for all concerned to hold the hearing here, and as soon as possible."

Le'ast hmmm-ed, and tugged on both sets of whiskers. "Your suggestion certainly merits consideration. Allow me to consult with Doctor Fulmer and Secretary Ernoul... and I suppose we must speak to the Earl and Countess also, about possible disruption to the schedule of this congress."

"It seems to me, sir, that the schedule is already somewhat fluid. And I strongly suspect that both the Earl and the Countess will be keen to see this matter resolved quickly." *And will Railu?* He was not so clear on that.

Worse still, he felt directly responsible for urging her into the actions which, after a sleepless night, he had felt compelled to report. *I think it would be better if Miss Railu took the lead.*

He was beginning to feel that those words might haunt him for a long time to come.

CHAPTER 31

RAILU

"Your name, please," said Fulmer.

"Skelber of Brinscal."

"Your rank and occupation?"

"Gentleman, physician."

"Your current position?"

"I'm a member of the Ethics and Enforcement Board of the Denvirran Association of Physicians."

"Doctor Skelber, you are the reporting party in this case, are you not?"

"That is correct, sir."

"You yourself observed the defendant engaging in the practice of medicine without a licence?"

"I did, sir, on two occasions. As such, and on reflection, I felt that my oath as a physician left me with no alternative—"

"—Yes, that goes without saying." Skelber frowned. Railu wondered what he had intended to follow *no alternative*. "Would you please describe the first occasion?"

"I was walking near one of the paddocks adjacent to the stables here when I became aware that some sort of accident had occurred. I saw a figure on the ground and a couple of people bending over him. I immediately hastened over to offer assistance."

"And when you got there?"

"I found Miss—the defendant—already in attendance. It transpired she had already reduced a dislocated shoulder and was about to tackle a splinter of wood which had penetrated the lad's thigh."

"I presume you immediately removed the woman and took charge."

"No, sir."

"Why not?"

"As she... explained to me, the splinter was dangerously close to a major artery. Changing places when she already had her hand on it would almost certainly have exposed the lad to greater risk."

"So you knowingly allowed an unqualified person to continue treating an injury?" There was a glint in Fulmer's eyes, thought Railu. All at once she saw something: Fulmer and Skelber were not friends. For Fulmer, this was no unwelcome duty, but one he relished. She had thought, as was only natural, of what might be at stake for herself. Now she wondered whether Skelber, too, could be damaged by this affair.

He gathered himself now, squaring his shoulders. "As any conscientious physician would, I made the decision I deemed in the best interests of the patient in those circumstances."

"By allowing an unqualified and untrained *woman* to continue with a risky procedure?"

"Doctor Fulmer, we have spent the past ten days consulting with *women*. It is clear to me, and I am sure to you—"

"—Is this in any way an answer to my question?"

"If you will allow me to proceed, my point will become clear."

"Proceed, then, but deliver an answer, not a lecture."

Skelber looked as if he wanted to grind his teeth. "We have all listened and learned from women: Dawnsingers. Miss—the defendant is not part of the official Sung Lands delegation but she has been advising them on matters connected with medicine and physiology. You've been in the room with them, as have I; you've seen how they pay attention to her. Do you really imagine they would take advice from someone who is, in your words, 'unqualified and untrained'?'

"It is for me to ask questions, Doctor Skelber, and the issue of the defendant's qualification and training—if any—will be addressed when I question her. In the meantime... you mentioned that you had observed the defendant indulging in medical procedures on two occasions. Would you please tell us of the second occasion?"

Skelber gave a concise account of the story of Ranguest and his dangerously inflamed appendix.

"Let me be clear, Doctor Skelber," said Fulmer. "On this occasion there was no pressing reason—as you claim for the first, where the defendant already had her hand on the splinter—to yield to her. You consulted together and then you allowed her to take the lead. Is that correct?"

"Perfectly correct."

"So on this occasion you not only allowed an unlicensed person to continue a procedure they had already begun... on this occasion you positively encouraged her to conduct the operation from the outset?"

"I did, sir." There was nothing apologetic or defensive about the statement.

"My next question is obvious: *why?* What possessed you, man?"

"Exactly what *possessed* me on the first occasion: my judgement of the best interests of the patient."

Fulmer sighed theatrically, as if he had all the cares of the world on his shoulders. In a fittingly weary tone, he asked, "And on what did you base that judgement?"

"I established that Miss Railu had performed more appendectomies, and more recently, and that she *had lost fewer patients*. In fact, none. In every respect, her record was better than my own."

That left Fulmer blinking for a moment. *Proper took the wind from his sails*, thought Railu. He managed a few more questions, but had lost his earlier impetus.

✳

"Your name, please."

"Ranguest of Winderkeer."

"Your rank and position?"

"Gentleman. I'm an Under-Secretary in the Denvirran Ministry of Roads and Waterways."

"Squire Ranguest, would you please tell us what happened four days ago?"

"Lunchtime, I had no appetite, hardly touched anything and then had to throw up. Bit of pain down here but not too much at first. Mid-afternoon, I started feeling feverish and the pain was getting worse— rapidly. Doctor Skelber examined me and then the woman—the one who isn't either a slave or a Dawnsinger—"

"The defendant, in fact?"

"Yes, that's her. She examined me also."

"And how did you feel about that?"

Ranguest frowned. "It was, well, odd, you know? But I wasn't thinking too clearly by then."

"And then Doctor Skelber suggested the woman also perform the operation? How did *that* strike you?"

"I suppose I wasn't best pleased at the time. Never heard of such a thing. But I have to say, fair and square, seems she did a fine job. Look at me, I'm up and about already, and Doctor Le'ast looked at the scar this morning and said he'd never seen a neater."

Fulmer looked sour. Clearly this wasn't the picture he'd wanted to paint. There was little more for him to do but thank Ranguest and dismiss him from the stand.

✳

"Your name, please."

"Evisyn."

"Is that your only name?"

Evisyn shrugged. "I had another name once, before I was Chosen, but that was over thirty years ago."

"Your rank and position?"

"Master Prime of the Guild of Dawnsingers."

"And how long have you known the defendant?"

"Depends what you mean by 'know'. I wasn't Master Prime when she first came to the College; wasn't even Master of Peripatetics 'til a few years later. Still, she'd have had a few lessons with me sometimes, on my rotations through Carwerid. Not that she made a particular impression, not in my classes; it was medicine, physiology, where her interest really lay, where she showed talent... But if you mean 'knowing' her in any deeper sense, only since we first arrived in Duncal at the start of this visit."

"So only a few weeks?"

"Over a month, now."

"Then you can hardly be placed to comment on her claims to competence as a doctor or surgeon." *Why are we wasting time with this witness?* his tone said.

"Don't be so hasty, young man," said Evisyn, and Railu had to smother a smile. "I may not have known her well in her time in the College, but I knew *of* her. We talk, Tutors and Masters, we talk a good deal about which Postulants and Novices show the most potential. I heard how the Healers, her teachers, spoke about her. I saw how devastated they were when she... left."

The Master Prime took a breath, looked about her; weighing up whether to add something, thought Railu. She decided. "They were certain she would take first place in Final Catechisms for their discipline. There was...

controversy when her declared marks were below expectations. Much later—too late—it turned out there had been an error."

Railu felt as if a bolt of lightning had speared her. She stared at Evisyn, then turned her gaze with equal intensity on Jerya, who gave a small shrug as if to say, *First I've heard of it.*

In that moment Doctor Le'ast was stepping forward, favouring his right hip as always. He held a brief whispered colloquy with Fulmer, then the younger man retreated to the tribunal table. Le'ast rested his forearms on the lectern, age-mottled hands hanging loosely.

"Master Prime, we understand that you were not closely acquainted with the defendant during her time at your College. We understand too that you are not a specialist in medical sciences or allied subjects. However... it would be true to say that your present, ah, eminent position requires you to have a good understanding of *all* the subjects covered in your, ah, curriculum?"

Evisyn smiled, waved a hand. "I can't claim to understand everything that's taught. Pure maths is probably even more of a mystery to me than advanced physiology. But I do have to... how shall I put it?... I have to grasp the *scope* of what is taught. And in my time as a Peripatetic, and then as Master of same, I had many opportunities to observe the practical applications of our knowledge, to set alongside what I knew of the theoretical background."

Le'ast returned her smile. "I should apologise, Master Prime; we have covered all this in much greater detail in our discussions at this congress. But you understand, I trust, that we must establish the key points once again, in this tribunal, and for the record."

"Of course, Doctor."

"Then may I ask you to tell us, concisely, about the training of Healers, as you call them, in your College?"

"Certainly. The Postulants—girls in their first year after Choosing—receive a basic grounding in all subjects."

"Including medicine?"

"Anatomy and physiology at that stage, rather than practical medicine. We assess them constantly, making the first judgements on their aptitude and inclination. As girls progress into their Novitiate, they begin to specialise, but not too much, too soon. However, when a Novice feels particularly strongly drawn to a subject, she may voluntarily undertake extra study or practical work. Girls who are drawn to medicine, for example, may help out in one of our Infirmaries. I understand that Railu was one of these from early Novitiate."

"The total duration of Novitiate is seven years?"

"Yes—and Postulancy is one year before that, so the combined total is eight."

"And at what stage in her Novitiate would a student truly be said to be specialising in one subject area?"

"For the final three years."

"You are aware that the training of a doctor in our academy in Denvirran lasts five years?"

Evisyn allowed herself another slight smile. "Yes, but don't be misled. By that time, as I've said, these Novices have already received a good grounding, including a broader study of biological science. And then you must remember that our students spend the entirety of their time within the College, with one partial exception. There are annual trips to our observatory at Kendrigg, where every Novice is able to observe the stars and planets, but unless a girl is specialising in astronomy these will occupy at most two weeks. And even then, though girls do not receive formal lessons in other subjects, they are encouraged to spend time in reading and discussion." She smiled again. "Until I visited the Five Principalities, I had never really encountered the concept of a 'holiday'.

"Consider the question not as a matter of years but of hours. In terms of hours spent in medical study and practical work, I would not be at all surprised if someone like Railu had surpassed most graduates of your academy, possibly by a substantial margin." She was well-briefed, thought

Skelber. A most impressive woman; well, he'd seen that already, in the discussions.

He thought of Railu, too, and of Countess Jerya. They also were impressive, each in her own way. He wondered if every alumna of the Dawnsingers' College was equally formidable.

"Thank you, Master Prime," said Le'ast. "Is there anything you'd like to add?"

"I did say that I've had some opportunity to get to know Railu better on this visit. We spent many hours in conversation on the journey here from Duncal, for example. I could say a little more about my impression of her, if you like."

"By all means." Railu saw Fulmer frowning; this was not entirely going the way he had hoped. Le'ast outranked him, she knew, and Le'ast was, apparently, rather less hostile toward her—or toward Skelber. She could only wonder; they had had minimal contact during the past fortnight, exchanging only a few sentences, though he had been unfailingly polite. The trouble with that kind of politeness, she thought, was that it could mask almost anything.

"What I have seen," said Master Evisyn, "Is someone who is highly dedicated, extremely skilled—so far as it's in my power to judge—and deeply caring. I can fully understand why the Master Healers thought she was a great loss to the College and the Infirmaries. I've told her that I would be delighted to welcome her back to the Guild, should she ever choose to return."

"Thank you, Master Prime," said Le'ast.

Chapter 32

Skelber

"Your name, please."

"Jerya of Skilthorn."

"Your rank and position?"

"Countess." She looked every inch a Countess today, in a full-skirted dress of a deep peach colour, a chandelier overhead sparking ruby highlights in elaborately-coiled hair.

"Would you be so good as to tell us how long you've known the defendant?"

"A little over fifteen years. We've gone through many experiences together in that time." A look passed between Jerya and Railu, one that spoke of exactly that deep well of shared experience. He wondered if he and Railu would ever look at each other like that. *Right now I'd settle for her looking at me at all.*

"Thank you, Countess. Were you witness to either of the incidents cited earlier, which precipitated this hearing?"

Skelber could not avoid the thought that Railu must think that it was he who had precipitated this hearing—and, really, who could blame her?

The Countess answered with a simple negative.

"Have you, in your long acquaintance with the defendant, witnessed her practising medicine on other occasions?"

The Countess smiled as if satisfied; as if that were exactly the question she'd been waiting for. "It seems to me, Doctor, that I cannot answer that unless you define what you mean by 'practise medicine'. After all, I could say *I* have practised medicine on many occasions." There was a sharp stir in the room, but she went on steadily. "I could say we all have. Before my husband—husband-to-be, then—and I set out on the Crossing four years ago, knowing that we would be days away from any help, we took advice and instruction on how to deal with the ailments and injuries that seemed most likely to occur, from frostbite to, yes, a dislocated shoulder." She hadn't said from whom they had taken instruction, but Skelber thought he could make an educated guess.

"Fortunately, we suffered nothing so serious. But I had to be prepared to deal with such eventualities. I had to know how to reduce a dislocated shoulder. If I had done so, would I be facing a tribunal now also?"

"Those are exceptional circumstances, surely, my lady."

"Are they? Someone needs help and you're the only—or the best—person to deal with it? Is that really so exceptional?" She gave a small shrug. "Let's talk about circumstances that everyone will be familiar with. Who hasn't bandaged a child's scraped knee, or applied arnica to a bruise? I frequently did such things when I was a governess. Should I have sent to Drumlenn for the doctor on every such occasion, and done nothing for the hour and a half it would take him to reach us, even supposing he wasn't out on another call? Should I have sat with an injured child all that time and offered him nothing but words?"

"I am sure no one is suggesting any such thing, my lady."

"No? Are they not? Then what are they suggesting? What *is* the practice of medicine? Unless you set clear limits, how is anyone to know what they may or may not do?" Le'ast opened his mouth, but Jerya gave him no chance to speak. "I'll tell you what Railu has *not* done. We already established I've known her longer and better than anyone else, so I think I know what I'm speaking of. What she has not done... She has never called herself 'doctor', nor, to my knowledge, allowed anyone else to refer to her as such. She has never nailed a brass plate to her door, nor charged a brass penny for any of the care she has given. She hasn't made a good income, or established herself in a fine house. She's never run a fine carriage or promenaded about the town on a Highday afternoon."

She fixed Le'ast with her gaze and the word came again to Skelber's mind: *formidable.* "I may be at fault here, Doctor Le'ast, but in my fifteen years' experience of the Five Principalities, and specifically of the Principality of Drumlenn, those are all things that I have come to associate with the practice of medicine, and with those gentlemen who call themselves doctors."

Le'ast stood for several long seconds before gathering himself. "Thank you very much, Countess."

❋

"Your name, please." After more discussion with Le'ast, Fulmer was back.

"Railu Kermey." Her voice was steady, but how could she not be anxious, beneath?

"Your rank and position?"

"Free-woman. I am housekeeper at Duncal, in the township of Drumlenn."

"You hold no other position?"

"No, I do not."

"You do not practise medicine?" If he'd left it there, it might have been a tricky question to answer honestly, but in his eagerness he over-reached: "You do not masquerade as a doctor?"

"I do not *masquerade* as anything," said Railu. "I have never claimed the title of doctor or represented myself as being licensed by your Association."

"But we have all heard clear testimony that you have performed a number of medical procedures, including reducing a dislocated shoulder and removing an inflamed appendix."

"Why do you say 'but'?" she asked, appearing genuinely puzzled. Skelber wanted to stand up and cheer. "Are those facts supposed to contradict what I just said?"

What a woman she is, he thought.

Fulmer blinked a few times, but regathered himself soon enough. "You will not, I take it, attempt to deny the facts themselves?" Again he should have stopped there, but again he hastened on. "After all, we have heard testimony from impeccable witnesses to both occasions. In the second case, we have heard from the victim himself."

"Victim?" said Railu with evident surprise, even indignation. "Pardon me, sir, but why do you use that word? We have heard from the patient, yes. And his testimony was clear; he is making a good recovery. What was it he said? *Fair and square, seems she did a fine job.* He mentioned, too, that Doctor Le'ast was complimentary about my work. That's so, is it not, Doct—"

"Madam!" snapped Fulmer. "It is for me to ask the questions, not you."

"Were you asking a question when you used the word *victim*? Or were you trying to insinuate that my work was not of an adequate standard?"

"The quality of your work is not the point at issue," said Fulmer, evidently eager to move on from his ill-advised choice of word.

"If that's not the point, then what is?"

For a moment Fulmer just stared at her. Le'ast was watching intently and Skelber sensed he was considering another intervention. But Fulmer was still not quite done. "The Charter of the Denvirran Association of Physicians states that only those who have undergone approved training and been licensed by the governing body may practise as doctors."

"As doctors," repeated Railu. There was no sign of anxiety now. "Haven't we already established that I've never called myself that?"

"Then what *do* you call yourself?"

"The word I use is 'healer'. You've heard from the Master Prime about the training of healers within the Guild of Dawnsingers. It's a pity none of the Master Healers are here to tell you more... Well, anyway, I completed that training. I graduated with honours. Since then, especially in the last few years, I have spent considerable time studying textbooks and journals from the Five Principalities. Earl Hedric was very helpful, providing material from the library here, even before his elevation. On several occasions he brought me things from the bookshops of Denvirran too. I'm sure he'd be happy to confirm, if you'd like to call him to the stand."

"I'm sure there's no need to trouble the Earl," mumbled Fulmer.

For a moment there was silence in the room, only the backdrop of people breathing. The Countess shifted slightly in her chair and her skirts rustled.

Railu gave Fulmer a look that seemed, now, almost sympathetic. "Have you any more questions for me, Doctor?"

What a woman, he thought again.

Chapter 33

Skelber

It took well over an hour. Skelber had been present at such hearings before, usually as a humble record-keeper, and he could not recall a tribunal ever needing more than fifteen minutes to reach a verdict. He hoped this protracted deliberation boded well, but he could not feel confident.

Perhaps if he could have spoken to Railu... but she and the Countess had disappeared rapidly at the close of the hearing. He did not know where they had gone and, even if he had, could hardly have barged in upon them.

As he picked desultorily at a plate from the cold buffet, his mind kept returning to the same thought. He had kept his eyes on Railu almost the entire time. Never once had she met his gaze and only a few times had she even glanced in his general direction.

I didn't truly realise how much her regard meant to me until now, when I seem to have to lost it.

"Railu Kermey," said Le'ast. "We have carefully considered all the testimony given before us this day, and we have come to a judgement.

"First, as to the substance of the complaint against you. It is our judgement that the Charter of the Denvirran Association of Physicians admits of no ambiguity. We are obliged to conclude that, on two occasions of which we heard testimony, and by implication many more, you did perform the office of a doctor without holding the requisite license from this Association or another with which we uphold reciprocal recognition."

There were indrawn breaths, a few protesting murmurs, one or two that sounded more like approval. The Countess's face was thunderous, but Railu kept watching Le'ast, intent and—superficially, at least—impassive.

Le'ast held up a hand. "Ladies and gentlemen, if you please. There is more. A good deal more."

Normally there would be nothing more to do but pronounce the penalty, which usually meant handing over the miscreant to the magistrate. Skelber wondered what 'a good deal more' could mean. He longed to believe it might be a good sign, but dare not yield altogether to hope.

"This tribunal took only a short time to reach the aforesaid verdict," resumed Le'ast. "We took a good deal longer to reach agreement on what sanctions were appropriate. Railu Kermey..." he met Railu's gaze, and suddenly Skelber began to hope again. "It is our judgement that no sanctions shall be imposed at this time."

Again there was a lively reaction in the gathering, but now the overarching tone was different. Railu's expression barely flickered, but the Countess turned to her husband and whispered something, smiling.

Le'ast repeated his quelling gesture. "I am aware that this judgement is exceptional. Indeed, as far as my memory stretches... which is no small number of years... it is unprecedented. This tribunal wishes it to be abundantly clear that this in no way represents a relaxation of the Association's general view on unlicensed practitioners. The circumstances of this case, and indeed of the defendant, are quite exceptional; I might even say unique. Let me expand a little on this.

"Miss Kermey, we recognise first the very significant service you have rendered during the present congress. We recognise that your efforts, though largely in the background, as an adviser to the Sung Lands delegation, have rested on your training as a Dawnsinger and a Healer of the Guild, and also on your, evidently extensive, grasp of the medical sciences of the Five Principalities.

"We recognise, too, that you *are* a trained and qualified practitioner under the aegis of the Guild of Dawnsingers. We acknowledge, as has become clear to us during this gathering, that this training, though different in many respects from that given to the young men of our Academy, is manifestly not inferior. It is also evident from the testimony of several witnesses, including the Countess herself, as well as Squire Ranguest and Doctor Skelber, that your practical skills are of a high standard." *Thank you,* Skelber crowed in his heart, *thank you for including my name.* He turned towards Railu but she still would not look at him.

"This tribunal further recognises that your situation has been not only unique but doubtless... awkward. Trained, and fully competent to practise, but officially disbarred because the compilers of our regulations never anticipated your particular circumstances." He gave Railu a slight frown. "If we wish to voice any criticism of you, it is only this; that you might at least have tried to seek our recognition. Not only might this... unpleasantness, and this disruption of the business of the congress, have been averted, you might also have enjoyed the freedom to practise openly for some time already."

Railu looked unconvinced, and Skelber thought he understood: there was no guarantee that approval would have been forthcoming if she had tried; and in doing so she would have tipped her hand, very possibly making it harder for her to practise discreetly as she had hitherto. Le'ast was a thoroughly decent fellow, but he had too great a tendency to think all his colleagues were equally fair-minded.

"This tribunal has also resolved to make an urgent recommendation to the Board of the Denvirran Association of Physicians. To wit, that a reciprocal recognition agreement be instituted with the Healers of the Guild of Dawnsingers. We further propose that we take advantage of the presence, here at Skilthorn, of representatives of both bodies, to ensure that provisional terms for such an agreement be drafted as part of the continuing business of this congress. And may I express my personal hope that Miss Railu Kermey will be closely involved in any such discussions?

"That concludes the statement of this tribunal. May I think all witnesses for their testimony and all others present for their attention. Good day to you all."

Railu immediately stood and a moment later she was talking earnestly with Le'ast. The Countess and the Master Prime joined them. Skelber waited at a discreet distance but they all moved off together.

As he wondered what to do next, Fulmer came toward him. "I can't work you out, Skelber. You initiated the complaint against the woman in the first place, and then in your testimony you seemed to bend over backwards to suggest extenuating circumstances."

"I see no contradiction, Doctor. It's a matter of principle. As a sworn member of the Association, I realised I was duty-bound to bring the matter forward. But I was equally bound, by duty and honour, to testify to the truth as I saw it."

"And you really think this woman is a competent physician? Even a competent surgeon?"

"I have only seen her in action twice. But based on that, and on conversations with her, I would say she is more than competent. Furthermore, as Doctor Le'ast just acknowledged, the Dawnsingers' practice is ahead of ours in some respects. Miss Railu informs me, for instance, that our attention to cleanliness—to what she calls sterilisation—would be deemed woefully inadequate."

"What they *deem* to be adequate or otherwise is not proof of anything."

"Perhaps not, but what she tells me about statistics on post-operative morbidity is highly indicative."

"Statistics," scoffed the younger man. "I believe in what I can see and touch."

"You'd do well, Doctor Fulmer, to recall that every entry on a ledger of post-operative mortality represents a life lost. Someone's mother, father, son, or daughter." Suddenly he could not bear to be in this room another moment, still less bandying words with this jackanapes. *But I must have a word with Le'ast about you...*

"I beg you to excuse me, Doctor Fulmer," he said with a courtly bow. He was always scrupulously polite with people he disliked.

※

He found both Earl and Countess in the lesser library, realised that he had intruded on what must be an all too rare moment alone together. He halted a few steps into the room.

"Did you want me, Skelber?" asked the Earl. "Or the Countess?"

"I'm sorry to have interrupted, my lord. It's not important."

"Your face just now told a different story. What's on your mind? Which of us do you require?"

"To be honest, my lord, I would be very grateful for a few minutes with either of you. You gave me wise counsel the other day, much food for thought. But it's my understanding that you, Countess, know Miss Railu better than anyone else."

"Since we are both here," said the Earl, "Why not bring your question to both of us? That way neither of us need move from our comfortable chairs."

He gestured to another of the arm-chairs. The Countess said nothing, but Skelber's impression was that she felt less welcoming.

"Well, my lord, I doubt you'll be surprised. When we spoke before I explained my dilemma; on the one hand, my growing regard for Miss Railu; on the other my sense of being compelled by my oath to... to a certain course of action." The Countess made a small sound deep in her throat. Her eyes, dark in the soft light cast by scattered reading-lamps, were fixed on him. "My dearest wish ever since has been to speak to her, at least to try to explain why I felt I had to do what I did, but thus far she has offered me no chance to do so."

"You can't be entirely surprised," said the Countess.

"No, my lady. I am not altogether a fool."

"Has it occurred to you that it would have been better to say something to her beforehand? At the very least the shock would have been less, and she would have had more time to prepare."

"It would, my lady. Though may I say that, however little preparation she had, she acquitted herself admirably."

"I think we can all agree on that," said the Earl. The Countess gave a small nod, but her steady gaze still demanded more.

"I don't attempt to absolve myself, my lady, but it may be some slight mitigation that my colleagues reacted much more swiftly than I anticipated. Setting the hearing for the very next day... Before I could find her, she had already received the news—the summons. The interval in which I could have told her before anyone else did was only an hour or two. But no, that is no excuse. I could have found her, should have... had I gathered my courage more swiftly."

"Are you telling us you've 'gathered your courage' now?"

He thought about that. "In truth, my lady, I do not know how much courage I have. I only know that if I do not at least try to explain myself to her I shall surely regret it till my dying day."

"And now you want us to do what? Plead your cause?"

"I must explain myself, my lady, or at least make my best attempt. I cannot ask anyone to speak for me. I only ask that you might assist me in gaining that hearing."

"I think," said the Earl, "That if Railu does not, at some point, hear your account of yourself... I think one day she too will regret it."

The Countess said nothing for some moments. Her eyes were cast down and she appeared deep in thought. Finally she stirred, looked at her husband. "I think you're probably right, Hedric." Her eyes turned back to Skelber, unflinching. "She was growing attached to you, too. Of course that's exactly why it was so painful for her."

"Believe me, my lady, I know that and I feel it. I know that I will feel better if I can speak with her. I deeply hope that she will feel better too."

"Well, I don't suppose it's likely to make things worse."

❉

He walked out of the room and almost collided with Railu. Automatically he extended a hand as if to prevent her falling. His fingers brushed her sleeve but he did not feel the solidity of flesh. For a moment he saw, as if magnified, the pleating where the sleeve gathered into the shoulder seam, the weave of the linen. There was a tiny flaw, perhaps a single broken thread.

She stepped back, but did not turn away.

"Miss Railu," he said, breathless as if he had just run a long race. "Forgive my clumsiness." She inclined her head, lifted one hand: *no matter*.

"I have just been speaking with the Earl and the Countess. I... I hoped they might intercede. With you." He heard how he sounded. A man should be able to speak for himself. *And I will.* "Not to plead my cause. Only to ask you to hear me."

She thrust her hands into her pockets. Yes, surely, her skirts would have capacious, practical pockets. "Do you really think there's anything you can say?"

"I know that there are things I want to say. That I need to say. And perhaps, dare I venture, you might feel better if you knew why I did—"

"—Why you denounced me?"

"Denounced?" He just managed to check himself before launching into why that was an unfairly loaded word. No, if that was how she felt, he needed to recognise that. "Miss Railu, just a little of your—"

"—Not here," she said abruptly, even brusquely.

"No, of course not."

"Outside? I think the rain has stopped."

He found himself looking at her shoes. "I believe so, but the grass will still be wet."

"Give me ten minutes to change my shoes."

Chapter 34

Railu

S he went out through the ballroom, empty but for a couple of enslaved sweeping the floor, tidying napkins and cake-cups that delegates had discarded. She thought, just for a moment, of what that implied, the un-thinking assumption that there would always be someone to clean up any mess you left.

He was waiting on the terrace, turned as she emerged. Her insides clenched at the sight of him; she didn't know if it was anger or something quite different. *Well, I'm here. Let's hear what he has to say.*

"There's a dell hidden in those trees," she said, gesturing across the lawn. "It's pretty, and usually quiet. It doesn't seem many people have discovered it."

"I for one have not, and I shall be delighted to go wherever you wish." He looked for a moment as if he was about to offer his arm. Railu knew this was a perfectly normal act for a gentleman about to take a walk with a lady, but she was not sorry, at this moment, that he thought better of it.

They descended and started across the wide lawn. Even with her boots on, with their thicker soles, within a few strides the hem of her skirt was darkening. She shrugged. A damp hem would do her no harm.

Under the trees it was almost as if the rain had not ceased. Everywhere the trees dripped, an occasional drop landing on her head and trickling coldly down her scalp. Ferns slumped heavy with the weight of moisture. The light was soft and green, and the air smelt of fertility.

Lower, as the path negotiated its way around outcrops of rock, she noticed how dark and rounded they were, quite unlike the crumbly, buttermilk-coloured limestone of the Wold. There must be a distinct geological boundary nearby. Jerya would know all about it; Hedric too.

As she descended, Skelber turned, then smiled. "I should have known that one who made the First Crossing would need no assistance in a place like this."

"When we made the Crossing, we were not wearing skirts."

There was a little sideways tilt of his head that he did when taking something in; an almost birdlike movement. She had not known till now that she had observed it before, yet found it curiously familiar. "I had not given thought to that."

She joined him on a more level path and he stepped back so as not to crowd her. "This is an intriguing place." *Intriguing*, she thought. *Yes, a good choice of word. An intriguing choice.* "However, these narrow paths are not the most conducive to conversation."

"It widens a little, further on."

Even then it was barely wide enough for two to walk side by side. Her skirt-hem, still damp, brushed frequently against his leg. She drew her shawl around her and kept her hands there, elbows drawn in.

For a few moments they walked in silence. The beck, spreading wider and shallower over a stony bed, burbled away to itself, almost as Embrel had done before he began to form words. Far above, the highest leaves glowed like minute scraps of the sun herself.

"Miss Railu," said Skelber, "May I speak frankly?"

"I see very little point in this if you do not."

"No, of course. Well..." He made an exasperated sound, between a sigh and a snort. "I thought I had planned exactly what I would say to you but now it comes to it..."

"Please, just say *something*."

"Yes, yes, indeed. Forgive me for being tongue-tied. It is only because this is of great importance for me. *You* are of great... Miss Railu, I have known you but a few days. I suppose the time we have spent together—truly together—amounts to not even a handful of hours. And yet it fills my mind, and my heart."

Railu said nothing. Clearly she had no intention of making it easy for him.

"From the first moment I saw you... no, not the very first. I had seen you many times, but always in the background, quiet, unobtrusive, advising the Dawnsingers. I suppose the truth—the *embarrassing* truth—is that I never really noticed you."

"In fairness," she said, "I cannot say I took much note of you either."

"No. I suppose our roles were somewhat alike. Let Le'ast and Fulmer speak for us, as Master Evisyn and Master Yanil spoke for the Guild." Yanil wasn't a Master, but she didn't correct him. "Well... If I had not truly seen you before, that changed that day in the paddock."

"When you were rude to me."

"I did apologise shortly after," he protested mildly. She acknowledged it with a brief nod. Another stray drip slithered down scalp and nape. "In the first moments I did not know what to think. I had never encountered a woman like you before. But soon thereafter I began to consider whether that might say rather more about the women I'd known before than it did about—"

"—About those women, or about what society allows them to be?"

"A very fair question, Miss Railu—and another distinction which I had scarcely considered. But in the past two weeks, observing the Dawnsingers—and the Countess, of course—well, any man who is not an utter fool would have to re-evaluate his assumptions about what women are or are not capable of. And in the last few days, having had the opportunity—the *privilege*—of observing you, I have been obliged to revise my ideas even more." He ran a hand through his hair, its russet tint almost lost in the green shade. "Not to beat about the bush any longer, I have conceived a very high regard for you. And I had begun to think—to hope—that you might feel something of the same for me."

She stopped so suddenly that he went on two paces before he realised. He turned back to face her. It gave her a moment to turn her impulsive, angry retort into something more measured. "Fine words, Doctor Skelber, but if that's true... then why did you..."

"Denounce you?"

"You didn't seem to like the word when I said it before."

"I don't like it now. But that doesn't mean it isn't accurate."

"Well, whatever you or I call it, we know what you did." There was a small cascade just a little way ahead, where a tiny tributary stream fell over sheaves of rock half-smothered in vivid green ferns. She walked on a few paces and stood facing across the main beck, looking at the cascade so she didn't have to look at him as he attempted to explain.

"Miss Railu," he said, alongside her. She could see enough in the corner of her eye to know he too was looking at the trickling water and the luxuriant ferns, "Please believe me when I say I debated long and hard with myself, and I took my dilemma to Earl Hedric. He was kind enough to find time for me, and said much that seemed both wise and kind, but he did not solve the problem for me. I would have given much to spare you the unpleasantness—"

"—It was more than unpleasantness," she said, catching a glimpse of his profile. "I was very much afraid I'd never be able to practise again."

"I am very sorry to put you through that—and let me say how delighted I am that that has not been the result. I wish I could claim that I anticipated from the start that it would go that way. I might have hoped; Le'ast is a reasonable man, and I know he has been much impressed by what he has learned of medicine and physiology in the Sung Lands. But it would be dishonest to claim that I had planned or anticipated the outcome. And honesty is the heart of the matter here. Try as I might—as I did—to see another way, in the end I could only conclude that my oath as a physician left me no alternative."

Then, and only then, she shifted position, turned to look at him, and he met her gaze. His eyes seemed pleading, even wounded. *Am I not the wounded party here?* she thought, but somehow conviction was lacking.

"I'm an oath-breaker," she said finally. "A Vow-breaker, as the Dawnsingers term it. Perhaps you knew that already?"

"The Earl mentioned it. He said more particularly that the Countess was—though she wasn't a Countess then, was she?"

In spite of everything, Railu laughed. "We'd never even heard of Earls and Countesses back then. Oh, heavens, there was so much we didn't know. We were so young… eighteen, nineteen. But still, we'd taken solemn Vows. Three times, in my case: Postulant, Novice, and Ordained Dawnsinger. And only weeks after the last occasion we ripped up those Vows and trampled them into the dust." *The dust of Delven*, she thought.

"Yes, Earl Hedric spoke of that. But he also said that he trusts his wife absolutely." His eyes rested on hers and she wondered if he was trying to convey *as I trust you*. "And he said this too: *Breaking a vow is a terrible thing, but it may not be the worst thing.*"

"But you could not do it."

"I have lived by my Physician's Oath since I first entered the Academy, almost twenty years ago. I am not sure who I would be if I breached it now."

She thought about that and suddenly she shivered. The humid air of the dell was anything but chilly, but for a moment it was as if an icy gust had infiltrated itself. "I don't think I knew who I was for some time after we walked out of the Sung Lands. Several years, maybe. Things happened to me; I didn't act for myself."

"You were enslaved," he said. It seemed nine-tenths statement, maybe one-tenth question.

"That, and other things." *Enslavement, and motherhood. Acting as wet-nurse to my own infant. And all the time watching Jerya stretch herself, watching her regain her freedom.* All she said was, "Those years, the first few years at Duncal, they were the hardest, the bleakest, of my life."

"I am sorry for it. But you have moved beyond all that, have you not?"

"Aye, but I feared..." She could not say it. *I feared to lose it all again.*

He stared at her. "I'm a fool. No, not an entire fool. I knew it would be hard for you, if the tribunal went badly. But I never truly understood quite how it would feel for you."

"Do you understand now?"

"Yes," he said and then, sharply, "No. No, how can I say that? I *am* a fool. But I look at you and I feel... I imagine that I can feel what you feel, or at least some shadow of it."

"Damn you," she heard herself saying. "Damn you, Skelber, for even trying to understand. This would all be so much simpler if I could go on hating you."

There was new hope in his eyes, but she wasn't ready to absolve him yet. "I need to think. Maybe for an hour, maybe for a day or two. Will you give me that? Leave me be and let me come and find you when I'm ready?"

"That's more than I dared hope for." It was a lie, she thought, but the kindest and bravest kind of lie.

"If you wait here a few minutes, I can find my own way back."

She looked back once, just as she came to the rocky passage. He was gazing toward her. Neither of them raised a hand or made any other sign. She gathered her skirt in one hand and began to climb.

CHAPTER 35

MAVRYS

I t was never too bad getting a sack of grain onto her shoulder when the stack was still two or three high. When there were only a few left, and she had to heft each one up from the floor, she struggled. There was no point pretending she was as strong as the others, especially Mardom or Tharshin. *I'm still not eighteen yet*, she told herself; *I'll get stronger.*

She had begun to work out a few tricks to make it as easy as possible. As long as there was more than one sack left, she could take it in stages: heave her chosen sack atop another, take a few breaths, then get her weight under it as far as she could. It was all about using the legs as much as possible. Even her legs were no broader than Mardom's arms.

Once she had the sack settled on her shoulders, properly balanced, she knew she could manage the rest. Her back and shoulders would be protesting by the time she got across the yard, but they would hold out.

As she emerged from the store, she almost collided with Mardom. Once you were in motion, with half your bodyweight on your shoulder, it was harder to stop. She kept on going as he dodged.

"Yow all reet wi' that?" he asked from half a pace behind.

"I've got it," she said tightly.

"S'no pro'lem..."

"I said I've got it. Thanks all the same."

He grunted. "Suit yowrsel' then."

"I will." But she hadn't gone more than another couple of steps when another thought struck her. "Mardom?"

"Changed yowr mind?"

"No, but... the grain store's almost empty. Do you know if there's more coming?"

He fell in beside her. "Renfrith allus use to ride down to th' mill on a Lunesday, give 'em th' week"s order."

"Today's Maresday, right?" One day was much like another in the routine of the stables, but after a moment they agreed it was so.

"D'you know if Haldrow went yesterday? Shouldn't we have had the delivery today?"

He puffed his cheeks, expelled a long breath, as he often did when cogitating. "Aye, shoulda had a cart first thing."

"Where's Haldrow now?"

"Exercisin' Oronsa."

Mav felt like grinding her teeth. Renfrith, for all his faults, had seen the sense that Oronsa fared better with a lighter rider. And, after the crazy run she'd had last week, she surely didn't need a long ride under a heavier one. Not that Haldrow had the bulk of, say, Mardom, but he was significantly bigger than herself.

"Which way did he go, did you see?"

"To'ards the West woods, them tracks."

That made some sense, at least. The tracks in the West woods were largely covered in wood-chips, making a forgiving surface under-hoof. But it was almost opposite the direction of the mill and granary; it was unlikely Haldrow would combine that business with Oronsa's exercise.

"Someone'd better go and check," she said.

"At th'mill?"

"Aye."

Finally she reached the feed-bin, rested the sack on the narrow shelf of its lip. She took a moment to catch her breath before reaching for her knife. She slit the strings of the sack and watched the golden cascade of oats tumble into the bin, then shook out the last few grains, folded the sack and added it to the pile.

"You're not jumping at the chance to ride down to the mill?" she asked.

Mardom frowned. "Haldrow bin on at me to clean those stalls where those two greys were. From Troq—Troha..."

"Troquharran."

"Aye. Why can't for'ners gi' their places easier names?"

That was a can of worms best left unopened. "All right, then. I'll go. And I'll give you a hand with the cleanout when I get back."

She rolled her shoulders to ease the ache as she headed back out into the hazy sunlight. *This wants doing quickly*, she thought. The mill was a fair way to walk and at this end of another busy day, she didn't feel much like running. But the time saved by riding could easily be lost to saddling and unsaddling a mount.

As if in answer to her thoughts, she saw Taalrix standing on the far side of the yard, idly swishing his long blond tail. If there was one horse in the stable that she could handle bareback, it would be the equable gelding. Better still, he still had bridle and reins. *No saddle? No problem.*

Without further debate, she led him the few steps to the mounting-block, and swung quickly onto his back. He turned his head, gave her an incurious look, flicked one ear. She smiled. "Let's go then, lad."

As they clattered out of the yard, Tharshin appeared from the tack-room. "Where th' hell d'yow think yow're goin'? He's already had his exercise."

"Just down to the mill," she said, and then they were past. "Won't be long," she added over her shoulder.

✳

"Nay," said the miller, "Nobod's bin this week. Figured they musta over-ordered last week. Heard some o'th fine folk bin leavin', like."

"Some, not all, and we're down to five sacks in the store."

He looked away, calculating in his head. "Yow're like to run out tomorrer, then."

"For sure. And I know we could put them all out on the grass. None of the horses'd starve. But it'd not do the paddocks much good, and it's not ideal for the horses either."

He looked at her curiously. Most people did; she was half-accustomed to it now. *A bald girl who speaks like a lady...*

"Well," she said. "Can you get us at least a part-load tomorrow? Please?"

"I c'd do yow a few sacks tonight... if'n yow wants to inspan th'horse *an'* load th'cart yowrsel". He grinned. "Or a proper load tomorrer, say by midday."

"That'd be wonderful. Thank—"

He stopped her with a hand. "But I need a chit first. Signed by th'Master o'Horse. Keep it all reg'lar, like."

"First thing in the morning?"

He wrinkled his freckled nose. "Tha's not *quite* reg'lar. But appen I c'n go along wi' that."

"Thank you so much," she said fervently. "Now there's just one more thing..."

"Wha'?"

"Could you give me a boost back onto the horse, please?"

"Th' devil? Where yow bin gall'vantin' off to? An' *bareback* an' all."

Saving your bacon, she thought, but she knew better than to say it. "I found out no-one had ordered grain for the week. I've been down to the mill to—"

"—Yow allus think yow know better, dun't yow? Wha' th'hell is th'world comin' to when a slave—an' a *girl* at tha'—reckons she knows better than th' Master o'Horse?"

I do know better. Today, this afternoon, I did know better than you. And somewhere inside, you know it too. He knew it, but he couldn't admit it to himself. That was the real reason he was so mad.

"Listen," he said, almost hissing in his fury. "If'n yow were a lad, I'd be *this* close to takin' a whip to yow right now. But I never hit a woman in my life an' I ain't about to start." For once, she thought, she wasn't going to protest about double standards. "But yow listen to me an' yow listen good. From now on, yow do 'xactly what I tell yow. *'Xactly*: no more, no less. Last chance. Yow got that?"

She thought about it for a moment. Even a moment was too long for him. "Yow hear me, girl?"

"I hear you, Master. But..."

"Do yow not know wha' *last chance* means?"

"Yes, Master. But I need to tell you. The miller needs a chit to confirm the order. Ordinarily he'd want it today for delivery tomorrow, but he said first thing in the morning'd do well enough."

He glared at her, jaw-muscles bunching. "All right. An seein' as yow're so clever an' so pally wi th'miller all on a sudden, yow can make out the chit and yow can tek it down there. An since he said first thing, yow make damn sure it is first thing. I wants yow back here for first walk-out."

As Haldrow stomped away, she realised Mardom was hovering nearby, having been lurking behind a water-butt. "D'you ever take one of these chits down to the mill for Renfrith?" she asked.

He nodded. "Aye, plenty o'times."

"What did it look like?"

He shrugged. "Piece o'paper. Folded over a couple o'times, like."

Her heart sank. "You never looked inside?"

"Yow knows I ain't much of a one for readin'."

I wonder if Haldrow is? she thought suddenly. *Maybe that's why he hadn't done it... and why he wants me to do it now.* It wasn't proof, but it made perfect sense.

Mav couldn't blame a man for struggling with reading and writing. It wasn't just slaves who missed out on schooling. But concealing the fact, and thereby risking the horses' welfare... that was less easy to forgive.

However, she had questions more pressing than ethical conundrums. What did the miller's requested 'chit' look like? The Carinnan stable had had pre-printed forms for feed orders, but they were for external merchants. The stable and mill here were just branches of the same estate.

Well, whatever the answer was, it almost certainly lay in the loft above the tack-room. Renfrith had had both his sleeping-quarters and his office there, but Haldrow still slept in the same tiny cottage he'd occupied before his promotion, one of a line built lean-to fashion against the North wall of the stable block.

She knew she didn't want to be discovered, certainly not by Haldrow, going through whatever the office might hold. It might take five minutes, or it might take an hour. *I'll have to wait until late.*

※

The Three were high enough to throw light across the yard, but the shadows were black. Mavrys crept around the shadow-side, not daring to unveil her lantern.

She kept the lantern turned low as she crept up the stair-ladder to the loft. At least the treads didn't creak. She didn't know who was on night-watch duty tonight, and didn't care. Her plan—her only plan—was not to be discovered by anyone.

In romance novels, it was always the heroes who did this sort of thing. The heroines... but 'heroine' was hardly the right word. The girls in those stories were there to be rescued, to be saved, not to save themselves, still less anyone else.

She knew that Renfrith was gone, and she'd seen a light in the window of Haldrow's cottage. Still she hesitated before the top, momentarily paralysed, unable to raise her head above the level of the upper floor. Almost for the first time, she felt a moment's regret for her hair. Even its light colour would be less conspicuous than a bald head in the Threelight that angled in from the end window.

But there's no one there, she insisted to herself. Still she hesitated, listening; wishing she could hear with every square inch of her skin, not just her ears. She held her breath, wished she could similarly suspend her racing pulse. Somewhere below, a horse whickered softly; then she heard the distant 'too-wit too-woo' of a pair of tawny owls. Her father had told her once that it was the female who called and the male who responded. She had never forgotten that.

Nothing else. Finally, hardly daring to breathe, Mav eased herself up another step. She could see no one, but of course she was still too low to be sure there was no one in the bed. She tried not to think that the last person to occupy it had been Renfrith. *He's gone.* Two more steps. The bedclothes were rumpled, as if no one had touched them since the day of Renfrith's dismissal, but no body humped the blankets.

Mav breathed again, but made her movements no less cautious as she completed the climb. A faint creak as she stepped onto the floorboards made her freeze, but nothing happened. She crept over toward the window, where a planed board atop a rough-made workbench served as a kind of desk. Papers were scattered haphazardly in the centre, with more orderly piles to either side.

She moved one of these piles so she could place the lantern out of line with the window. With the wick still low, and with the Threelight mirrored in the dusty glass, she did not think anyone outside would see anything suspicious, even if they had reason to look up. She was still taking a chance, but the chance had to be taken, or there had been no point to the whole exercise.

Mav leafed through the loose papers first. There was a scrawled list of tasks—*'Pass vet bill to (illegible); farrier (Hindsday); order carots,'* and so on. She had no way to be certain but she felt sure anyway; the angular, left-leaning script, smudged in a couple of places, was Renfrith's, not Haldrow's. There were misspellings—'stalion' for 'stallion' as well as 'carots'—but only a few, and apart from two or three proper names, nothing was indecipherable.

None of the ordered piles yielded anything more useful. She drew the lantern towards her, and noticed for the first time that drawers had been installed below the work-surface, their joinery noticeably finer than the original bench. At last, in the lower of these, Mav found what seemed to be what she was looking for. In a folder marked 'Acounts Compleat', she found a sheet of the estate's printed notepaper, with handwritten annotations below; dated last week, then 'Required for Main Stables; 40 bushel Oat; 20 Dr. Myx; 15 Bran'. There was a scrawl below that, a different hand; she guessed it to be the miller's signature. At the bottom, in a slightly lighter ink, were the following day's date, and then 'Del'd & Ch'kd'. A second signature below was also illegible, but looked very much as if it began with an R.

Mav had already seen a pen and inkpot on the work-surface. Now she only needed some blank notepaper, but there was no sign of this either on the top or in the drawers. She was beginning to think the whole desperate nocturnal venture would fall at the final hurdle, when she noticed a couple of shelves, almost invisible in the shadows off to her left. Once she had all the pieces, it took only a few moments to write out the order; remembering how bare the store had seemed, she added five to each of the quantities. Then, in case the miller needed a copy, she made a duplicate. She waited a seeming age to be sure the ink was dry before placing the sheets together and folding them twice. She thrust this inside her shirt and at long last began her descent.

❋

A grey-headed man was just dismounting from a smoke-black stallion. Mavrys recognised the horse first, the man second: the local veterinary. As she drew closer she heard him grumbling, apparently to his horse. "Where the devil's Renfrith? And why aren't the horses ready for inspection?"

Speak like a slave, she reminded herself. "Beggin' yowr pardon, sir. Can I help yow?"

He looked at her suspiciously, perhaps surprised to encounter a female. It was quite possible he hadn't noticed her on the previous occasion. "Where's Renfrith?"

"Master Renfrith dun't work here no more, sir."

"What? Why? Anyway, who's in charge now?"

"Haldrow, sir."

He sniffed. Mav couldn't tell whether he'd never heard of Haldrow, or merely had a low opinion of him. "Then where's *he*? And, more to the point, why aren't the horses ready? I've been coming at nine every Downsday for years."

"I'll find someone. But... might I make a suggestion?" He looked at her oddly, and she realised the slave-voice had slipped. Or perhaps slaves didn't make suggestions. But this made sense... "So there's no waste of your time. Could you take a look at the Countess's Oronsa? She had a hard run last Hindsday, harder than she should have. I think she might be a touch lame in the left fore."

She had to bear a few more seconds of the hard stare, then he shrugged. "Is she in her usual stall?"

"Aye, sir."

"Left fore, you say? Has Renf—no, dammit, has Haldrow seen it?"

"He says I'm imagining it. But I think there's heat in the gaskin."

He grunted. "Well, I'll take a look. Find Haldrow, and get the horses ready."

"Aye, sir."

As he strode into the stable, she turned to find Mardom a few paces away. "Have you seen Haldrow?" she asked.

"Not lately."

"Well, one of us needs to find him and the other needs to start getting the horses from the paddocks lined up for the vet's inspection. You have a preference?"

He shrugged. "Six and two threes to me."

"Fine, I'll go after Haldrow, and any of the other hands I see I'll tell them to help you."

"Very kind," he said. As she darted away her first thought was that he was being sarcastic, but as she rounded the corner she began to question her own assessment.

✳

The gelding from Sessapont was definitely favouring his right forefoot. She looked around, but there was no one else in the paddock. She sauntered casually across, staying in the horse's eyeline, before going through the usual routine of introducing herself and asking permission. It was always time well spent, especially with a horse you didn't know, had barely heard a report of.

The gelding seemed accepting enough, offering no resistance as she lifted the foot. The issue was obvious at once. "Now that's a thorn and a half," she murmured. "Where did you pick that up, I wonder? And are there any more out there? Has someone been trimming a hedge beside one of the tracks and not cleaned up properly? Pity you can't tell me, eh?"

The thorn came out easily enough, and she was just dipping into her pocket for some salve when... first she heard a momentary whizzing sound, then a distinct thump. An instant later her world dissolved into pain.

When the darkness cleared, maybe only a few seconds later, she was lying on her side in the grass. The pain had narrowed to a spot just above her right knee.

She heard running footfalls, then Mardom was crouching beside her. "Are yow all right, Mav?"

"Do I look like I'm all right?"

"Sorry, no. Want me to tak a look?"

With unexpected gentleness he rolled up the leg of her divided skirt. There was no mistaking the sharp intake of breath as he got his first sight of the wound. Mav propped herself up on an elbow, then felt sick as she saw.

"Well," he said with forced cheeriness, "That were some kick, but at least he din't catch yow on th' knee. If'n yow'd bin tall as me, he'd have catched yow bang on."

"Don't say bang," she begged. She tried to grin, but her head swam and she sank back to the ground.

"D'yow want me to fetch some'un?"

"Miss Railu if you can find her. And someone needs to make sure the horse is all right. I'd just pulled a nasty thorn out of his right forefoot, but I hadn't cleaned it or anything."

❋

"Lucky it missed your knee," said Railu, unwittingly echoing Mardom. "A smashed patella can be very nasty. Funny, I had another injury very like this the day before I left Duncal."

"*You* had?"

"On a patient, I mean. But that was a cow, not a horse. Sharper gash, cows don't wear shoes, but not greatly different. Now this is going to sting a bit..."

"A *bit*?" she gasped a moment later.

"If I say it's going to hurt like blazes, people tend to tense up, and that's rarely helpful. But..." She slipped on spectacles, peered closely at Mav's leg. "I think we can avoid stitches if I bind this just right, but you're going to have to keep your weight off it for a few days."

She glanced round and up at the round-faced slave-girl who'd accompanied her, and had been watching attentively. "Dortis, when the old Earl was getting sick, did he use crutches?"

"Yes, ma'am, he did. Used to whack folk wi'em sometimes—" The girl stopped, her naturally rosy cheeks getting pinker.

"Do you know where to lay your hands on a pair?"

"Surely do, ma'am."

"Then would you be so kind and fetch them?"

"For...?" Mav knew the full question would be: *for a slave?*

"For a patient who needs them," said Railu firmly. Dortis hurried away. "That should do for now. I'll check again tomorrow. Right, I'm just going to wash my hands. Where did you say there was hot water?"

"End door. The red one."

"Don't move till I get back."

Mav was happy to comply. She leaned back against the wall of the stable block. The sun was off the stones now, but its heat lingered, almost pulsing into her. She closed her eyes and let the familiar sounds of the work of the stable come to her.

Then an all too familiar voice broke in. "What th'hell's this?"

She peered up at Haldrow. "I got kicked."

"So? Lads get kicked every day."

If true, that doesn't say much for the lads. Horses don't kick for no reason. Instead of saying it, she pulled up the leg of her riding habit to reveal the bandage.

He grunted, unimpressed. "Any'un can wrap a bit o'cloth round their leg."

"You think I'm faking it? Just wait, Miss Railu'll be back in one minute."

"Or I could just take a look for mesel'." He reached toward the dressing.

"Don't touch that!" Railu's voice cracked like a whip. Heads—equine and human—appeared at several of the stable doors.

"Who th'hell are yow?"

"My name's Railu. I'm a physician. Mavrys got a nasty gash. It was touch and go whether it'd need suturing."

Haldrow blinked; Mav had a sudden certainty that he didn't know what 'suturing' meant. She wondered about that. It wasn't just human doctors who did it; vets did too. Perhaps he only knew the commoner term, stitching.

"She'll be on crutches for at least a week," added Railu. "I don't want her putting weight on that leg till I give the all-clear."

"What about riding?" asked Mav.

"Same thing. Not till I say so."

Wonderful, she thought. *I haven't had a chance on Oronsa since Haldrow took over, and now... who knows when—if—I'll get another?*

Haldrow clearly had a different view of the situation. "Well, that's mighty *con-veen-yent* for yow, ain't it?"

"What d'you mean?"

"Don't play stupid; yow've been too busy playin' smart to get away wi' tha'. Can't walk, can't ride, wha' hellin' use are yow? Yow might as well go lie on yowr feather bed for a week."

Mav had made a stern resolve not to rise to his taunts, but this was too much. "You call that convenient? You think I *want* to be laid up for a week? You think I got myself kicked *deliberately*?" She drew a ragged, angry breath. "When have you ever seen me shirking? Last I remember you were moaning because I'd taken on a job you hadn't asked me to do, not because I was lazy."

"Moanin', was I?" he began, but she couldn't stop now.

"Why the hell do you think I'm here? Why the hell do you think I've been putting up with the filthiest jobs? Why the hell do you think I've not been biting back at your gibes and insinuations? Because I love the horses and I love working with the horses... and this spragging leg is starting to hurt like bloody murder about now but that's not the worst thing about it. The worst thing about it is that it's going to keep me away from the horses. Though it might keep me away from you as well, so it can't be all bad."

"Have yow quite finished?" Haldrow drew himself up to his full height. "Because I've had a bellyful of yowr insolence... Now, some on'us have work to do, but have no doubt, girl, yow ain't heard the last o'this."

He turned on his heel. As he strode away Mav heard him murmur to himself, "In-so-lence *and* in-do-lence." He chuckled, obviously delighted with his own wordplay.

"Oh grief..." she said to Railu. "I said too much, didn't I?"

Railu settled beside her, pressed her hand. "It might have been better to forgo that final sentence. Although..." She smiled. "I'm not saying he didn't deserve it."

"I don't know what I'll do if I lose this position." *Go back to being a domestic*, I suppose. *Not the worst thing in the world. If they'll have me back. If not...* There were still ten long weeks to her birthday and freedom. Whatever 'freedom' might mean.

"Try not to worry too much. Why imagine the worst when it might never happen? Now... you said the leg was hurting badly?"

"I did exaggerate a bit... it's achy, sort of throbbing, but not too bad."

"Hmm... Where do you sleep now? Here, or still in the enslaved quarters?"

"Quarters. It seemed best, with no other females here."

"Right. Here's Dortis. How about we walk back that way together? We can see how you manage the crutches, and then I'll fetch you something to help you sleep."

✵

Halfway to the house, she heard fast, heavy footsteps on the shale behind. She stopped, looked round with a sense of dread, imagining it must be Haldrow, but it was Mardom. He stopped a couple of paces short. Mav gazed at his face. "You been in the wars too, Mardom? I hope it wasn't that horse gave you that shiner?"

"T'weren't any horse, it were Tharshin." He grinned. "But he looks worse."

"You were fighting? Why?"

"He said yow been tryin' to make him look bad. I said yow din't have to try."

She stared at him, unsure if she had heard aright. "Tharshin said that? And you...?"

"Dun't yow b'lieve me?"

"No, I do, I'm just surprised. I thought you and he were thick as thieves."

"Not when he pulls a stupid stunt like tha'."

"Like what?"

"Why d'yow think tha' horse kicked yow? Soft geldin' like that'un, he's not a kicker."

"I didn't think so either."

"Till Tharsh lobbed tha' stone."

The memory flashed clear. A whizz and a thud. "Tharshin threw a stone...? *That's* why the horse kicked me?"

"Ain't tha' what I just said?"

"Sorry to be slow. I just didn't think he'd be that much of a..."

"Of a spraggot? No more did I, afore now."

"And he thinks I'm trying to make him look bad?"

"Aye."

"I'm just trying to do *my* job best as I can."

"Aye, but that's all it takes. An'..." He paused as if weighing his words. 'Appen he might not be th'only 'un."

Mav groaned silently to herself. *It gets worse.* "And now with this, Haldrow's convinced I'm trying to dodge work... I'm going to have to think of things I can do sitting down."

"There's allus fixin' and cleanin' th'tack. No'un ever fancies tha'. Mebbe sortin' through some o'th' old stuff too."

"Anything I can do. Long as it keeps me near the horses."

"Aye," he said. "Tha's th' thing, for yow. I can see it, even if some can't."

CHAPTER 36

MAVRYS

"It's a funny thing," said Haldrow. "Every time there's trouble, seems I find yow there."

"It doesn't mean I'm the cause," she protested, aware she was speaking not only to him but to all the hands. They'd followed him into the tack room; now they clustered behind, all but the closest near-silhouettes against the light of the end-window. Haldrow stood a few paces away, close enough to loom. She levered herself upright, rested her rear against the bench, trying not to put weight on the right leg. It wasn't comfortable, but she felt better facing him on a level, or close enough.

"Dun't it?" he said. "I ain't so sure. Though mebbe I should thank yow, seein' it was yow got Renfrith sacked."

"*I* got him sacked?"

"You ain't denyin' he were sacked 'cause o' yow?"

"He was sacked because he conspired with those so-called Rangers."

"We've only yowr word for that."

Her anger swelled: *calling me a liar!*, but she forced herself to think. "Not true. Mardom saw how he reacted when I came back, didn't you—where is Mardom?"

"Slipped out," said someone.

That was a puzzle; all the others were watching avidly. Mardom, who'd seemed more of a friend than anyone else in the yard: Mav felt abandoned. But she couldn't dwell on that. "If Renfrith didn't plan the whole thing, he certainly knew what might happen. He sent me down that road, on that day, when those men were waiting. It's only thanks to Oronsa that I'm not lying somewhere in the forest even now."

"Ah, aye, Oronsa. Her ladyship's own precious horse. What the vet'n'ry said had gone lame in her left fore."

"And who was it asked him to look at her? Lame in her left fore; I said those exact words to the vet myself. I could have told him you'd been riding her for three days since the day I—" She broke off, shying away from those memories. "How much do you weigh, Master Haldrow?"

"What sort o' fool question is tha'?"

"Twelve stone, maybe? Maybe twelve and a half?" They'd known the weights of all the riding-hands at Carinnan; it was important when it came to matching horse and rider, doubly so in preparing for a 'chase. "I'm barely nine, last time I checked. The Countess might be heavier; she's a good bit taller than me, but she's slender. Maybe she's ten stone. And that's what Oronsa's used to."

As he listened, his face had grown darker, a purple tint creeping in beneath the sun-ripened amber. "I dun't believe this. Yow hearin', lads? She's only tryin' to blame *me* for Oronsa goin' lame."

"If she was lame after Hindsday how is it you never noticed? How is it you'd been on her three days running and never spotted anything wrong?" Over Haldrow's shoulder she saw a head tilt, very much the posture of someone considering a point. *Maybe they've not all made up their minds,* she thought. It was encouraging, if only faintly; but it didn't make any real difference. The moment she'd gripped the crutches and risen from the stool to face Haldrow, she'd known she was going to stand her ground, no matter the consequences.

He folded his arms. "Injuries can take time to work out. Any'un what knows horses knows tha'."

"Of course—but I also know if a horse has had a hard run, you don't overwork her for a few days. And that run Oronsa had… all right, there weren't any jumps, but it was as hard on her as any 'chase. At Carinnan we'd just have walked her to the paddock and let her move as much or as little as she liked for the first couple of days."

"Yow allus know best, dun't yow?"

Trouble is, she thought, *I rather think I do. Not all the time, not about everything... but I'm right about this. And I'd stake my life I've been right about a few other things too.*

Even resolved to stand up for herself, she had a good idea that wasn't the wisest answer she could give. She gazed back at him a moment, wondering, then said, "All right. Apparently it's my fault Renfrith arranged for me to be waylaid by those ruffians. Apparently it's my fault I had to run Oronsa hard to save my life. What else am I accused of?"

"Yow overstep th'mark," said Haldrow. "Not just once; it's all the time."

"*All* the time?"

"Spraggit, most o'th'time yow dun't even have to say anythin'. It's obvious just in th'way yow looks at me, at th'others."

"What, it's a crime to look at someone now?" Someone, one of the silhouetted figures, chuckled. "Don't flatter yourselves. None of you are that handsome. I'm much more interested in looking at the horses." There was another chuckle, a different voice. Haldrow heard it too, and scowled. "All right, I overstep the mark. Any real examples, or is it just that I look at people?"

"Yow took it on yowrsel' to give instructions to the vet'n'ry."

"Oh, yes, that. When he arrived for his weekly visit, which he's been doing regular as clockwork for years and nothing was ready for him. What should I have done? Left him kicking his heels and gone looking for you? How long would that have taken? All right, I took it on myself... to *ask* him, very politely, if he'd mind looking at Oronsa... which gave me time to find some of the other hands and get some horses ready for him to inspect."

"And the veterinary was quite appreciative," said a new voice. Every head turned, and then there was a scramble, boots scraping on tile, as the hands jostled to make way for Earl Hedric. Behind him, Mav saw Mardom, grinning broadly. Now she knew why he'd made his exit earlier.

"In fact," said the Earl, "He wrote me a note about it. And with your permission, Master Haldrow, I'd like to read you some of what he said."

He took station to one side, facing both Haldrow and Mavrys. He pulled a sheet from a pocket, unfolded it. The crackle of stiff paper was intensely audible in a suddenly clotted silence. "I'll skip the polite greetings and all that... yes, here we are.

'Imagine my surprise, on arrival, to be greeted only by a young woman—no more than a girl, really. I would have taken her for a slave, but it seems that these days, around your lordship's estate, one can no longer be so sure who, or what, one is dealing with.

"Be that as it may, she immediately divined my displeasure, and promptly invited me to look in on her ladyship's Oronsa, which—as the girl correctly suggested—was slightly lame in one leg. By the time I had completed this inspection, a number of the horses had been led out and more were following, allowing me to perform my usual offices without any undue delay.

"I cannot know all that transpired behind the scenes, or why your stable-master—your new stablemaster, I am led to understand—was not present from the start, so I make no charge against him. It is clear to me, however, that this young female, whoever and whatever she may be, deserves principal credit for ensuring that all of your lordship's horses, and those of your guests, received due attention, and that I was able to continue on to my next call with minimal delay."

Mav's gaze had been shifting between the Earl and the Master of Horse as the reading progressed. Haldrow's face had only grown grimmer and more set.

The Earl refolded the paper and replaced it in his pocket; slowly, deliberately, precisely. No one else spoke. Mav shifted slightly, trying to take a little more weight through the crutches.

"Haldrow," said the Earl at last. "It seems to me you really should be thanking Mavrys, not castigating her."

"I don't know *castigatin'*, m'lord, but she were underminin' my authority."

"Really? How would it have looked if she hadn't intervened, if she'd just left the vet to stew in his own juices? Would that have been better for your authority?" The stress on the final word was subtle, perhaps even unintentional... but it was there.

"With all due respect, m'lord, yow ain't bin here this week. Yow ain't seen... I said it afore yow came, and I'll say it again, when there's trouble, she's allus there."

Mav sensed Hedric was about to speak, but Haldrow was too caught up in his own indignation to see it. It wasn't exactly interrupting his master, but it was too close for comfort. "M'lord, I can't be doin' wi' her any longer. Either she goes, or I do."

Hedric sighed. He took off his glasses, inspected them nearsightedly, brushed a speck off one lens with his cuff, and replaced them. "Haldrow. Take a moment. Take a deep breath. Consider very carefully if you really want to stand on that statement."

Haldrow did not take a breath. "I'm sure, m'lord."

The Earl sighed again. "I'm sorry you feel that way, but if that's your decision, I must respect it." Haldrow's chin came up, a gleam entered his eye, but it died instantly as the Earl went on, "I think, under the circumstances, it will be best if you take a month's pay in lieu of notice."

Whatever Mav thought of the man, it was hard to watch his face crumple, his body sag, as he registered what his master had just said. Finally he stumbled out a few words. "M'lord, yow can't mean... Am I really to understand yow're takin' her side over mine?"

"The problem, Haldrow, is that there didn't have to be two sides. You made it so, and you sealed the deal by issuing that ultimatum." Haldrow looked as if 'ultimatum' was another word he didn't know, but it became clear enough as the Earl went on, "Even after I specifically invited you to reconsider."

"I only thought yow meant... somethin' short o' dismissal, for her."

The Earl removed his glasses again, this time pulling out a crisp white handkerchief and wiping the lenses thoroughly. He looked younger without them, yet also more weary.

There were motes of dust in the air, clear in the light from door and window, but Mav realised they weren't why he did it. It was something he did to give himself time, when he needed to think or when a strong emotion threatened to cloud his judgement.

The Earl replaced his glasses, settling them carefully. "I don't believe I gave you reason to think that. You set the choice yourself: *she goes or I do.*" he paused, glancing to left and right in the watchful silence. "I'm sorry it's come to this, Haldrow. You've served the estate well for... what is it, fifteen years?"

"Nearer twenty, m'lord."

"I suppose it is. Aye, I must have still been a lad, first time you held my horse for me. You've always been a good man with horses, and I shall gladly give you a character to say so. But a stable-master needs also to be good with people..."

Then there seemed to be nothing left to say. Haldrow stood for a moment, swaying very slightly, then gave a small bow, and turned away. The other hands parted to let him pass, but he stepped out into the daylight alone.

The Earl gave another heavy sigh. "*Good with people...*" he repeated softly, as if talking to himself, his eyes focused on nothing, or else on the motes that spiralled in the air disturbed by Haldrow's departure.

Finally he drew himself up, rolled his shoulders, turned towards Mavrys. "You told me a week ago that you could do the Master's job. Do you still think so?"

She weighed her answer carefully. "I am less certain now, my lord."

"Why so?"

"Because of what you just said. I thought the job was all about horses, and I know horses; I've known them all my life. I know what needs to be done to keep them healthy, and fit, and content. But you said the Master of Horse needs to be good with people. And I see what you mean. He—or she—cannot do everything, even oversee everything. He or she must rely on others." She looked past him to the assembled hands but their faces, shadowy or simply expressionless, were too hard to read. "And Haldrow taught me something about that."

"Did he now?"

"Yes, my lord. He... the problem with the feed, and with the vet, didn't need to happen. He wasn't a week into the job, and before that, lately, he'd been working with the carriage-horses. No one could expect him to know every last detail of the routines this side. But he didn't *ask*, not that I ever saw or heard. He didn't *listen.*" *And he didn't read Renfrith's charts and notes, possibly because he couldn't.* "He thought it was enough to go around giving orders, telling everyone, do this, do that."

"And you would do things differently."

"Aye, my lord." She didn't think—didn't *dare* think—that he might be offering something, made herself believe he was merely soliciting advice. "Most of the time, caring for horses is simple enough. They need food, water, exercise, grooming. Young ones need schooling, and then you're looking to see if they're suited to the 'chase, or the hunt, as a carriage-horse, or as a regular riding-horse. But that's the other thing. Horses aren't all the same—like people, I suppose. And it's hard for a Master to know every horse that well."

She paused, wishing for a sip of water, but there was none to hand. The room seemed to have grown stiflingly hot. "Everything I just said, everyone in this room knows it. But each hand knows some of the horses better than others—and better than the Master does. A Master needs to understand that." She thought of her father, and her eyes prickled. It seemed to her now that she'd rarely heard him give a direct order, had spent most of his time with the Carinnan hands asking questions. "A Master needs to trust the hands, listen to what they say, and then—most of the time—stand back and let them get on with it."

The Earl smiled. "A Master—or a Mistress?"

There seemed to be no words. She could only gaze at him, knowing that he—probably all of them—could see that her eyes were brimming.

✳

"I know this is a shock for you all," she began. "Believe me, it's a shock for me too. I'm sure you're all thinking, she's very young, she's a girl, she's a slave... Well, I am young and I am a girl and I can't change that. But I'm telling you now... I'd really appreciate if it didn't go any further, so I'm putting my trust in you, but I think you need to know. One or two of you know already, or may have guessed.

"I'm not truly a slave; I've only been living as one for a while. Maybe one day I'll tell you why... but my father was a gentleman. A gentleman, and one of the most admired breeders and trainers in Denvirran, perhaps in all of the Principalities. I could ride almost as soon as I could walk, and I spent every possible moment in the yards and the paddocks. So I may be young, but I've lived and breathed horses for fifteen years. It doesn't mean I know everything; there's always more to learn. But I'm not a novice, far from it.

"Most of all, though, I meant what I said before, to his lordship. You'll all know things I don't know. You'll all know particular horses better than I do. I expect you all have your favourites... and the horses have theirs. I'd like to match you up as best I can, make sure each of you has particular responsibility for the horses that suit you best. And then, with visiting horses, make sure they're shared out as fairly as possible."

There were a few nods, she thought. That seemed encouraging. Then a voice from the back. It sounded like Crimmon: "S'pose yow'll want to keep Oronsa for yowrself."

"Want to, for sure. Whether I'll be able to... Besides, before long, all these visitors'll be gone and her ladyship'll be back riding Oronsa herself. Till then... I am less than nine stone, after all.

"But we'll talk about this more soon. Meanwhile, there's a more pressing problem. We've been stretched anyway, with all these visitors. Renfrith's gone, and now Haldrow. We're two men down—"

"Three," said another voice.

"Tharsh..." said Mardom, trying for a placatory tone.

"We all know yow reck th' sun shines out o' her arse," said Tharshin.

"Dun't yow talk 'bout her like tha'," snapped Mardom, moving forward.

"Enough," said Mavrys. When nothing happened, she repeated it, louder, trying to make her voice crack like a whip, the way some gentry habitually spoke to their 'inferiors'. This time, it worked; seven startled faces turned toward her, and Mardom and Tharshin fell still, though they quickly renewed their intersecting glares.

Mav thought for a second. *Maybe that was just surprise. Need more...* In three paces she placed herself between them. She was all too aware they both stood almost a head taller than she, might weigh half again as much. She reminded herself that every time she stood in front of a horse she faced a creature far heavier again. Even a lightweight like Oronsa would be four times her mass. She had faced horses fearlessly when she weighed half what she did now. "It's all right, Mardom. Let Tharshin speak."

Tharshin looked down at her. His gaze was anything but friendly, but he unclenched his fists and folded his arms. "Yow're no coward, I'll give yow tha'. Though 'appen yow reck his lordship'll protect you."

"His lordship isn't here. But you're not going to hit me anyway, are you? You're not a thug like Renfrith and those so-called Rangers he conspired with."

In truth, she wasn't entirely certain. She was gambling; but even if Tharshin did have the impulse to strike her, she knew he wouldn't get more than one blow in. Mardom was close behind her, and she was pretty sure most of the others would not stand idly by either, not for that.

"No," said Tharshin after what had seemed an age. "I wun't hit a woman. But I wun't work under one either. Slave, free, gen'leman's daughter, dun't make no differ."

"That's your choice. And... I can't speak for his lordship, but I'll wager he'll say the same as he did to Haldrow. A decent character, and a month's wages in lieu of notice."

He looked at her a moment longer, then gave one curt nod and strode from the room.

Mavrys turned slowly, looking at each of the men in turn. All taller and heavier than she, all older, by five years or ten or twenty. "Is there anyone else who'd care to follow him?"

No one moved, and she knew then that the task she had taken on might not be altogether impossible.

"Very well," she said. "We're *three* men down. And with the stables as full as they are, we need help as soon as we can get it. Does anyone have any ideas?"

"There's horses down on th'home-farm," said Crimmon. "And they're 'tween plough-time and harvest-time. 'Appen they might lend us a lad or two while they're not too busy."

"That sounds an excellent idea. Even if it's only for a few days, till some of the visitors are gone. Would you like to head down there and ask? Do you need a note from me to make it official?"

Crimmon shrugged. "Reckon they knows me well enough."

"Aye," said Mardom, "He's down there every chance he can get."

"Oh, why so?"

"He's sweet on one o'th lasses in th'milkin' parlour."

Mav grinned. "Well, Crimmon, I'd like to know the answer as soon as you can... but I'm not going to know the difference if you take a few minutes to pay your respects."

"*Pay your respects?*" repeated Barrian. "Never heard it called that afore." Then he checked himself.

Before he could apologise, Mav smiled again. "I'm a gentleman's daughter. I'm sure I don't know what you mean."

CHAPTER 37

MAVRYS

A woman in the yard, stepping down from the block beside an unfamiliar dapple-grey. A woman in a smart, if well-worn, green riding-habit, pushing back a fashionable token veil on a small-brimmed hat. Mav's heart seemed to land in her boots. Lady Deneval of Carinnan... No, Mav recalled, she was *Dowager* Lady Deneval now. And Carinnan was gone...

"Mamma..."

Deneval's expression changed, shock rippling over every feature as if she'd been physically struck. "No..." she said, on an almost voiceless breath. Then, a little stronger. "Irmavel? Is it really you, or is this some nightmare?"

I'm very much afraid it will be, thought Mavrys. "Yes, Mamma, it's me, and I am very well, thank you very much. I hope you are—"

"If you're well, why are you walking with a stick?"

That was actually a good question. "I'm getting over a bit of an injury."

"What? Did you fall? I've told you a thousand times, horses are dangerous."

"You have, Mamma. I don't even think 'a thousand' is an exaggeration. But, no, I wasn't—"

"You're very saucy all of a sudden. Are you planning on acting like a boy as well as dressing like one?"

Mav looked down. Not half an hour before she had been thinking how well her new outfit was working out. Dressing more like the lads did was another way of minimising the distance between them. *Meanwhile, the distance between me and my mother is wider than ever.*

She sighed. Her mother was here, now. They would have to talk; they didn't have to do it in front of the entire yard. "I'll get someone to look after your horse. And then, if you come this way, I'll make you some coffee."

❋

"Who told you I was here? Was it Brellas?"

"No, it was not. As far as I am aware, he doesn't yet know I'm here."

"Then who was it?"

"You have no right to demand an answer. You have no rights at all. You forfeited any right when you absconded, when you made yourself ridiculous."

"I'm ridiculous now, am I?"

"Well, just look at yourself. Shaven like a slave, and—"

"—Stop. Have you not taken in that there are Dawnsingers here? The *Master Prime* is here, at Skilthorn. She is the ruler of the Sung Lands, or the nearest they have to a ruler. In the Sung Lands a shaved head is a mark of honour."

"We are not in the Sung Lands. And I am sure even Dawnsingers don't dress themselves in boy's clothing."

"Really? How would you know what Dawnsingers do or don't do?"

Lady Deneval sighed. "Do you really think all I read is society title-tattle and fashion reports? But I'm not here to bandy insults with you. I'm here to take you home."

It was hardly unexpected. Indeed, Mav had considered more than once, usually while on Oronsa's back, what she might say if the worst should happen. She didn't feel fully prepared, but she did have an answer to hand. "Home? What home? Carinnan is gone."

"You know what I mean."

"And then what? Brellas isn't going to marry me now, you know."

"No man is going to marry you looking like *that*," snapped Deneval, "But put you in a decent dress, and a wig... Or fine head-wraps are acceptable. Admittedly usually for the more mature lady, but—"

"—You really think that's all it takes? That as long as I look acceptable he'll take me back? Do you really think the way I look is all that matters?"

"No, of course not... but it'd be a mighty improvement over the way you look right now."

"That's your opinion. Not mine."

"You're still a minor. You have no right to an opinion."

"Really?" Mav didn't know whether to laugh or cry. She found herself doing a little of both. "I have no right to an opinion? No right to have feelings? You can say that and yet you still call yourself my *mother*?"

Perhaps because she was half-blinded by tears, the slap took her completely unaware. There wasn't even a great deal of force behind it; her mother wasn't a big woman, or a strong one; but, caught off balance, Mav staggered back to fetch up against the saddler's bench. Suddenly she was all too aware of all the sharp tools there. What would be most effective? A hawkbill knife? Or perhaps just an awl?

She shuddered. *I'm not* that *far gone.*

"Mother," she said, forcing calm into her voice, though she hardly felt it. "Let's just stop a minute. Stop screaming at each other. I would bet every lad in the yard is out there listening to us by now. Can we just talk, quietly, like civilised women?"

"Are *you* behaving like a civilised woman?" said Deneval; but she did at least say it in an even tone.

Mav grasped the edges of the bench behind her, feeling its rough texture, the deep gouges and score-marks: settling herself, until she could reply in like manner. "We keep coming back to how I look. And... I know it must have been a shock to you. But did you ever stop to wonder *why*? Why am I here, looking like this? Why did I leave home in the first place?"

"Of course I asked myself."

"Well, you know, I tried to tell you. It seems to me I spent weeks trying to tell you. Trying to explain how I felt about being married to a man I scarcely knew, didn't care for, a man twice my age... d'you know, he must be closer to your age than mine?" She laughed. "Maybe *you* should marry him. That would solve all our problems, wouldn't it?"

Deneval stared at her. "I suppose you're right; he is closer to my age. But there's still a decade between us. Men don't marry women ten years older than themselves unless the woman has a fortune in trust."

"The Earl did. Oh, maybe not ten years, but five. And J—the Countess—I mean, she wasn't the Countess then, obviously. She certainly didn't have a fortune."

"You seem very well acquainted with the affairs of the Earl and Countess."

"She's the reason I came here. You remember the stories, around the time of their marriage, and again more recently. I read every one I could lay my hands upon. Something about her, her story... it called to me. I thought if anyone would understand how I felt, she would. And she did."

"She did?" repeated Deneval, bemused. Mavrys could easily imagine the confusion her mother might feel. On the one hand, *my daughter is acquainted with a Countess*; on the other, *this Countess aided and abetted my daughter's rebellion.*

"She did," said Mavrys. "She agreed that the best way for me to escape notice was to appear as an enslaved. And not just as a masquerade; she said I would have to live the life. Just as she once did herself."

Deneval looked thoughtful. Mav recalled her words: *Do you really think all I read is title-tattle and fashion reports?* No, her mother was not surprised by the reference to Jerya's time as a slave. "Irmavel," she said, and Mav decided not to protest—this time. "I truly am I trying to understand. But... you said the Countess said you would have to live the life of a slave. But I walk in here not even three weeks later and I see you giving orders to free men."

Mavrys considered. "One moment." She walked past her mother to the door, looked out, was not in the least surprised to see every one of the hands in the yards, trying with varying degrees of success to appear occupied with some useful task. "Have none of you anything better to do?" she asked, but mildly. "Mardom, could you step in here for a moment, please?"

"O'course, ma'am." Mavrys choked back a laugh. He'd never called her 'ma'am' before.

"Mardom," she said as he stepped into the relative gloom of the tack-room. "This is my mother, Lady Deneval."

"Honoured, my lady." Mardom made a decent attempt at a bow.

"Now, I am sure you all must have heard a lot of what we said in here."

"Aye, ma'am. At th'start, anyhows."

"And did anything occur to you?"

"Aye, ma'am, sohappen I was wonderin' if'n I should run up to th'house, tell th'Earl?"

"Why would you think that?"

Well, 'tain't even a week since he lost a second Master o'Horse. Dun't think he's like to be best pleased losing another so soon."

"Master of Horse?" said Deneval, staring in turn at the hefty lad, then at her daughter.

"I prefer to say Mistress of Horse," said Mav.

"Master, Mistress, it makes no difference. How can you... it's ridiculous!"

"Mardom, I think you were absolutely right. I think you should ask the Earl if he can come down." She turned back to Deneval. "You can tell him to his face that putting me in charge is ridiculous."

"The Earl himself put you in charge?" said Deneval, looking and sounding utterly bewildered. Mav almost felt sorry for her, but then she remembered what her mother had tried to do, and hardened her heart. Outside, she heard Mardom's steps racing across the yard, light on his feet considering his size, turning fainter as he reached the track, fading away. "You're not even an adult, for heaven's sake. And you're—"

"Please, Mamma, don't even say it."

❋

Lordship sends his respecks, had been Mardom's message, *but he's unavoidably detained. He'll come when he can.*

With that she would have to be content, for now. She could almost see the wheels turning in Deneval's head: was that a genuine message from the Earl, or just some stalling tactic that Mav and the lad had somehow cooked up? The doubt was clear: could Mav really have the Earl's backing? Could she really bear the unheard-of, probably scandalous, title: Mistress of Horse?

Several times in the couple of hours that followed, Mav had to leave her mother alone, to go and check on something, to answer a query from one of the hands, to help walk some of the horses down to the main paddock. Between whiles they circled around each other, metaphorically and occasionally literally. Mav felt they were having the same conversation each time, in slightly different words, but it could be distilled down to this:

"I'm your mother, darling. Of course I want you to be happy."

"Mamma, I *am* happy, truly. Just lately, running this yard, it's the happiest I've been since Papa..."

"You may think you're happy now—" This with an inflection on 'think' that made it very clear Deneval thought Mav was deluding herself. "—But will you still feel that in a year's time? Five years? Ten?"

Crimmon looked in to report some problem with the harness for the carriage-horses, and Mav went out to discuss it with him. On the way back she glanced at the track leading to the house, and stopped in mid-stride. A moment later she was hurrying back to the tack-room just as fast as she could while still leaning on her stick.

She found her mother still moodily picking at oat-farls and cheese. "Mamma, come out here."

Deneval mumbled a protest, but complied. She moved stiffly, Mav noticed; no doubt the ride had been longer than she was used to. For the first time she wondered why she hadn't come by carriage... and then wondered if there was still a carriage for her to use.

Deneval followed her to the gates of the holding-paddock. She was a few steps behind when Mav stopped and bobbed a curtsey, but Mav clearly heard the sudden intake of breath.

"Mamma," she said, struggling to contain the smile that tugged at the corners of her mouth, "May I present the Lady Jerya, Countess of Skilthorn? Countess, this is my mother, the Dowager Lady Deneval."

Deneval's eyes were cast down as she held a deep curtsey. Jerya's smile was for Mav's benefit, a promise; *Today, for you, I'll play the part.* "Lady Deneval, this is an unexpected pleasure." She held out a hand, encouraging Deneval to rise. "And may I present to you my friend and honoured guest Master Evisyn, the Master Prime of the Guild of Dawnsingers."

This was as close as Mav had even been to the Master Prime; serving in the house, she had seen her many times, but only at some distance. She was taller than Jerya, lean, sharp-featured, with the look of one who'd spent much of her life out of doors.

Deneval was saying something about being honoured. After a few moments, Jerya grasped an opening. "I am delighted you are here, my lady, and I hope we shall have more converse very soon. I trust you can stay a few nights at least? Perhaps you would care to join my husband and me at dinner tonight?" As Deneval fumbled out a reply, Jerya went on, "At this moment, however, Master Evisyn and I have limited time. You might say we are playing truant... but we both felt the pressing need for some fresh air, a little exercise." She turned to Mavrys. "How is Oronsa? Is she fit to ride?"

"The vet gave her a clean bill of health yesterday, my lady. I was thinking I'd take her out for an hour myself, ease her back into the swing of things. But of course now..."

"I'm sorry to deprive you." She looked down, taking in the stick. "You are fit enough also?"

"I reckoned I'd give myself the same medicine as Oronsa."

"There must be another horse you could take, if you'd care to join us. We won't be going far or fast if Oronsa's—" There was a snort from behind her, then a great grey head nuzzled her arm. The Countess laughed uninhibitedly. "There you are, my darling. I'm glad to see you still remember me." Mav handed her a half-carrot from her pocket, and Jerya held it out to Oronsa.

"I'd be very happy to join you, if you're sure..." said Mav.

Jerya gave her a mock-severe look. "I wouldn't have said it if I wasn't."

"Thank you, my lady. The dapple gelding, there, hasn't been out today. And that tall roan is yours, I think, Master Prime? I'll get some help to fetch them over and get them saddled up."

"I've saddled my own horse hundreds of times," said Jerya, with a darting look at Master Evisyn.

"I don't have the luxury of owning my own horse, but I must've thrown a saddle on a thousand times."

"Is that a challenge?"

"Why not?"

"Why not?" echoed Jerya. "What about you, Mavrys? Are you up for a contest?"

"I think I'm at a disadvantage," she said, brandishing the stick. "Perhaps I should be referee."

"You think we might cheat?" Jerya's tone was indignant, but there was merriment in her eyes. Mav was aware of her mother watching every moment, dumb-struck in disbelief, if not awe.

The saddles were fetched, the horses lined up, and Mav gave a count of three. It was clear within moments that Jerya was fast—but Evisyn was faster. When both had declared themselves finished, she checked both horses carefully before confirming the winner. A few minutes later, Mardom having saddled the gelding for her, they were riding down the track that led to the mill and then up towards the Wold.

"I can't thank you enough," she said, bringing the gelding alongside Oronsa as Evisyn drifted a few paces ahead.

"It's no trouble," Jerya shrugged. "We'd been planning to grab some time today anyway, and if we can do you a favour into the bargain... I'm glad to see your leg's nearly healed. I was sorry to hear about that. And of course the other... incident."

"I'm sorry Oronsa got over-run."

"Don't be. Sounds like she got you out of a nasty spot."

"Couldn't have had a better mount."

"Yes, and I'm sure you don't want to relive it all again." Jerya glanced around, called ahead. "Take that fainter track on the right." Turning back, she remarked, "I like your new outfit, by the way."

"Thank you, my lady. I'm not sure my Mamma was so taken with it."

"Or with your..." She glanced across. "You know you're not even acting the part of an enslaved any longer? You don't have to keep shaving."

"I know, but I'd started out on the basis I'd keep it up until my birthday. And... I found I like it."

"Yes, I did too." Jerya gave her a smile. "Your birthday's, what, a couple of months away?"

"Nine weeks yesterday."

The track dipped and they splashed through a ford. Watercress beds filled the stream either side, swaying gently in the current. "Yes, it was a shock when I was shaved the first time," said Jerya pensively, "But I soon got used to it. Had to, with everyone around me being bald too. Got used to it, learned to love it, especially when a fresh shave meets a fresh pillowcase. And I always found shaving myself was kind of a meditative experience."

"You shaved yourself? That sounds risky."

"We had better razors back there. But, yes, you had to be careful. That was rather the point, I think."

They rode on as the slope ahead began to steepen. The track swung right then back left to ease the gradient. "Mavrys," said Jerya as they came out onto the bare crest. "I think I understand why you might want to stay bald for a while longer. And why shouldn't you have that right? But there is a... a new factor in the equation. I don't know how your mother found you...?"

"I have an idea about that." *Tharshin...*

"Anyway, the point is, she has. And in law we can't keep you here if she wants to remove you. She could, in theory, have us arraigned as accessories..."

"I'm sure she won't..."

"In theory. But perhaps it's encouraging that she came here alone. She might have brought a carriage, a couple of burly footmen to drag you into it. And I hope that seeing the way things are here, seeing how we value you, may make her reconsider what's best for you."

"I'm very grateful to you for everything you've done. Especially today."

"Today?" Jerya laughed. "Yes, we put on a bit of a show for her, but it was *fun*. Which is something that my life's been rather lacking lately... And now, going for a ride, talking like this... none of it is any hardship, Mavrys. No, indeed, this is the most purely enjoyable afternoon I've spent in weeks." They came up alongside Evisyn, who had reined in by the pillar that marked the high point. For a few moments the three women sat and simply gazed out over Skilthorn.

From here, Mav had learned, you could see more of the estate than from any other vantage point. A vast mosaic of fields and woodland, the velvety green of the parkland, the inset jewel of the lake. And from here, as nowhere else, you could take stock of the house and all the other structures that surrounded it: the slave-quarters, the stable-blocks, the walled gardens, orchards and glasshouses. A little further off, down the valley, the home-farm, the mill and granaries, the outlying barns and byres, the open-sided shelters for the deer, the saw-mill and the great racks where timber was seasoned. She knew that there were still other structures that she could not see, hidden in the forest or masked by the escarpment behind her, including some that remained a mystery; what exactly was a bloomery, for example?

Beside her, Evisyn let out a breath. "It even exceeds the scale of our College. I suspect more of our supplies come in from outside: it really looks like you produce everything for yourself here, that you could be your own little self-contained world." She leaned forward to see past Mav, grinned at Jerya. "You could have another College of Dawnsingers here."

Jerya grinned too. "I'm sure that would go down well."

"Like I say, self-contained. Who'd even need to know?" She chuckled. "We could all pretend to be enslaved, eh?" Sobering, she transferred her gaze to Mavrys. "As I hear you did, for a while."

"I did, Master Prime. And I had intended to continue for longer. Though I... with respect, I do not like the word 'pretend'. I tried, as best I could, to live that life."

"Aye," said Jerya. "You did... for the most part." She glanced at the timepiece she wore on a slender bracelet. "And still we are all slaves to time." She heeled Oronsa and moved off North along the ridge.

A little later, descending through the shallow combe that disrupted the line of the escarpment, Mav found herself riding alongside the Master Prime.

"This fellow doesn't quite seem to like the descents," said Evisyn.

"Try him with a longer rein," said Mav. "Some horses like to look further ahead. Or just to feel free."

"Hm," said Evisyn after a moment. "That seems to help. Thank you." She looked across. "I'm told you once expressed interest in becoming a Dawnsinger?"

"I did, but..." Mav felt almost too embarrassed to speak. "It was a silly notion. I didn't know what I really wanted to do. Only that I needed to escape the fate my mother had planned for me. I had no idea what it means to be a Dawnsinger, or whether you would even consider me."

"I gather Railu set you straight."

"She did... I think I'd have been a very bad Dawnsinger."

"And now you have another role... which seems to suit you much better."

"Yes, very much. If only my mother could see that."

Evisyn sighed. "As a Dawnsinger, you might think that I know nothing of motherhood. But of course I had a mother, and still do. And as a Peripatetic... you know what that means? Most Singers do not travel much, but the Peripatetics do. I still see my mother, every few years." She looked about her, gaze settling on the mill just below, with its lazily turning wheel. "And, as Peripatetics, we see much more of everyday life than most Singers, especially those who live in the College... and all that is a very roundabout way of saying I am no expert in motherhood, but I'm not altogether ignorant. And it is very much my impression that mothers love their children. If there are exceptions, they are so rare as to have escaped my notice. Maybe some are more openly affectionate than others, but... sometimes it is the ones who seem less demonstrative who are most affected when a daughter is Chosen. Even when there is little outward display, one can sense deep feelings behind the facade."

Mav hesitated to ask, but curiosity won out. "Are the mothers—or the girls—are they allowed to refuse?"

Evisyn pursed her lips. "Traditionally, that is not the case, but we are trying now to work out how we can be less rigid. I am not sure it is in the best interests of the Guild if some of our Postulants start out feeling resentful, even traumatised."

There was much more that Mav wanted to know, even if it was nothing more than idle curiosity about places she would surely never see. However, though Evisyn was surprisingly easy to talk to, still she was the Master Prime of the Guild of Dawnsingers. They rode on a way in silence, companionable enough, down past the mill, across the bridge with its low parapets, onto the homeward track.

It was a few minutes more before Evisyn spoke again. "You know your own mother, and I do not. Still, sometimes one can be *too* close to something. Just as making the Crossing and coming here, seeing a different way of life, may help me see my Guild more clearly when I return.

"Perhaps I should not say this. Perhaps it is presumptuous of me. Perhaps it is simply too much to claim on a few minutes' observation. But I am the Master Prime, and rather too accustomed to people hanging on my every word, so I will say it. I watched your mother when we met, and when you were talking with Jerya, and I am quite convinced that she loves you. I am far less sure that she *understands* you, but if there is willingness on both sides, understanding can grow."

"Aye," said Jerya, coming up on Mav's other side as the track broadened. "I'd listen to this woman, Mavrys. She's no one's fool." She leaned forward, waving a wasp away from Oronsa's ears. "There was one more thing I didn't quite get to say to you on the way up earlier. You said you like being bald and you had a mind to stay that way at least until your birthday. And I said you should have that right. What I didn't say was... if your mother hates it, and I saw how she was looking at you... I won't suggest full skirts and corsets and all the other folderol; that's hardly compatible with your duties, is it? However, letting your hair grow—at least for now—wouldn't impede your work, and it might help reconcile your mother just a little more to the rest of your... You know, to her, it must be a shocking transformation."

"Yes... but, you know, I think that's *why*... why I want to be this way."

"What, to rub her nose in it?"

"Perhaps... no, I felt the same before she appeared. I want it for *myself*; to be transformed."

"Well, I'll say no more about it, though I do urge you give it further thought."

The track curved slightly, and up the long gentle rise ahead Mavrys could see the roofs of the stables, and a gleam of sunlight on the flank of a bay horse. Even at their languid pace, she knew it would be only a few minutes before they were back. *I don't want this ride to end.*

Mav's sigh drew Jerya's gaze. Her eyes seemed sympathetic, but she made no direct comment. "There is something I want to ask you, if I may. If it seems intrusive you must tell me, but I am asking for my own sake, not to pry into your life."

"Please, Countess, ask me anything."

"Countess." Jerya repeated the word with a kind of heavy amusement. "Aye, there it is. They tell me I am part of the nobility now but, as you know, my birth was humble by any standards. You, however, were born and raised among the gentry..."

"The lowest rank of the gentry, my lady. And yours is the next-to-highest rank of nobility."

"Nevertheless, in some ways you have more experience of all this than me. Let me get to the point. I suppose you had wet-nurses and nursemaids and all that; governesses too, later."

"Nursemaids and governesses, certainly. I suppose I had a wet-nurse too, but I don't remember."

"No, you'd be too young." Jerya lapsed into pensive silence.

Thinking to fill it, Mav said, "I think I must have been a trial to my governesses, always running off to the stables."

"Having been a governess myself, they have my sympathy... But really I'm thinking about your mother. About the generality of mothers in what people call the polite strata of society. How, having given birth, they seem to delegate the rest of the care of their child, all the most intimate aspects, to servants. Sometimes to enslaved. I wonder... doesn't this create a distance between mother and child? A... detachment?"

Mav wondered at the question. If Jerya were really asking for her own sake... then why? Still, she owed this woman a lot; the least she could do was give the best answer she could manage. "I am not sure what I can tell you. You have lived in several different worlds; I've only ever known the one. I think I was unusual, not because I didn't spend much time with my mother, but because I *did* spend so much with my father."

They were back between the paddocks now. On their left, a grey, one of the horses the Dawnsingers had ridden in on, tracked them, matching their ambling pace.

"Well, you *are* unusual," said Jerya. "Whatever the reason may be. It's why I like you so much. I only hope your mother can see it too."

CHAPTER 38

JERYA

"I find it hard to grasp that this Congress is so nearly over already. I look back and ten days seems like no time at all... until I recall... I seem to have spent half my time running about making sure there's enough food and drink for everyone, that the right rooms are ready for the right people at the right times. I could probably have left all that to our wonderful staff, free and enslaved, who've done such extraordinary work. And if I had, then I might have found a little more time for an activity which I feel I've neglected over this time... thinking."

Jerya let her gaze roam, relieved to see she had everyone's attention, or at least the appearance thereof. "There's been plenty of talking, and you might say, what's that but thinking out loud? Perhaps I should say that what I've missed is *reflection*. Well, perhaps that will come later, as we disperse over the next few days, back to our homes and our regular occupations."

She sipped water. "I dare say you all know that I was once a Dawnsinger. Four months, near enough, as Postulant and Novice. Then, too, I felt almost bombarded with new knowledge, new ideas, but never quite had the time to step back and ponder, to absorb and digest it all. That was fourteen years ago, yet I sometimes still feel as if I'm coming to terms with it all.

"Anyway, I've been reminded of one particular moment from that time." She refrained from mentioning that it was Railu's 'trial' that had sparked the memory. "A moment when I got myself into trouble by asking a question... though perhaps that's not quite fair. What I was hauled over the coals for was asking the question in the wrong way at the wrong time.

"I'd been in a history class—in those days I was flitting about the College, taking in all sorts of classes, trying to cram eight years of Postulancy and Novitiate into... well, I didn't know then just how short my time would be; and, yes, it's entirely my own fault that it was so short." She met Evisyn's gaze, and received a small nod.

"The question I asked was one of the simplest, and yet most profound, that anyone can ask: *how do we know?* Specifically, in this case, how do we know that the Journal-Keeper was female?" She gave a brief account of the Four Fragments, and the place of the Journal-Keeper in the history of the Guild. "I'd already raised this question with some of my contemporaries—Railu will remember—and seen that it shocked them, so I might have anticipated what would happen when I asked it in class, in front of fifteen third-year Novices. Ostensibly, that's what I was disciplined for, disrupting the class and disturbing the other students, and maybe that's fair. But what stayed with me—and Tutor Yanil, I'm sure, remembers a conversation we had about it—what stayed with me was that no one could actually give me a convincing answer. Nowhere in the First Fragment does the Journal-Keeper state that she is female, or make any other reference that would establish the fact. One of her close companions, also, is never referred to by any pronoun that would tell us whether they are female or male.

"Of course, the Journal-Keeper and her companions—if that *is* the correct pronoun—were the forerunners of a Guild which for three and a half centuries has been exclusively female. This certainly *suggests* that the four of them, also, were female...but it's only inference, however compelling, not established fact. When I was being disciplined over it, someone used the term 'axiomatic'. I could have put it differently; I could have said *taken for granted*."

She sipped again, eyes darting around the room. "Well, Dawnsingers aren't alone in sometimes taking things for granted. I've often observed that, even among people who are thoroughly committed to better conditions for the enslaved, they're often startled when I raise the question of whether we really need slavery at all.

"Today, of course, I can say, look to the West, to the Sung Lands. When I arrived in the Five Principalities, I was nineteen years old and I'd barely heard the word 'slave'. I found out what slavery was in the most..." She smiled. "The most *empirical* way. I found out by *being* a slave.

"That's just one example. Just as slavery still seems, to many here, perfectly natural, so it seems perfectly natural that schools and universities are reserved for males. You don't have to go further than our own library, not fifty paces away, to find learned tomes that earnestly proclaim that men are rational, women intuitive... even, in one case, 'man's mind is orderly, woman's is chaotic'." Again she looked around, gaze resting momentarily on one male delegate and then another. "I must admit that my first impulse was to throw that particular volume on the fire... but of course that would have been a *chaotic* response." She was pleased to catch a flurry of soft chuckles and snorts of amusement, not all in a female register. "Instead, let me just say that the hands that make your beds, clean these rooms, put food in front of you, are almost all female... and the minds that arrange all this, exclusively so. We—I include myself, but only as one of four or five—have organised a Congress for more than forty people, at exceedingly short notice, with remarkably few stumbles. Could *chaotic* minds really have done all this?

"Well, I mustn't be sidetracked by my indignation, however justified, over certain things. I'm aiming at a broader point.

"We can look back on several specific advances at this Congress, not least the mutual recognition of qualifications between the Denvirran Association of Physicians and the Healers of the Guild of Dawnsingers. We very much hope the corresponding bodies in the other Principalities will follow suit, and I'm sure this is something the Guild delegation will hope to raise in their visits to Sessapont and Troquharran.

"But more than this, or any of the other specific agreements, I hope this Congress will serve as a catalyst in spurring all of us—and many more, thousands of people, who aren't here—people in both lands, high and humble... in spurring all of us to take stock and reflect afresh about things we've taken for granted; things we've always regarded as inevitable, as perfectly natural."

She gave a soft, low chuckle. "I guess I've always been given to asking awkward questions. When I was just a girl, growing up in Delven, in a place that only had twenty-three books in its library, I asked a lot of questions that no one could, or would, answer. The response I got most often from the aunts who raised me was, 'it's the way things are'.

Jerya paused a moment, then repeated, "*The way things are*. Even at an early age, ten or eleven, if not younger, I knew that wasn't good enough. I wanted better answers, and I still do. Why do sticks float and stones sink? Is slavery really fixed for ever in the Five Principalities? Why can't girls go to school, to university? What is a nebula? 'It's the way things are' isn't a good enough answer to any of them. It's an insult to every curious child." *I'll never say it to my own child*, she vowed inwardly. "'Perfectly natural' isn't good enough. Taken for granted isn't good enough.

"If, in years to come, this Congress is to be remembered for anything, let it be this: it made us—every one of us—stop and reflect and question our most cherished assumptions. It made us ask, again and again, 'how do we know?'"

She stopped again, smiled. "One thing I do know. Our kitchens have once again served up a fine feast. I hope it will give you all energy for dancing. To give the staff time to clear this room, I must ask that everyone now move promptly. It's a pleasant evening if you would like a short stroll outside, or drinks are available in the picture gallery. I hope to see all of you here again in an hour or so."

CHAPTER 39

MAVRYS

She did love the green silk dress. It had also been the practical choice, because when you were cramming things into saddle-bags in the small hours, silk packed smaller and lighter than most fabrics. Even so, it had looked a little sorry for itself when she finally unpacked it, but hanging for a couple of days had refreshed it fairly well.

There were still problems. It was not designed to facilitate dressing oneself. A brief trial had shown her that ridiculous contortions would be required to lace the back. She had to hope she could find Vireddi. One of the others would do at a pinch, but it ought to be Vireddi. The dining-hall seemed the best place to start, and for once her luck was in. *"She brav?"*

"Me proper brav. She?"

"Firm. Howver, me need she help."

Vireddi did not hesitate. *"Now?"*

"If she go for can."

"Me go for. How?"

"Sheme go for go room?"

In the room they still shared, Vireddi's eyes widened as Mav unbundled the green dress. *"Me see what for she need me help."* She lifted it from Mav's arms, laid it on the bed, smoothed out what creases there were. Mav quickly shed chemise and breeches, then lifted the petticoat to let Vireddi settle the former round her hips. *"Brav,"* she said, stroking the velvet. *"All go for same?"*

"*All same.*" Mav thought of the formers that house-slaves wore under their skirts, tubes of scrap fabric stuffed with more scraps, or, for the unlucky, with horsehair. There wasn't time to show Vireddi how the velvet rolled up, but she sketched the elongated triangle with her hands, mimed rolling it tightly. Vireddi nodded, her own hands tracing the smooth taper the former made on each side.

Initially, Vireddi laced the dress too tight, as if compensating for the lack of a corset. "*Nen, me go for dance. Me need breathe.*" If there was a Patter word for breathe, or indeed dance, she hadn't learned them.

Once she was dressed, Vireddi stood gazing at her, even lighting a second candle to see better. "*She proper fetchin,*" she said at last. "*Granduns go for laud she. Only...*" She reached to run a hand over the faint stubble that had begun to darken Mav's scalp.

Mav thought about what she wanted to say and decided it was beyond her command of Patter. "You think I should have long hair?"

Vireddi shrugged. "*Hair brav, spose. Me reck proper bal' go for more brav.*" Again she trailed her fingers up the back of Mav's head. It felt like when the hair stood up of its own, in fear or excitement, but almost *more* so.

"In a minute I won't want to go at all," said Mav, abandoning Patter.

"*Me brav for she stay.*"

"*Nen, me hafta.*" She wondered how to say *my whole future might be at stake*. She could say it in Plain... but Vireddi seemed to understand well enough.

"*Me ken.*"

"*Vireddi. She brav...*" But what was the word for friend? "You're a good friend. You're the best friend I could have found here."

Vireddi said nothing, just stepped in and kissed her on the mouth.

The impulse to stay was more powerful than ever. Mav had to steel herself to step away and begin her journey out of the slave-quarters into wider passages and grander surroundings.

❋

"I'm not a very good dancer," she said.

Brellas smiled. "I, however, am an excellent dancer."

"I see you don't indulge in false modesty."

"You do me credit, then, in accepting that such modesty would be false?"

How different this was from the directness of her talk with Vireddi, half an hour before. Obviously Patter could be used for lies and deceit, but surely it would be hard to skirt elegantly around things, to dress them up in metaphor and allusion.

"Be assured," he said, taking her silence for reluctance, "If you agree to dance with me, I shall take it for nothing but what it is. I think, however, your lady mother will be most gratified to see us on the floor together."

Directness, she decided, was best. "That is what I'm worried about. If I dance with you, she's bound to start thinking I might still be... open to persuasion."

"Whereas, I take it, your mind is as resolved as when last we spoke?"

"Very much so. Perhaps even more so. I believe I see my future more clearly than I did before."

"And my delegation is due to depart tomorrow." *Yes, and most of the others too. At least a dozen horses to get ready. I'm going to be late to bed and early to rise.* "We may, then, regard this dance as a valediction."

"Very well," she said. "I will dance with you. One dance, and on one condition."

"And what might your condition be?"

"That you ask my mother to dance also. And when she says no, you will be at least as persistent as you have been with me."

✹

As it turned out, one dance was enough for her anyway. Not because she hadn't enjoyed it: Brellas was indeed an excellent dancer, and she had soon found herself caught up in the movement and the music. But her leg had begun to ache, causing her to miss a couple of steps which she should have made easily. Brellas, swiftly grasping the situation, had guided her expertly through the swirling couples to a clearer space near the windows, which stood open to the soft summer evening. He made solicitous enquiries; she explained, and he offered to fetch a drink.

While he was gone, her mother appeared at her side. Recalling Jerya's advice, and her own resolve to be pleasant, Mav gave her a cheerful smile.

"Did you enjoy that, my dear?"

"I did, very much, but I shan't dance again this evening."

"Surely Brellas will be glad to oblige you once more?"

"I'm sure he would. It's not that. My leg isn't quite ready for this."

Deneval frowned, no doubt thinking about how Mav had received her injury, but before she could say anything Brellas was back, bearing two glasses. He handed one to Mav and gallantly offered the second to her mother.

"Thank you, sir, but I am sure your need is greater than mine."

"The gavotte *is* rather thirsty work," he agreed. "And when one hopes to dance as long as the musicians keep playing, refreshment is essential. But only if you are sure..."

"Quite sure, thank you, sir."

He tasted the wine. Mav sipped her own more cautiously. Stable work started early, but balls generally ran late. She'd be lucky to get more than four hours sleep tonight: she didn't need to meet the morning with a sore head too.

"Speaking of dancing," said Brellas, "I am avid for more, but the young lady is sadly incapacitated."

"Sadly," agreed Mav, though she really didn't mind. "But one dance was sufficient to show me that you are most accomplished."

He gave a polite bow. "You are too kind. But I do believe I can lay claim to some modest proficiency in the art."

You told me straight out you were an excellent dancer, she thought. But if he thought such a direct claim might work less well with Lady Deneval, he was probably right. Indeed—a slightly strange thought—he probably knew Mav's mother better than he knew Mav herself. He had surely spent more time with her. *Arranging things,* she thought with the usual flare of indignation. *Well, now you can arrange to dance with her.*

Perhaps he read her mind, or her look; perhaps he was simply ready to ask anyway. He drained half of his wine, deposited the glass on the nearest table, then gave a slight bow. "I believe the next dance commences in a few minutes. Lady Deneval, if you are not already engaged, might I dare to claim the pleasure?"

"Regretfully, I must decline your kind invitation."

"Then you *are* already engaged?"

"No, I am not. I have come to the conclusion that my dancing days are over."

"My dear lady... may I dare to ask why?"

Deneval said something about her age, and Brellas protested dutifully, but Mav hardly heard them. She had a sudden suspicion that she knew the real reason, and it was, in the end, the same reason that her mother had come to Skilthorn alone, on horseback, and not in a carriage. The same reason that the dress she wore was one Mav had seen at several balls before. A lady who could no longer afford to host a ball, to entertain in other ways, might, sooner or later, find herself also receiving fewer and fewer invitations. If you declared yourself too old to dance, perhaps that made it easier to bear the lack.

She came out of this reverie just in time to hear her mother sigh and say, "Well, perhaps one last dance would do no harm." It wasn't the most graceful way to accept an invitation, but it was the result that counted.

Clutching her wine-glass, still almost full, Mav picked up a plate of dainties from the table, then wandered out through the open window onto the terrace. She placed plate and glass on the broad stone parapet, then leaned her hands on it, taking a little weight off her right leg. The evening air was cool on her shoulders and scalp, but for now she welcomed it.

Behind her she heard the music start up again. Further along the terrace, a couple emerged from another of the tall windows, began to dance again, moving into the shadow. She heard a foot scrape, a slight gasp, then a muffled laugh; evidently the woman was an unschooled dancer. A moment later, as the couple spun into the light again, she saw a bald head. The woman, laughing at her own missed steps, was Railu.

Mav withdrew her gaze, but she was loath to venture back inside. She had encouraged her mother to dance with Brellas; she was not so sure she wanted to witness it. Instead she stayed where she was, sipping occasionally, picking at the food, looking out over lawns and woods in the deepening twilight, and thinking.

She was as sure as she could be that her suspicion was right. Her mother's circumstances—and presumably also her uncle's—must be even more straitened than she'd realised. *And Mamma no doubt believes I can solve it all for her by marrying Brellas.*

Never mind that she didn't want to. Never mind that she had made it abundantly clear to him that she had no such desire... and, being an astute man (as well as a more honourable man than she had previously imagined), if she now changed her tune, he would surely smell a rat. No, even if she could bring herself to sacrifice all that she had found here, all that she had become, marriage to Brellas was no longer on the cards.

On the other hand, despite all the friction that had arisen between them, she could not bear to think of her mother reduced to penury. *But why is it up to me to put things right?*

Along the terrace, the laughing couple had fallen quiet, and were moving away. Mav was glad of it. She could not begrudge Railu her happiness, but it contrasted too pointedly with the trend of her own thoughts.

She was still no nearer an answer, if there was one, when her mother emerged beside her.

"You were right," said Deneval, "He is a wonderful dancer."

"Yes, Mamma, but you mustn't think—"

"—Stop, darling, stop. Just for once, don't jump straight in as if you know what I'm going to say before I say it. Your father did the same and it was not his most endearing habit. I wanted to say thank you. I know you told him to ask me to dance. I suspect you told him not to take no for an answer... And thanks to you I've had a delightful half-hour. So let's not mar the moment."

"I am glad, Mamma, I truly am. I do want you to be happy, you know."

"And I you. What else should a mother want for her only child, after all?"

"I know. I only want you to understand that what makes you happy isn't necessarily what makes me happy. I think if you can just accept that, then we can move forward, we can talk to each other instead of endlessly talking past and around each other."

"Perhaps... but it is hard for me to believe that the life you seem to be living now, the way you look, the way you've been dressed... that these will really make you happy. It's hard..."

"And yet you know that, ever since I was a little girl, my happiest times were in the stables, around the horses, or riding."

Deneval uttered a long sigh, looking away into the twilight. Beyond the yellow bands of light from the interior, colour seemed to be draining from the grass and trees, everything in shades of grey beneath an indigo sky. "I always thought that was all about... you and your father."

The last words seemed almost to be wrenched from her; and in that moment a lot of things made sense to Mav in a way they never had before. "Oh, Mamma... yes, I loved him. But a lot of the time what I loved was the sharing. Feeling the same way about the horses, about riding, about breeding a winner... You know I was devastated when he died, but it became ten times worse because I was losing everything else too."

Her mother took her hands, held them for a time. "You know he's gone."

"I know. Oh, every now and then I'll be doing something, something really inconsequential, fiddling with a bit of tack or reckoning up the next feed order, and I'll think I hear his step behind me. Just for a moment I'll expect him to say something, or simply lay his hand on my shoulder in passing..." Her voice faltered, steadied. "And in a way he is there, he'll always be there, inside me. But the other things are there all the time. They're real."

"And you truly believe it will still be the same in five years, ten years time?"

"As far as anyone can know how they will feel five or ten years ahead, yes, I do. And, you know, it is the most incredible luck that I have this opportunity." *It didn't feel lucky when Oronsa and I were running for my life, but now...*

"I think I understand, my dear, or at least I begin to see a glimmer. But what am I to say to your uncle? He is your legal guardian, you know."

Mav's spirits plunged. *Just when we seemed to be getting somewhere.*

She forced herself to think rationally about it. Or try to, anyway. At least when it came to her uncle, things were not so complicated by... well... love. Still, she wasn't sure why the first question that came to mind was, "Does he know you've found me?"

"I haven't written. I was hoping to be able to give him definite news—more than simply that I found you, I mean. But, Irmavel—or must I call you Mavrys now?"

"Call me whatever you like." It couldn't hurt to be magnanimous, like refraining from shaving her head for a few days.

"Irma, darling, there is something I haven't told you. The horse you took... he was threatening to report it stolen. He still could. He is quite a valuable beast, I believe?"

"Yes," she said bitterly. "The best of the few that were left. I didn't take him by chance, you know. Perhaps it might be thought spiteful of me... but do you understand my anger? It was a good business that my father, and his father before him, made. And in not much over a year, uncle Thiseman has contrived to run it down to almost nothing."

"I confess I do not understand these things, my dear, but he says the market has been difficult."

"Markets are always difficult. It's not as if Father never took a loss on anything. But... he first showed me something of the accounts when I was eleven, and between then and his death he always came out ahead, or at worst broke even, in every single quarter."

Lady Deneval gazed at her daughter. Half her face was painted gold by the light leaking from the ballroom, the other half in deep shadow, relieved only by the slightest glimmer of the eye. It made her expression unfathomable.

"Mamma, I can hardly feel as if I 'stole' the horse. More as if I rescued him. Can you understand that?"

Deneval nodded slowly; that at least was clear. "Perhaps. But my brother will not see it that way."

"In any case, I can get him back. He's only at livery somewhere, half a day's ride away. Or if you let me do it, I can have him sold. I'll get a better price than uncle Thiseman ever could. And whatever I might think about the true rights and wrongs of it, he can have every penny."

"No doubt that would relieve his worry considerably, and soften his anger."

"What does *he* have to be angry about?" demanded Mav. Receiving no answer, she went on in a softer tone, "I can put him in a sale under the authority of the Earl, probably within a week. I know his bloodlines by heart."

"That sounds well, my dear, but you know the horse is legally Thiseman's property." Mav snorted in disgust, but the fact was inarguable.

"I imagine there is a pigeon-post, or a relay, between Skilton and Cleaving," she said. "We could secure his permission within a few days."

"*If* he sees fit to give it."

"He'd be a fool not to."

Deneval said nothing. Mav suspected they were both thinking the same thing: *unfortunately, he is a fool.* "I suppose you will have to be particularly persuasive."

"I can try... but I wonder...?"

"What?"

"Since you are on such good terms with the Earl and Countess... a few words from them would go a long way."

"I've had a lot from them already. But I suppose asking one of them to pen a few lines is not excessive."

Suddenly, Lady Deneval shivered, and in the same moment Mav was freshly aware of the steadily chilling night air on her stubbled scalp, her bare shoulders. "I suppose it's time to go in," she said, but reluctantly, loath to exchange the fresh stillness of the night for the stuffy, noisy, ballroom.

"I would appreciate another drink."

"I could take another half a glass, I suppose." They turned away from the night.

Mav took one sip from her fresh glass, before applying herself more diligently to a new plate of food.

"You should be careful," said her mother, softening the apparent rebuke with a smile, "It's all too easy to put on weight once you stop growing. And then your corsets need to be laced ever tighter."

As if I care about corsets... But she only said, "I don't believe I *have* finished growing. And I can eat more, with the active life. Besides, I've hardly eaten anything tonight."

And one place I'm sure I am still growing is across the shoulders. She'd caught herself in a mirror on the way to the ballroom, and sight had confirmed what feeling had already indicated; the dress was definitely tighter around the chest and shoulders than last time she'd worn it.

She did not mention the observation. Concord between herself and her mother was still delicate, and she did not think Lady Deneval would relish the notion of her daughter developing her muscles.

"You know," said Deneval, "To you, selling the horse here seems much the best plan, and I really can see why... but I cannot guarantee Thiseman will see it the same way. The idea that you can get a better price than he can would be an affront to his pride."

"It's a damnfool kind of pride that can't face facts. Especially when there's a profit in it."

"Doubtless you're right. Still... fool or no, for the next eight weeks he is your legal guardian, and—"

"And he may as well be yours too," said Mav, suddenly seeing the picture. "Oh, *I'm* a fool. All along I've been thinking this was between you and me. That it was all about you trying to control my life. But it's not like that. You're... you're just caught in the middle. Not you trying to control me, but him trying to control you. I should have seen... I'm so sorry, Mamma."

She reached, took her mother's shoulders, held her gently. For the first time she saw clearly that they were the same height now. "If there are sides, Mamma, we have to be on the same one."

Deneval smiled, but weakly. "I'm glad to hear you say so, darling... but what can we do? Eight weeks from now you will be free—free of him, anyway. You will have a life here. It still seems a strange life to me, but if it's what you want... but I have no other life. I can't train horses. I can't... I can't do *anything*."

"They made you believe that," she said. "Especially uncle Thiseman. Don't let them...."

All at once the hubbub and heat of the room, the smells of candles and wine and rich food, were too much. She would have accepted the chill of the night air for the sake of its clarity, but there had to be another alternative. And as soon as she framed the question she had an answer. "Let's go somewhere quieter, where we can think."

Her mother had no objection, and willingly followed Mav towards the exit. But just before they reached the doors a few overheard words almost stopped her in her tracks. "Mamma," she said in an urgent whisper. "Go down the passage straight ahead. Third door on the right; a small library. Wait for me there. I'll just be a few minutes."

To keep her backtracking inconspicuous, she headed first for a slave carrying a tray, and smilingly accepted a couple of glasses of wine, though for her own part she had no intention of drinking any more. Returning, she slowed as she passed the group; it would look innocent enough, if anyone was looking, as a slight knot formed momentarily in front of her.

"—time should we assemble, then?" the voice said. A dart of certainty almost made her spill the wine in her hands. She could clearly hear the same voice, the words, *reassemble the force...*

All doubt vanished, she changed course again, deeper into the room, scanning for a glimpse of Earl or Countess. Failing that, Railu would also do well, but Railu was nowhere to be seen. She did, however, soon locate Earl Hedric, and hurried towards him as fast as swirls of bodies would allow.

"Forgive me for interrupting, my lord," she said breathlessly, "But I must speak with you urgently."

He nodded to the Dawnsinger he'd been conversing with; Mav thought her name was Yamil or some such. "What is it, Mavrys? Trouble in the stable?"

"No, nothing like that. It's—do you see that man over there? Azure coat with yellow lining?"

"The pale fellow who keeps sweeping his hair back?"

"That's the one."

"What of him?"

"He's the one I heard."

It took him only a second. "As in *over*heard?"

"Yes, exactly."

"You're sure about this? I seem to recall you said the man was a Troqu'er? That fellow's with the Denvirran delegation."

"He has the accent, my lord."

"Then I had better have a word with him as soon as may be. Do you—no, let's keep you out of this."

"Thank you, my lord. I need to talk to my mother anyway. She's waiting for me in the small library."

"Go, Mavrys, with *my* thanks. I must find my wife."

✳

Lady Deneval looked up from the hearth, in the act of adding another log to the fire. She brushed her hands as she straightened. "Didn't seem worth finding a slave to do it," she said. "And I have thought I may need to accustom myself to doing more of these things for myself."

Mavrys, who had raked out the ashes from that very grate more than once, said nothing.

"I've been thinking, my dear. Trying to remember exactly what I said."

"What you said when?"

"Leaving home. I was in such a hurry I only left a message with Landrup. If I'd written it down I'm sure I'd remember more clearly. You know how you can see—"

"—Mamma! Just tell me."

"Sorry, darling. I don't think I said Skilthorn, I really don't, but I'm sure I said I was taking the South-West road... and I... I might have said I was going to meet a Countess."

Why would you say that? Mav had to wonder, but she had a more acute worry now.

There had always been a copy of *The Peerage* on the family bookshelf, but she had only looked into it when obliged to do so, when a governess was trying to drum some 'important' information into the head of a girl whose heart was elsewhere.

She had read little and retained less, but she did recall that Denvirran Principality had only three or four Dukes; the number of Earls might just reach double figures. The North-East road surely led to at most two or three of them. And if Deneval had said 'Countess', thoughts might readily turn to the one Countess who had recently been in the public eye.

"I'm sorry, darling." Her mother had been studying her face anxiously. "I didn't mean to. I wanted to find you myself."

"And bring me back."

"Because I thought it was best. Not just at his instigation, because I genuinely believed it."

It was all too tempting to issue a stinging retort, or simply to burst into tears, but Mav could see that her mother was thoroughly sensible of the grievous consequences likely to follow from her actions, and needed no further burden.

"Well," she said bleakly, "What's done is done. Chances are he'll be here in a few days. The question is: what are we going to do about it?"

"I don't know, darling, but if there's anything I can—"

"Wait here. I have an idea."

When she returned to the ballroom, the evening seemed to be winding down. Neither Earl nor Countess were in evidence—and neither was the man in the azure coat. Nor, she quickly saw, was Brellas, and she didn't know where his room was. *And even if I did, would knocking on his door after he's retired be such a good idea? Last time I did anything like that...* She hastily quelled that thought; it was not a memory she savoured.

I'll just have to catch him in the morning.

"We're just discussing a few things about the horses," she said, manoeuvring so Brellas's horse screened them from the rest of his company. "They'll need water mid-morning. There's a pond in Pentshank that's always fresh. Feed them when you feed yourselves... well, you know, I'm sure."

He nodded, grasped the saddle, about to lift his foot to the stirrup, but Mav had more to say. "Master Brellas, tell me honestly, why did you want to marry me? It can't have been for money."

He smiled slightly. "May I speak frankly?"

"Please do. I know your time is short."

"Very well. I am not exactly in want of funds, but supporting a bachelor establishment is one thing; sustaining a marital home is quite another. If I can progress my career as I believe my talents and application merit, then my income will appreciate significantly. The obstacle is that, in courtly circles, position matters. I have the education of a gentleman, but not the social standing."

I'm glad you gave me the concise version, she thought wryly. She knew how delicately any discussion of financial matters was generally approached, and any admission of impecuniosity could be social suicide. He had, by those lights, spoken both candidly and concisely.

"And by marrying me you would gain that attachment to the gentry?" She hardly needed to wait for his affirmation. "Then let me ask you this: isn't it the case that you would achieve the same result by marrying my mother?"

He blinked rapidly, and seemed lost for words.

"The difference being," she pressed on, "That instead of acquiring a step-mother who would be a constant presence, you would gain a step-*daughter* who would trouble you rarely, if at all?"

"I cannot believe that your mother would be content to see you so infrequently," he said, adding gallantly, "Nor indeed can I conceive of such sporadic intercourse as anything to be wished."

"You're too kind, sir. But I am sure the Earl and Countess would welcome you any time." *And such a connection couldn't harm your social standing either.*

A brusque voice called his name. Leaning to look past the horse's head, Mav saw that his companions were already mounted.

"All I can say is that you have given me food for thought," he said as he swung up into his own saddle.

"I hope you find long rides conducive to contemplation."

"If Finshal is not in one of his excessively garrulous humours, I should." Mav held the horse's head as Brellas made a small adjustment to the length of the reins. "And I suspect he has a sore head this morning. Whereas I, having danced much and drunk but little—"

The impatient voice was raised again, and hooves began to clatter on the setts.

"Tell your mother I shall write," he said hurriedly. "But pray do not allow her to build any further expectation. I must ponder... and now, I must go." She released the bridle. He gave her a swift, uncertain, smile as the horse eased into motion.

CHAPTER 40

RAILU

The far side of the lawn lay in deep shadow, as if full night had already arrived. Beyond, the trees of the arboretum, in all their diversity, were silhouetted against the Western sky, a pale citrine glow behind plum-coloured clouds. Pipistrelles flickered over them, just as they had on summer evenings in the College of the Dawnsingers.

Turning to face Skelber, Railu saw how their footprints appeared as dark absences in a lawn no longer green but dove-grey. She knew that her shoes, and perhaps the hem of her skirt, would be damp. Well, the skirt would survive, and she could hope the shoes would be retrievable. If they were no longer immaculate, they would serve for less exalted occasions.

"Miss Railu," said Skelber, "May I speak frankly?"

"Please do. I hope you always will. I haven't been schooled to delicacy and euphemism like a gentle lady."

"No, and I believe... I believe that is part of what I wanted to say, even at risk of repeating myself...Miss Railu, you are like no other woman I have ever met. I doubt very much I shall ever meet another like you. And that fills me with..." He stopped.

"Whatever you have to say, please say it."

"I am trying... but unlike you I *have* been schooled in the *proper* way of addressing a lady. It now seems inadequate, but old habits are hard to break." He drew a deep, ragged breath. "The first thing I must say is... only a few days ago I feared you might never speak to me again. Let alone *dance* with me."

"I hope your toes recover soon."

"I'm sure they will... but I would endure more than bruised toes, much more, for—" He stopped. "But I should not bleat of endurance, not to you. What have I ever had to endure, compared to you?"

"Your wife died, did she not? If... you don't mind if I mention it?"

"It was a long time ago."

"And so were the hardest times of my life. So maybe we shouldn't dwell on them. I only meant you shouldn't belittle your own trials."

"I think you are too kind," he said, "But I thank you."

"You were saying? Before we digressed, you were saying about dancing with me?"

"Yes. Dancing with you is a delight—" He pressed on over her stifled giggle; she knew her own limitations all too well. "—That I never dared hope to enjoy. However... It was borne in on me this evening that only a few more days remain. Then my delegation, too, will depart, and naturally I shall be expected to go with them."

"Of course."

"In the normal course of events, I do not know that there is much hope that our paths will ever cross again... And that is a thought which fills me with... should I hope that you feel similarly, or should I think it would be kinder if you didn't?"

"Well," she said, "I don't know what I *should* feel. I'm not even sure what I *do* feel in lots of ways... But when you raise the prospect of our never meeting again, I think I know how I feel about that."

He looked directly at her then, the fading sky-glow catching in his eyes. His face was unreadable, but the sudden grasp of his hand and the fervour in his voice were clear. "Miss Railu..." Again she wanted to say how she detested 'Miss', but there would be a better time for that. "When you agreed to dance with me tonight, I felt as if I had everything I could wish for. But of course it's not so. As soon as I think about leaving here..."

"I won't always be here either. I'll stay a few days longer, till the Dawnsingers leave, but then I must get back to my own home, my own work." *Since I still* have *my own work.* There was more to be said between them about that, but now was not the moment. "And you know Duncal is a lot closer to Denvirran than Skilthorn is."

His gaze, as best she could tell, was locked on hers. She wondered, if she could see so little of him, how much he could see of her. Perhaps a little more, since she was half-facing the light that spilled, tangled with music, from the ballroom.

"That is true," he said thoughtfully. "Though not as close as I might wish."

"And I suppose both of us are rooted where we are."

"Yes, indeed. At least it is not an impossible distance. But will you forgive me if I..." He broke off. "You said I could speak frankly, so I hope you will not find it offensive if I say that we are not... not in the first flush of youth."

"That's nothing but the simple truth. I'd be a fool to be offended by that."

"Yet it is generally considered ill-mannered to allude to a lady's age."

"I am thirty-two years old," she said. "Am *I* ill-mannered for saying so?"

"Not at all. We are not children, and we have—in our different ways—considerable experience of the world. I would hope we might know our own minds where the young might hesitate."

She could not resist teasing him a little. "Some might say that it's youth which acts on impulse; maturity reflects before action."

"I believe that what I feel now goes far beyond mere impulse.. However... as you know, my wife died, fully twelve years ago. Whatever else I take from that, it bore in on me that life is short. I have probably squandered too much of it already, feeling sorry for myself, brooding on loss. Time is a fleeting thing."

"And so is daylight, I fear. If we don't go in soon, we shall have trouble finding our way."

"Another reason to get to the point. Miss Railu, do you believe that there is a possibility that our futures, yours and mine, might be tied together?

And is that... for you, is that not only possible but something to be wished for?"

She thought for a moment, standing on the dew-silvered lawn, hands still joined with his. The first cool breath of a night-breeze brushed across her scalp.

"To be wished for... I can't even quite grasp the *possibility*. It's too new... it seems fantastical."

"Perhaps we might step over here..." he said. She looked where he indicated. There was a tree, artfully placed at an angle of the lawn; just a shape in the night, but she thought from an earlier walk it might be a cherry. It would shield them from view, if anyone were looking out of one of the dark windows of the house. Not that an observer would be able to see much in any case. In the East it was no longer possible to distinguish trees from sky; clouds blocked all sight of the stars. Only in the low West was there still a faint amethyst glow through rents in the spreading clouds.

He moved towards her so slow and tentative she almost urged him to hurry up. The first kiss was a brief, featherweight touch. Then he pulled back, as if examining her expression, though surely he could see nothing. She could barely see his outline, the gleam of an eye.

The second time, the kiss lasted far longer, and when he finally broke away he was trembling. "Miss Railu, I dare not continue, or I fear I shall be unable to contain myself. I only hope I have not already overstepped...?"

She rested her hands on his shoulders. He was only a little taller than herself. "Have no fear, Skelber. I too feel the urge to prolong these moments. But you're right, I'm sure. It would be prudent to go in now, take some time for reflection."

"Also," he said with that disarming dry chuckle, "Our absence might be remarked. In fact... you might prefer that we return separately? For your reputation."

Railu gave a chuckle of her own. "You're assuming that I *have* a reputation."

He said nothing, only moved close again for one final kiss. This time one hand cradled the back of her head, and when he pulled away again he let his fingers trail slowly across her scalp above her right ear.

She thought a little about that as they walked, not speaking, back across the lawn toward the ballroom terrace. It was a fact, though never publicly discussed, that many, perhaps most, young men of the more prosperous classes had their first sexual experiences with enslaved women. She had attended the births of several babies whose origins lay in just such couplings. She thought, too, of the youths who had attempted to *buy* Jerya and herself. Close on fourteen years ago, but the memory was clear. In the night she shivered, hoping at once that Skelber had not noticed or that, if he had, he put it down to the cold air.

Some men continued to pleasure themselves on the enslaved all their lives. The Prince of Sessapont, evidently, was one such, and the old Earl, Hedric's uncle, had been another, as long as he was able. It almost seemed to her that Dortis's apparent tenderness towards that vile old man sprang from the fact that he had not 'taken advantage' of her, even when he might still have been—just—capable. In the warped values of a slave society that might be enough to suggest that he was doing her special honour.

She had no grounds to suspect that Skelber was one of those men who were forever drawn to slaves, or those who looked like slaves. No, she had every reason to believe that he valued and respected her, as a physician, as a person... as a woman.

Every reason to believe... but not certainty. Not yet.

PART THREE
PARTINGS AND MEETINGS

CHAPTER 41

JERYA

"That was a fine address you gave last night," said Evisyn. "And a bit of your history I never knew about."

"The time I was disciplined?"

"That would have been in Brinbeth's class, I take it?"

"It was."

Her face must have given her away, for Evisyn smiled. "Brinbeth's a stickler, but she's fair. And she's not one of Perriad's cronies."

"They seemed close enough that time."

"Agreeing on one thing doesn't make them best friends. Anyway, Jerya, thank you for the reminder about not taking things for granted." Her raptor gaze was firm on Jerya. "Though... do you really think the Journal-Keeper might not have been female?"

"I think it highly likely that she *was*. I was only ever trying to say that we don't know."

"The point is well made, and you may be sure that I take it." There was a voice behind her. "I'm sorry, Jerya, I must check my harness. It's a long road to Sessapont."

"I wish you a good road—and a good reception when you get there."

"Well, we have some idea what kind of man the Prince is. Always better to be forewarned—yes, Tanour, one more moment." She turned back to Jerya. "Time always harries us—as you also said last night."

"Did I?"

Evisyn grasped Jerya's shoulders. "I'll tell you this, Jerya, whatever else we may achieve this season, I can already go back to the Conclave and tell them my making the Crossing was fully justified."

"Does that mean you'll be back?"

"Not next year. Probably not for a few years. But the Master of Peripatetics is an able deputy." She smiled. "And there will be letters. By the start of next Crossing season, we'll have a mail service of some sort... and that's another achievement of the Congress."

She gave a firm squeeze, released her grip, and with a last quick smile turned away.

A moment later Yanil was there in her place. "I'm sorry I didn't get to spend more time with you," said Jerya.

Yanil made a 'no matter' gesture. "It seems to me you've spent most of these weeks trying to be in two places at once—if not more. Don't apologise because you can't do everything."

Jerya knew that was good advice, though she also knew she might struggle to stick to it. "You always were the voice of reason for me." Yanil only smiled. "I know, I know, I didn't always follow..."

"Where would we all be now if you had?"

"Who can say? Especially as I didn't even consult you on the biggest choice of all."

"You still count that the biggest?" Yanil looked around. Jerya could guess what she was thinking: *This house. This estate. Two thousand slaves. Being a Countess...* "Seems to me you must have made a few big decisions since then."

"True enough. But I'd never even have faced any of the others if I hadn't made that first choice."

"For ten years and more I thought that was a sad day for the Guild. Now I'm not so sure."

Jerya only looked at her. For once, she had no words.

Then Evisyn was there, and the horses were led out, and there was no more time.

"May I hope we'll see you in Drumlenn before we start the return Crossing?" asked Yanil.

"I hope so. But..." She thought for just a moment about what to say. "If I can still ride with a big belly."

Yanil looked bemused for a moment; Jerya recalled her thought about how Dawnsingers, especially those who rarely left the College, were removed from the realities of others' lives. Then her face cleared. "Something else that would never have happened had you remained, eh?" A direct gaze, eyes keen behind the lenses. "I trust you're happy about it?"

"Happy, bemused, delighted, terrified... Tell you true, Yanil, these past couple of weeks I've hardly had time to think about it."

"May I tell Sharess when I get home? Or would you rather write?"

"I'll write to her, of course. I'll hope to put the letter in your hands myself, but if I can't I'll send to Duncal, care of Railu. But by all means tell her, if you'd like."

"I believe I'd like that very much. Thank you, Jerya."

Evisyn was mounting, and the other Singers were following. There was no time for more words, only a swift but strong embrace.

CHAPTER 42

MAVRYS

Each day she could try to convince herself just a little more that the worst would never happen, that Uncle Thiseman had not perceived the implications of her mother's reference to 'a Countess'. Surely, if he had, he would have been here already. After further discussion, they had decided that they would wait until her birthday to notify him of the whereabouts of his horse and offer to sell him profitably.

Each day she began to feel just a little bit closer to safety.

Until…

In a soft afternoon drizzle Mavrys was walking back from the farther paddock when she spotted a young slave leading a brindle gelding. The slave she knew by sight if not by name; the horse, however, was all too familiar. Her heart made a dive for her boots and for a moment she wanted to flee, but she collected herself, told herself she'd faced worse things than her own uncle.

By the time she met slave and horse she was able to speak evenly. "I'll take him from here, thank you."

"Thank *yow*, Mistress." Many, and not only among the enslaved, were still uncertain how Mav should be addressed, but 'Mistress' suited well enough. *I am Mistress of Horse, after all.*

"The gentleman left him at the front of the house, I presume?"

"Aye, Mistress." The lad didn't question how she knew the rider was a gentleman. It was possible, but not very likely, that a lady would choose a horse of this size. "'Appen he weren't th' sort to be received at any door but th' front."

Some would have classed that as impertinence, but Mav let herself smile at the lad. He had just summed up her uncle in a sentence.

She thanked him again and led Belhati toward the yard. The horse had cocked his ears when he heard her speak; now he nuzzled her neck as if checking by smell what sound had already told him. Under other circumstances she would have laughed, but knowing the confrontation had always been likely did not make its imminence any easier to face.

✳

The horse had recognised her immediately. Her uncle, at first glance, did not, barely sparing her a glance as he strode past, making instead for Mardom. He was, after all, a considerably more imposing figure; and he was, at that moment, still rubbing down Thiseman's horse. "Are you in charge here?"

"No sir, not me, just one o' th' hands."

"Well, no matter. I'm looking for my niece. Seventeen, not o'er-tall, light red hair. Name of Irmavel."

"Ain't seen anyone looks like that round here, sir. Nor anyone answerin' to tha' name." Mardom's reply was perfectly truthful, and perfectly respectful, but Mav could clearly see he was enjoying himself. *Possibly a little too much...*

For one wild moment she entertained the thought. *I could still make a break, run up to the house. Get myself freshly shaven, put on a slave's skirt and apron, disappear into the crowd.*

She knew, though, that it would be futile. At best it would delay the inevitable—and her uncle would be all the more wrathful when she was discovered.

She stepped forward, stopping where her uncle could, she guessed, just see her from the corner of his eye. "He means me, Mardom."

The reaction was almost comical, but she knew that to laugh would be a grave mistake. Thiseman stared, jaw slack, then shook his head, drew breath as if to speak, then snapped his mouth shut again. The entire pantomime was then repeated almost exactly before he finally gave himself a shake and found words. "Where's m'damn horse?"

Mav's hackles rose. It wasn't just the accusatory tone, irritating though it was; what really rankled was the way he simultaneously laid claim to and yet dismissed the 'damn horse'. She almost demanded if he even knew the animal's name. She herself had known Garrenva since he was a very new foal teetering on spindly legs.

With an effort she tamped down her ire, answered with a cool she assuredly did not feel. "D'you mean Belhati, uncle, or Garrenva?"

"Garrenva, o'course, damnit."

"He's perfectly safe, uncle. He's some distance from here, but you can fetch him tomorrow if you wish."

"Why the devil wouldn't I wish it?"

"My mother informs me that you received an offer of six hundred for him. If you would allow me to place him in an auction instead, I believe—"

"Allow *you?*" he said.

Mav's hackles rose at his scoffing tone, but she wrestled her anger into submission. "I do have some experience. The Earl would allow me to sell under his auspices."

"Even if that were true," he said, "Your mother misled you. It's not merely an offer. I have agreed the sale. Lorzon and I shook hands on it."

"At six hundred?"

"Aye, your mother had that right."

Then you're a fool, or you've been swindled. She took a deep breath. "Uncle," she said carefully, earnestly. "If I were selling him, I would set a reserve of a thousand at least. I would expect the sale to realise a minimum of twelve hundred, probably fifteen."

He shook his head, scepticism doubtless battling with avarice. "Six hundred is a perfectly fair price for a decent riding horse."

"For an everyday mount, yes. But Garrenva is no everyday horse. Do you know his full stable-name?"

He blinked. His silence spoke volumes.

"He is Carinnan Garrenva," she recited, "By Eirnyerey out of Susinda. The dam is Carinnan born and bred but she was served at Tallentine by Ramspent, himself by Daychant out of Kenmilt. And a notable champion."

"But Garrenva's never been raced."

"True, but he's been well-schooled over jumps." *Often by me,* she thought with a sharp pang. "Papa would have tried him in races this year. Any prospective owner will know he's a gamble, but if he was a proven winner, the price would be still higher." She let that thought hang a moment, wondering if it would give him pause, make him think for a moment about the opportunities he'd squandered. "But he's still only four years old, and even if he doesn't achieve everything he might have done, with those bloodlines he'd be able to command decent stud fees."

"Fees?" he said, showing interest as if for the first time. Then he shook his head. "All very well, but I gave my word, and as a gentleman—"

This was too much. "A *gentleman?* Does a *gentleman* impose a husband on a girl who has no interest and no attachment to him?"

"I have your best interests at heart." It almost sounded as if he believed it.

"Well, it doesn't matter now. Brellas won't marry me anyway."

"You are still a minor, still my ward. You have no right to refuse."

"No, uncle, I didn't say I wouldn't marry him. I said he won't marry me. I've spoken to him more than once—"

"—What, he's here?"

"He was until three days ago." *I wonder if he's written to my mother yet...*

"What did you say? What the devil have you done?" Face darkened, Thiseman stepped toward her, right hand raised, but then he became aware of Mardom's bulk, looming menacingly. Mav realised for the first time that the other hands were also clustered around, and none of them were looking at Master Thiseman in any friendly manner. Their loyalty made her eyelids prickle.

"Stand away from me, oaf," said Thiseman furiously.

"I ain't no gen'leman, I knows that," said Mardom. "Yow may be in rights callin' me an oaf. But I do know I'd never feel right in myself if'n I hit a lady—nor any female, come to tha'."

"I'll take no lectures on morality from a stable-boy," growled Thiseman, but he slipped his hands into his pockets and took a pace back.

Mav tried for a calming tone. "Brellas told me he aspires to the gentry. But it seems to me he has the qualities of a gentleman already. As soon as he learned he had been misled about my feelings on the matter, he withdrew his offer."

"Never mind your *feelings*, you stupid girl, what about your future?"

"I *have* a future. For the first time since my father died, I can see my way. I have a position here, an income."

"A *position?* What the devil do you mean by that?"

"The Earl and Countess have been good enough to appoint me Mistress of Horse."

"Mistress of — ? I begin to believe you have entirely taken leave of your senses."

"'Tis true, sir," said Mardom.

"Did I ask you? What is this, a prank, and you're all in on it? Well, think on this, no one makes a fool of me without consequences. What did she offer you to—"

"—How dare you!" cried Mav. Mardom's fists bunched.

Thiseman only laughed. "I'll believe it when I hear it from the Earl himself, and not a moment before."

'Appen yow wun't have to wait long," said a voice Mav recognised as Elenby. "His lordship's comin' down th' track now. An' th' Countess, an' your lady mother, Mistress."

"Come to bid you welcome, no doubt," she said. "But we have a couple of minutes. Tell me, please, who was it you agreed to sell Garrenva to?"

"Lorzon of Flemby."

The name sounded vaguely familiar. Had he been a client of her father's, or some other sort of associate? She couldn't remember clearly, but she was sure there was a connection. "He knows something about horses...?"

"He runs a few in local 'chases. Used to ride himself, but crocked his hip in a tumble a few years back, so now his son rides 'em."

"I have to say, uncle, you may have been a perfect gentleman throughout, but I don't think he has."

"What the devil d'ye mean?"

"He must know the horse is worth at least twice what he offered you."

Thiseman scowled and did not answer. *Yes*, she thought, *Nothing's harder to stomach than admitting you've been duped.*

"You'll be pleased to know I have resolved the situation," said Thiseman.

Mav turned, swinging in her chair to face him. She had heard the feet on the ladder, but assumed it was one of the hands with a message or a request. "Uncle..." she greeted him warily. She had not been overburdened with his company since his arrival, but she had never dared think all was well. She had immersed herself in work to keep the gnawing dread at bay.

"Niece." He bestowed a benign smile, but Mav's unease did not abate. He seemed altogether too pleased with himself.

She had to ask. "You said you've resolved the situation?"

"Indeed I have. The past few days I have been riding regularly to the town." He sniffed. "I would have expected somewhere a little more impressive, given its proximity to a great estate such as this, but at least it has an avian service."

This explained a few things. He had ridden off every morning; nothing unusual or untoward in itself, but Mav had noticed that he had always turned toward the house, a direction which offered no good riding routes save the main drive to the road. Each time he had been full of bonhomie towards all the stable hands, and their Mistress—almost as if he had truly come to terms with her new incarnation.

But the thing that set a small alarm sounding now was the mention of the avian service.

He smiled. "Are you not intrigued as to whom I've been in communication with?"

'Intrigued' is one word for it. "I'm sure you are eager to enlighten me."

"I sent to Lorzon to tell him the horse was safe and well." He smiled again. "But also to inform him that I had been made aware that he had perhaps not dealt entirely in good faith. For a man like him, reputation is worth a great deal more than the value of any one transaction."

This was no doubt true. And, thus far, quite harmless; but she could not shake the feeling that there was more to come.

"In composing my first missive to Lorzon, I recalled that we have more in common than just an interest in horseflesh. As I have a beloved niece, he has a nephew. Younger than you, not long past sixteen—"

Mav could contain herself no longer, and sprang from her chair. She had moved too suddenly; a startled Thiseman took a step back, but his foot found only the hole in the floor. It seemed for a moment that he hovered on the brink, arms flailing for balance, but then he dropped out of sight. A horrible succession of meaty thumping sounds ended with a final deadly thud.

For one brief, interminable, moment, she stood paralysed by horror. *I've killed him...* A dark corner of her mind observed that a dead uncle might solve all of her problems. Sick with shame, she dismissed the thought, shook herself from her rigor, and hastened down the ladder.

He lay like a rag doll on the floor. Her eyes went at once to the dark, spreading pool of blood. She knew another awful instant as she feared it might be coming from his head, but then she spotted the splinter protruding from the meaty part of his right forearm. It might still be bad, but she began to dare to believe it was not as bad as it could have been. He was breathing, albeit a rough panting, and a twitch of one leg suggested his spine might be intact.

"Help!" she yelled, straining for maximum volume, words rasping her throat. "Help in here now!"

It seemed an age, but it was probably only a few seconds before Crimmon appeared, with Mardom and several others close behind. "Who's the fastest runner?" she demanded.

"That'd be me, likely," said Leithen.

"Get to the house, then. Find Miss Railu—you know who I mean?"

"I reckon so."

"Ask if you're not sure. But do it quickly. Get her here."

He nodded and disappeared.

Mav had been around horses all her life, and where there were horses there could always be injuries, whether from falls or the occasional kick. She had picked up a rough knowledge of first aid, and she knew—her mind strangely calm now—that her first priority was to stem the bleeding. "Mardom, pass me a cinch strap off the bench. Or anything I can make tight." The wound was high on the forearm; she decided the tourniquet was better placed above the elbow.

"I am aware what you did for me," he said. His voice, as he lay nestled among pillows, might lack its usual resonance, but he spoke clearly and without any obvious evidence of pain or shortness of breath. "The... lady physician made it clear to me that your prompt action saved me from permanent damage to my arm. I am aware, and I am grateful."

He smiled, and Mav did her best to smile back, but... "I am sorry, Uncle. It feels like my fault you fell."

"No, it was stupid of me. I should have moved away from the opening. I knew it was there; I had climbed that same stair just moments earlier."

"And I'd been meaning for a couple of days to fix that splinter. Instead it got left and it went right through your arm."

"Please, Irmavel, do not distress yourself... I am aware you have thought me indifferent to your feelings. No doubt I have given you some grounds... I fear you believe I consider only my own position and my own comfort. I pray I may disabuse you of such notions. Having no children of my own..." A shadow crossed his chiselled features. Mav recalled hints and allusions, words overheard from her parents. There was some tragedy in Thiseman's past that she had never been made aware of.

"You are my only niece, but more than that, you are the closest thing to a daughter I ever had. I should have revealed my feelings more, been a better uncle to you, but... Well, what's done is done, and all we can do is strive to do our best in the here and now.

"And you must never think me indifferent or dismissive of your feelings. I know of old—and if I did not, I could see for myself now—how you feel about horses and their care."

He smiled again, and again Mav made herself smile back; but she wasn't ready to believe it would all be sweetness and light from here on.

"Which brings me to what I wanted to tell you the other day, before..." He shrugged, then winced as the movement jarred something in him. "I should have known all along that Brellas was not the right choice—however close to the ideal in some ways. A man so much older than you... and of course a city fellow, not a countryman. No, an admirable fellow in many respects, but hardly destined to be a harmonious partner for you."

He laughed. "I could have kicked myself for not thinking of him sooner; it can only be that the lad is so young. But it was always part of your objection to Brellas that he was twice your age. Riccart won't be able to lord it over you the way an older husband would; instead you can grow together. And—even better—he is another lover of all things equine. Quite as ardent as you, Lorzon tells me. A perfect partner for you."

He let his head loll back on the pillow. He was beaming, but Mav's heart had plummeted. *Think hard,* she commanded herself, *and think fast.* "I wonder you didn't think of him first, if he's so perfect."

"I know. I could kick myself, as I said. It can only be that he wasn't of marriageable age till very recently. Not in respectable circles."

Chapter 43

Railu

As the bride entered, Railu allowed herself a small smile. Mavrys had made it very clear she did not want to be escorted down the aisle by her uncle—still less 'given away'—and a search in the codices in Skilthorn's main library had revealed that the Sessapontine Rite specifically allowed this departure from the norm.

Her smile widened as she saw that Mavrys had indeed changed out of the green dress and now appeared in her plum-coloured riding-habit. It was clean, and decent quality, but it was not what people generally expected to see a bride wearing. There were indrawn breaths, a few mutterings, in the rows behind. She wasn't even sure who most of the people were; probably many were townsfolk who fancied the spectacle of a wedding, or—more likely—hoped for some free food and drink afterward. Well, unless they had the means to convey themselves to Skilthorn, they would be disappointed in that.

She saw a frown on Thiseman's face. He was a good-looking man, at least when he smiled. Older brother to Mavrys's mother, he had to be past forty, but appeared neither overly worn, nor softened, by time. One of those, perhaps, for whom an active life counterbalanced an equal love of good wine and food; she'd seen evidence of the latter with her own eyes. But smiles, even then, were on the rare side. She had a feeling the frown was nearer to his natural expression. She preferred the honest puzzlement that she saw on the broad young face of the groom, Riccart.

He was looking earnestly at Mav as she took her place. Railu could not see her face, but she suspected she was not meeting the lad's gaze. *I can't say I blame her.*

When the young couple were in place, the Reeve stepped forward, stopping at arm's length from them. He adjusted his elaborate robe, cleared his throat. "Noble Lord and Lady, members of the gentry, citizens, we are gathered here to solemnise the marriage of these two young people." A faint emphasis suggested he was well aware just how young they both were. "I should first make known to all that I have been asked to perform the ceremony today under the Sessapontine Rite rather than our familiar Denvirran observance. The differences are not great, in most respects, and mostly concern the order in which elements of the ceremony are taken. I must beg you to make allowance for any unfamiliarity, and excuse me if I occasionally need to consult this paper." He brandished a sheet.

"As with the Denvirran Rite, we begin with the identification of the participants. And I remind all present that the penalties for bearing false witness in a public ceremony may extend all the way to enslavement." He turned a fraction to his right. "Young man, do you solemnly swear and pledge that you are Riccart of Flemby, son of the late Cabus of the same estate?"

"I do so swear and pledge," said Riccart, his voice soft.

"Young lady, do you solemnly swear and pledge that you are Irmavel of Carinnan, daughter of the late Birtler of the same estate and ward of Thiseman, also of the same?"

Mav's voice was firmer and clearer, and it shocked everyone. Even Railu, who was expecting it, felt the jolt. "I cannot swear to that."

The Reeve looked startled. "And why is that?"

"I no longer answer to the name Irmavel. My name now is Mavrys."

"Are you then prepared to swear that you are Mavrys of Carinnan?"

"I am not."

A weary kind of half-smile ghosted across the Reeve's brown face. Railu had some sympathy. He was only trying to do his job, after all; this situation was none of his making. "Why not?"

"My place of residence now, and the place I call my home, is Skilthorn."

"Then do you solemnly swear and pledge that you are Mavrys of Skilthorn, daughter of the late Birtler of Carinnan and ward of Thiseman, also of Carinnan?"

Mavrys sighed; Railu knew that admitting to Thiseman's guardianship pained her. But she could not honestly deny it. In renaming herself, she was already sailing close to the legal wind. "I do so swear and pledge."

At last... the thought was clear in a communal sigh of relief, and in the Reeve's expression. "Then we proceed to the next step. I am required to confirm that the participants are entitled in law to marry. Riccart of Flemby, do you solemnly swear and pledge that you have no prior wife living, and that you have made no promise of matrimony to any other woman?"

"I do so swear."

"Thiseman of Carinnan, as guardian, do you solemnly swear and pledge that your ward, Mavrys of Skilthorn, has no prior husband living, and that she has not been promised in matrimony to any other man?"

Railu felt Jerya tense beside her. She would not have been surprised if her friend were grinding her teeth in indignation; the lad was fifteen months younger than Mav, yet he was allowed to speak for himself and she was not.

"There was a prior promise, your honour," said Thiseman, "But it has been rescinded by mutual agreement on both sides before any marriage ceremony could take place."

"It is certain that this other gentleman will make no claim? I remind you that everything you say is to be considered as being under oath."

"It is certain, your honour."

"Very well. I must now throw this marriage open to general question...

"If any man know of any just cause or lawful impediment that shall invalidate this marriage, let him declare it."

At every previous wedding Railu had attended, the only thing that followed this challenge had been an awkward hiatus. This time, the silence lasted but a moment. Then there was a rustle of skirts and underskirts as Jerya got to her feet.

She was dressed, if anything, even more splendidly than when she had been hosting a Prince. Formers at her hips spread her skirts near twice as wide as her true figure; her sleeves too were exaggerated out of all proportion, till her corseted body seemed scarcely more than an afterthought. Everything was in rich brocaded fabrics in shades of lavender. Her hair was coiled up around and behind a tall slender hat from which hung a half-veil, a light gauze in the same lavender hue.

She would take no pleasure in such a costume, Railu knew: it was purely for effect.

"I am Jerya, Countess of Skilthorn." Her words dropped into absolute silence. "And I object to this marriage. I object because I believe in marriage. I believe in marriage as I know it, the willing commitment of two people one to another. What we are called to witness today is no such thing; it is a mockery."

"My lady," said the Reeve, "You speak with power, and if there is truth in your avowal, then the parties to this marriage should most certainly reflect on it and interrogate their consciences. However, I must take note of the wording of the Rite we follow today: *If any* man *know of any just cause*, and so forth."

Jerya sat down, the sound of her skirts resonating even louder in the startled stillness. The veil was thin, but Railu could only see her in profile, and it was intuition rather than direct observation that told her just how furious her friend was.

On Jerya's left, Hedric now stood. "I am Hedric, Fourteenth Earl of Skilthorn, and I object to this marriage."

"On what grounds, my lord?"

"As my wife has already said, marriage is meant to be the willing commitment of two people. What we are presented with today is nothing of the kind. The two young people had never even set eyes on each other until yest—"

"Not so, my lord," said Thiseman, standing and glaring at Hedric. "They met several times as young children."

Hedric waved a hand dismissively. "I stand corrected. Before yesterday, they had never set eyes on each other since they were young children. And you will not dispute, Master Thiseman, that until a week ago there had not even been any discussion of a marriage between them?"

Thiseman, still standing, glared at Hedric, but made no immediate answer. "Master Thiseman," said the Reeve, "Is this true? I remind you again, you are under oath."

"It's true, I suppose."

"You suppose? Surely it is either true or it isn't."

"All right, it's true. But what has that to do with *lawful* impediment? I know of no law that requires a long engagement. Or any engagement, for that matter."

"Master Reeve," said Hedric, "I believe the words you read to this assembly were *just cause or lawful impediment*. Have I recalled correctly?"

"You have, my lord."

"*Just cause*," he repeated. "Does that not indicate that we must pay attention to justice as well as to the narrow letter of the law? And does not justice suggest that my wife was entirely correct when she referred to this marriage as a mockery?"

"I am beginning to think you are right, my lord," said the Reeve, "But I am not sure that abstract considerations of justice provide the certainty I would need to declare this wedding null and void."

"I repeat, Master Reeve, the two young people are scarcely acquainted with each other, and there was no suggestion of a marriage between them until a few days ago. I cannot speak to the young man's state of mind, but I know the young lady well, and I know that she has no wish whatever to be married to him, or to anyone else at this time in her life."

The Reeve looked at Mavrys. "Is this true?"

She stood. "It is, sir," she said quietly; but then she turned to face the assembly and said in a clear, ringing voice, "I am Mavrys of Skilthorn, and I object to this marriage."

"Pesk, sir!" said Thiseman, "Have you not declared already that only men may make objection?"

"That is true," said the Reeve. "That is the wording of the Sessapontine Rite, and it is my understanding that this Rite is being used at the request of the bride. Nevertheless—"

He was interrupted by another rustle of skirts. Beyond Jerya and Hedric, another figure was getting to her feet. "I am Deneval of Carinnan. I am the mother of the bride, and I object to this marriage."

"Damn me, sister," snapped Thiseman, "What the hell are you doing? You've always been at least as keen as I was that she should be married in due time."

"I was," said Deneval. Railu saw Mavrys staring at her mother, her eyes suspiciously bright. "But now I see things diff—"

"—And you are a woman and have no right to be heard."

Deneval began to respond, but another voice broke through. At first it seemed no one knew who had spoken, but within moments all eyes were on the young bridegroom. "I am Riccart of Flemby," he said, obviously repeating what had been inaudible the first time, "I am a man, so I do have a right to be heard... and *I* object to this marriage." The young man's voice grew firmer. "I see now that I have been brought here under false pretences. My uncle, and Master Thiseman, assured me that Irm—I mean Mavrys—was quite willing to be my wife. They promised me that we had compatible interests, that we would make a fine partnership, that we would have a bright future." He faced Mavrys. "They lied to me, didn't they?" He ignored shouts from both Thiseman and—for the first time—Lorzon. "You have no wish to marry me, do you?"

Mav shook her head almost regretfully. "I have no wish to be married to anyone at this time in my life. It is no particular reflection on you. As my lord the Earl said, I do not know you... and that's rather important, isn't it?

As my lady the Countess put it, marriage should be a willing commitment of two people one to another. I think that implies that the two people should know each other, and well."

"I believe I should like to know you better, my lady."

"Well," she said, "I have no objection to that. But let us be very clear that there is no promise of anything more."

"It shall be as you say, my lady."

"I believe," said the Reeve, "That these two young people have just shown a... decorum and dignity that some of their elders would do well to emulate. It only remains for me to declare that there shall be no wedding here today... and to wish both of you happiness in whatever the future may bring you." He smiled at the two, then removed his robe and slung it over his arm.

"You know," he added in a different tone, "I haven't been so entertained by a wedding since the day the bride's waters broke halfway down the aisle."

As the Reeve moved away, Hedric stepped into the space he had vacated. "There will be no wedding today, but let's not waste all the good food and drink that our people have worked hard to prepare. All here are welcome to enjoy the hospitality of Skilthorn. We shall reconvene there in one hour.

CHAPTER 44

JERYA

Her skirts seemed to fill most of the carriage-seat, which normally had room for three. Rearranging them with brusque gestures, she said, "Look at me. Dressed up like a... like a performing turkey." Ignoring a splutter from Hedric, she went on, "Two hours, near enough, to get dressed this morning, my hair done... I don't put myself through all this rigmarole for my pleasure. I had the notion—obviously a stupid one—that looking the way a Countess is supposed to look might give my words more weight. And what happened? He as good as said they counted for nothing because I'm a woman. Would he still have ignored me if I'd had irrefutable evidence that the—what the draff are you laughing at?"

"I'm sorry, my love," said Hedric, pink-faced. He took off his glasses, fished a cloth from a pocket. "It's just the notion of a performing turkey."

Jerya allowed herself a grudging smile, but her indignation would not be so easily mollified. "If any *man* knows... Is it the same in all the marriage rituals?"

"I'm sorry," said Railu, "We didn't think to look at that."

Jerya shook her head. "If dressing up and bearing children is all a noble-woman's good for, I think I'd rather go back to being a slave."

Hedric choked back a last chuckle, resettled his glasses, composed his features. "Fortunately that's not all you're good for. Very far from it, I would say. A trade agreement—"

"—A *draft* trade agreement."

"A draft trade agreement between the Sung Lands and the Five Principalities. Brokered, principally, by you. That is no mean achievement within a few months of assuming the title. A joint commission to establish a full concordance of weights and measures; a mutual recognition agreement between the Guild of Dawnsingers and the Denvirran Association of Physicians. Half a dozen pacts to begin the exchange of correspondence, books and journals in specific subjects. Next... who knows, a school for girls, maybe?"

"If we can find any teachers," said Jerya. She'd had hopes of Kamrine Ishe, the wife of Embrel's housemaster, but she had not yet responded to her letter: and where else was she to start looking? "And if anyone will send their daughters to us."

"Might I make a suggestion, my lady?" said Mavrys tentatively.

"I suppose so." Jerya knew she sounded ungraceful. It only made her more angry, but now the anger turned in upon herself.

"Well, this summer you gathered several Dawnsingers at Skilthorn, and I was privileged to speak with Master Evisyn more than once. And I have heard you, and Miss Railu, speak about your experiences as Dawnsingers. Perhaps... perhaps if more Dawnsingers are to travel to the Five Principalities in future, you might suggest that some of them gather at Skilthorn, to offer some of their learning to young ladies?"

"A seasonal school," said Hedric thoughtfully. "A *summer*-school."

"A few months," said Jerya. "It's not an education."

"Jerya," said Railu from her corner. "Don't let your rightful anger make a fool of you."

Jerya stared. There were very few people in the world who could get away with calling her a fool, but Railu was one, perhaps even first on the short list. Even so... "What do you mean?"

Railu smiled. "Remind us. How long were *you* a Dawnsinger?"

Jerya's anger collapsed like a pricked balloon. After a moment she gave a rueful chuckle. "Draffit, I *am* a fool."

"Performing turkeys are not renowned for their sagacity," said Hedric, and then they were all laughing.

Collecting herself, Jerya said, "Thank you, Mavrys. An excellent idea. I must write to Master Evisyn."

"I expect I'll see her, too," said Railu. "They'll pass through Duncal again on their way home."

"Aye, and you'll be heading back soon, I guess?"

"I'd love to stay longer, but I've neglected my practice long enough."

Jerya only nodded, feeling a twinge of envy at Railu's single-mindedness. "When do you think...?"

"I'll have to press Dortis for a decision. And I suppose there will be documentation to complete, if you are making her over to me."

Aye, thought Jerya, *welcome to the world of ownership.* "Yes, and it's more complicated because it has to be under trust... these damn laws. It might take a few days."

"Let's hope she's ready to decide, then."

Jerya turned back to Mavrys. "Dare we truly believe the threat of a forced marriage has finally been lifted? I doubt your uncle can conjure yet another potential husband in the few remaining weeks."

"I hope so," said the girl, rubbing at her frizz of hair. Jerya remembered that stage of regrowth; the itching had sometimes driven her to distraction. "But I won't feel truly safe until my birthday arrives."

"Early Veremander, isn't it?"

"Aye, my lady... but till then—and maybe after, too—he will no doubt try to fill me with guilt. As if I am consigning my mother to destitution. I have already said she can have my stipend. I don't need it. I have room and board, and I have the horses."

"You shouldn't do that," said Hedric. "Not all of it, anyway. Surely you'll want to save for a horse of your own."

"I would bid on Garrenva myself, if I had the money... but of course I can never own him."

"Under proxy, you can. I've already told Railu I will stand as trustee if she acquires Dortis; I'll gladly do the same for you. The deed can be written so that your right of disposal is inalienable."

"Thank you, my lord," said Mav, and clearly she meant it. "But..."

"Yes, your mother," said Jerya. "Well, she is welcome to remain at Skilthorn as long as she wishes."

"My lady, I..."

"I make one condition. She must make herself useful. I don't care in what way she does so, and she can of course take time to find her feet. But it's a firm rule from now on. As long as there are enslaved here, they don't work as they do simply to maintain others in idleness."

"Aye," said Hedric, "No more performing turkeys from now on."

Jerya stamped on his foot.

CHAPTER 45

RAILU

"It's time for you to choose," she said.

Dortis sighed. "I'm sorry, m'm. I dun't know how." The quickly-mumbled m'm had been inescapable ever since Railu had insisted that Dortis not call her 'my lady'. It seemed like a reflex in her, as with the other enslaved at Skilthorn.

Of course, reflected Railu, *She's been a slave her whole life. When was she ever asked to choose anything, never mind anything important? How do I help her do so now?* "It's two choices; stay here or come with me. Let's think about what each of those looks like..."

Dortis looked doubtful, but managed a slow nod.

"Well, you could stay here. That's what you know, what's familiar. Coming with me, now, that's different, isn't it? Everything different, living in a new place... I guess you've lived here your whole life?"

"Yes, m'm."

"Have you ever been further than Skilton?"

"No, m'm."

"Well, Duncal's a lot further; a long day's ride—probably two, as you're not used to riding either... D'you like the idea of seeing new places, or does it just scare you?"

"Some o'both, I reck'n, m'm."

"Fair enough. And when we get there, Duncal's a bit different from here too. The house is a lot smaller, for a start. Only a handful of enslaved in home-quarters. But there are more in the farmstead, and my work—our work, as it would be—takes me to other estates in the area. You'd get used to riding pretty soon, you'll be doing enough of it."

"Yes, m'm." Dortis did not sound convinced.

"We'll find a nice placid little pony for you. It's always better when you know the horse. In fact... we should ask Mavrys if there's anything going at a reasonable price. You know Mavrys, don't you?"

"Know who she is, m'm, I seen her a few times, like when I he'ped yow treat that gen'l'mun what fell down the stairs in th' stables. I wun't say I knows her."

"Maybe you should..." It was an intriguing thought. Mavrys must be about the same age Dortis had been when she first saw her, serving as the old Earl's main carer. "Well, the big thing is what that life will be like. But you've had some taste of it lately, helping me. I wouldn't be asking you now if I didn't like what I've seen... but I already knew; the Earl and the Countess told me you'd done an amazing job caring for the old Earl for years."

"Kind on 'em to say so, m'm."

"I think they were being truthful, not kind... Those years can't have been easy for you."

Dortis shrugged vaguely, looking into some unseen distance. "Dun't know about easy, but I din't mind it. I mean, he weren't a nice man, he weren't kind... but he never did me no harm. Even afore, he had me warm his bed a few times, but he never... imposed." The old man had been impotent by then, Railu inferred. Though he hadn't really been so very old; sixty-six when he died. "And carin' for him, I kind of liked it." The girl sighed in frustration. "I dun't know how to say it, I ain't smart wi' words like yow. I din't like *him*... should I of said that? It's disrespeckful..."

"Say whatever you like. Say it in Patter if it's easier for you."

The girl blinked at that but, continued in Plain. "I din't like him, but I did like carin' for him. That's best way I can say it."

"We don't have to like our patients," said Railu, recalling some of her earliest lessons, a long way away and half a lifetime ago. "We don't have to think they deserve our care. The old Earl doesn't sound like he deserved much of anything. Al that matters is that our patients *need* us. And it seems to me you understand that part very well already."

"I allus did my best for him, m'm."

"I'm sure you did. And that's what I'm... if you come with me, if you let me train you, then you'll be able to do much more for your future patients. Do you understand that?"

"Aye, m'm, I think so."

"I'll be honest with you: it won't be easy, and it'll take a long time. I spent seven years learning the healing arts as a Dawnsinger, and ever since... well, I'm still learning how to apply them in practice. I think I can speed it up for you, but we won't really know till we start. Anyway, one of the first things you'll have to do is learn to read."

"To *read*?" Dortis's voice rose sharply, and for once there was no 'm'm'. "I couldn't."

"I don't see why not. You're not... you're smarter than you think you are. And reading isn't that hard. Three-year-olds can do it. Why, Jerya once told me she learned to read just by watching her—watching someone's finger tracing the words as he read. And upside-down compared to how everyone else reads."

"It's not that, m'm. But I'm a slave. It's 'gainst the law."

Railu shook her head. "Not exactly. What the law actually says is *no free person shall teach any slave to read or write*. That's all. It doesn't say slaves may not learn. There's a fellow on an adjoining estate, enslaved for bad debts a few years ago." Punitive enslavement was steadily gaining in popularity; it was a lot more 'efficient' than keeping people in prison. "He'd be your teacher. At least for purposes of record." Ever since Jerya's manumission, her interpretation had been: *no free person shall be* seen *to teach any slave to read or write,* and Railu had taken the same view. She wasn't sure Dortis grasped the point, but that could wait.

"One more thing, Dortis, to be sure you understand what this all means. If you're to come with me, to be my apprentice, I have to... acquire you. I'm sure you know the law says women can't directly *own* slaves, but it does allow us to acquire what are called *rights of use and disposal*. It's all..." *It all stinks, is the simple truth.* "It's all a bit complicated and there's a lot of legal language about trusteeship and proxies, but what it means in practice is that Earl Hedric would sell you to me, under his own proxy."

Railu stopped, because she could barely get the words out. She longed for a drink, not just to soothe her throat but to numb the inner pain. "I've always said I would never want to be an owner, not even a proxy owner. I've been there myself, you know, been put on a platform, auctioned off. I'd never put you through the humiliation we endured that day, but even so..." Again she had to pause. "I know Jerya—the Countess—felt the same way." *Marrying Hedric meant marrying into the owner-class; she really struggled with that.* "She's still uncomfortable with it, but she believes she can do more to improve the lives of the enslaved this way. And that's the only reason I can reconcile myself to it, to being your... owner. Because it's necessary if I'm going to offer you this new life."

Dortis looked at her solemnly, barely blinking, but said nothing.

"It would be my plan to free you as soon as I can," said Railu. "But... how old are you, do you reckon?"

"Pro'ly two-an'-twenty, m'm. Mebbe three-an'-twenty."

"And unfortunately, under the new law, no slave can be freed until she's thirty at the youngest. Save in exceptional circumstances, by petition to the Court of Special Pleas...

"Well, we need to check the estate records; I'm sure your exact date of birth will be in the ledgers, and we'd need that before I can free you officially, but it's clearly some years off. Till then, as far as the law is concerned, you'll be my slave-by-proxy. But I don't think of it that way. You'll be my apprentice, my student. Do you understand?"

"I think so, m'm." Railu wondered briefly; how much did Dortis really understand of words like 'student' or 'apprentice'? She smiled to herself. *Equally well call her Postulant, and then Novice.*

"Is there anything you want to ask me?"

"I dun't think so, m'm."

"I expect you need some time to think. It's a big decision for you."

"No, m'm."

"No?"

"I dun't need no more time, m'm. I knows."

Railu took a deep breath, hardly daring to ask what the answer was.

CHAPTER 46

JERYA

"I'm sorry," said Jerya. "The mail has arrived, and there's nothing from Skelber... you're sure he won't have written to Duncal?"

Railu shrugged. "He knew I was staying on a while longer. Have you had other mail from Denvirran?"

"We had something yesterday. And today there's a letter from Sessapont, from Master Evisyn."

Railu shrugged again, but said nothing. She could dispense consoling platitudes when a patient required them, but hated to receive them herself. Jerya opted for blunt honesty. "If he hasn't the decency to tell you what he's decided, he's not the man you thought he was."

"That's true, I guess." There was a significant pause, but Jerya knew Railu had more to say. "It was probably never meant to be. It's not as if I was unhappy before. I didn't mope around like something was missing from my life. And now I have Dortis as well, her training to think about..." She laughed, though Jerya thought it rather forced. "I'd never have time for a *husband* anyway."

She squared her shoulders. "And speaking of Dortis, I should take a walk down to the stables, make sure everything's ready for her to ride tomorrow. Have you got time to walk with me?"

"I'd love to, but I have a few things to attend to. I'm hoping to get out for a ride this afternoon."

"Would you like company?"

"If you need to talk more..."

"No, Jerya, it's fine.... Don't tell me, you want some veil-time."

"You know me too well."

"I know I'm not the only one with things to think about... Well, I'll mention it to Mavrys, so Oronsa's ready for you."

※

Veil-time.

Railu did indeed know her well; even now, she thought, her oldest friend understood her in ways Hedric didn't, and perhaps never could. Hedric was a patient and sympathetic listener, but he had never sung the Dawnsong with a thousand others, crossed the mountains without the first idea what lay beyond. Nor had he ever been paraded on a public platform, naked apart from a metal collar and a placard.

It was Railu she wanted to think about first. *Not as if I was unhappy before. I didn't mope around like something was missing from my life.* Those had been her words. In the past, Jerya had heard her use the word 'content'.

Contentment. It didn't sound like too much to ask out of life. But when in her own life had she felt such a thing, and what did it mean anyway?

Railu was content because she had her work; she had said as much more than once. Jerya was well aware that not every such protestation was to be taken at face value, but she believed her friend. The work was never finished, she could never do enough, it stretched her every day and there was always more to do.

Perhaps that was what real work, true work, looked like. She had read an account of an artist who had said, late in life, *I'm never completely satisfied with any of my work. I always believed that the next piece would be better. Of course, I never told any of my patrons. I had to let them believe I had given them my best work, and in a way I did, but it was only ever the best I could do at that time. I don't believe a true artist can ever be completely satisfied. Where would the fun be in that? What would be the point of carrying on?*

The painter's words suggested one could be content in life without ever being satisfied. Perhaps satisfaction was only a step or two away from complacency, and then smugness.

By that reckoning, Jerya supposed, she had been content for most of her time in the College of the Dawnsingers. Never satisfied, because there was always more to learn, but content, and often exhilarated, to be *learning*. Perhaps that was what art was too: a continual exploration.

She had found a similar sense of equilibrium at Duncal, after her manumission, especially when she was combining her work for the campaign with being Embrel's governess. After meeting Hedric, her equilibrium had been shaken, but before long she found a new balance. In fact, there was more than contentment; there was *joy*. Working with him on original research, like measuring the distance to the moons, had been joyous. *And there will be more*, she pledged to herself, though a voice inside muttered darkly about when that might be. It was true: the coming of a child represented another break of equilibrium. But then, she had not really found her balance since becoming a Countess.

They came to the steeper slope up the scarp-face of the Wold, and she said a few encouraging words to Oronsa. Something else came to her then.

She had never been more content in her life than on her first two Crossings: with Railu and Rodal, and later with Hedric and Lallon. Both had been hard, often uncomfortable, occasionally terrifying, and both times ultimate responsibility had rested squarely on her shoulders. At times she had hated it, but always she had loved it.

She grinned sardonically to herself. The veil was more symbolic than effective concealment, but there was no one around to see anyway. *Am I only happy when I'm uncomfortable? When life's a struggle?*

She had no ready answer; she wondered if it was really the struggle and discomfort she missed, or whether what she hankered for was the simplicity, the clarity, of those moments.

The question set her thoughts on a new path, resonating with a passage in Evisyn's letter. She ran through the whole again in her mind.

❋

My dear Jerya,

Greetings from Sessapont.

And what a place this is. So beautiful, and yet so... the word that comes to me is 'corrupt', but even that somehow misses the mark.

I know you've been here, so I need not describe the beauty of the setting, the fineness of many of the buildings, the play of light on the waters, or the ceaseless hither-and-yon of vessels of all shapes and sizes. But, equally, having visited, you will not need me to tell you of the darkness that lurks beneath, not least at the Court. Perhaps especially at the Court.

On that subject, I must say our reception from the Prince was entirely cordial. As far as I can judge we were accorded high honour, but of course I have no way to compare with how other guests might be welcomed. At the same time, nothing was said by the Prince or in his presence to take us further than our discussions at Skilthorn. It remains to be seen whether we make more progress at the University; time—starting tomorrow—will tell.

At least there is nothing to suggest that His Highness bears us any ill-will, as we might have anticipated following his abrupt departure from the Congress. I detected no allusion, however veiled, to his notion of making an incursion into the Sung Lands. Perhaps it was never more than a passing fancy, and had it not been for Mavrys we would never have suspected even that.

Regarding that young woman, I recall you saying, before she even went to him, 'why couldn't he have brought one along with him? Then we could turn a blind eye.' There is no turning a blind eye here. There always seems to be at least one young female slave close by him, scantily clad and wearing a gilded collar. In the streets I have seen others being led around on leashes, though their collars are of bronze or leather. But you've been here and I'm sure you've seen it all.

Of course slavery is a stain across this entire land, as you know far better than I. I know you've struggled with becoming an owner yourself. Take heed,

Jerya: all that any of us can ever hope to do is shine a little light into whatever darkness we face, be it slavery, ignorance, hunger, pestilence, suffering in all its forms.

I know you fret that you aren't doing enough. I feel the same. That feeling only grows as greater responsibility accrues, whether as a Countess or as a Master Prime. I'd be surprised if you didn't *feel that way. But don't let it overwhelm you; remember that you have your own needs too. There is a reason why we call it* recreation. *Re-creation. It refreshes you to renew the work.*

Well.

I'm looking out of a window about two-thirds of the way up the Palatine hill. Over the harbour, the barrier-islands, the Inner Reach. The Outer Isles are grey outlines today, no more substantial than if they were cut out of paper, but I can see the deeper sea beyond; I can just about distinguish the horizon. And it calls to me.

You and I, I believe, are kindred spirits. From our first meeting, in that tavern in Carwerid, I sensed something in you, and I fancy you sensed the same in me. I have no other explanation for the feeling I had; a rapport, an ease of comprehension.

I think both you and I have the souls of wanderers. It's one reason I found such satisfaction as a Peripatetic, and then as Master of same. I can fully justify my decision to make the Crossing in person this year, but I cannot pretend that my motives were entirely disinterested. Having seen the Southern Crossing I now yearn to see your Northern route also—and, as I gaze out of this window, I feel a powerful longing to see what lies beyond that vague horizon.

I could make a case that such exploration is no mere indulgence. Who would deny it's a good thing that the Sung Lands and the Five Principalities are now known to each other? Well, we can think of one... Certainly there are challenges, and there are risks. I cannot suppose that either side will be unchanged. And you, Countess, have already played a significant role in advancing the process—more significant, I suspect, than you give yourself credit for. I think I see the impact more clearly now, in our reception here, than I did when I left you. I am certain that you will make further noteworthy contributions, but more of that anon. I was writing of our wandering souls, but my pen has wandered from that track.

I said that exploration is no mere indulgence; call me presumptuous, but I am sure you would agree. No doubt you saw the globe at the Kendrigg Observatory, on which the bounds of the Sung Lands are marked, and you surely did not fail to remark how tiny an area it was. As we now know, the Sung Lands and the Five Principalities together amount to barely one percent of the total surface of the globe. Historical sources suggest that in the Age Before, more than half the total was ocean, but that would still leave vast areas of land of which we currently know nothing. Given the energies that shattered the One Moon, it is possible that the surface of the Earth was also resculpted to some degree, but we do not know—and that, it seems to me, is very much the point.

Navigators from the Five Principalities have reached several days' sailing beyond the Outer Isles, but have as yet found no other inhabited land, nor any clear traces of former civilisation. Well, this too, you will surely know better than I. And I am sure that, like me, you would love to see those empty isles and coasts. Empty, at least, of human life; you'll have seen the tales of cliffs white with birds, of abundant game when mariners have achieved a landing.

Still, all the lands and waters that have been charted represent no more than three or four percent of the world's surface. Is it likely that our two small, adjacent, lands are the only ones in which human life has survived? And even if this should be so, is it credible that there are no remains from the Age Before elsewhere? Remains which would, perhaps, give us a clearer picture of that lost time?

It seems inevitable that exploration will soon reach further. It pains me to admit, but the Principalities, specifically Sessapont and Troquharran, have ships and crews far better equipped for this than the Sung Lands. I very much hope, however, that we can play some part in these voyages—but by 'we', to my regret, I must mean the Guild as a whole. I will not be an active participant. Whatever my heart may crave, the Conclave would never countenance it. You will easily imagine how the whole idea would be portrayed by our mutual friend, Perriad, and her acolytes. I cannot give them that opening. In any case, even my strongest allies on the Conclave would, I think, argue that I have too many other responsibilities.

There is, of course, one way I could free myself from all such constraints, and that is to resign (or abdicate, as some would call it). And as soon as I contemplate that path for even a moment, I see that it is not one I can take. It may sound arrogant, but I believe the Guild needs me. The times are turbulent enough without any further upheaval. Ex-Master Perriad might well find a point of leverage to swing more doubters behind her plan to close the borders and cease all intercourse with the East.

And so I can do no more than dream, and share my dreams via the mails with the one person, at least on this side of the mountains, I think most likely to understand.

Responsibility, Jerya; it's a burden, isn't it? I strongly suspect you are finding exactly the same as you adjust to your new position. (As I'm still adjusting to the Primeship after the best part of four years.) I have little doubt you feel much as I do about the prospect of voyaging into the wider world, but I fear you too are restrained by responsibility.

In one way, at least, I think I have it easier than you. There is an established model of how a Master Prime should conduct herself. I had seven years on the Conclave to observe my predecessor closely, to see how she did things and to think about those (relatively few) things I would do differently. In my observations of the Five Principalities, and in all my listening and reading of reports, I have seen no model for any of the things you and Hedric are planning or hoping to do. I am sure this makes your task more daunting, but I have no doubt of your courage and resolve.

I doubt you need my encouragement, but I'll say it anyway: do it, Jerya. Shine a little more light. It's all you can do, all any of us can do.

Your friend
Evisyn

Responsibility, she thought. Yes, she empathised with everything Evisyn had to say. But there was another responsibility about to be thrust upon her, one that Evisyn never had and never would face.

CHAPTER 47

RAILU

"There'm a gen'l'mun to see yow."

Railu didn't dare allow herself the indulgence of hope. She tried not to even consider the possibility. She merely thanked Lutrin in a calm tone, gave Dortis brief instructions to continue copying the alphabet, then gathered her skirts and headed for the hall at a dignified walk.

Inside, however, she was far from calm. Try as she might to contain her hopes, seeing anyone other than Skelber would be a bitter blow. And she had grounds for cautious optimism. Lutrin had said only 'a gentleman'; but she knew all the local gentry well enough, so the visitor had to be someone new. And he had asked for her specifically.

She turned the corner into the hall. Her immediate reaction was a wave—a veritable flood—of relief; but at once new doubts assailed her. He was a gentleman; perhaps he would have felt himself obliged to break bad news in person.

The moment hung in the air, weightless as thistledown, heavy as lead. They stared at each other. Finally his face opened into a smile, and he offered a deep bow. Railu returned her best curtsey, averting her face in conventional fashion, which made it easier to rein back the grin that tugged at her own features.

"Miss Railu," he said when they had finished their genuflections. "I would be most grateful if I might speak privily with you."

She thought quickly. Dortis was at the kitchen table, and though she could be moved, there was every chance of Lutrin bustling in and out;

Rhenya, too, would probably soon be back from her business. As far as she knew the mistress was in the parlour and the squire was in his library. "The day is still fine, I think? Shall we take a short walk?"

He assented gladly, and without further ado she led him outside and turned towards the knowe.

"You have ridden far this morning?" she asked.

"Only from Drumlenn. I put up at the Windhover last night."

"I trust it's proved satisfactory?"

Inconsequential pleasantries filled the few minutes it took to reach the stile. She hitched her skirts and clambered quickly over.

"I suspect most young ladies would have expected to receive assistance there," he said as he followed, "But climbing a stile must seem trivial to one who participated in the First Crossing of the Dividing Range."

"Stiles are designed to be climbed; mountains are not." She lifted her skirts again as they reached the steepest part of the slope. "But then again, I was barely nineteen, I wasn't wearing skirts, and I was just following Jerya's lead anyway." She did not mention Rodal: she and Jerya had long ago agreed that, though they would not lie, they would also not draw attention to the fact there had been three on that crossing. Mention of Rodal would likely lead to questions about what became of him, and from there it was but a step to the delicate matter of Embrel's parentage.

"I am sure there is more to it than *following Jerya's lead*," he said, "Though I freely admit she is a most remarkable woman."

"I completely agree."

They came onto the level and in a few more strides were enclosed in the ring of trees, filled with dappled green light and a soft insectile murmuration. Railu settled onto the fallen beech where she had sat many times before. Skelber perched beside her, arm's length away, but almost at once he sprang up again with an air of agitation.

"Miss Railu," he said, shifting from foot to foot. "The Countess is indeed a remarkable woman, but in my estimation you are no less so. I must tell you... when we left Skilthorn, my masters soon decreed that it was too late to make the journey all the way back to Denvirran in the day, so we put up at Blisco and made a more relaxed schedule.

"I had always hoped to use the time on the journey to give fuller consideration to... to all that passed between us during that time at Skilthorn. I needed to weigh my feelings, to test the true depth of my regard for you. It would be unfair—to both of us—to do any less. Those days at Skilthorn were, to me, like a time out of normal life. To go to work every day with the feeling—the *knowledge*—that we were making history—or, at least, given my own secondary role, that I was present as history was being made. And to rub shoulders, almost literally, with a Prince, not to mention an Earl and a Countess... all that was intoxicating. I was filled with a sense that everything and anything might be momentous, but... I had to consider that in that intoxicated condition, I might have fallen into the trap of building a great edifice on slender foundation. And that if I had, if I were to act without reflection, it would be grossly unfair to you.

"I needed also to consider—however reluctantly—questions of a more practical nature. Of course you and I had already spoken of some of the implications of any alliance we might enter into. I was duty-bound to take time to weigh all of my responsibilities. And, perhaps not least, I was obliged to consider what... complications might arise, given the difference in our social standing."

"I am beneath you, is that what you're saying?"

"Some might think so," he acknowledged, adding quickly, "But for me the whole question is ambiguous. You are the intimate friend of a Countess. Even, I think, her closest confidante, after her husband." He smiled wryly. "Some might say that places *you* above *me*. Therefore I asked myself whether I was overly impressed, even dazzled, by your closeness with Her Ladyship."

He took a few steps, soundless on ground more moss than grass, stood a few seconds looking at the trees, or perhaps at nothing, then turned back. "Miss Railu. The plain fact is that with every passing day I have grown more certain that I was *not* deceiving myself. I stand before you now in a sure conviction that my regard for you is of the truest and deepest kind... and I can only hope and trust that your feelings toward me are of similar measure."

Railu could not sit any longer; she rose, took the three short steps needed to reach him. His hands were clasped tight in front of him; she teased them apart, grasped one in each of her own. "I cannot say I have dissected my feelings in quite the way you have done. So I hope you will not think me superficial when I say... I feel as I did that evening when we stood on the lawn under the gathering night. Just the same."

"Then may we do as we did that night?"

Some time later they separated and, without words, seated themselves on the fallen tree; but now they sat just inches apart.

Skelber looked at her, smiling; but then he sighed. "I could not be more glad that I made this journey today. Still, there remain matters of practicality to be resolved. And I must tell you now that there are certain... considerations that I did not mention before."

"What kind of considerations?" she asked with sudden unease.

"I think it would be best... Miss Railu, how soon would you be free to ride into Drumlenn with me? There is someone I would like you to meet."

Sumyra had something of her father in the broad brow and tapered jaw, and in her grey eyes, but her skin was noticeably darker. Her near-black hair seemed determinedly unruly, wispy strands escaping the two tight braids which hung, not quite symmetrically, down her back. Railu had no memory of ever having hair, herself, but she had a distinct, if inexplicable, feeling that her own hair, left to itself, would have been similarly hard to contain.

They had barely progressed past the introductions when a slave in the distinctive livery of a messenger was ushered into the inn-parlour. He presented Skelber with a slip of paper which Railu recognised as the transcript of an avian message. Originals of more than a few short lines were written, using special apparatus, in script too small for the naked eye to read. Skelber fished a small hand-lens from an inside pocket to read it, then sighed. "I really should respond to this. To draft a reply and get it transcribed and sent will take at least half an hour. Probably longer, to be realistic."

Railu looked at Sumyra. "We could take a tour of the town, if you're agreeable." The girl's face declared her more than agreeable, and her father assented willingly.

'Tour of the town,' was all very well, Railu reflected as they emerged onto the bustling street, pausing a moment to let eyes adjust to the brightness. "To be honest," she said, "There's not a great deal of note in the upper town. Shops, inns, all the usual... but what *is* interesting is the port."

Sumyra gave her a curious look. "Did you say 'port'? Are we not two hundred miles inland?"

"Not quite two hundred as the messenger-bird flies, but rather more as the river wanders." They began to walk. "But you can have river-ports as well as seaports. We'll go by the Overlook and then you'll see."

They turned into a quieter street. "Miss Railu," said Sumyra, "It is of course polite to say one is delighted to meet someone, but I wish you to know that when I said it earlier I meant it from my heart. Since my father came back from Skilthorn, he has spoken of you several times."

Railu smiled. "I hope he has not flattered me overmuch. I should hate to disappoint you."

The girl darted a shy glance at her. "I'm sure you won't. I am glad he told me you are bald." She dropped her gaze, a sudden blush bruising her cheeks. "I beg your pardon, was that overbold of me?"

"Not at all. I *am* bald. I have been bald since I was—may I ask how old you are?"

"I turned twelve in Tuulander."

"I've been bald since I was younger than you are now; more than twenty years. I can't remember being any other way... but I do understand. Many people take me for a slave at first, or are perplexed because my position seems... anomalous." She laughed. "I think your father was among them. We hadn't even been introduced and I started giving him orders."

"Yes, he said. You were mending a... a broken shoulder?"

"Dislocated, not broken. A good deal quicker to fix, but exceedingly painful for the victim until it is."

The girl nodded solemnly. "But it—being bald—it is because you were a Dawnsinger?"

"Yes. And explanations are easier, now most people have at least heard of Dawnsingers."

"But you're not one now."

"No. I went through eight years of training—a year as a Postulant, seven as a Novice—and I was Ordained, as they call it, but I never practised as a full-fledged Singer. I left very shortly after Ordination, and I ended up here. And of course in those days no one had heard of Dawnsingers, or even knew that there was life West of the mountains, so we were taken for slaves—"

"You and the Countess?"

"Yes, though she wasn't a Countess then, of course; just plain Jerya."

Sumyra nodded. She would have heard of Jerya; who, now, had not? Very likely she had read one or more of the accounts that had appeared in most of the Principalities' newspapers and journals. Accounts of highly variable accuracy; it would be interesting to see exactly what the girl knew, or thought she knew.

Conversation lapsed briefly as they crossed the Garslet road and turned again, down the final lane to the Overlook. As the rumble of iron-shod wheels on setts faded behind, Sumyra gave Railu another side-glance. "One thing I don't understand, if you aren't a Dawnsinger any longer..."

"Yes?"

"Why are you still bald?" Again colour bloomed in the girl's cheeks.

Railu smiled, and tried to make her tone reassuring. "I have no choice about it." She explained about the lotion girls began to use when they progressed from Postulancy to Novitiate, how eventually its effect became permanent. *No choice... but I've been bald two thirds of my life; would I want to change now?*

This brought them to the Overlook, and as the view began to unfold, Sumyra almost ran the last few steps to the railing. Railu followed more sedately. "It's quite something, isn't it?"

"How high are we?"

"Almost two hundred feet above the river, I believe. And now you see how Upper Drumlenn is but half of the whole."

Sumyra stepped up onto the low plinth that supported the railings, the better to lean out, with no sign of nervousness.

"The bluff is steepest about here," said Railu, "That's why the Overlook is here. The course of the river is nowhere so steep, but there are some cataracts, so obviously it's no longer navigable. I hear the occasional dare-devil tries descending it in a canoe."

"You said 'tries'?"

"Yes, I've not heard of any making it down unscathed. Look, you can see one of the river-ships there, in the distance."

"Will we see it come in?"

"It'll be a while yet, I should think, with this light wind. But you can see the masts of one at the staithe, there. And you can see how the road winds to and fro across the slope—but even so, it's hard for laden beasts or waggon-teams to tackle. So they came up with an ingenious solution... look, there."

She pointed out one of the cargo-carriages beginning its descent. Sumyra stared. "Oh my, what's that?"

"They call it a *vertical tramway*. Though you can see it isn't truly verti-cal." The second carriage appeared from below and they watched the two pass each other. Railu explained to the attentive girl about the endless cable, the skill of the loadmasters. "Sometimes they can simply match the weight of ascending and descending cargo, but there are tanks in the base of each carriage which can be filled with water for ballast."

The ascending carriage came to rest at the top station, close enough to hear a dull thud as it reached the buffers, a distinct clank as the brake was applied. "That's wonderful," said Sumyra, watching as several brawny slaves began unloading. "I do like to know how things work."

"You do?"

The girl looked around, lowered her voice, though there was no one else on the terrace. "I had a clockwork mouse when I was little. When I got bigger I took it apart to see how it worked."

Railu smiled. "And did you put it together again?"

"I tried, but it was held together with lots of little metal tabs that were folded over. I could pry them open with my knife, but I couldn't flatten them down again, not tightly enough."

"You needed better tools?"

"I think so."

"Well, you know, your father and I, being doctors... when we take people apart, we have to be very sure we can put them back together."

Sumyra nodded solemnly. "I look at the insides of the clock on my mantel sometimes, but I can never quite see how all those wheels and things make it work. I think I might understand if I took it apart, but I'm sure I'd get into trouble."

"You mean if you couldn't put it back together?" Railu pondered briefly. "Would you like to do that? If you had the right tools? Take things apart, put them back together, make them work when they're broken?"

"I *would*... but people wouldn't understand. They'd say it's not fit work for young ladies."

"I'm sure some people say that... but do you know who makes the finest clocks and watches in the Two Lands? Dawnsingers."

"Really?"

"Really."

"Do *you* know how?"

Railu shook her head. "Sorry, I didn't study horology."

"You don't know how clocks work, but you do know how bodies work?"

"I know a lot about that, but there's always more to learn."

Sumyra nodded. "My father says that too." She gave Railu a keen look. "I can't tell you how I felt when he told me about you. A lady doctor... but... you only learned in the Sung Lands. I can't go and study to be a Dawnsinger, can I?"

"Well, there's no prospect of that for the present. And they start girls a year or two younger than you anyway. However..." She wondered if Skelber would welcome her introducing such thoughts into his daughter's mind. *If he doesn't, he may not be the man I take him to be.* "Well, as you know, my friend Jerya—"

"—The Countess?"

"We've been friends for fifteen years; to me she's simply Jerya. Anyway, she wants to do something about the lack of proper education for girls..."

Chapter 48

Skelber

"She's an absolute delight."

Sumyra's chatter had finally been stilled by the fatigue of an eventful day, and Skelber had excused himself to see her to bed before returning to the inn-parlour.

"I'm glad to hear you say so," he said now.

"I say it because I think it... but I also think bringing her here was a smart move on your part."

"I'm not sure what you mean."

"Really?" Railu sipped daintily at her wine. "Had you never considered that meeting her might make it harder for me to refuse you?"

He took a taste from his own glass. "If anything, I feared it might tip the balance the other way, that a step-daughter might be a complication you would prefer to avoid. And also that you might be angry that I did not tell you of her existence before."

"I have been wondering..."

He sighed, made a vague gesture with his free hand. "I should have, I know; and I know it's too easy to say 'I never found the right moment'... Perhaps there's some truth in that, but if I'm honest what I really never found was courage. It is asking a lot of any woman to take on another woman's child, I know, and at this particular time in her life... You will know better than I what the next few years will hold. I have done my best as her father—"

"—And judging on what I've seen you can be proud."

He raised his glass. "Thank you... but it seems to me that I may find it harder to guide her through the coming years. It has focused my mind on the... drawbacks of my bachelor state. But I cannot but be aware, also, that taking on a step-daughter at this time would be, as they say, like being thrown in deep water to learn to swim." He sighed again, took more wine. "None of this, of course, excuses my lack of candour, but perhaps it does go some way toward explaining it."

"Well, if we're making up for lost time, I haven't been entirely open with you either. You need to know that if you marry me you will not be marrying a virgin."

He supposed she had to say it: a marriage could be annulled if the bride were found not to have been a virgin. He thought carefully before responding. "I suppose... we are neither of us in the first flush of youth. I suppose it would be asking a lot for you never... but I'm sure you said you have not been married before."

"No, and the truth is that I only ever lay with a man once in my life."

He stared at her. The question was immediate, but he could not see how to phrase it with any vestige of delicacy. To his relief, Railu seemed to read his thought. "I was not forced, no, but the circumstances were... before I say any more, I must have your word that you will not repeat any of this to another soul."

He was bemused, but gave his promise. Railu seemed to take his word as good. "Very well. The first thing is that there were not two of us on the First Crossing, but three."

"I always thought..."

"It was just Jerya and me? Yes, we don't hide the truth, but we don't shout about it either. But we had a companion. A man from Jerya's village, Rodal. He'd seen her to Carwerid when she first arrived."

"But surely there's no shame..."

"In accepting his help? No, and I really don't know if we would have made it across without him. Both he and Jerya were far more at home in the mountains than I, and stronger. And Hedric freely admits she was the strongest, the leader, on the Second Crossing, too. Maybe she would have got me across on her own the first time; I don't know. But at the time... well, I'd had moments of terror, been exhausted most of the time, three-quarters convinced we were all going to die on some bleak slope... when we did get down to somewhere we could rest, where the sun was warm, where there were fish in the river, I was dizzy with relief. I was hardly in my right mind. And just at that time, Jerya was off somewhere and Rodal and I were alone together and..."

"I don't suppose you need to spell out the details."

"Thank you."

He picked a scrap of cheese from his plate, ate it slowly, then studied the wine in his glass, swirling it around. "Every man wishes for his bride to be a virgin, of course... but it would be a very hard man who would condemn you for a single... lapse under such circumstances."

"That's not all," she continued. "The very next day, Rodal was away hunting, when Jerya and I were... taken." Her throat tightened, as it always did when she tried to speak about that time.

"Taken for slaves, you mean?"

"Yes. We were both bald, it's no wonder they took us for runaways. I don't need to go into all of that now. I only mention because I need to explain why Rodal wasn't there. When he found out what had happened, he made a decision—and both Jerya and I think he was quite right—not to come to us right away. We were at Duncal by this time, we weren't in danger, we weren't being ill-treated. He decided he would take some time to find out how things worked on this side of the mountains, and to earn some money, so that he'd be better-placed to do something for us later."

"And did he...? But I presume he must have come back, since you know what his choice was."

"Yes, he did, some time later. But we told him, Jerya and I, we were well enough as we were; we didn't want to be fugitives again." That was glossing over a lot of the story, but she still hadn't reached the meat. "And he had... an obligation back in the Sung Lands too, so he went back. With our blessing," she added, clearly not wanting Skelber to think ill of Rodal. He nodded slowly, still looking mostly at candlelight refracted through wine.

Railu took a long, shaky breath. "The thing is, we never told him... but in between those times, I had a child." At last he looked at her, could not avoid it. "Either I've drunk too much, or I truly trust you. There are only six people in the Principalities who know this. When they discovered my... condition, the squire and his lady made me an offer. They would take the child and raise it—him—as their own. And they have."

"So the boy—what is he, fifteen, now?— does he know?"

"Fourteen, still... As far as he knows, I was his wet-nurse, his nursemaid, and ever since I've been housekeeper. That's all."

He shook his head. "Have you never wanted to tell him?"

"Jerya always argued I should. She still thinks he should know when he reaches his majority, but I can't see what it would achieve. I could never have given him the life he's had, the opportunities, the education."

"And the boy's father, this Rodal, doesn't know either."

"No."

"You don't think he's entitled to know he has a son?"

"He's married," she said. "Back in the Sung Lands, in Carwerid. Three children now."

"And they have a half-brother they know nothing of."

"But what would it do to his wife, to Annyt? I knew her, a little, back then, before any of this, and... if anyone in all of this is entirely blameless, it's her. And the children."

He didn't answer, and she left him to his thoughts as a slave-girl cleared plates and cutlery. When she was gone, Skelber stirred. "And now I'm thinking, if I do marry you, Sumyra will have a step-brother she can't know about. I've often thought she would have liked a brother or a sister." He drained his glass and sighed. "And... I'd be a poor father if it didn't at least give me pause to learn that my daughter's potential step-mother once gave up a child of her own."

Railu sighed. "I am scarcely the same person I was back then. I was only nineteen when I bore him, and I'd been raised for eight years as a Dawnsinger. Can you understand...? Dawnsingers do not have children. It was never even a remote possibility. And then we'd just crossed the mountains, been captured, been sold as slaves—and it was only by chance that we were bought by well-meaning people." As always, she shuddered at the memory, the lustful eyes that had raked her naked body; she had known that what they had in mind would be very different from what had happened between herself and Rodal. "My world had been turned upside down anyway, even before I found out I was... pregnant. As far as I knew I was always going to be a slave; one of the more fortunate ones, no doubt, but a slave nonetheless. My child could be born into slavery, or he could grow up as heir to Duncal." She regarded him steadily until he met her gaze. "Can you even begin to imagine what it was like for me?"

He gestured with the bottle and she accepted a little more wine. He refilled his own glass before answering. "You're right, of course: I cannot imagine, though I owe it to you to try. It must all have been terrifying; bewildering. But let me ask you one more thing; you must see the boy often..."

"Every day, until he went away to school."

"Seeing your own flesh and blood being raised as the child of others... Surely that was hard."

"Sometimes, yes. And I do love the lad; we all do. He's not exactly scholarly, but he's bright, and he has a sunny disposition. But in many ways Jerya was closest to him. She was his governess for—what?—five years?"

"A governess for a boy. An unusual choice."

"Possibly, but she had a lot more success than any of his previous tutors."

He nodded thoughtfully. "The Countess's interest in education is nothing new, then."

"We were Dawnsingers. We were educated. Of course, her main interest now is in education for girls."

"Ah, yes... Sumyra did say something about a... what was it, a summer-school?"

"That's right... I did think I maybe should have mentioned it to you first, but it was too late by then."

"Well, maybe so, but having seen how she took to the notion, I'd be a harsh father to deny her the opportunity. I'll still need reassurance on a few points, but... I have met a few educated women this summer, and my eyes have been opened."

"Should I take that as a compliment?"

He raised his glass to her. "If you like. But we are talking, above all, about the future of my daughter. And she said something this evening, as I saw her to her bedchamber... well, I should be interested to know what you say to it."

"And what was that?"

"She said, 'Is Miss Railu to be my new mother?'"

"And what did you say to that?"

"I equivocated, to tell the truth. But I should be very interested to know how you would have answered her."

Had he intended to set her a test? He suspected that was how she felt as she gazed at the candlelight refracted and reddened by the wine in her glass. "I should say... she may not remember her mother, but her mother knew *her* and, I am sure, loved her very much. I cannot take a place which is not vacant. I will not be her mother, but I do wish to be a true friend to her; perhaps more than a friend, but I don't know what the right word would be. 'Stepmother' is merely a shorthand. Exactly what we can be to each other... we'll only discover that in time."

If that was a test, he thought, *she could hardly have done better.*

He couldn't stop himself smiling—beaming—as he reached out with both hands, grasped both of hers. "My dear Miss Railu, you could hardly have put it bet—"

He was stopped by the loud grating scrape of a chair. Sudden silence fell across the room.

A florid, beetle-browed man loomed over them, swaying slightly like one who's had too much to drink. "I've held my peace long enough. It's bad enough you entertain your slave trollop in a respectable inn at all, but I'd resolved merely to speak to the landlord about it. But I cannot sit by when you start pawing at each other, and with ladies—"

Skelber sprang to his own feet. "*Pawing*, did you say?" His fists clenched and unclenched at his sides.

"Sir!" said Railu loudly. The angry man stared at her, apparently astonished at being addressed by a 'slave'. Railu's return look was cool and self-possessed. Skelber suspected she'd had many chances to perfect it. "Clearly you are not from around here."

"What the deuce?"

"If you were, you would know—"

"—Enough! I don't take correction from slaves, still less ones of easy virtue."

"How dare you, sir!" growled Skelber. "You have no idea whom you are addressing and, if I may say so, no idea how to behave."

"You, *sir*, are the last person to lecture any gentleman on good behaviour."

"I repeat, you have no idea whom you are addressing or what you are talking about, but as a gentleman, I give you one last chance to withdraw your hasty and offensive remarks about my companion. Otherwise I—"

"—*Companion*? Ha, is that what they're calling it now?"

Skelber stepped forward until they were almost toe-to-toe. He was fractionally the shorter, but surely the fitter. "As you said, sir—almost the only thing you have said to which I do not take exception—there are ladies present. Shall we therefore step outside and settle this like gentlemen? Even if you are no such thing."

The man flushed even redder, and threw a punch at Skelber's head. Skelber blocked it easily, and followed up with a quick left jab to the ribs. The reach was too short for the punch to have full power, but it made the angry man still angrier. He threw a wild roundarm swing. Skelber dodged back nimbly, and the momentum of his own flailing arm made the man stagger. Perhaps he tangled his own feet; all Skelber knew was that he went down. Railu gave a horrified gasp as they saw and heard him clip the side of his head on the table. He crashed to the floor and lay still.

Quicker than he was himself, she sprang from behind the table and knelt beside the fallen man. Already blood was pooling on the floor.

"I'll get my bag," said Skelber. "And send someone to the hospital for a stretcher."

"I'll see what I can do about the bleeding."

By the time he got back, she had obviously obtained water and clean napkins, washed the wound site, and made a thorough examination.

Skelber was soon back, kneeling alongside her. "There's no skull fracture," she said, "I'm sure as I can be. But it's a nasty scalp wound and you know how they bleed."

"It's going to need a dozen stitches. And it's really a two-m—a two-person job."

"I'll go on stabilising the site if you want to do the suturing."

"I wish we could shave the area."

Low enough for no one else to hear, she said, "It would serve him right if we shaved his entire head."

Then they dared not look at each other. It would not do to laugh.

CHAPTER 49

RAILU

"Still up, then?" said Skelber, peering round her door, which she'd left ajar.

"Awaiting news. How is he?"

"Still a fool, but a penitent one." He laughed softly. "Hard to know whether he'll have more of a sore head from the wine or from his injury." His face grew serious again. "There's something else, though…"

"Why don't you come in, then?"

"I didn't want to cause another scandal."

"You're more visible standing there."

Since there was only one chair, she yielded it to him and perched herself on the edge of the bed. "Now…?"

"Yes," he said, crossing his legs, "While we were waiting for our patient to come round, I had an interesting talk with a young doctor who's recently arrived."

"I'd heard some mention."

"Name's Gorennie. Seems like a smart fellow, keen on the latest ideas, and very interested in what's coming out of the Sung Lands."

"He'll not see eye-to-eye with the Director, then."

"Exactly." He leaned forward. "He's only been there a few weeks, maybe a month, and already he's feeling some frustration. And I have an inkling he may not be alone."

"No, far from it." Railu sighed. "I don't go near the place if I can help it, but people talk. Nothing's really changed in that hospital in all the years

I've been in this district. That Director, Arvend... well, let me just say I doubt he'll be joining in the congratulations on my qualifications being recognised. Call me biased, but it's often seemed to me he's more concerned with maintaining tradition than about the outcomes for his patients."

"And people know this?"

"I hear it all second-hand, you know, through my employers. But they're friends, or at least acquaintances, with at least half of the Board of Management. I think the Board knows they have a stagnating hospital and a Director who's become an obstacle to progress, but they've never quite dared even to discuss asking him to step down. One reason might be that they've never had a strong candidate ready to replace him. Talented subordinates tend not—" She stopped abruptly. "Skelber, what are you thinking?"

He smiled. "You've already guessed. If you think they'd consider me a strong candidate..."

She gazed at him, hardly daring to hope.

"Gorennie started me thinking," he said. "He was saying it's natural for anyone travelling to or from the Crossing to come through here. That's right, isn't it?"

"Well, the first habitation you'd meet, coming from the West, is a hamlet called Redfork. There's a hunting-lodge and a logging outpost. From there, there are two possibilities. The direct route toward Denvirran, but that's a rough hill path; I guess mules could make it, but certainly not carts, and it's most of a day's walk before you reach a carriage-road. Or there's the track to Drumlenn. Smaller carriages and carts can manage it, with care, and there are some improvements in hand."

"How do logs get out from there at present?"

"They float them down the river."

"I see. Sorry, a digression. Well, we may suppose, especially after the Congress, that there will be continued, and almost certainly increased, traffic across the mountains each summer. And that most of it will pass through Drumlenn... including Dawnsingers."

"Actually, there's one more reason why Dawnsingers prefer this route."

"And that is...?"

"Me." He blinked in surprise, and Railu smiled. "Perhaps I should say, the house at Duncal. They're assured of a friendly welcome and they can get the news, learn how things lie, before continuing."

"I see... well, you can guess how I've been thinking. The hospital here needs a new lease of life anyway, but there is a chance to do something more. To create a focal point for the exchange of medical knowledge between Sung Lands and Five Principalities. And this could, of course, be of great benefit to the people of this region." He gazed into her eyes. "Does this sound possible to you?"

"Possible, yes... but I cannot speak for the Guild. You would need to speak to someone, preferably the Master Prime."

"And she is in Denvirran at present...?"

"Last I'd heard, she was in Sessapont, but that was a week ago. She's probably in Troquharran by now."

"Ah... Well, there are others I should speak to, like Le'ast. It may be that I should return sooner than... I originally planned on spending a few days here, but now this scheme has come to me..."

"Wonderful as it sounds, you might at least want to sleep on it."

"Yes, wise words, I'm sure."

"Besides, it's certain, or as certain as anything can be, that they'll spend at least one night at Duncal on their way home."

He nodded. "Also worth considering. Yes, I should give it more thought. Fools rush in, as they say... But, whatever else, the revitalisation of the hospital would be a worthy challenge in itself. Other things may need to follow more slowly. And it occurs to me..." Again his eyes sought hers. "As I'm sure it has to you, that this gives me a strong motive to base myself in Drumlenn."

He shook his head, gave her a rueful smile. "But then I already have a strong motive... Miss Railu—"

"—Please, just call me Railu."

"Railu... my dear Railu, all this time I have been talking to you, I have had the cart before the horse. Yes, my new notion about the hospital excited me, but... when I came to find you, I intended only to inform you briefly of our patient's condition before moving on to... to what I had been about to say when we were so rudely interrupted."

Railu looked at him expectantly. He sprang to his feet, halved the distance between them, but then stopped. She was conscious that she was sitting on the bed, and he was a man who respected the proprieties. She rose also.

"My dear Railu," he said again, "Your answer to Sumyra's question freed me from the last of my doubts. And the way you and she have taken to each other had already dispelled most of them. I think you know what I am about to say—what, indeed, I was about to say nearly three hours ago—but it behoves a gentleman to speak for himself, so—"

She put a finger to his lips. "I believe I do know, so let me save you the trouble. My answer is yes."

For a while they didn't speak, until they heard the clock at the end of the landing strike once. She rested her hands on his shoulders, leaned back. "I suppose there's no pressing reason why we cannot be married reasonably soon."

"If you can be content with a simple ceremony, then I see no reason at all. I'll need a couple of months to wind up my affairs in Denvirran; three at the outside. Let's hope by then we have some progress on matters here, too."

She put fingers over his mouth again. "I wasn't thinking quite so practically. More... here we are, a bed two steps away. We're neither of us virgins, are we? It's been a long time and I'm not sure I want to wait any longer." He didn't answer and she felt a twinge of concern. "I haven't shocked you, have I?"

"No, no," he said hastily. "Perhaps you surprised me a little, but no more." He ran a hand over her scalp, a slow caress that made her shiver deliciously. "I can hardly tell you how tempted I am... but I think if I make love to you now, I am all too likely to fall asleep after. And I do not like to think of Sumyra waking to find me absent."

"I suppose so..."

"Have a little patience, my dear. Only a little... although..." He laughed softly. "Speaking of Sumyra, she may take some persuasion to embrace the idea of a simple ceremony. Well, we shall see; but first we shall have the immense pleasure of telling her our news. I shall say nothing to her until we are all together... we shall see you at breakfast, I trust?"

"Yes, but can we make it early? I must be heading back to Duncal. I've neglected my practice quite enough this summer... and I have another thought."

"Oh?"

"Yes, if you agree, I'll try and secure a dinner invitation for you. For tomorrow night, if you're free. I think a conversation with the Squire and Lady would be a good way to begin exploring the prospects for change at the hospital."

"An excellent notion. I shall endeavour to have another conversation with young Doctor Gorennie, under cover of checking on our patient, but he is not in a position of influence, while your employers can introduce me to those who are."

"I'll ask them as soon as I get back, and send a message by the midday diligence to confirm it."

"I shall have to bring Sumyra, but it may be a dull evening for her if we are all talking about hospital administration."

"I'll endeavour to keep her entertained." She chuckled. "Let the three of you worry about weighty matters."

"I'm sure she'll like that... but she and I will have some free time to-morrow—I suppose it's today, now. She can show me the tramway; do you recommend we take a ride on it?"

"Yes, why not? And then you can see the port and the lower town. Walk up to the cascades if you have time, they are quite impressive."

"And now I suppose I must convince myself to leave you. A solitary bed is less appealing than a shared one, but still... well, you did say breakfast should be early."

✳

"One day you will be the one getting married," said Railu. "Who do you want making the final decisions then? That will be your day; yours, and whichever young man is lucky enough to win your heart. This wedding is our day, your father's and mine. Of course we want you to be happy with everything, but you do see we must be comfortable with it all too."

"I do see that," said Sumyra, but there was no missing the lack of enthusiasm.

Railu reached for her hand; it was slender, almost fragile, compared to her own. They were sitting on a bench at the Overlook, which had become Sumyra's favourite spot in Drumlenn. "Let's talk about this business of giving me away. I've said before that, in my mind, it is I, and no one else, who will give myself to your father. But I haven't told you about Jerya's wedding, have I?"

"The Countess?"

"She wasn't a Countess then, you know. This was almost four years ago; Hedric was heir to the old Earl and they had no idea when he might inherit. And his uncle—who was a very unpleasant man, by the way—wasn't over-keen on the marriage. He could have invited them to celebrate at Skilthorn, but he never did, and as he wasn't well enough to travel, he didn't attend when they held it here. Well, that's by the by. The point is that Jerya—and she was very much plain Jerya Delven then, a governess and secretary—felt much as I do about having anyone 'give her away'. So we found a form of ceremony that didn't require those words... and can you guess who escorted her down the aisle?"

Sumyra shook her head, loose hair swishing across her shoulders.

"It was me," said Railu; the girl's eyes widened. "I suppose you still thought it had to be a man? Well, we happen to know that there's no such condition in the Sessapontine rite."

"I'd wager people were surprised, though?"

Railu grinned. "Does your father know you gamble?"

"I don't gamble; it's just a figment—a *figure* of speech."

"Best keep it that way, if you'll take my advice. I learned enough maths in my time as a Dawnsinger to understand a little about odds and probability." She studied Sumyra's face a moment. "Anyway... you know a little of our shared history, Jerya and me."

"I should like to know more."

"You shall. And she'll tell you a few stories about me, too." Sumyra's face brightened; meeting a Countess was still a thrilling prospect. "But you know already that we've been through a lot together. We've had a few minor fallings-out, but never for terribly long, and we always seem to end up even closer afterward. For almost fifteen years she's been my dearest friend. And I believe, without boasting, I've been similarly important to her. It's a bit different since she's been married, but we're still close. I don't suppose she had one second's doubt that she wanted me to walk with her down the aisle; and now the positions are reversed, I feel exactly the same."

"It would be something to have a Countess at the centre of the wedding," said Sumyra thoughtfully. "And will the Earl be there too?

"I'm sure he will. And here's another thing: if we can arrange it before the end of Fructander, there is a good chance of having some Dawnsingers there too, including the Master Prime. That would be something too, wouldn't it?"

"Of course... but that's only just over two months. And I don't know if we can find anywhere that won't already be booked."

"That's going to be easier, though, if the numbers aren't too many." She smiled. "If you think I'm trying to bribe you with Countesses and Master Primes, maybe you're right... but there's something else I'd like you to think about. Two things, in fact. First, both your father and I would like to be married soon so we can properly begin our life together. And you'd like that too, wouldn't you?" Sumyra nodded cautiously. "Second... I just can't think of that many people I really want to invite."

The girl's face suggested scepticism. "I'm serious," said Railu. "I know lots of people as patients, but not so many as friends. I thought about this as I was writing to Jerya yesterday, and I could only name about half a dozen people whose presence really matters to me. Among free-folk, that is. I could name some more among the enslaved, but you know how difficult it is to include them in any gathering more formal than around the kitchen table at Duncal." She sighed. "I wish it were different, but it isn't."

"Only half a dozen?"

"Whose presence really matters, I said."

CHAPTER 50

MAVRYS

Mavrys sat back, stretching her arms wide. Finally she felt she had the paperwork under control. Renfrith, she thought, had had a system, though its logic was known only to himself. Haldrow had simply let papers pile up. She could almost feel sorry for Haldrow; his difficulty with reading surely wasn't his fault. *If you'd only spoken up about it, I could have helped.*

Pride had prevented that. Pride, or its ugly sibling, shame. Haldrow hadn't been one to ask for help, still less from a female—and least of all from one who looked like a slave.

Don't look so much like a slave now. Mav scratched at the base of her neck, feeling how the hair was just beginning to curl. She wondered how it looked. She hadn't seen her own reflection for months. There had been a mirror in the shaving room; she always looked at it, occasionally paused a breath or two, getting acquainted with the young slave who gazed back at her.

Mirrors... she thought. There were none anywhere around the stable-block. Unless...

She pushed the chair back, strode past the stair-head—now safely railed around three sides—and the new partition, still unpainted and doorless. Through what was now her bedroom. The further door led into a chaotic lumber-room. She had looked in on an early inspection tour of her new domain, entertained the fleeting notion that if cleared out it might make some kind of sitting-room, but nothing had come of it. There was never enough time. Even time to think had been scarce these past months.

There was enough clear space to open the door and enter, but the rest was a crazy jumble; she could barely see the far wall, estimate the size of the room. On one side, piles of old tack and miscellaneous tools had slumped into hip-high hummocks. On the other, a motley assemblage of furniture, too confused for swift inventory; but she could see a large table—how had they manoeuvred that up the stairs?—and six or eight upright chairs.

There was no mirror to be seen, though anything might lurk in the deeper recesses, but the table and chairs sparked a new thought. On that same tour of inspection, Mav had noticed an old black kitchen range half-filling one wall in another room that had been taken over by discarded stuff.

Mav's father had instilled in her an aversion to clutter. Anything worth keeping at all should be stored in an orderly fashion, allowing for easy retrieval. If a thing had no further use, it should be moved on altogether.

There was that; and there was another thing. It made little sense that the lads—and the overburdened Mistress of Horse—had to troop up to the house three times a day for their meals. A few times a week, perhaps; it was good to keep in touch with the household staff. But just because they met other friends there, and because there was rarely room for nine at one table, gave no chance for them to talk together as a team. Meetings had to eat into other time; time, the great bugbear; and there was nowhere better than the tack room. Mav had tried perching on the bench, but everyone else was standing, and so disposed among the racks of saddles and harnesses that they could not all see each other.

If they could gather round a table regularly, no front and back, all equal...
Equal...

Another thought crystallised. Back in her bedroom, she glanced out of the grimy window; still drizzling. At least it was now only grimy on the outside, but that was a reminder of another job. Two jobs, really, because window-cleaning could not proceed before the ladder was repaired.

Mav sighed, clattered down the stairs, and plucked a jerkin from its hook on the way out. Mirrors were forgotten.

❋

The slaves' dining-hall was still busy, but she didn't see Vireddi. She turned to the three waiting outside the shaving-room. Curious looks greeted her. They might not know her, but they'd all seen her; seen her as a slave. "Excuse me... have you seen Vireddi?"

"Aye, miss, she'm in there."

"Thank yow."

She barely glanced at the mirror on her way in, but she saw enough to confirm she no longer looked like a slave. *Hair's long enough.* The thought sparked new questions... but Vireddi was just rising from the chair. Her eyes widened as she saw Mav, but neither spoke until they were outside again.

"Can I talk to you for a minute? Have you had breakfast?"

"Aye, got up early."

"Is there anywhere private?"

Vireddi thought a moment, then led her down a passage to a linen-room. "Shudn't be anyone in here till th' bell's gone."

Mavrys had had things ready to say, but now they just stood, looking at each other. Finally: "It's good to see you, V."

"Yow too—" Vireddi stopped. "I dun't know what I should call yow now."

"Mavrys. Mav. Always."

"Dun't seem quite proper."

"When we're alone..." She dismissed the thought that they hadn't been alone together since before her birthday, more than two months ago. "Besides, when were we ever quite proper?"

Again they looked at each other.

"I swear you're taller, V." Their gazes were level; surely they hadn't been when they first met. Five months... was that really all it had been?

Vireddi chuckled. "Reckon I might be. Needed a new skirt, like. Gettin' prop'ly fed these days."

"You're looking good on it."

"Yow too. I like your hair."

"You do?"

Vireddi reached out and her hand lifted an incipient curl on Mav's brow. Not thinking, hardly breathing, Mav let the back of one finger trail lightly above Vireddi's ear. Freshly-shaven, sweetly smooth. She thought of her own days of baldness with a pang of... regret? nostalgia?

She could not have said who moved to initiate the kiss. It seemed as if the distance between them simply dissolved.

Some time later, she said, "I missed you, V."

"Missed yow too, Mav."

"I should have come sooner, but I've been so busy. We're shorthanded still, and I'm—" She stopped herself from babbling about paperwork and bloodlines and the covering of mares, and everything else that had filled her mind. "But I have thought about you... and I've had an idea." She flung straight into an explanation.

"I dun't know nothin' 'bout cookin'."

"I'm sure you could learn. It'll be a while before there's a kitchen to cook in, anyway. But the question is... would you want to?"

"Yow'd have to speak to Shevra."

"Not 'will they allow it'?. I said, 'would you want to?'"

"Work in th'stables? Wi' horses all around?" Vireddi sounded distinctly dubious.

"There won't be horses in the kitchen. Or in the sleeping quarters. And you know how to do all the rest, laundry, sweeping..."

"Aye, reckon so."

"And simple cooking. Nothing fancy, and for ten, not a hundred."

"Well, mebbe..."

"Look, V, I want you to be sure. But there's another thing. You could live there too."

"Live there?"

"Yes. I've got a big bed..." She hadn't known she was going to say that until the words were out. Vireddi's face showed a flicker of surprise and then... what? Sudden nervousness made Mav say, "Or you could have your own room." *What would I want a sitting room for? When would I ever have time?* "Either way, V, I don't want you to feel like I'm pressing you. You could even stay on here... I mean, for as long as you want. See how everything goes."

Still Vireddi seemed hesitant. Mav knew she should probably just shut up now, give her time to think, but her head was too full. I know it's a lot to think about. It only came together for *me* this morning. But... I'm sure, V."

"Yow an' me?"

"You and me."

"E'en though I'm a slave an' yow ain't? Now yow're th' Mistress o' Horse."

"It's a fancy title, I know. But I'm the same person. The same one who cried in your arms after..." She saw in Vireddi's eyes there was no need to say more. "Anyway, I know what I want." *And I think you want it too.* The kiss had suggested she did. But she held her peace and waited.

Finally Vireddi's face relaxed. "You'll still have to talk to Shevra."

"I'll talk to the Earl and Countess to if I need to."

This time the kiss was ended by a jangle of bells in the passage.

Three days later; the same linen-room. This time, a kiss before anything else.

"Sorry I couldn't get away before," said Mav, a little breathless.

"So'm I."

Mav would have liked to explore all the reasons why Vireddi might be sorry, but time was pressing, as ever. There were things she wanted to say, and things she needed to say. "Have you thought about what I said?"

Vireddi grinned. "Might ha' done. Just a little, like."

"Don't keep me in suspense, V, please."

The grin deepened. "*She yen me-she go for same room?*"

Mav sighed inwardly. She'd hardly begun to get comfortable with Patter before her time as a slave had come to an end, and she'd had no practice since. But if this was how Vireddi wanted it... "*Me yen proper. She proper brav for me.*" Her grip on Vireddi's hands underlined her words.

"*Brav a me.*" Vireddi could have been a governess.

"*She proper brav a me.*"

"*She proper brav a me'n'all. She tellem she gotten gran' bed?*"

"*Yem, vrai, proper gran'.*"

"*Gran' room an' all?*"

"*Yem.*"

As abruptly as she'd switched into Patter, Vireddi switched out again. "Not too big, I hope. I dun't know as I could be doin' wi' one o'them great big rooms. Feel lost tryin' to sleep in one o'them, I reckon. Reckon that's why they have them curtains round th'beds?"

Mav, who'd had a tester-bed of her own at Carinnan, knew it was more for warmth than anything else; but that was another point; big rooms took a lot of heating. All very well when you had a maid to come in and light a fire before you were even out of bed; not so fine when you had none, let alone when you *were* the maid. She only smiled and—perversely sticking to Patter—said, "*Yem, she 'stute.*" And then, thinking Vireddi hadn't sounded over-keen on a big room, she added, "*Nen* vrai *gran'. Gran-er'n room me-she go for kip afore. Nen gran' com en rooms den fine folks kip.*"

Vireddi nodded but said nothing immediately. Mav, who felt the pressure of time all day and every day, could not resist saying, "*So?*"

"*So?*"

"*She apt go for trav dan stables?*" If there was a word for 'stables' in Patter, she'd never heard it. And then the bigger question: "*She apt go for kip same room a me?*"

"*Me apt go for same room, same bed.*" Mav felt as if her heart swelled with relief. "*Ma... Afore me go for trav dan stables, she gotten go for parl av Shevra.*"

"*Me proper apt go for doso.*" She thought a second. "She *yen go for look see em place?*"

Vireddi's answer was cut off by the bells, but Mav saw her nod.

They had just emerged from the passage when they saw Shevra turn into it.

Shevra looked her up and down. It felt all too much like their first meeting. Was Shevra thinking how Mav had been (or not been) a slave the first time? Or just taking in her breeches and jerkin? Mav had a strong feeling Shevra would prefer ladies to dress more decorously. But Mav had had enough of such constraints.

After a long moment, Shevra said, "Mistress." There was no curtsey, not even a dip of the head, but Mav was happy with that.

"I've messed up, haven't I?"

Vireddi said nothing, looking out across the paddock to where Oronsa stood, looking in the shade of the sycamores almost like just another grey horse.

"It all seemed like a perfect plan. You could come and work here and we'd live together. I didn't think about giving you orders and you calling me 'Mistress'. But I still treated you like my slave. I might as well have been giving orders, mightn't I? Come here, learn to cook... and for all I know you might hate cooking."

"I mightn't be no good at it, 's'true." Vireddi's voice was soft, almost musing. "No way o' knowin'."

"When we started, V, and I was learning how to be a slave, you were my guide, my instructor. I'd rather go back to that, to be a slave again, then mess everything up between us."

If anything, Vireddi's response was even quieter, but it was definite. "No, yow wouldn't."

"What?"

"I saw how yow was wi' th'horse afore, what's her name?"

"Oronsa."

"Yow dun't want to give that up. It'd break yowr heart."

"It feels like it's going to break anyway, one way or the other."

Now Vireddi turned to face her. "Mav, *hark a me*. Yow said, 'learnin' how to be a slave'. I never had to learn. I's allus been a slave. Yow tried, I saw it, but it were hard for yow. Born a slave, yow jus' know it. Know it in th' bone. And, see, the thing is, no one ever asked me afore, would I like to do this, would I like to work here?"

Distant bells intruded into the edge of Mav's consciousness. Vireddi did not seem to hear, and Mav dare not interrupt her.

"Yow did," said Vireddi. "Yow said, 'would yow want to?', an' 'I want yow to be sure'. No one ever said things like that to me afore."

In one way, this was as heartbreaking as anything Mav had felt before. As much as any tales of whipping or tonguing, of bad food and endless drudgery, it summed up the essential lot of every slave. But above that, what she felt now was hope. "Are you saying...?"

Vireddi treated her to her most wicked grin. "I still might be terrible at cooking'. Yow wouldn't want me if I poisoned all yowr lads. "

"I'll always want you, V."

Vireddi said nothing, but her eyes said, *Well, mebbe.*

Epilogue

JERYA

"Accompanying Railu down the aisle has been one of the proudest moments of my life. I'm glad finally to repay the honour she did for me at my own wedding but, more than that, I'm glad because Railu is my oldest and dearest friend and because she deserves every honour that I or anyone else can pay her.

"Which makes it my duty—my very pleasant duty—to tell you a little about Railu, and why I honour her so highly.

"I've known Railu all my adult life. I met her on the day I arrived at the College of the Dawnsingers. I was a half-educated girl from one of the remotest villages in the Sung Lands, and I was terrified. Railu wasn't the only one to show me kindness, but her welcome was particularly warm, and very soon we became friends. When I was wrestling with my conscience about whether I could remain in the Guild it was Railu whose understanding I needed—and she was the most patient of listeners.

"My next step was a madcap scheme to cross the mountains. Mountains which, to the best of my knowledge—then and now—had never been crossed in this age of the world. I say 'madcap'; I suspect Railu might think that an understatement." Glancing down, she saw Railu nodding emphatically, though with a broad smile. "Madcap, crazy, perhaps bordering on the suicidal... and yet she agreed to accompany me. Simply, I suppose, because she didn't believe I should be allowed to go alone.

"Well, we made that journey." *Three of us, not two, but that's for another day.* "We crossed the mountains... and the next thing we knew, we were being taken for runaway slaves. I'm sure Railu would agree that was the darkest hour of all we've been through together. But that's the point: that, too, we endured *together*.

She paused for a sip of water, leaving the wine for the toasts. "So much in life depends on happenstance, it seems to me. If we had attempted the crossing of the mountains at any other point. If Squire Duncal and Lady Pichenta had not been passing by the slave-market on that particular morning. If they hadn't, nine years later, played host to a young man with a passion for astronomy—who just happened, unbeknown to me, to be the heir to an Earldom. So many points at which, if any one thing had been different, *everything* that follows would have been different.

"And yet it feels to me as if I was always meant to meet Railu. It sounds superstitious; I don't really believe things are 'meant'. Yet that's how it feels. I can't imagine my life without her.

"Whether living in the same house, or following her progress from afar— we've been pretty diligent correspondents—I've been constantly impressed with what Railu has achieved in those years. Clandestinely, and with only a fraction of the resources available to male doctors, she's provided essential care to dozens, probably hundreds, of people. It's wonderful—though no more than she deserves—that she is finally able to call herself Doctor, to practise openly." She nodded down the table at Doctor Le'ast. "I'm really excited to see what new things flow from her partnership with Skelber.

"And of course I'm delighted to have played a part, however unwittingly, in bringing her and Skelber together.

"You all know that we were once Dawnsingers, and Dawnsingers, of course, do not marry. We left the Guild—" She darted an apologetic look toward Evisyn. "—But thoughts of marriage never entered our heads, not then. For years after I don't think either of us really envisaged that we would ever wed. I did, of course, and I'm very happy that I did, but I still... I suppose I wondered if there was any man out there who would be worthy of Railu's hand.

"It seems there is one, after all." She looked toward Skelber; he raised his glass. "My subject today is the bride, not the groom, but there is one thing I've learned about him which I think worth mentioning. He has been sole parent to Sumyra for most of her life. Having had the very great pleasure of getting to know her in the last few days, I am even more inclined to think well of her father. Today Sumyra has gained a wonderful stepmother, and Railu has gained a wonderful stepdaughter. And both those things make me very happy."

Jerya smiled at the girl, who was proudly beaming back at her. *I hope that does the trick, Rai*, she thought. Railu had explained that Sumyra had been dreaming of a grander wedding, but the presence of a Countess and a Master Prime would do much to alleviate her disappointment; and being singled out for mention by that same Countess would do a good deal more.

"And that, really, is all I have to say. Railu is my oldest and dearest friend and I am happy beyond my capacity to express that she has found this place in the world, and this man to share it with. I am full of a... a hopeful curiosity to see what they can achieve together here in Drumlenn."

The tables had been cleared and the musicians were tuning up before she caught up with Embrel. "Having a good time?"

"Good evening, Countess," he said with his cheekiest grin.

She scowled back ferociously, but only for a moment, before mirth gained the ascendancy. "Would you do something for me? And for Railu?"

"What is it?"

"Dance with Sumyra."

"She's just a kid."

"She's only two years younger than you."

He looked rebellious, briefly, then shrugged. "For Railu?"

"Well, if you won't do it for me..."

"But you're asking for Railu, really."

That was true, and quite an acute observation. *He's growing up.* "For Railu, and for Sumyra. I think it will mean a lot to her."

"And it's not like any of the fellows from school are here to see."

"That's not the *most* graceful way to say yes, but thank you anyway."

❋

She danced the first dance with her husband, the second with the groom. After that, her back began to feel tight, and the room felt stuffy, so she wandered out onto the verandah. She leaned back on the wooden balustrade, taking some weight on elbows and forearms, easing her back, thrusting out her burgeoning belly.

She was in this position when Railu found her. Her friend smiled. "Tired?"

"Back's a little tight, that's all."

"Five Principalities doctors talk a lot of nonsense about pregnancy. They'd have you do nothing for three months. That's what you get when all your doctors are men, I suppose."

"When they also say pregnant slaves should get three months off work, I'll pay attention."

"I don't think that's likely any time soon... I might have a word with... with my husband." She shook her head. "I never thought I'd hear myself saying that."

Jerya laughed softly. "It takes some getting used to. But then I never imagined any of this when we were Novices, did you?"

"Never imagined, never even guessed it was there to be imagined."

"And now look at us..."

"Suddenly I'm married. Suddenly I've got a twelve-year-old daughter. And you..." Railu grinned. "You're a fucking Countess."

Jerya laughed out loud in shocked delight. Railu almost never swore, but this was perfect; she'd deployed the profanity with the precision of a scalpel and the force of a hammer. "It still means nothing unless I can make it *fucking* count."

Railu gave a little nod as if to say, *you're kind of handy that way too.* "Seems to me you've made a good start."

"And I'm not going to spend the next three months doing nothing. Or the three months after that."

"Of course, but... I learned medicine from Sister Berrivan and the other Healers. And with all due respect to my husband..." Again she paused over the new word. "...And every other decent doctor in the Five Principalities, I'd go to the Healers every time for questions about women's health. They wouldn't say 'do nothing', not unless you actually get sick... but they would say be careful. Look after yourself. Let your body tell you when to keep going and when to stop."

"Like coming out here rather than lining up for another dance?"

"It's a good start."

Together they looked back towards the open doors. A moment later they saw Embrel and Sumyra spin past, the girl's skirts flaring wide as she twirled under her partner's arm. They could not hear over the music and the pulsing rhythm of two dozen pairs of feet on the wooden floor, but it certainly looked as if both youngsters were laughing.

"Is that their third dance?" asked Jerya.

"At least."

"I only suggested he ask her for one."

Railu shrugged. "He seems happy enough."

"They both do." They looked at each other and Jerya knew they were both thinking much the same thing. "*Well, this could be interesting.*

It was probably nothing. The occasion, the music, the euphoria of the dance; for Sumyra at least the added spice of being allowed to stay up well past her usual bedtime. After the weekend Embrel would be returning to school and wouldn't see Sumyra again till Year-End.

Probably nothing. But... "Does it occur to you they're almost related now? What would she be? His step-half-sister?"

Railu gave her a sceptical look. "Now you're inventing whole new ways in which two people with absolutely no shared blood are 'related'... Just be happy to see them both happy, Jerya."

"Aye, no doubt you're right."

Jerya looked back toward the dance-floor, but Embrel and Sumyra were no longer in sight. "Let me ask you something else. And you might not think this so fanciful." She drew breath. This was a delicate topic, and though she had already given close thought to what she wanted to say, it was still important to get the tone right. "When I look at Embrel, I can see his kinship with you. But I already know it's there. Without that, I don't reckon anyone seeing you and him together would suspect anything. But you can see as clearly as I can, the older he gets, the more he looks like Rodal."

"It's true," said Railu, her tone guarded. "But no one's ever going to see them together."

"Well, that's the thing. You know I made him—Embrel—a promise. Years ago, before I set off back to the Sung Lands. I promised I'd take him travelling. *One day I said, when you're older, we'll go on a journey together. A real journey.* So far, I've never taken him further than Troquharran. I don't want this... I broke one vow in my life, I don't want to break any more."

Railu only nodded, her face guarded.

"Well, this is where it gets complicated. Since he's met Master Evisyn and the others... now he wants to go to the Sung Lands. Next time I make the Crossing."

"Jerya. You're pregnant. Three months from now you're going to have a daughter or a son. And I know you're not going to leave her or his care to someone else for months on end. It's going to be a few years at least before you make another Crossing."

"I know that. Embrel knows it too. He understands. *Even if it's ten years,* he said." Her eyes searched Railu's face, but the light spilling out from the hall made it enigmatic. "Even if it is ten years—even if it's longer... Rai, you know how much Embrel means to me. If it's still what he wants, when the time's right, how could I say no? But then again, how could I go the Sung Lands, go to Carwerid, and not see Rodal? You see the problem? Do you really want that to be how the lad finds out who his real father is?"

Railu was silent for a while. The music changed: a fourth dance. Jerya wondered if Embrel and Sumyra were dancing this one together too. Finally Railu gave a long sigh. "I could wish you hadn't brought this up on my wedding day. It's not like it's urgent..."

"I'm sorry, bad timing. I hadn't really planned it this way, but then there were Embrel and Sumyra dancing together and it just sparked from there. Shouldn't have done it on your wedding night, but, you know, if you never talk about something when it isn't urgent then you can get caught on the hop when it suddenly is."

"It's not like we've never talked about it before."

"We've talked about telling Embrel. We never talked about the possibility of him actually meeting Rodal."

Railu sighed again. "All right. I'll think about it. When I get a chance." A smile began to steal back into her face. "It's not exactly like I've nothing else on my mind right now."

Jerya returned the smile. "That's true." *But let's not keep putting it off indefinitely either*, she didn't say.

"You know," said Railu after a moment. "I really came out to say thank you for what you said."

"I meant every word. In fact I'd like to have said more, but there were things I could not say in front of... well, some things I could not say in front of *anyone*. Not even Hedric. Things he doesn't know, things he maybe would rather not know. You were everything I said, Rai, but you were my first lover too. And you didn't just teach me about... about the physical side. You taught me about love itself."

Railu said nothing. After a second Jerya realised she probably couldn't.

Perhaps it was fortunate that Evisyn chose that moment to appear beside them. "I've danced with both your *husbands*," she said with an impish grin, "And that's about as much intimacy with males as I'm comfortable with."

"I imagine even that would shock some of your Conclave," said Jerya, as Railu brushed at her eyes.

"No doubt," said Evisyn, "But I know you won't be telling them. Anyway, I was wondering if either of you—or even both, in due course—would care to take wobble round the floor with me?"

"If you'd asked me at the ball in Skilthorn," said Jerya, "I'd have been delighted, but I'm afraid my back's protesting now."

Evisyn nodded, then turned to Railu. "What about you, Doctor?"

Railu smiled. "Honoured, Master Prime. When does the next measure start?"

"Two minutes, they said, and that was probably a minute ago."

"Then we should take our places. Do you think I'd better lead?"

MAVRYS

As she watched the ceremony, an idea had begun to form in Mavrys's mind. Some of the Countess's words had sharpened it. Now, it was quite beyond her to keep her mind on the steps.

It was true she had agreed to dance with Brellas. Now she could call him brother-in-law, or at least brother-in-law-to-be, with no fear of ever having to call him husband, she found she liked him a great deal better. Dancing with him pleased her mother too.

Mav was glad to know they had set a date, though not so thrilled that the wedding was to be in Denvirran. Drumlenn was a long day's journey from Skilthorn; Denvirran was two, and she could hardly avoid the expectation of spending a few days with her mother beforehand, helping in the preparations. It would be at least a week away from home, and the horses, and Vireddi. Right now, having only left home yesterday, she already missed her.

But there it was. Vireddi was on her mind, and weddings were in the air.

Then the evolutions of the dance brought her briefly face to face with Earl Hedric. In the moment, as if without conscious thought, she heard herself asking, "Might I speak to you, my lord?"

There was no time to catch a reply before they were whirled apart, and then it was minutes before they came together again. "After this measure," he said. "The garden?"

Drumlenn's Assembly Rooms did not have expansive grounds like Skilthorn, but there was a modest garden. The stiffness of its clipped shrubs and parterres was softened in the moonslight, and it was both cool and blessedly quiet. Skilthorn's dance floor seemed to soak up the sound; Drumlenn's seemed to amplify the clatter of feet.

"Well," said the Earl, "It is a relief to escape out here, and I thank you for that, but I dare say we shall both be required again soon enough. So, if you don't mind, Mavrys, we should get right to, well, whatever it is."

"Of course, my lord. I'm grateful for every minute you can spare. And I'm very aware how much you've done for me already."

He waved a hand. "As to that... my stables seem to be running as smoothly as I've ever seen them. All my horses are in the pink. I rather think I've done *myself* the greater favour."

"Well, my lord, all I'm really asking at this moment is some advice."

"Which costs me nothing. Please, proceed."

As she began to outline her idea, he pulled off his glasses and held them up, angling them to the light to check for smears or specks. As she went on, he polished them assiduously.

He did not replace them until she had finished. "Well," he said then, "It's a bold notion, to be sure. But that's not to say it's a bad one. Jerya walking Railu up the aisle was a bold step; Railu playing the same part at our wedding was a bolder one. And their embarking on the First Crossing was the boldest of all... but I can only ever be glad that they did it."

"Because it brought Jerya here."

"Indeed. And because it brought Railu too. Let's not underestimate her boldness, her resolve, practising as she has for so many years."

"I admire her very much. And I'm very happy to see her married. To a man she loves and who clearly loves her."

"Yes, true marriage is a fine thing."

"And false marriage is a foul one," she said with a vehemence that surprised them both. "Of all the reasons I am grateful to you and the Countess, your support on that day is one of the greatest." She took a slow breath. "But that's what irks me the most. When a sham of a marriage can be perfectly legal, but Vireddi and I can't be married at all."

Though his glasses had surely had no time to collect so much as a speck of dust, he removed them again. "I'll tell you a little story, Mavrys, if I may. I don't know if it will help, but it might. When Jerya and I had known each other maybe six months…"

"Before the Second Crossing?"

"Actually, ours was the third, but let's not be sidetracked. Yes, before. We were pretty sure by then how we felt about each other, but the question of marriage was not so simple. My uncle, the thirteenth Earl, was still alive, and growing ever more irascible. He was hardly likely to think Jerya the most suitable bride, and I could readily imagine him disinheriting me. In fact he almost did… but that's another digression."

He examined his lenses once more, gave a small shake of the head, and resettled them on his face. "But as I say, we were already sure how we felt about each other, but the question of marriage… Well, Jerya said some words to me, and I've never forgotten them. I never shared them with anyone before…"

"You do me honour, my lord."

"And I know you will not abuse my trust; but if you wish to share the words, or the thought, with Vireddi, you have my leave. Well, this is what Jerya said: *'If marriage is just the vows two people make to each other, we could do that right now. We wouldn't need anyone else.'* There was more, of course; a good deal more; but those are the words I think most fitting to your situation."

We wouldn't need anyone else. The words almost rang in Mavrys's head. She was almost dizzy for a moment. "Thank you my lord… but you *did* want more."

"I'm not sure we *wanted* anything else, but we *needed* it. For the public face… I mean, had Jerya and I lived as man and wife without benefit of wedlock, you can be sure my uncle would have cut me off. And for ourselves, we would not have cared; we would still have Kirwaugh." He sighed, and Mavrys had a flash of understanding: Skilthorn, and the other properties, were more burden than privilege. "But the estates would have gone to my cousin, and nothing much would have changed for the people."

Mavrys knew something of how the old Earl had been. Vireddi was never keen to speak of those times, but her reticence, foreign to her usual nature, spoke volumes. And... had Hedric not inherited, had Jerya not become Countess, she, Mavrys, would never have gone to Skilthorn, and then she would never have met Vireddi.

Distantly, she heard a new measure beginning; they were now missing a second dance. She hardly thought she would be much missed, but the Earl surely would. He had given her much time already; time to draw this to a conclusion. "*'For the public face,'* you said, my lord. But the public face is firmly set against the marriage of free and slave."

"And of woman and woman," he said, very gently.

"It hardly matters whether it's forbidden once or forbidden twice; it's still forbidden."

"'Tis true, I'm afraid. Well, you cannot be married in the eyes of the law... and we cannot ignore the law. You and Vireddi cannot marry; we cannot free a hundred slaves a year. Well, as both instances illustrate, law and justice do not always align. You have heard me speak of this before."

"Aye, my lord; on the day of my... my *un*wedding."

"Unwedding?" He chuckled. "I like that."

"The law would have sanctioned that marriage, but forbids the one I truly want."

"Well, Mavrys, there are a number of laws in this land I would wish to change, but I have slim hopes of speedy success with any of them. That being the case, all I can suggest is that we work around it."

"How so, my lord?"

"Well, I suppose you have not the same concern about the public face that we had. So I remind you of Jerya's words: *'If marriage is just the vows two people make to each other...'* And I recall she said a little more: *'Whatever words we need, we choose.'* Choose your own words, Mavrys, you and Vireddi; and if you wish to say them before witnesses, I will stand with you. I don't like to take my wife's name in vain, but I would lay odds she would be there too. It may not be everything you wish for, Mavrys, but I hope it's something."

"It is, my lord. It's very much something." She could not, at that moment, have said another word. Almost she threw her arms around him, but he was still an Earl.

She looked up at the moons, but they were just smears of pale light, as if seen through a rain-streaked window. When she wiped her eyes and blinked her vision clear, the Earl was gone

❉

"I suppose," said the Countess, "You'll be wishing you could just get on a horse and ride straight back to Skilthorn?" She sipped at her coffee and made a face. Mavrys understood; the brew was as weak as the wan sunlight that slunk past the curtains of the inn-parlour.

"I would, my lady, but I know I'm needed. And I have been learning a great deal about driving, and the management of the carriage-horses."

"In any case," said the Earl, practically, "It's too late now. By the time we'd procured a horse and everything else you'd need... well, you could hardly hope to reach Skilthorn before midnight. And I'm not keen on the idea of you riding some of those roads alone, after dark."

Mavrys had to admit she, too, was daunted by the prospect, but she did not want to say so out loud. "I fear the expense would be too much for me, my lord."

"Are we not paying you enough?"

"I have no complaint about my salary, my lord... I've been sending most of the money to my mother. Since my uncle cut her off."

"After the... unwedding?" He smiled.

The Countess required an explanation of 'unwedding' before the Earl could ask, "Where is your mother living now?"

"In an hotel in Denvirran."

"At your expense?"

"Largely, yes, my lord." She felt it necessary to explain that Brellas was not neglectful, but he was bearing the costs of the forthcoming wedding, as well as renting, and decorating, a larger house.

"I don't know him well, but he seems a decent fellow."

"He is, my lord. I'm not sure they love each other quite as... as Railu and Skelber do, but I think they *like* each other well enough."

"That's more than many people have," said the Countess

"I'm not sure it's not greedy to expect more," said the Earl. "But I suppose I did."

The Countess flashed him a quick smile, turned back to Mavrys. "Your mother seems quite... conventional to me. And she's already been obliged to accept quite a lot that's *un*conventional from her only child."

"I see your thought, my lady. Yes, I think marrying Vireddi might be a step too far for her. She took a good deal of persuasion to agree that I could walk her down the aisle. But she wouldn't ask uncle Thiseman, and I said, who else was there?"

"It's becoming quite the tradition," said the Earl. "First Jerya, then Railu, and now Lady Deneval... Dare we hope the habit will spread further?"

"It's a small thing," said the Countess, "But it's not nothing."

"Even an inch, in the right direction, is better than nothing."

"We were hardly going to be publishing wedding notices in the *Denvirran Remarker* anyway. We'll have the ceremony, good food... I'll say a few words if you wish, or Hedric will. Dancing after... it can all be however you wish it to be, unconstrained by any of the conventional Rites."

"*'Whatever words you need, you choose,'*" said the Earl. "That's quite a privilege, when you think about it." A look, full of private meaning, passed between him and his wife.

"Is there anyone beyond Skilthorn you'd wish to invite?" asked the Countess.

"Railu," said Mav at once. "And Skelber, of course."

"That probably means inviting Sumyra too."

"Then I shall hope to get to know her in the next two weeks." Sumyra would be accompanying them to Skilthorn while her father and her new stepmother were on their sweetmoon.

"Had you thought about a date? Railu and Skelber are likely to be extremely busy once they get back, and I'm also going to have other things on my mind in a few weeks..."

"I shall have to speak to Vireddi... Foof! I don't even know for sure she'll agree." There was nothing Earl or Countess could helpfully say to that.

"Well," said Mav, regathering herself, "Supposing she does, and to give time to prepare, and to give Railu some notice... and to work around my mother's wedding... I can hardly see it being possible in less than eight weeks. Maybe ten. But first... first I have to get back to Skilthorn and ask Vireddi to marry me."

"Tomorrow," said the Countess. "We'll make an early start."

About the Author

Jon Sparks has been writing fiction as long as he can remember, but for many years made his living as an (award-winning) outdoor writer and photographer, specialising in landscape, travel and outdoor pursuits, particularly walking, climbing and cycling. He lives in Garstang, Lancashire, UK, with his partner Bernie and several bikes.

If you enjoyed this book...

There are several more volumes to come. To be the first to hear about these, and to get other news and insights, please consider signing up to my mailing list: go to tinyurl.com/4dvf7pt. There's a free short story as a thank you.

The Shattered Moon website is at https://www.jonsparksauthor.com. I also have a Facebook Page at https://www.facebook.com/profile.php?id=100089266940531, and I'm on Substack too: http://tinyurl.com/3nmmmsm4

Finally, a small plea. Reviews and ratings are really valuable to indie authors like me. If you can find a moment to leave a few thoughts, or just to add a star rating, it all helps. You can do this on whatever platform you got the book from, and there are also general review platforms, notably Goodreads, where my profile is at https://tinyurl.com/2p9znuhh. Thank you.

ACKNOWLEDGEMENTS

Terry Pratchett once said, "Writing a novel is as if you are going off on a journey across a valley. The valley is full of mist, but you can see the top of a tree here and the top of another tree over there. And with any luck you can see the other side of the valley. But you cannot see down into the mist. Nevertheless, you head for the first tree."

This perfectly encapsulates what writing a novel feels like for me. But what Terry didn't say, at least on this occasion, is that few, if any, writers undertake the journey entirely alone.

I reiterate my thanks from earlier volumes to all who've read and commented on my work, notably Marion Smith and Jago Westaway. Thanks to the many excellent editors I've worked with in my non-fiction career, particularly Ronald Turnbull, Sue Viccars, John Manning, and Seb Rogers. Many other members of the Outdoor Writers and Photographers Guild have helped me too.

First, last, and always, I cannot overstate what I owe to my partner Bernie, with whom I've shared unforgettable experiences from Morocco to New Zealand, as well as a host of hikes, climbs and treks in the Lakes, Scotland, and across the UK. She's also my principal beta-reader, and so much more besides. Our conversations on walks and in pubs and cafés have helped refine my ideas and I'm sure this book, and this series, are much the better for them.

Of all the places we've had such conversations, none means more to us than Cobblers Bar and Bistro in Garstang. Passages from all the books have been written or edited here too. It's a particularly welcoming and nurturing place.

It's very likely I wouldn't have been around to bring this book, and this series, to fruition without the amazing work of many dedicated health professionals. Deepest thanks to all of them, notably Dr David Howarth and Dr Scott Gall.